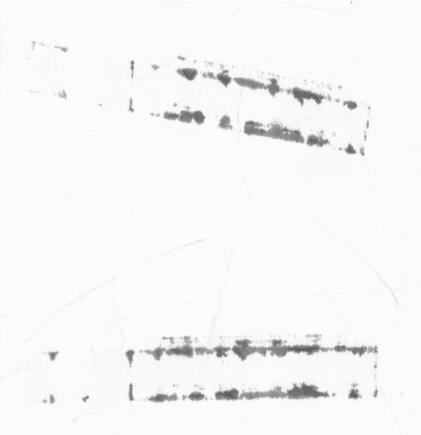

SPRING SNOW

ALFRED · A · KNOPF

1972 NEW YORK

THE SEA OF FERTILITY

A CYCLE OF FOUR NOVELS

SPRING SNOW

YUKIO MISHIMA

Translated from the Japanese by

Michael Gallagher

UNESCO COLLECTION OF REPRESENTATIVE WORKS/JAPANESE SERIES
This book has been accepted in the Japanese Series
of the Translations Collection of the United Nations
Educational, Scientific and Cultural Organization (UNESCO)

THIS IS A BORZOI BOOK
PUBLISHED BY ALFRED A. KNOPF, INC.

Library of Congress Cataloging in Publication Data
Mishima, Yukio, pseud.   SPRING SNOW.
(His The sea of fertility, [1]) (UNESCO collection of
representative works: Japanese series)
Translation of Haru no yuki.
I. Title. II. Series: UNESCO collection of representative
works: Japanese series.
PZ3.M6878Se vol. 1 [PL833.I7]   895.6'3'5s [895.6'3'5]
ISBN 0–394–44239–3   74–154940

Manufactured in the United States of America

First American Edition

SPRING SNOW

1

WHEN CONVERSATION at school turned to the Russo-Japanese War, Kiyoaki Matsugae asked his closest friend, Shigekuni Honda, how much he could remember about it. Shigekuni's memories were vague—he just barely recalled having been taken once to the front gate to watch a torchlight procession. The year the war ended they had both been eleven, and it seemed to Kiyoaki that they should be able to remember it a little more accurately. Their classmates who talked so knowingly about the war were for the most part merely embellishing hazy memories with tidbits they had picked up from grown-ups.

Two members of the Matsugae family, Kiyoaki's uncles, had been killed. His grandmother still received a pension from the government, thanks to these two sons she had lost, but she never used the money; she left the envelopes unopened on the ledge of the household shrine. Perhaps that was why the photograph which impressed Kiyoaki most out of the entire collection of war photographs in the house was one entitled "Vicinity of Tokuri Temple: Memorial Services for the War Dead" and dated June 26, 1904, the thirty-seventh year of the Meiji era. This photograph, printed in sepia ink, was quite unlike the usual cluttered mementos of the war. It had been composed with an artist's eye for structure: it really made it seem as if the thousands of soldiers who were present were arranged deliberately, like figures in a painting, to focus the entire attention of the viewer on the tall cenotaph of unpainted wood in their midst. In the distance, mountains sloped gently in the haze, rising in easy stages to the left of the picture, away from the broad plain at their foot; to the right, they merged in the distance with scattered clumps of trees, vanishing into the yellow dust of the horizon. And here, instead of mountains, there was a row of trees growing taller as the eye moved to the right; a yellow sky showed through the gaps between them. Six very tall trees stood at graceful intervals in the foreground, each placed so as to complement the overall harmony of the landscape. It was impossible to tell what kind they were, but their heavy top branches seemed to bend in the wind with a tragic grandeur.

The distant expanse of plains glowed faintly; this side of the mountains, the vegetation lay flat and desolate. At the center of the picture, minute, stood the plain wooden cenotaph and the altar with flowers lying on it, its white cloth twisted by the wind.

For the rest you saw nothing but soldiers, thousands of them. In the foreground, they were turned away from the camera to reveal the white sunshields hanging from their caps and the diagonal leather straps across their backs. They had not formed up in neat ranks, but were clustered in groups, heads drooping. A mere handful in the lower left corner had half-turned their dark faces toward the camera, like figures in a Renaissance painting. Farther behind them, a host of soldiers stretched away in an immense semicircle to the ends of the plain, so many men that it was quite impossible to tell one from another, and more were grouped far away among the trees.

The figures of these soldiers, in both foreground and rear, were bathed in a strange half-light that outlined leggings and boots and picked out the curves of bent shoulders and the napes of necks. This light charged the entire picture with an indescribable sense of grief.

From these men, there emanated a tangible emotion that broke in a wave against the small white altar, the flowers, the cenotaph in their midst. From this enormous mass stretching to the edge of the plain, a single thought, beyond all power of

human expression, bore down like a great, heavy ring of iron
on the center.

Both its age and its sepia ink tinged the photograph with an
atmosphere of infinite poignance.

*

Kiyoaki was eighteen. Nothing in the household where
he had been born would account for his being so sensitive, so
prone to melancholy. One would have been hard pressed to
find, in that rambling house built on high ground near Shibuya, anyone who in any way shared his sensibilities. It was
an old samurai family, but Kiyoaki's father, Marquis Matsugae, embarrassed by the humble position his forebears had
occupied as recently as the end of the shogunate fifty years
before, had sent the boy, still a very small child, to be brought
up in the household of a court nobleman. Had he not done so,
Kiyoaki would probably not have developed into so sensitive
a young man.

Marquis Matsugae's residence occupied a large tract of
land beyond Shibuya, on the outskirts of Tokyo. The many
buildings spread out over a hundred acres, their roofs rising
in an exciting counterpoise. The main house was of Japanese
architecture, but in the corner of the park stood an imposing
Western-style house designed by an Englishman. It was said
to be one of four residences in Japan—Marshal Oyama's was
the first—that one might enter without removing one's out-
door shoes.

In the middle of the park a large pond spread out against
the backdrop of a hill covered with maples. The pond was big
enough to boat on; it had an island in the middle, water lilies
in flower, and even water shields that could be picked for the
kitchen. The drawing-room of the main house faced the pond,
as did the banqueting room of the Western house.

Some two hundred stone lanterns were scattered at random
along the banks and on the island, which also boasted three
cranes made out of cast-iron, two stretching their long necks
to the sky and the other with its head bent low.

Water sprang from its source at the crest of the maple hill and descended the slopes in several falls; the stream then passed beneath a stone bridge and dropped into a pool that was shaded by red rocks from the island of Sado, before flowing into the pond at a spot where, in season, a patch of lovely irises bloomed. The pond was stocked both with carp and winter crucian. Twice a year, the Marquis allowed school-children to come there on picnics.

When Kiyoaki was a child, the servants had frightened him with stories about the snapping turtles. Long ago, when his grandfather was ill, a friend had presented him with a hundred of these turtles in the hope that their meat would rebuild his strength. Released into the pond, they had bred rapidly. Once a snapping turtle got your finger in its beak, the servants told Kiyoaki, that was the end of it.

There were several pavilions used for the tea ceremony and also a large billiard room. Behind the main house, wild yams grew thick in the grounds, and there was a grove of cypresses planted by Kiyoaki's grandfather, and intersected by two paths. One led to the rear gate; the other climbed a small hill to the plateau at its top where a shrine stood at one corner of a wide expanse of grass. This was where his grand-father and two uncles were enshrined. The steps, lanterns, and torii, all stone, were traditional, but on either side of the steps, in place of the usual lion-dogs, a pair of cannon shells from the Russo-Japanese War had been painted white and set in the ground. Somewhat lower down there was a shrine to Inari, the harvest god, behind a magnificent trellis of wisteria. The anniversary of his grandfather's death fell at the end of May; thus the wisteria was always in full glory when the family gathered here for the services, and the women would stand in its shade to avoid the glare of the sun. Their white faces, powdered even more meticulously than usual for the occasion, were dappled in violet, as though some exquisite shadow of death had fallen across their cheeks.

The women. No one could count exactly the multitude of

women who lived in the Matsugae mansion. Kiyoaki's grandmother, of course, took precedence over them all, though she
preferred to live in retirement at some distance from the main
house, with eight maids to attend to her needs. Every morning, rain or shine, Kiyoaki's mother would finish dressing and
go at once with two maids in attendance to pay her respects to
the old lady. And every day the old lady would scrutinize her
daughter-in-law's appearance.

"That hairstyle isn't very becoming. Why not try doing it
in the high-collar way tomorrow? I'm sure it would look better
on you," she would say, her eyes narrowed lovingly. But when
the hair was arranged the Western way next morning, the old
lady would comment: "Really, Tsujiko, a high-collar hair-do
simply doesn't suit an old-fashioned Japanese beauty like you.
Please try the Marumage style tomorrow." And so, for as long
as Kiyoaki could remember, his mother's coiffure had been
perpetually changing.

The hairdressers and their apprentices were in constant
attendance. Not only did his mother's hair demand their services but they had to look after more than forty maids. However, they had shown concern for the hair of a male member
of the household on only one occasion. This was when Kiyoaki
was in his first year at the middle school attached to Peers
School. The honor had fallen to him of being selected to act
as a page in the New Year's festivities at the Imperial Palace.

"I know the people at school want you to look like a little
monk," said one of the hairdressers, "but that shaved head just
won't look right with your fine costume today."

"But they'll scold me if my hair is long."

"All right, all right," said the hairdresser. "Let me see what
I can do to improve it. You'll be wearing a hat in any case, but
I think we can arrange things so that even when you take it
off, you'll outshine all the other young gentlemen."

So he said, but Kiyoaki at thirteen had had his head clipped
so closely that it looked blue. When the hairdresser parted his
hair, the comb hurt, and the hair oil stung his skin. For all

the hairdresser's vaunted skill, the head reflected in the mirror looked no different from any boy's, yet at the banquet Kiyoaki was praised for his extraordinary beauty.

The Emperor Meiji himself had once honored the Matsugae residence with his presence. To entertain his Imperial Majesty, an exhibition of sumo wrestling had been staged beneath a huge gingko tree, around which a space had been curtained off. The Emperor watched from a balcony on the second floor of the Western house. Kiyoaki confided to the hairdresser that on that occasion he had been permitted to appear before the Emperor, and His Majesty had deigned to pat him on the head. That had taken place four years ago, but it nevertheless was possible that the Emperor might remember the head of a mere page at the New Year's festivities.

"Really?" exclaimed the hairdresser, overwhelmed. "Young master, you mean to say you were caressed by the Emperor himself!" So saying, he slid backward across the tatami floor, clapping his hands in genuine reverence at the child.

The costume of a page attending a lady of the court consisted of matching blue velvet jacket and trousers, the latter reaching to just below the knees. Down either side of the jacket was a row of four large white fluffy pompons and more were attached to the cuffs and the trousers. The page wore a sword at his waist, and the shoes on his white-stockinged feet were fastened with black enamel buttons. A white silk tie was knotted in the center of his broad lace collar, and a tricorn hat, adorned with a large feather, hung down his back on a silk cord. Each New Year, about twenty sons of the nobility with outstanding school records were selected to take turns— in fours—bearing the train of the Empress, or in pairs to carry the train of an imperial princess during the three days of festivities. Kiyoaki carried the train of the Empress once and did the same for the Princess Kasuga. When it was his turn to bear the Empress's train she had proceeded with solemn dignity down corridors fragrant with the musky incense lit by the palace attendants, and he had stood in attendance behind her during the audience. She was a woman of great elegance and intelligence, but by then she was already elderly, close to sixty. Princess Kasuga, however, was not much more than thirty. Beautiful, elegant, imposing, she was like a flower at its moment of perfection.

Even now, Kiyoaki could remember less about the rather sober train favored by the Empress than about the Princess's broad sweep of white ermine, with its scattered black spots and its border of pearls. The Empress's train had four loops for the pages' hands, and the Princess's two. Kiyoaki and the others had been so exhaustively drilled that they had no trouble in holding firm while advancing at a steady pace.

Princess Kasuga's hair had the blackness and sheen of fine lacquer. Seen from behind, her elaborate coiffure seemed to dissolve into the rich white skin-textures of the nape of her neck, leaving single strands against her bare shoulders whose faint sheen was set off by her décolleté.

She held herself erect, and walked straight ahead with a firm step, betraying no tremor to her trainbearers, but in Kiyoaki's eyes that great fan of white fur seemed to glow and fade to the sound of music, like a snow-covered peak first hidden, then exposed by a fluid pattern of clouds. At that moment, for the first time in his life, he was struck by the full force of womanly beauty—a dazzling burst of elegance that made his senses reel.

Princess Kasuga's lavish use of French perfume extended to her train, and its fragrance overpowered the musky odor of incense. Some way down the corridor, Kiyoaki stumbled for a moment, inadvertently tugging at the train. The Princess turned her head slightly, and, as a sign that she was not at all annoyed, smiled gently at the youthful offender. Her gesture went unnoticed; body perfectly erect in that fractional turn, she had allowed Kiyoaki a glimpse of a corner of her mouth. At that moment, a single wisp of hair slipped over her clear white cheek, and out of the fine-drawn corner of an eye a smile flashed in a spark of black fire. But the pure line of her nose did not move. It was as if nothing had happened . . . this fleeting angle of the Princess's face—too slight to be called a profile—made Kiyoaki feel as if he had seen a rainbow flicker for a bare instant through a prism of pure crystal.

His father, Marquis Matsugae, watched his son's part in the festivities, absorbing the boy's brilliant appearance in his beautiful ceremonial costume, and savoring the complacency of a man who sees a lifelong dream fulfilled. This triumph dispelled completely his lingering fears of still seeming an imposter, for all his attempts to establish himself as someone fit to receive the Emperor in his own home. For now, in the person of his own son, the Marquis had seen the ultimate fusion of the aristocratic and the samurai traditions, a perfect congruence between the old court nobles and the new nobility.

But as the ceremony continued, the Marquis's gratification at the praise people had lavished on the boy's looks changed to feelings of discomfort. At thirteen, Kiyoaki was altogether too handsome. Putting aside natural affection for his own son, the Marquis could not help noticing that he stood out even in comparison with the other pages. His pale cheeks flushed crimson when he was excited, his brows were sharply defined and his wide eyes, still childishly earnest, were framed by long lashes. They were dark and had a seductive glint in them. And so the Marquis was roused by the flood of compliments to take note of the exceptional beauty of his son and heir, and he sensed something disquieting in it. He was touched by an uneasy premonition. But Marquis Matsugae was an extremely optimistic man, and he shook off his discomfiture as soon as the ceremony was over.

Similar apprehensions were more persistent in the mind of young Iinuma, who had come to live in the Matsugae household as a boy of seventeen the year before Kiyoaki's service as a page. Iinuma had been recommended as Kiyoaki's personal tutor by the middle school of his village in Kagoshima, and he had been sent to the Matsugaes with testimonies to his mental and physical abilities. The present Marquis's father was revered as a fierce and powerful god in Kagoshima, and Iinuma had visualized life in the Matsugae household entirely in terms of what he had heard at home or at school about the exploits of the former Marquis. In his year with them, however, their luxurious way of life had disrupted this expectation and had wounded his youthfully puritanical sensibilities.

He could shut his eyes to other things, but not to Kiyoaki, who was his personal responsibility. Everything about Kiyoaki —his looks, his delicacy, his sensitivity, his turn of mind, his interests—grated on Iinuma. And everything about the Marquis and Marquise's attitude toward their son's education was equally distressing. "I'll never raise a son of mine that way, not even if I am made a Marquis. What weight do you suppose the Marquis gives to his own father's tenets?"

The Marquis was punctilious in observing the annual rites for his father, but almost never spoke of him. At first, Iinuma used to dream that the Marquis would talk more often about his father and that his reminiscences might reveal something of the affection in which he held his father's memory, but in the course of the year such hopes flickered and died.

The night that Kiyoaki returned home after performing his duties as an imperial page, the Marquis and his wife gave a private family dinner to celebrate the occasion. When the time came for Kiyoaki to hurry off to bed, Iinuma helped him to his room. The thirteen-year-old boy's cheeks were flushed with the wine that his father, half as a joke, had forced upon him. He burrowed into the silken quilts and let his head fall back on the pillow, his breath warm and heavy. The tracery of blue veins under his close-cropped hair throbbed around his earlobes, and the skin was so extraordinarily transparent that one could almost see the fragile mechanism inside. Even in the half-light of the room, his lips were red. And the sounds of breathing that came from this boy, who looked as though he had never experienced anguish, seemed to be the mocking echo of a sad folksong.

Iinuma looked down at his face, at the sensitive darting eyes with their long lashes—the eyes of an otter—and he knew that it was hopeless to expect him to swear the enthusiastic oaths of loyalty to the Emperor that a night like this would have invoked in any normal young Japanese boy striving toward manhood, who had been privileged to carry out so glorious a task.

Kiyoaki's eyes were now wide open as he lay on his back staring at the ceiling, and they were filled with tears. And when this glistening gaze turned on him, Iinuma's distaste deepened. But this made it all the more imperative for him to believe in his own loyalty. When Kiyoaki apparently felt too warm, he pulled his bare arms, slightly flushed, out from under the quilt and started to fold them behind his head; Iinuma admonished him and pulled shut the loose collar of his nightgown: "You'll catch cold. You ought to go to sleep now."

"Iinuma, you know . . . I made a blunder today. If you promise not to tell Father or Mother, I'll say what it was."

"What was it?"

"Today, when I was carrying the Princess's train, I stumbled a little. But the Princess just smiled and forgave me."

Iinuma was repelled by these frivolous words, by the absence of any sense of responsibility, by the tearful look of rapture in those eyes, by everything.

 2

IT WAS HARDLY SURPRISING, then, that by the time Kiyoaki turned eighteen, his preoccupations had served to isolate him more and more from his surroundings. He had grown apart from more than just his family. The teachers at the Peers School had instilled in their pupils the supremely noble example of the principal, General Nogi, who had committed suicide to follow his Emperor in death; and ever since they had started to emphasize the significance of his act, suggesting that their educational tradition would have been the poorer had the General died on a sickbed, an atmosphere of Spartan simplicity had come to permeate the school. Kiyoaki, who had an aversion to anything smacking of militarism, had come to loathe school for this reason.

His only friend was his classmate Shigekuni Honda. There were of course many others who would have been delighted to be friends with Kiyoaki, but he didn't like the youthful coarseness of his contemporaries; he shunned their rough, coltish ways and was further repelled by their crude sentimentality when they mindlessly roared out the school song. Kiyoaki was drawn only to Honda, with his quiet, composed, rational temperament, unusual in a boy of his age. Even so the two had little in common in appearance or temperament.

Honda seemed older than he was. Though his features were quite ordinary, he tended to assume a somewhat pompous air. He was interested in studying law, and was gifted with keen intuition, but it was a power he tended to disguise. To look at him was to believe that he was indifferent to sensual pleasures, but there were times when he seemed fired by some deep passion; at these moments, Honda—who always kept his mouth firmly shut, as he kept his somewhat nearsighted eyes severely narrowed and his brows in a frown— was to be caught with a hint of parted lips in his expression.

Kiyoaki and Honda were perhaps as different in their makeup as the flower and the leaf of a single plant. Kiyoaki was incapable of hiding his true nature, and he was defenseless against society's power to inflict pain. His still unawakened sensuality lay dormant within him, unprotected as a puppy in a March rain, body shivering, eyes and nose pelted with water. Honda, on the other hand, had quite early in life grasped where danger lay, choosing to shelter from all storms, whatever their attraction.

Despite this, however, they were remarkably close friends. Not content to see each other in school, they would also spend Sundays together at one or the other of their homes. And because the Matsugae estate had more to offer in the way of

walks and other amusements, Honda usually came to Kiyoaki's house.

One October Sunday in 1912, the first year of the Taisho
era, on an afternoon when the maple leaves were almost in
their prime, Honda arrived in Kiyoaki's room to suggest that
they go boating on the pond. Had this been a year like any
other, there would have been a growing number of visitors
coming to admire the maple leaves, but as the Matsugaes had
been in mourning since the Emperor's death the previous
summer, they had suspended normal social activities. An
extraordinary stillness lay over the park.

"Well, if you want to. The boat will take three. We'll get
Iinuma to row us."

"Why do we need anybody to row us? I'll row," said
Honda, remembering the dour expression of the young man
who had just needlessly escorted him with silent but relentless obsequiousness to Kiyoaki's room.

Kiyoaki smiled. "You don't like him, do you, Honda?"

"It's not that I don't like him. It's just that, for all the time
I've known him, I still can't tell what's going on inside his
head."

"He's been here six years, so I take him for granted now,
like the air I breathe. We certainly don't see eye to eye, but
he's devoted to me all the same. He's loyal, he studies hard,
you can depend on him."

Kiyoaki's room was on the second floor facing the pond. It
had originally been in Japanese style, but had been redeco-
rated to look Western, with a carpet and Western furniture.
Honda sat down on the windowsill. Looking over his shoulder, he took in the whole sweep of the pond, the island and the
hill of maples beyond. The water lay smooth in the afternoon
sun. Just below him, he could see the boats moored in a small
inlet.

At the same time, he was mulling over his friend's lack of
enthusiasm. Kiyoaki never took the lead, though sometimes
he would join in with an air of utter boredom only to enjoy
himself in his own way. The role of exhorter and leader,

then, always fell to Honda if the pair were to do anything at all.

"You can see the boats, can't you?" said Kiyoaki.

"Yes, of course I can," Honda replied, glancing dubiously behind him.

*

What did Kiyoaki mean by his question? If one were forced to hazard a guess, it would be that he was trying to say that he had no interest in anything at all. He thought of himself as a thorn, a small, poisonous thorn jabbed into the workmanlike hand of his family. And this was his fate simply because he had acquired a little elegance. A mere fifty years before, the Matsugaes had been a sturdy, upright samurai family, no more, eking out a frugal existence in the provinces. But in a brief span of time, their fortunes had soared. By Kiyoaki's time, the first traces of refinement were threatening to take hold on a family that, unlike the court nobility, had enjoyed centuries of immunity to the virus of elegance. And Kiyoaki, like an ant that senses the approaching flood, was experiencing the first intimations of his family's rapid collapse.

His elegance was the thorn. And he was well aware that his aversion to coarseness, his delight in refinement, were futile; he was a plant without roots. Without meaning to undermine his family, without wanting to violate its traditions, he was condemned to do so by his very nature. And this poison would stunt his own life as it destroyed his family. The handsome young man felt that this futility typified his existence.

His conviction of having no purpose in life other than to act as a distillation of poison was part of the ego of an eighteen-year-old. He had resolved that his beautiful white hands would never be soiled or calloused. He wanted to be like a pennant, dependent on each gusting wind. The only thing that seemed valid to him was to live for the emotions—gratuitous and unstable, dying only to quicken again, dwindling and flaring without direction or purpose.

At the moment nothing interested him. Boating? His father had thought the little green and white boat he had imported from abroad to be stylish. As far as his father was concerned the boat was culture; culture made tangible. But what of it? Who cared about a boat?

Honda, with his inborn intuition, understood Kiyoaki's sudden silence. Although they were the same age, Honda was more mature. He was, in fact, a young man who wanted to lead a constructive life, and he had made up his mind about his future role. With Kiyoaki, however, he always took care to seem less sensitive and subtle than he was. For he knew that his friend was quite receptive to his careful displays of obtuseness—the only bait that seemed to draw a rise from Kiyoaki. And this streak of deception ran through their whole friendship.

"It would do you good to get some exercise," said Honda brusquely. "I know that you can't have been reading all that much, but you look as if you'd read your way through a library."

Kiyoaki smiled by way of reply. Honda was right. It was not his books that had drained him of energy but his dreams. A whole library wouldn't have exhausted him as much as his constant dreaming night after night.

The very night before, he had dreamed of his own coffin, made of unpainted wood. It stood in the middle of an empty room with large windows, and outside, the pre-dawn darkness was shading to a deep blue; it was filled with the sound of birdsong. A young woman clung to the coffin, her long black hair trailing from her drooping head, her slender shoulders wracked with sobs. He wanted to see her face but could make out no more than her pale, graceful forehead with its delicate peak of black hair. The coffin was half covered with a leopard-skin bordered in pearls. The first muted glow of the dawn flickered on the row of jewels. Instead of funeral incense, a scent of Western perfume hung over the room with the fragrance of sun-ripened fruit. Kiyoaki seemed to be watching this from a great height, though he was convinced that his body lay inside the coffin. But sure as he was, he still felt the need to see it there by way of confirmation. However, like a mosquito in the morning light, his wings lost all power and ceased beating in mid-air; he was utterly incapable of looking inside the nailed-down coffin lid. And then, as his frustration grew more and more intense, he woke up. Kiyoaki took out his secret journal and wrote all this down.

*

Finally, the two of them went down to the landing and unfastened the mooring rope. The calm surface of the water reflected the flaming scarlet maples beginning to turn on the hill beyond. As they stepped into the boat, its wild rocking evoked in Kiyoaki his favorite feelings about the precariousness of life. At that instant, his inner thoughts seemed to describe a wide arc, clearly reflected in the fresh white trim of the boat. His spirits rose.

Honda pushed against the stone landing with an oar and maneuvered the boat out into the water. As the prow shivered the brilliant scarlet surface of the water, the smooth ripples heightened Kiyoaki's sense of liberation. The dark water seemed to speak in a deep, solemn voice. "My eighteenth autumn, this day, this afternoon, this moment: never to come again," he thought, "something already slipping irrevocably away."

"Shall we take a look at the island?"

"What's the fun in that? There's nothing to see."

"Don't be a kill-joy. Come on, let's go and look," Honda urged. His voice sounded deep in his chest as he rowed with a lively vigor that suited his years.

As Kiyoaki stared fixedly down into the pond, he heard the faint sound of the waterfall far away on the other side of the island; he could not see a great deal because of the cloudy water and the red of the maples reflected in it. There were carp swimming down there, he knew, and at the very bottom snapping turtles lurked in the shelter of the rocks. His childhood fears flared for a moment, then died.

The hot sun struck the backs of their close-shaven necks. It was a peaceful, uneventful, glorious Sunday afternoon. Yet Kiyoaki remained convinced that at the bottom of this world, which was like a leather bag filled with water, there was a little hole, and it seemed to him that he could hear time leaking from it, drop by drop.

They reached the island at a spot where a single maple stood among the pines, and climbed the stone steps to the grassy clearing at the top with the three iron cranes. The boys sat down at the feet of the pair that were stretching their necks upward in an eternal, mute cry, then lay back on the grass to stare up at the late autumn sky. The rough grass pricked through the backs of their kimonos, making Kiyoaki rather uncomfortable. It gave Honda, however, the sensation of having to endure an exquisitely refreshing pain that was fragmented and spread out under his back. Out of the corners of their eyes, they could see the two cranes, weathered by wind and rain and soiled by chalky-white bird droppings. The birds' supple, curved necks, stretched against the sky, moved slowly with the rhythm of the shifting clouds.

"It's a beautiful day. In all our lives, we may not have many like this—so perfect," said Honda, stirred by some premonition.

"Are you talking about happiness?" asked Kiyoaki.

"I don't remember saying anything about happiness."

"Well, that's all right then. I'd be much too scared to say the things you do. I don't have that kind of courage."

"I'm convinced that the trouble with you is, you're horribly greedy. Greedy men are apt to seem miserable. Look, what more could you want than a day like this?"

"Something definite. What it might be, I've no idea," the young man answered wearily, as handsome as he was indecisive. Fond as he was of his friend, there were times when Kiyoaki found Honda's keenly analytic mind and his confident turns of phrase—the very image of youthful promise—a severe trial to his capricious nature.

All at once, he rolled over on his stomach on the grass and raised his head, staring across the water at a spot some distance away, in the direction of the garden that fronted the drawing room of the main house. Stepping-stones set in white sand led from it to the edge of the pond, which was intricately scalloped with small inlets crossed by a network of stone bridges. He had noticed a group of women there.

3

HE TAPPED HONDA on the shoulder and pointed in that direction. Honda raised his head and peered across the water until he too spotted the women. And so they stared from their hiding place like two young snipers. His mother went for her daily walk whenever the mood struck her; but her company was not confined to her personal maids today; two guests, one old and one young, were walking just behind her. All except the young girl were wearing kimonos of muted, quiet colors. And although she was in pale blue, the material was richly embroidered. As she crossed the white sand to walk along the water's edge, it shone pale and silky like the sky at daybreak. The women's laughter, carrying on the autumn air, betrayed her uncertain footing on the irregular stepping-stones, but it rang too pure and sounded a little artificial. It always irritated Kiyoaki to hear the women of the household laughing like that, but he was well aware of the effect it had on Honda, who had a glint in his eye like a rooster alerted to the clucking of hens. The brittle stalks of dry autumn grass bent under their chests.

Kiyoaki felt sure that the girl in the pale-blue kimono would never laugh that way. In a great flurry of merriment, his mother's maids were leading their mistress and the guests hand-in-hand from the edge of the pond to the hill of maples along a path deliberately complicated by a maze of stone bridges that threaded to and fro across the inlets. Kiyoaki and Honda soon lost sight of them behind the tall grass in which they lay.

"You certainly have a lot of women around your house. We have nothing but men," said Honda, putting a good face on his interest, which was keen enough to make him get up and move to the other side of the island. Here, from the shelter of the pines, he was able to follow the awkward progress of the women. To the left of him, a hollow in the slope held the first four of the nine waterfalls. The stream then followed the curve of the hill and finally splashed down in front of it into the pool below the red Sado rocks. The women were now making their way below these last falls, testing their footing on the stepping-stones. The maple leaves here were especially beautiful, so thick as to blot out the white ribbon of the falls and stain the water at the edge of the pond a deep scarlet. The maids were leading the young woman in the aquamarine kimono across the stepping-stones, her head bent forward, and even at that distance the white of the nape of her neck was visible to Kiyoaki. It made him think of Princess Kasuga and her creamy white neck, something that was never far from his mind.

After the path crossed below the falls, it leveled out for a time, following the waterline as the shore began to come toward the island. Kiyoaki had followed the women's progress with concentration. But now he caught sight of the profile of the woman in the aquamarine kimono and recognized Satoko. His fantasies were shattered. Why hadn't he recognized her earlier? Probably his whim that the beautiful girl should be a total stranger.

Now that she had destroyed his illusion, there was no point in remaining hidden. Brushing the burrs from his kimono,

Kiyoaki got to his feet and parted the lower branches of the pines that had been his cover.

"Hello," he called.

This sudden cheerfulness took Honda by surprise, and he craned his neck for a better look. Aware that Kiyoaki's high spirits were by now a reflex response to the interruption of his dreams, Honda did not mind his friend seizing the initiative.

"Who is it?"

"Oh, it's Satoko. Did I never show you her picture?" answered Kiyoaki, speaking her name with cool indifference. Satoko, the girl on the shore, was certainly a beauty. Kiyoaki, however, seemed determined to ignore this. For he knew that Satoko was in love with him.

This instinctive rejection of anyone who showed him affection, this need to react with cold disdain, were a failing of Kiyoaki's that no one could have known better than Honda, who saw this pride as a kind of tumor that had taken hold of Kiyoaki when he was no more than thirteen and had first had to endure people making a fuss over his looks. Like a silvery bloom of mold, it would spread at the slightest touch.

Perhaps, in fact, the dangerous attraction that Kiyoaki's friendship held for Honda was rooted in the same impulse. So many others had attempted to befriend Kiyoaki, only to be rewarded for their pains with his mockery and contempt. In challenging Kiyoaki's caustic reserve, Honda alone had been skilled enough to escape disaster. Perhaps he was mistaken, but he wondered if his own acute dislike for Kiyoaki's gloom-faced tutor sprang from the latter's expression of perpetual defeat.

Although Honda had never met Satoko, Kiyoaki's stories were full of her. The Ayakura family, one of twenty-eight among the nobility that bore the lofty rank of Urin, was descended from an ancestor named Namba Yorisuke, a skilled player of *kemari*, the version of football popular at the Imperial Court in the time of the Fujiwaras. The head of the family was appointed a chamberlain of the Imperial Court when it established residence in Tokyo at the time of the

Meiji Restoration. The Ayakuras moved to the city and lived in a mansion in Azabu formerly occupied by one of the retainers of the shogun. The family excelled in the sport of *kemari* and in composing *waka*. And since the Emperor had seen fit to honor the family's young heir with a court rank of "fifth degree, junior grade," even the post of Grand Councillor of State now seemed within reach.

Marquis Matsugae, who was conscious of his own family's lack of polish and who hoped to give the next generation at least a touch of elegance, had entrusted the infant Kiyoaki to the Ayakuras after obtaining his own father's consent. And so Kiyoaki had been raised in the atmosphere of the court nobility with Satoko, who was two years older and lavished affection on him; until he went to school, she was his only companion and friend. Count Ayakura himself, a warm and personable man who still retained his soft Kyoto accent, taught the young Kiyoaki calligraphy and *waka*. The family would play *sugoroku*, an ancient form of backgammon, far into the night, as was the custom in the Heian era, and the lucky winners would receive traditional prizes, among them candies molded like gifts from the Empress.

Moreover, Count Ayakura arranged for Kiyoaki to continue his early cultural training by going to the palace each New Year to attend the Imperial Poetry Reading Ceremony, in which he himself figured prominently. At first, Kiyoaki had seen this as a chore, but as he grew older, his participation in these elegant and ancient rituals came to hold a certain charm for him.

Satoko was now twenty. And thumbing through Kiyoaki's picture album, one could see the changes as she grew to maturity, from when she was a child with her cheek pressed affectionately to Kiyoaki's until the previous May, when she had taken part in the Matsugae Omiyasama festival. At twenty she had passed the stage that was popularly supposed to mark a girl's greatest beauty, but she was still unmarried.

"So that's Satoko. And the other one, the woman in the gray tunic everyone's making such a fuss over, who's she?"

"Her? Oh yes; that's Satoko's great-aunt, the Abbess of Gesshu. I didn't recognize her at first because of that curious hood."

Her Reverence the Abbess was indeed an unexpected guest. This was her first visit to the Matsugaes, hence the conducted tour of the garden—something that Kiyoaki's mother would not have undertaken just for Satoko but was quite happy to do for the Abbess. Her great-aunt's visit to Tokyo being such a rarity, Satoko had no doubt brought her to see the maple leaves. The Abbess had taken great delight in Kiyoaki when he first came to the Ayakuras, but he could not remember that far back. Later, when he was in middle school and the Abbess had paid a visit to Tokyo, he had been invited to the Ayakuras, but he had had the opportunity to do no more than pay his respects. Even so, the Abbess's pale face with its air of quiet dignity and the calm authority in her voice had made a lasting impression on him.

Kiyoaki's voice had brought the group on the shore to an abrupt halt. Startled, they looked toward the island as if pirates had risen before their very eyes from the tall grass beside the decorative iron cranes.

Pulling a small fan from her obi, Kiyoaki's mother pointed toward the Abbess to indicate that a respectful greeting was expected. Kiyoaki, accordingly, made a deep bow from where he stood on the island. Honda quickly followed suit, and Her Reverence acknowledged them both. His mother then opened her fan and waved it imperiously, its golden sheen suddenly giving off scarlet reflections. Kiyoaki urged Honda to hurry up, knowing that they must come back from the island at once.

"Satoko never misses a chance to come here. She's taking advantage of her great-aunt," grumbled Kiyoaki with a show of bad temper, while helping Honda by hurrying to cast off the boat. Honda, however, viewed Kiyoaki's haste and his grumbling with some skepticism. The way Kiyoaki had lost patience with Honda's steady, methodical movements and had seized the rough rope in his own unseasoned white hands to

try to help with the unpleasant task of unknotting it was
enough to raise doubts about the Abbess being the cause of
his eagerness.

As Honda rowed back to the shore, Kiyoaki looked dizzy,
his face picking up a red flush from the reflection of the maple
leaves floating on the water. He nervously avoided Honda's
eyes in an attempt to deny his vulnerability to Satoko. For
each moment brought him closer to the young woman who
knew altogether too much about him, about his childhood,
even about his body's most intimate details, and to whom he
seemed tied by almost overwhelming bonds of emotion.

"Why, Mr. Honda! What a good oarsman you are!" said
Kiyoaki's mother admiringly when they reached the shore.
Her pale, classic face had a persistently melancholy cast, even
when she laughed. Yet her expression was a façade rather
than a true indication of her deeper emotions. She was in fact
almost invariably insensitive. She had raised Kiyoaki to tolerate his father's dissipation and boorish energy, but she was
quite incapable of grasping the complexities of her son's nature.

Satoko's eyes were riveted on Kiyoaki from the moment he
stepped out of the boot. Strong and calm, affectionate from
time to time, they invariably unnerved Kiyoaki. He felt, not
without reason, that he could read criticism in their glance.

"Her Reverence has honored us with a visit today, and we
shall shortly have the pleasure of listening to her speak. But
first we wanted to show her the maple leaves. Then you gave
us such a fright by that rude shout of yours. What were you
doing on the island in the first place?"

"Oh, just watching the sky," Kiyoaki replied, being as
enigmatic to his mother as possible.

"Watching the sky? And what's there to see in the sky?"

His mother was quite unembarrassed about her failure to
grasp the intangible, which struck him as her sole admirable
characteristic. He found it comical that she could adopt such
a pious expression for the Abbess's sermons. The Abbess
maintained her role of guest throughout this exchange, smil-

ing unassumingly. And he would not look at Satoko, who
gazed steadily at the thick, glossy, tousled black hair that
brushed his smooth cheeks.

The group now started up the steep path, admiring the
maples as they went and amusing themselves by trying to
identify the birds singing in the branches above their heads.
However much the two young men tried to check their stride,
they inevitably drew ahead to walk some distance in front of
the women around the Abbess. Honda took advantage of this
to discuss Satoko for the first time, and admire her beauty.

"You think so?" Kiyoaki replied, well aware that although
Honda's finding Satoko unattractive would have been a severe
blow to his pride, he must make a show of cold indifference.
He was firmly convinced that any young woman in Satoko's
relationship to him would have to be beautiful, whether he
chose to acknowledge her or not.

At last their climb ended at the bridge below the topmost
waterfall, and they stood looking up toward its rim. Just as
his mother was savoring the compliments of the Abbess,
whose first view of the falls this was, Kiyoaki made an ominous discovery which cut across the mood of the day.

"What's that? At the top there, what's damming the water
like that?"

His mother responded at once. Using her fan to shade
her eyes from the bright sunlight that shone through the
branches, she peered upward. The landscape artist had painstakingly built up walls of rock on either side of the rim to ensure a graceful fall of water, and could never have intended
the flow to be diverted so awkwardly at the middle of the
crest. A mere rock wedged up there could never have caused
such a disruption in the flow.

"I wonder what can be the matter. Something seems to
have lodged itself up there," his mother said to the Abbess,
openly puzzled.

The Abbess, though she seemed to be aware that something was wrong, said nothing and smiled as before. If anyone was to speak out clearly, regardless of the effect, it would

have to be Kiyoaki. But he held back, fearing the impact of his words on the happy mood of the group. He realized that everyone must have recognized what it was by now.

"Isn't it a black dog? With its head hanging down?" said Satoko quite plainly. And the ladies gasped as if they were noticing the dog for the first time.

Kiyoaki's pride was hurt. Satoko, with a boldness that might be construed as unfeminine, had pointed out the dog's corpse, ignoring its ominous implications. She had adopted a suitably pleasant and straightforward tone of voice, which bore witness to her elegant upbringing; she had the freshness of ripe fruit in a crystal bowl. Kiyoaki was ashamed of his hesitation, and felt cowed by Satoko's capacity for directness.

His mother issued some quick orders to the maids, who left at once to look for the negligent gardeners. But her profuse apologies to the Abbess for such an unseemly spectacle were cut short by Her Reverence, who made a compassionate proposal that was totally unexpected.

"My presence here would seem to be providential. If you will bury the dog under a mound, I'll offer a prayer for it."

The dog had probably been mortally sick or wounded when it came to the stream to drink, and had fallen in. The force of the current had wedged its corpse into the cleft of rocks at the top of the falls. Satoko's courage had excited Honda's admiration, but at the same time he felt oppressed by the sight of the dog hanging dead in the falls under a bright sky only faintly flecked with cloud. The dog's black fur glistened in the clear spray, its white teeth shining in the gaping, dark red, cavernous jaws.

Everyone adjusted quickly to the shift in attention from the red maple leaves to the dog's burial. And the maids in attendance suddenly livened up, becoming almost frivolous. They had all crossed the bridge and were resting in the arbor designed as a vantage point from which to view the falls when the gardener came rushing up, babbling every cliché of apology in his repertoire. Only then did he climb the steep, treacherous rock face to remove the dripping black body and bury it in a suitable spot.

"I'm going to pick some flowers. Kiyo, won't you help?" asked Satoko, effectively ruling out any assistance from the maids.

"What kind of flowers would one pick for a dog?" Kiyoaki countered, his obvious reluctance drawing a burst of laughter from the women.

Meanwhile the Abbess removed her drab tunic to reveal the purple habit beneath and the small stole that hung around her neck. She had a presence that radiated grace to those around her, her brightness dissipating the atmosphere of ill-omen.

"Goodness, the dog is blessed to have Your Reverence offering a requiem for it. Surely it will be reborn as a human being," said Kiyoaki's mother with a smile.

Satoko did not bother to wait for Kiyoaki, but started up the hill path, stooping now and then to pick a late-flowering gentian that she had spotted. Kiyoaki found nothing better than a few withered camomiles.

Each time she bent to pick a flower, Satoko's aquamarine kimono was an inadequate disguise for the roundness of her hips, surprisingly generous on such a slim figure. All at once Kiyoaki felt unsettled, his mind a remote lake of clear water suddenly clouded by a disturbance deep below its surface.

After picking the gentians necessary to complete her bouquet, Satoko suddenly straightened up and stopped abruptly in Kiyoaki's path, while he did his best to look elsewhere. Her finely shaped nose and huge bright eyes, which he had never yet dared to look into directly, now confronted his vision at uncomfortably close range, a threatening phantom.

"Kiyo, what would you do if all of a sudden I weren't here any more?" Satoko asked, her words coming in a rushed whisper.

4

THIS WAS A LONG-STANDING trick of Satoko's for disconcerting people. Perhaps she achieved her effects without conscious effort, but she never allowed the slightest hint of mischief into her tone to put her victim at ease. Her voice would be heavy with pathos at such times, as though confiding the gravest of secrets.

Although he should have been inured to this by now, Kiyoaki could not help asking: "Not here any more? Why?"

Despite all his efforts to indicate a studied disinterest, Kiyoaki's reply betrayed his uneasiness. It was what Satoko wanted.

"I can't tell you why," she answered, deftly dropping ink into the clear waters of Kiyoaki's heart. She gave him no time to erect his defenses.

He glared at her. It had always been like this. Which was why he hated her. Without the slightest warning she could plunge him into nameless anxieties. And the drop of ink spread, dull and gray, clouding everything in his heart that had been pellucid only a moment ago.

Satoko was still watching him intently, and her eyes, which had been sad, suddenly twinkled.

On their return, Kiyoaki's bad temper surprised everyone and gave the women of the Matsugae household something to gossip about.

*

Kiyoaki was so capricious that he tended to exacerbate the very worries that gnawed at him. Had it been applied to love affairs, his stubborn persistence would have been that of almost any young man. But in his case it was different. Perhaps this was why Satoko deliberately sowed the seeds of dark and thorny flowers, rather than brightly colored ones, knowing what an unhealthy fascination they held for Kiyoaki. Indeed he had always been fertile ground for such seeds. He indulged himself, to the exclusion of all else, in the cultivation of his anxiety.

Satoko had caught his interest. Although a willing prisoner of his discontent, he was still angry with Satoko, who always had a ready supply of fresh ambiguities and riddles to disconcert him. And he was also angered by his own indecision when faced with finding a solution to her teasing.

When he and Honda had been resting in the grass on the island, he had indeed said that he was looking for "something absolutely definite." What it was he didn't know, but whenever this bright certainty seemed to shine within his grasp, the fluttering sleeves of Satoko's aquamarine kimono interposed themselves, trapping him once again in the quicksands of indecision. Though he had sensed something definite, a flash of intuition, distant, unattainable, he chose to believe that Satoko was the barrier that prevented him from taking a single step toward it.

It was even more galling to have to admit that his very pride, by definition, cut him off from all possible means of dealing with Satoko's riddles and the anxiety they provoked. If, for example, he were now to ask someone: "What does Satoko mean about not being here any more?" it would only betray the depth of his interest in her. "What could I do," he thought. "No matter what I did to convince them I wasn't interested in Satoko but only in an abstract anxiety of my own, nobody would believe me." A multitude of such thoughts raced through his head.

Ordinarily a bore, school under these circumstances offered Kiyoaki some relief. He always spent his lunch hours with Honda, even though Honda's conversation had taken a somewhat tedious turn of late. On the day of the Abbess's visit,

Honda had accompanied the others to the main house. And there Her Reverence had addressed them with a sermon that had completely seized his imagination. Now he couldn't wait to assault Kiyoaki's inattentive ears with his own exegesis of each point.

It was curious that while the sermon had left the dreamy Kiyoaki quite indifferent, it struck rationalistic Honda with the force of cogency.

The Gesshu Temple on the outskirts of Nara was a convent, quite a rarity in Hosso Buddhism. The gist of the sermon had strongly appealed to Honda, and the Abbess had been careful to introduce her listeners to the doctrine of Yuishiki * by using simple examples of no sophistication at all.

"Then there was the parable that Her Reverence said came to her when she saw the dog's body hanging over the falls," said Honda, thoroughly caught up in himself. "I don't think there's any doubt whatever that her use of it shows how fond she is of your family. And then her way of telling it—court phrases blending with old-fashioned Kyoto dialect. It's an elusive language that is filled with all sorts of subtle nuances. It certainly did a great deal to heighten the impact.

"You remember that the story is set in Tang China. A man named Yuan Hsaio was on his way to the famous Mount Kaoyu to study the teachings of Buddha. When night fell, he happened to be beside a cemetery, so he lay down to sleep among the burial mounds. Then in the middle of the night he awoke with a terrible thirst. Stretching out his hand, he scooped up some water from a hole by his side. As he dozed off again, he thought to himself that never had water tasted so pure, so fresh and cold. But when morning came, he saw what he had drunk from in the dark. Incredible though it seemed, what had tasted so delicious was water that had collected in a human skull. He retched and was sick. Yet this experience taught something to Yuan Hsaio. He realized that as

* The fundamental doctrine of Hosso Buddhism: all existence is based on subjective awareness.

long as conscious desire is at work, it will permit distinctions
to exist. But if one can suppress it, these distinctions dissolve
and one can be as content with a skull as with anything else.

"But what interests me is this: once Yuan Hsaio had been
thus enlightened, could he drink that water again, secure in
the knowledge that it was pure and delicious? And don't you
think that the same would hold true for chastity? If a boy is
naïve, of course, he can worship a prostitute in all innocence.
But once he realizes that his woman is a slut, and that he has
been living an illusion that merely serves to reflect the image
of his own purity, will he be able to love this woman in the
same way again? If he can, don't you think that would be
marvelous? To take your own ideal and bend the world to it
like that. Wouldn't that be a remarkable force? It would be
like holding the secret key to life right there in your hand,
wouldn't it?"

Honda's sexual innocence was matched by Kiyoaki's, who
was therefore unable to refute his strange ideal. Nevertheless,
being headstrong, he felt that he was different from Honda,
that he already had the key to existence within his grasp as
a sort of birthright. He did not know what gave him this confidence. Ominously handsome and a dreamer, so arrogant yet
so much a prey to anxiety, he was certain that somehow he
was the youthful repository of a peerless treasure. Because at
times he seemed to wear a quite physical radiance, he bore
himself with the pride of a man marked down by a rare disease, even though he suffered neither aches nor painful
swellings.

Kiyoaki knew nothing about the history of Gesshu Temple
and saw no need to remedy this lack. Honda by contrast, who
had no personal ties with it at all, had taken the trouble to do
some research in the library. Gesshu, he discovered, was a
comparatively new temple, built at the beginning of the eighteenth century. A daughter of the Emperor Higashiyama,
wishing to observe a period of mourning for her father, who
had died in the prime of life, devoted herself to the worship of
Kannon, the Goddess of Mercy, at the Kiomizu Temple. She

soon came to be deeply impressed by the commentaries of an old priest from the Joju Temple on the Hosso concept of existence, and consequently she became a fervent convert to this sect. After her ritual tonsuring, she declined to accept one of the benefices reserved for imperial princesses, deciding instead to found a new temple, one whose nuns would devote themselves to study of the scriptures. And it still preserved its unique place as a convent of the Hosso sect. Satoko's great-aunt, however, though an aristocrat, had the distinction of being the first abbess who was not an imperial princess.

Honda suddenly turned on Kiyoaki.

"Matsugae! What's the matter with you these days? You haven't paid the slightest attention to anything I've said, have you?"

"Nothing's the matter," Kiyoaki replied defensively, for once caught off guard. His beautiful clear eyes looked back at his friend. If Honda thought him insolent, it did not bother Kiyoaki in the least. What he feared was that his friend should become aware of his agony of mind. He knew that if he gave Honda the least encouragement in this direction, there would soon be nothing at all about him that Honda did not know. As this would be an unforgivable violation, he would have lost his only friend.

Honda was immediately alert to Kiyoaki's tension. He knew that to retain Kiyoaki's affection he must check the unthinking roughness that friendship ordinarily permitted. He had to treat him as warily as one would a freshly painted wall, on which the slightest careless touch would leave an indelible fingerprint. Should the circumstances demand it, he would have to go so far as to pretend not to notice Kiyoaki's mortal agony. Especially if such assumed obtuseness served to point up the elegance that would surely characterize Kiyoaki's ultimate suffering.

At such moments, Honda could even love Kiyoaki for the look of mute appeal in his eyes. Their beautiful gaze seemed to hold a plea: leave things as they are, as gloriously undefined as the line of the seashore. For the first time in their relationship—a protracted, warily transacted negotiation in the coin of friendship—Kiyoaki's composure was about to shatter; he was pleading. Honda was thus transformed into an aesthetic observer. Those who considered Kiyoaki and Honda to be friends were not mistaken, for as it stood, their relationship gave to each of them exactly what he desired.

 5

ONE EVENING about ten days later, Marquis Matsugae happened to return home unusually early and so Kiyoaki had dinner with both his parents, something that happened very rarely. Since the Marquis was fond of Western food, dinner was served in the small dining room of the Western-style house, and he himself had gone down to the wine cellar to choose the wine. He had taken Kiyoaki with him and had gone to great lengths to expound on the characteristics of the various wines cradled in the shelves that filled the cellar. His father had gone on to explain what wine went with which foods, what wine should be served only on the occasion of the visit of a member of the Imperial Family, and so on, beaming all the while. The Marquis never seemed as happy as when dispensing useless knowledge of this kind.

While they were sipping their aperitifs, his mother, who had been driven to Yokohama two days before by her young coachman, described the shopping expedition as if it were an event of great significance.

"I was simply astounded at the way people stared at my Western clothes, and in Yokohama of all places! Some dirty little children actually ran after the carriage shouting, 'Foreign lady! Foreign lady!'"

His father ventured something to the effect that he was thinking of taking Kiyoaki with him to the launching of the warship *Hie*, but he spoke as though it were a foregone conclusion that his son would not be interested.

At this point, both parents were at a loss for viable topics of conversation and began to flounder, their discomfiture evident even to Kiyoaki. Somehow, however, they finally happened upon the congenial subject of Kiyoaki's Otachimachi, the divination ritual that had taken place three years before when he was fifteen.

This ancient ceremony fell on the seventeenth of August according to the lunar calendar. A large wooden basin filled with water was placed in the garden to catch the reflection of the moon, and appropriate offerings were made. If the sky was overcast on this August night of his fifteenth year, bad fortune was expected to dog the boy who stood before the basin, for the rest of his life.

As his parents talked, the scene came back to Kiyoaki vividly. Flanked by his parents and dressed in his *hakama*, a divided skirt, and kimono blazoned with the family crest, he had stood in the middle of the dew-drenched lawn, the new basin filled with water before him, and a chorus of chirping insects ringing in his ears.

The trees that encircled the now-darkened garden, the tiled roofs of the mansion itself beyond, even the maple hill— the reflection of all this, and more, had been fixed in jagged outline, compressed into the circle of water that was defined by the rim of the basin. That rim of blond cyprus wood had become a frontier where this world ended and another began. Since this ceremony during his fifteenth year was to determine his lifetime fortune, Kiyoaki felt as though his very soul, naked, had been set there on the wet grass. The wooden sides of the basin expressed his outer self; the disk of water, which they in turn defined, expressed his inner.

Everyone was silent, so the sounds of insects throughout the garden filled his ears as never before. He gazed earnestly into the basin. The water within was dark at first, shadowed

by clouds as thick as clustered seaweed. A moment later the
seaweed seemed to wave and he thought he had seen a faint
glow suffuse the water, but then it faded. He could not remember how long he had waited after that. Then all of a
sudden the black water in the basin, which had seemed im-
penetrably obscure, cleared, and there directly in its center
shone a tiny image of the full moon.

Everyone broke into exclamations of pleasure, and his
mother, rigid all this time, was greatly relieved and began to
wave her fan to drive away the mosquitos swarming around
her skirt.

"Oh, I'm so glad! Now the boy will have a fortunate life,
won't he?" she said.

Then Kiyoaki was congratulated by everyone present.

But still he felt a certain dread. He could not bring himself
to look up into the sky at the moon itself, the origin of the
image in the water. Rather he kept looking down into the
basin and into the water contained by its curved sides, the reflection of his innermost self, into which the moon, like a
golden shell, had sunk so deep. For at that moment he had
captured the celestial. It sparkled like a golden butterfly
trapped in the meshes of his soul.

Yet, he thought, were these meshes fine enough to hold it?
Once caught, would the butterfly not slip out soon and fly
away? Even at fifteen he feared its loss. His character was already formed, and each of his triumphs would bring this fear
in its wake. Having gained the moon, how much then would
he dread life in a world without it. The oppression of such
fear! Even if this moon aroused nothing but hatred in him.

For even in the triviality of a single playing card missing
from a deck, the world's order is inevitably turned awry. And
for someone like Kiyoaki, the smallest incongruity took on
the proportions of a watch deprived of one cogwheel. The order of his universe collapsed and he found himself trapped
in terrifying darkness. The lost playing card, of no value in
itself, would, in his eyes, assume the significance of a crown
over which rival claimants were locked in a struggle that

would plunge the world into crisis. His sensibility was thus at the mercy of every unforeseen occurrence, however trivial, and he had no defenses at hand.

As he thought back to his Otachimachi, that night of August 17 three years before, he suddenly shuddered with the realization that Satoko had somehow impinged on his thoughts.

At that moment, to Kiyoaki's relief, the butler entered in his cool *hakama* with a rustle of Sendai silk to announce that dinner was ready. Kiyoaki and his parents went into the dining room, each to sit in front of a place set with fine English china decorated with the family crest. Since early childhood Kiyoaki had had to endure the tedium of his father's lessons in Western table manners. As it was, his mother had never become accustomed to the Western way of eating and his father still behaved with the ostentation of a man eager to seem at home abroad, so he was the only one who ate naturally and at ease.

When the soup course arrived, his mother lost no time in raising a new topic in her calm voice.

"Really, Satoko can be very trying. Only this morning I discovered that the Ayakuras sent a messenger with her refusal. And for a time she gave everyone the distinct impression that she had decided to accept."

"She's twenty already, isn't she?" his father replied. "If she continues to be so demanding, she may find herself left an old maid. I've been worried about her myself, but what can one do?"

Kiyoaki was all ears as his father went on casually. "I wonder what's the matter with her? Or did they think he was too much beneath her? No matter how noble a family the Ayakuras once were, their present fortunes hardly allow them to turn down a young man like that, with a bright future ahead of him in the Ministry of the Interior. They should have been glad of him, shouldn't they, without bothering about what kind of family he came from?"

"That's exactly how I feel. And that's why I'm disinclined to do anything more to help her."

"Well now, we owe them a great deal because of what they did for Kiyoaki. I feel obliged to do all I can to help them build up their family fortunes again. But what could we do to find a suitor whom she'd accept?"

"I wonder if such a man exists?"

As he listened, Kiyoaki's spirits rose. His riddle was solved. "Kiyo, what would you do if suddenly I weren't here any more?" Satoko had asked. She had simply been referring to the offer of marriage then pending. At the time she had been inclined to accept but had dropped her hint out of concern for Kiyoaki's reaction. Now, ten days later, it would appear from his mother that she had formally refused. And her reason for doing this was clear to him. She had done so because she was in love with Kiyoaki.

And with that the clouds faded from his horizon. He was no longer beset by anxieties. The water in the glass was clear once again. For ten days he had been excluded from the small, peaceful sanctuary that was his only refuge. But now he could return to it and breathe easy.

Kiyoaki was enjoying a rare moment of acute happiness, a happiness that without question sprang from his regaining his clarity of vision. The card that had been deliberately concealed had reappeared in his hand. The deck was complete. And so once more it became a mere pack of cards. His happiness shone clear and unmarred. For a moment at least, Kiyoaki had succeeded in breaking the grip of his emotions.

The Marquis and Marquise Matsugae, however, were still looking at one another across the table, their insensitivity blinding them even to something as obvious as their son's sudden rush of happiness. The Marquis confronted the classic melancholy of his wife's face, and she, in turn, the coarseness of his. Features proper to a man of action had become blurred by the ravages of indolent living that spread beneath his skin.

Despite the seemingly erratic course charted in his parents' conversation, Kiyoaki had always been aware of adherence to a definite ritual; it was as set as the Shinto ceremony of offering the gods a branch of the sacred sakaki tree, a ceremony in which each syllable of the incantation is meticulously pronounced and each lustrous branch carefully selected.

Kiyoaki had observed the ritual countless times since early childhood. No burning crises. No storms of passion. His mother knew exactly what was coming next. The Marquis knew that his wife knew. Their expressions blank, innocent of foreknowledge, they glided downstream like twigs hand in hand on clear waters mirroring blue sky and clouds, to take the inevitable plunge over the crest of the falls.

Just as predictably, the Marquis left his after-dinner coffee unfinished and turned to his son. "Now, Kiyoaki, what do you say to a game of billiards?"

"Well, then, please excuse me," said the Marquise.

Kiyoaki was so happy tonight, however, that this kind of charade did not grate on him in the least. His mother returned to the main house and he went with his father into the billiard room. With its English-style oak paneling, its portrait of Kiyoaki's grandfather, and its large map done in oils depicting the naval battles of the Russo-Japanese War, this room was much admired by visitors. One of the disciples of Sir John Millais, famous for his portrait of Gladstone, had done the huge likeness of Kiyoaki's grandfather during his stay in Japan. And now his grandfather's figure loomed in ceremonial attire from the shadows.

The composition was simple, but the artist had evinced a high degree of skill in his judicious blending of idealization and realistic sternness to achieve a likeness that expressed not only the indomitable air expected of a Restoration peer but also those more personal traits dear to his family, down to the warts on his cheek. According to household custom, whenever a new maid came from the ancestral province of Kagoshima, she was taken before the portrait to pay reverence. Some hours before his grandfather's death, though the billiard room was empty and it was unlikely that the picture

cord could have become so worn, the portrait fell to the floor
with a crash that echoed throughout the house.

The room contained three billiard tables covered with layers of Italian marble. Though the three-ball game had been
introduced at the time of the war with China, no one ever
played it in the Matsugae billiard room; Kiyoaki and his father used four. The butler had already placed the red and
white balls on the table in proper order and now he handed a
cue to both the Marquis and his son. Kiyoaki looked down at
the surface of the table as he rubbed the tip of his cue with the
Italian chalk of compressed volcanic ash. The red and white
ivory balls lay motionless on the green baize, each casting a
round shadow like a shellfish making a hesitant foray into the
open. They stirred not the slightest interest in him. He had
the sensation of standing alone on an unknown street at the
height of the day and suddenly finding himself face to face
with these odd shapes devoid of all meaning.

The Marquis was always made uneasy by the boredom on
his son's handsome face. Happy as Kiyoaki felt tonight, his
eyes remained dull. "Did you know," said his father, hitting
on a subject of conversation, "that two Siamese princes are
coming to Japan to Peers School."

"No."

"Since they'll be in your class, we might have them staying
here with us for a few days. I've mentioned it at the Foreign
Ministry. It's a country that's made great strides recently.
They've abolished slavery and they're building railroads and
so on. Be sure to keep that in mind when you deal with them."

His father lined up his shot. Kiyoaki stood behind him and
watched him crouch like a fat leopard twisting his cue with
a show of fierceness. Kiyoaki could not suppress a sudden
smile. His sense of happiness and the image of a mysterious
tropic land fused in his mind with a soft click as appealing
to him as the contact of the red and white ivory balls on the
table. And then his elation, which had been as abstract as
pure crystal, suddenly took on the green extravagance of the
tropical jungle.

The Marquis was an expert at billiards, and Kiyoaki was never a match for him. After each had taken the first five shots, his father turned abruptly from the table with the suggestion Kiyoaki had long been expecting. "I think I'll take a little stroll. What would you say to that?"

Kiyoaki did not answer. His father then made a totally unexpected proposal: "You can come just as far as the gate, can't you? The way you used to when you were a child."

Startled, Kiyoaki turned dark, flashing eyes on his father. In any event, the Marquis had scored a point over his son for surprise.

His father's mistress was installed in one of the houses just outside the gate. European families rented the other two. Each house had its own back gate in the fence that separated it from the Matsugae estate. The European children were free to make use of this opportunity and played every day in the grounds of the estate. The only gate with a lock on it—and this was covered with rust—was the gate behind his mistress's house.

From the front door of the main house to the front gate was half a mile. When Kiyoaki was a child, his father would take him by the hand and walk with him as far as the gate en route to his mistress's. There they would separate, and a servant would bring Kiyoaki back.

When his father went out on business, he invariably used the carriage. When he left the house on foot, therefore, his destination was obvious to everyone. Accompanying his father on these occasions had always been painful for Kiyoaki. While some naïve instinct of boyhood urged him to hold his father back for his mother's sake, the realization of his own helplessness stirred bitter frustration in him. His mother of course was not at all pleased at Kiyoaki's accompanying her husband on these evening strolls. But the more she resented it, the more her husband persisted in taking Kiyoaki by the hand. Kiyoaki had been quick to detect his father's covert desire to make him an accomplice in his mother's betrayal.

This walk, however, on a cold November night, was something quite new. As his father put on the overcoat proffered by the butler, Kiyoaki left the billiard room to fetch the uniform coat with metal buttons that he wore at school. As always, the butler was waiting at the door with the usual present wrapped in purple crepe; then he followed his master at the customary distance of ten paces.

The moon was bright, and the wind moaned through the branches of the trees. Although his father did not trouble to glance back at the wraithlike figure of Yamada the steward, Kiyoaki was concerned enough to look over his shoulder more than once. Without so much as a cape over his *hakama*, Yamada came along behind, swaying slightly on his unsteady legs, his hands, white-gloved as always, cradling the package in its purple wrapper. His glasses had a frosty sparkle in the moonlight. Kiyoaki wondered at this man, loyal beyond a doubt, allowing almost nothing to pass his lips. How many passions lay spent within his body like a tangle of rusted springs? Far more than the jovial, extrovert Marquis, his reserved and seemingly indifferent son was capable of detecting depth of feeling in others.

The hooting of the owls and the wind in the trees reminded Kiyoaki, still wine-flushed, of the branches blowing in the photograph of the memorial service. As they walked through the bleak, wintry night, his father was anticipating the moist warmth and intimacy of the rosy flesh that awaited him, while his son's thoughts turned toward death.

As the Marquis went along elated by the wine and scattering pebbles with the tip of his walking stick, he suddenly turned to Kiyoaki: "You're not much of one for having a good time, are you? I couldn't tell you how many women I'd had at your age. Look here, suppose I take you with me next time? I'll see that there are plenty of geishas there and for once you can kick up your heels. And bring along some friends of yours from school if you want."

"No, thank you."

Kiyoaki shuddered as he blurted this out. He felt his feet suddenly glued to the ground. At this one remark of his father's, his elation shattered, like a vase striking the floor.

"What's the matter?"

"Please will you excuse me? Good night."

Kiyoaki turned on his heel and walked rapidly back past the dimly lit entrance of the Western house in the direction of the main residence whose distant lights, burning at the front door, gleamed faintly through the trees.

Kiyoaki was unable to sleep that night. But it was no thought of his mother or his father that troubled him. On the contrary, he was absorbed in revenging himself on Satoko. "She has been cruel enough to lure me into a petty trap. For ten days she let me suffer. She had just one thing in mind: to keep me in agony. I can't let her get away with it. But then I'm no match for her when it comes to inventing ways of torturing people. What can I do? What would be best would be to convince her that I have no more respect for female dignity than my father has. If only I could say or write something absolutely outrageous to her that would strike home. But my trouble is that I'm always at a disadvantage since I'm not bold enough to let people know bluntly how I really feel. It wouldn't be enough to tell her that she doesn't interest me in the least. That would still leave her plenty of room to scheme. I have to insult her. I have to humiliate her so completely that she'll never come back for more. That's what I have to do. For the first time in her life, I'm going to make her sorry for what she's done."

Despite all this, Kiyoaki's resolutions were feeble. No specific plan had yet occurred to him.

A pair of threefold screens stood on either side of his bed, each decorated with poems of Han Shan. At the foot of the bed, a carved jade parrot looked down from its perch on a sandalwood display shelf. Kiyoaki had little interest in anything as currently fashionable as a Rodin or a Cézanne. His tastes were rather conservative. Sleepless, he stared at the parrot. Every detail of its clouded green jade, even down to the fine carving of the wing feathers, seemed to glow more clearly. Thus the figure of the bird appeared to hover, disembodied, in the dark, a phantom image that made Kiyoaki uneasy. Realizing that the phenomenon was caused by a stray shaft of moonlight coming in through the window, he pulled the curtain all the way open in an abrupt movement. The moon was high in the sky, and its light spilled over the bed.

It was dazzling enough to suggest frivolity rather than solemnity. He thought of the cold gleaming silk of Satoko's kimono. With unearthly clarity he saw her eyes there in the moon, those splendid large eyes which he had seen so disconcertingly close to his own. The wind had died.

The burning heat of Kiyoaki's body could not be explained by the mere warmth of the room, and something like fever seemed to tingle in his earlobes. He threw off the blanket and opened the collar of his nightgown. The fire still burned and seethed under his skin, and he felt that he would find no relief until he took off his nightgown and bared his body to the cold moonlight. Finally, wearied by his thoughts, he rolled over on his stomach and lay with his face buried in his pillow, his naked back to the moon and the hot blood still throbbing in his temples.

And so he lay, the moonlight washing over the incomparable smooth white of his back, its brilliance highlighting the graceful lines of his body to reveal the subtle but pervasive hint of firm masculinity that made it clear that this was the flesh not of a woman but of a still immature young man.

The moon shone with dazzling brightness on Kiyoaki's left side, where the pale flesh pulsed softly in rhythm with his heartbeat. Here there were three small, almost invisible moles. And much as the three stars in Orion's belt fade in strong moonlight, so too these three small moles were almost blotted out by its rays.

6

IN 1910, His Highness King Rahma VI had succeeded his late father, Rahma V, to the throne of Siam. One of the princes now coming to study in Japan was his younger brother, Prince Pattanadid, whose titular name was Praong Chao. His companion, eighteen like himself and also his best friend, was his cousin Prince Kridsada, a grandson of King Rahma IV, whose titular name was Mon Chao. Prince Pattanadid nicknamed him "Kri." But Prince Kridsada, in deference to Pattanadid's place in the succession, addressed him more respectfully as "Chao P."

Both princes were fervently devout Buddhists. But they not only dressed for the most part like young English gentlemen, they also spoke the language with perfect fluency. Indeed it was precisely because the new king had been concerned about their becoming too Westernized that he had decided upon Japan for their university studies. Neither of the princes had raised any objections, despite one unfortunate aspect to it. Leaving Siam entailed the separation of Chao P. and Kri's younger sister.

The love of these two young people for each other was the delight of the court, since their engagement at the end of Chao P.'s studies was a foregone conclusion and their future was secure in every way. Yet when he sailed, Chao P.'s grief was so intense as to give rise to alarm in a country whose customs did not favor such direct expressions of feeling.

The sea voyage and his cousin's sympathy had helped considerably to alleviate the young prince's distress, and when

they arrived for a stay at the Matsugaes', Kiyoaki found their
swarthy faces alight with happiness.

The princes were free to follow the school routine as they
liked until the winter holidays began. Though they were to
start attending classes in January, it was decided that they
would not be officially enrolled until the new term began in
the spring, by which time they would have had the chance to
acclimatize and also to study the language intensively.

While they were at the Matsugaes', the princes were to oc-
cupy two adjoining guest rooms on the second floor of the
Western-style house, which had been equipped with a steam-
heating system imported from Chicago. The period before
dinner with the assembled Matsugae family was awkward for
Kiyoaki and his guests, but when the three young men were
left to themselves after the meal, stiff formality suddenly
eased as the princes began to show Kiyoaki photographs of
the golden temples and exotic scenery of Bangkok. Kiyoaki
noticed that Prince Kridsada was no younger than his cousin
and yet still retained a certain childish capriciousness, but he
warmed to Prince Pattanadid in whom he sensed a dreamy
nature like his own.

One of the photographs was a general view of the monastery of Wat-Po, famous for its huge sculpture of the reclining
Buddha. Since a skilled artist had applied delicate tinting to
the photo, it was almost like having the temple itself before
one's eyes. Palm trees were blowing gracefully, every detail
of their clustered leaves carefully etched in color against a
background of tropical sky whose vivid blue contrasted
sharply with the sheer white of the clouds. The monastery
buildings were incomparable; they overwhelmed the spectator
with a brilliant sunburst of gold, scarlet, and white. Two
golden warrior gods stood guard on either side of a scarlet
gate outlined in gold. Delicately carved golden bas-relief
climbed the temple's white walls and columns to form a kind
of frieze at the top. Then there was the roof with its array of
pinnacles, each one also covered with intricate bas-relief of

gold and scarlet; from the treasure house in their midst, the gleaming spires of the triple tower soared up into the bright blue of the sky.

The princes were delighted with Kiyoaki's look of unfeigned admiration. Then Prince Pattanadid began to speak; there was a distant look in his fine, wide, sloping eyes, whose keen glance contrasted strongly with his soft, round face.

"This temple is special for me. On the voyage here to Japan, I often dreamed about it. Its golden roofs seemed to float up out of the night sea. The ship kept on moving, and even by the time the entire temple was visible, it was still a long way off from me. Having risen from the waves, it glistened under the stars the way the light of the new moon shines across the surface of the water. Standing on the deck of the ship, I put my hands together and bowed in reverence toward it. As happens in dreams, although it was night and the temple was so far away, I could make out the smallest details of the gold and scarlet decoration.

"I told Kri about this dream and said that the temple seemed to be following us to Japan. But he laughed at me and said that what was following me to Japan was not the temple but the memory of something else. He made me angry at the time, but now I'm inclined to agree with him. For everything sacred has the substance of dreams and memories, and so we experience the miracle of what is separated from us by time or distance suddenly being made tangible. Dreams, memories, the sacred—they are all alike in that they are beyond our grasp. Once we are even marginally separated from what we can touch, the object is sanctified; it acquires the beauty of the unattainable, the quality of the miraculous. Everything, really, has this quality of sacredness, but we can desecrate it at a touch. How strange man is! His touch defiles and yet he contains the source of miracles."

"He certainly puts it in a difficult, roundabout way," said Prince Kridsada, breaking in, "but what he's really thinking

about is the girl he loves back in Bangkok. Chao P., show
Kiyoaki her picture."

Prince Pattanadid flushed, but his dark skin hid the rush
of blood to his cheeks. Seeing his guest's discomfiture, Kiyoaki
turned the conversation back to their previous topic.

"Do you often dream like that?" he asked. "I keep a diary
record of my dreams." Chao P.'s eyes flashed with interest as
he replied: "I wish my Japanese were good enough to let me
read it."

Kiyoaki realized that even though he was having to speak
in English, he had just succeeded in conveying to Chao P. his
fascination with dreams, something he had never dared reveal
even to Honda. He felt himself liking Chao P. more and more.
From then on, however, the conversation lagged, and Kiyoaki,
noticing the mischievous twinkle in Prince Kridsada's eyes,
suddenly realized the difficulty: he had not insisted on seeing
the picture, which was what Chao P. had wanted him to do.

"Please show me the photo of the dream that followed you
from Siam," he hastened to ask.

"Do you mean the temple or the girl?" Kridsada inter-
jected, as playful as ever. And although Chao P. scolded him
for his frivolous bad manners, he was unrepentant. When his
cousin finally took out the photograph, he thrust out his hand
eagerly to point.

"Princess Chantrapa is my younger sister. Her name means
'moonlight.' But we usually call her Ying Chan."

Looking at the picture, Kiyoaki was rather disappointed to
see a much plainer young girl than he had imagined. She
wore Western clothes, a dress of white lace. Her hair was tied
with a white ribbon and she wore a pearl necklace. She looked
modest and unsophisticated. Any student at Peers might well
be carrying a picture of a girl like her. The beautiful, waving
fall of her hair to her shoulders showed signs of care. But the
rather strong brows over wide, timid eyes, the lips slightly
parted like the petals of an exotic flower before the rains come
—her features all gave the unmistakable impression of girlish

innocence unconscious of its own beauty. Of course that had
its charm, but much like a young nestling quite oblivious of
its power to fly, she was too passively content.

"Compared with this girl," Kiyoaki thought, "Satoko is a
hundred, a thousand times more of a woman. And isn't that
why she is often so hateful to me—because she is so much a
woman? Besides, she's far more beautiful than this girl. And
she knows how beautiful she is. There's nothing she doesn't
know, unfortunately, including how immature I am."

Chao P., seeing how Kiyoaki was staring at the picture of
his sweetheart and perhaps feeling slightly alarmed that he
might be too attracted to her, suddenly reached out his fine-
boned, amber-skinned hand and retrieved it. As he did so,
Kiyoaki's eye was caught by a flash of green, and for the first
time he noticed Chao P.'s beautiful ring. Its stone was a rich,
square-cut emerald. On either side of it, the fierce beasts'
heads of a pair of yaksha, the warrior gods, had been finely
etched in gold. All in all, it was an immense ring of such
quality that for Kiyoaki to have overlooked it until now was
proof of how little he was inclined to take notice of others.

"I was born in May. It's my birthstone," Prince Pattanadid
explained, slightly embarrassed again. "Ying Chan gave it to
me as a farewell present."

"But if you wore something as magnificent as that at Peers,
I'm afraid they'd order you to stop," warned Kiyoaki.

Taken aback by this, the two princes began to confer
earnestly in their native language, but quickly realizing their
inadvertent rudeness, they switched back to English for
Kiyoaki's sake. Kiyoaki told them that he would speak to his
father about making arrangements for them to have a safety
deposit at the bank. After this had been settled and the atmosphere had warmed still further, Prince Kridsada brought
out a small photograph of his own sweetheart. And then both
princes urged Kiyoaki to do the same.

"In Japan we are not accustomed to exchanging pictures,"
he said hastily, under the spur of youthful vanity. "But I'll
certainly introduce her to you very soon." He did not have the

courage to show them the pictures of Satoko that filled the album he had kept from early childhood.

It suddenly dawned on Kiyoaki that although his good looks had excited praise and admiration all his life, he had nearly reached the age of eighteen in the gloomy confines of the family estate without a single female friend other than Satoko.

And Satoko was as much an enemy as anything else; she was far from being the ideal of womanhood, sweetness and affection incarnate, that the two princes would admire. Kiyoaki felt his anger rising against the many frustrations that hemmed him in. What his somewhat tipsy father had said to him on that "evening stroll"—though his tone had been very kind—now seemed in retrospect to contain a veiled scorn.

The very things that his sense of dignity had made him ignore up to now had suddenly gained the power to humiliate him. Everything about these lively young princes from the tropics—their brown skin, the flashing virility in their eyes, their long, slender, amber fingers, already so experienced in caresses—all this seemed to taunt Kiyoaki: "What? At your age, not even a single love affair?"

Feeling his poise evaporating, Kiyoaki, with his last reserves of aloofness and elegance, hurriedly said, "I'll introduce her to you very soon." But how was he to arrange matters? How to show off Satoko's beauty before his foreign friends? For the very day before, after a long hesitation, Kiyoaki had finally sent a wildly insulting letter to Satoko.

Every phrase in that letter, a letter whose premeditated insults he had worked and reworked with the most painstaking care, was still vivid in his mind. He had begun by writing: "I am very sorry to say that your effrontery toward me compels me to write this letter." And from that curt opening, he had gone on:

> When I think how often you have presented me with these senseless riddles, withholding any clues in order to make them seem more serious than they really are, numbness strikes this hand of mine holding its writing brush until it withers me. I,

have no doubt that your emotional whims have driven you to do this to me. There has been no gentleness in your method, obviously no affection whatever, not a trace of friendship. There are deep-seated motivations in your despicable behavior to which you are blind, but which are driving you toward a goal that is only too obvious. But decency forbids me to say anything further.

But all your efforts and schemes have now become a mere froth on the waves. For I, unhappy though I once was, I have now passed one of life's milestones, a transition for which I owe you some debt of gratitude, however indirect. My father invited me to go with him on one of his excursions to the Gay Quarters, and now I've crossed a barrier that every man must cross. To put it bluntly, I spent the night with a geisha my father had chosen for me. Nothing but one of those exercises in pleasure that society sanctions for men.

Fortunately enough, a single night was sufficient to bring about a complete change in me. My previous concepts of women were shattered. I learned to see a girl as nothing but a plump, lascivious little animal, a contemptible playmate. This is the wonderful revelation to be found in my father's kind of society. And having had no sympathy for his attitude toward women until that night, I now endorse it completely. Every fiber in my body tells me that I am my father's son.

Perhaps at this point you may feel that I am to be congratulated on having finally outgrown the dead old-fashioned views of the Meiji era in favor of more enlightened ones. And perhaps you are smiling contemptuously, secure in the knowledge that my lust for paid women will only serve to enhance my esteem for pure ladies like yourself. No! Let me disabuse you of any such notion. Since that night (enlightenment being exactly what it says) I have broken through all these standards into territory where there are no restraints. Geisha or princess, virgin or prostitute, factory girl or artist—there is no distinction whatever. Every woman without exception is a liar and "nothing but a plump, lascivious little animal." All the rest is makeup and costumes. And I must say that I see you as being just like all the others. Please believe that gentle Kiyo, whom you considered so sweet, so innocent, so malleable, is gone forever.

The two princes must have been somewhat taken aback when Kiyoaki said an abrupt good night and hurried out of their room fairly early in the evening, although he smilingly observed all the usual proprieties expected of a gentleman, such as checking that their bedding was correctly laid out, inquiring after any further needs, and finally withdrawing with the ritual courtesies.

"Why is it that at times like this, there is never anyone to rely on," Kiyoaki muttered to himself as he fled through the long corridor that led back to the main house from the Western one. He thought of Honda, but his exacting standards of friendship made him dismiss that possibility.

The night wind howled at the windows of the passageway with its line of dim lanterns stretching into the distance. Suddenly afraid that someone might see him and wonder at his running and being out of breath like this, he stopped, and as he rested his elbows on the ornamental window frame and pretended to stare out into the garden, he tried desperately to put his thoughts in order. Unlike dreams, reality was not so easy to manipulate. He had to conceive a plan. It could not be anything vague and uncertain; it had to be as firmly compact as a pill, and with as sure and immediate a result. He was oppressed by a sense of his own weakness, and after the warmth of the room he had just left, the cold corridor made him shiver.

He pressed his forehead to the wind-buffeted glass and peered out into the garden. There was no moon tonight. The island and the maple hill beyond formed one mass in the darkness. In the faint glow of the corridor lamps he could make out the surface of the pond ruffled by the wind. He suddenly imagined that the snapping turtles had reared their heads out of the water and were looking toward him. The thought made him shudder.

As he returned to the main house and was about to climb the stairs to his room, he encountered his tutor Iinuma, and looked at him very coldly.

"Have Their Highnesses already retired for the night, sir?"

"Yes."

"The young master is about to retire too?"

"I have some studying to do."

Iinuma was twenty-three and in his final year of night school. In fact, he had probably just returned from class since he was carrying some books under one arm. To be young and in his prime seemed to have no other effect on him than to deepen his look of characteristic melancholy. His huge dark bulk unnerved Kiyoaki.

When the boy returned to his room, he did not bother to light the stove, but began to pace about anxiously, tossing up plan after plan after plan.

"Whatever I do, I must do it quickly," he thought. "Is it too late already? Somehow, in the very near future I have to introduce a girl to the princes as being on the fondest terms with me, when I have just sent her this letter. And furthermore, I have to do it in a way that won't cause gossip."

The evening paper, which he had no time to read, lay on the chair. For no good reason, Kiyoaki picked it up and opened it. An announcement for a Kabuki play at the Imperial Theater caught his eye, and suddenly his heart began to thump.

"That's it. I'll take the princes to the Imperial Theater. And as for that letter, it can't have arrived already since I sent it only yesterday. There's still hope. My parents won't allow Satoko to go to a play with me, but if we met by accident, there'd be nothing wrong with that."

Kiyoaki rushed out of the room and down the stairs to the room beside the front entrance where the telephone was. Before he went in, however, he looked cautiously in the direction of Iinuma's room, which was emitting streaks of light. He must be studying.

Kiyoaki picked up the receiver and gave the operator the number. His heart was pounding; his customary ennui had been swept away.

"Hello, is this the Ayakura residence? Please may I speak to Miss Satoko?" Kiyoaki asked, after the familiar voice of an old woman had answered. From distant Azabu, her voice

expressed a certain displeasure, though remaining agoniz-
ingly polite.

"It's young Master Matsugae, I believe? I'm terribly sorry,
but it's so late, I'm afraid."

"Has Miss Satoko gone to bed?"

"Well, no, I don't believe she has retired yet."

After Kiyoaki persisted, Satoko finally came to the phone.
The sound of her warm, clear voice cheered him immensely.

"Kiyo, what in the world do you want at this time of night?"

"Well, to tell the truth, I sent you a letter yesterday. Now I
must ask you something. When it comes, please, whatever
you do, don't open it. Please promise me that you'll throw it
right into the fire."

"Well really, Kiyo, I don't know what you're talking about
. . ." Something in Satoko's apparently calm voice told Kiyoaki that she had started to weave her usual net of ambiguities. And her voice on this cold winter night was as warm
and ripe as an apricot in June. He said impatiently, "I know
you don't. So just please listen and promise. When my letter
comes, throw it in the fire right away without opening it,
please?"

"I see."

"Do you promise?"

"Very well."

"And now there's something else I want to ask you . . ."

"This certainly seems to be the night for requests, doesn't
it, Kiyo?"

"Could you do this for me: get tickets to the play at the
Imperial Theater for the day after tomorrow for yourself and
your maid."

"A play . . . !"

The abrupt silence at the other end made Kiyoaki afraid
that Satoko might refuse, but then he realized that, in his
haste, there was something he had forgotten. Given the
Ayakuras' present circumstances, the price of a pair of tickets,
at two yen fifty sen apiece, would represent quite an extravagance.

"No, wait, excuse me. I'll have the tickets sent to you. If your seats are next to ours, people might talk, but I'll arrange it so that they are somewhere nearby. I'm going with the two princes from Siam, by the way."

"How kind of you, Kiyo! Tadeshina will be delighted, I'm sure. I'd love to go," said Satoko, making no effort to conceal her pleasure.

7

THE NEXT DAY AT SCHOOL, Kiyoaki asked Honda to join him and the Siamese princes at the Imperial Theater the following night; Honda was pleased, and accepted at once, although not without a vague sense of awkwardness. Kiyoaki, of course, did not choose to tell his friend the part of the plan that provided for the chance encounter with Satoko.

At home that evening during dinner, Honda told his parents about Kiyoaki's invitation. His father had some reservations about the theater, but felt that he should not restrict the freedom of an eighteen-year-old in matters of this sort.

His father was a justice of the Supreme Court. He saw to it that an atmosphere of decorum reigned in his household. The family lived in a large mansion in Hongo with many rooms, some of which were decorated in the oppressive Western style popular in the Meiji era. Among his servants were a number of students, and books were to be found everywhere. They filled the library and study and even lined the hallways, in an expanse of brown leather and gold lettering.

His mother, too, was the opposite of frivolous. She held office in the Women's Patriotic League, and she was rather pained that her son should have struck up a close friendship with the son of Marquise Matsugae, a lady who had no taste for such worthwhile activities. Aside from this, however, Shigekuni Honda's school record, his diligence, his health, and his unfailing good manners were a source of constant pride to his mother, and she never tired of singing his praises to other people.

Everything in the Honda household, down to the most trivial utensil, had to meet exacting standards. Starting with the bonsai in the front entrance, the screen behind it with the painted Chinese ideogram for harmony, the cigarette case and ashtrays laid out in the drawing room, the tasseled tablecloth, and ending with the rice bin in the kitchen, the towel rack in the toilet, the pen holders in the study, and even the various paperweights in the study—each item was perfection of its kind.

And this same care extended to the conversation of the household. In the homes of Honda's friends, one or two old people could always be counted on to come up with absurd stories. In all seriousness, for example, they might recall the night when two moons had appeared at the window, one of them a badger in disguise who immediately resumed his normal shape on being roundly abused, and lumbered away. And there would always be an appreciative audience. But in his own home, a severe glance from his father would make it clear even to the oldest of the maids that to indulge in such ignorant nonsense was out of the question.

In his youth, his father had spent some years studying law in Germany, and he revered the German respect for logic.

When Shigekuni Honda compared his own home with Kiyoaki's, one aspect of the contrast particularly amused him. Although the Matsugaes seemed to lead a Westernized life and although their house was filled with objects from abroad, the atmosphere of their home was strikingly and traditionally Japanese. In his own household, on the other hand, the day-to-day life-style might be Japanese, but the atmosphere had much that was Western in spirit. And then his father's regard for the education of his student houseboys was in marked contrast to Marquis Matsugae's attitude toward his.

As usual, once he had finished his homework, which tonight was French, his second foreign language, Honda turned to some law digests. These were written in German, French, and English, and he had had to order them through the Maruzen bookstore. He read these every night in anticipation of the future demands of college work, and also, more significantly, because he had a natural bent to trace everything to its source. Lately, he had begun to lose interest in the European natural law that had exercised such a fascination on him. From the day of the Abbess of Gesshu's sermon, he had become more and more aware of such a system's inadequacies.

He realized, however, that although natural law had been comparatively neglected in recent years, no other system of thought displayed such a capacity for survival: it had flourished in different forms suited to each of the many epochs in two thousand years of history—from its apparent origins in Socrates and its powerful influence on the formulation of law in the Roman era through the medium of Aristotle's writings, to its intricate development and codification during the Christian Middle Ages and its renewed popularity in the Renaissance; this indeed reached such a peak that the period could be called the Age of Natural Law. In all probability, it was this recurrent philosophy that preserved the traditional European faith in the power of reason. Still, Honda could not help thinking that despite its tenacity, two thousand years of its strong, bright, Apollonian humanism had barely sufficed to hold off the assaults of darkness and barbarism.

Nor was the assault limited to these forces. Another, more blinding light had also threatened it, since natural law had to rigidly exclude the very possibility of a concept of existence based on romantic and irrational nationalism.

However that might be, Honda did not necessarily cling to the historical school of law, which was influenced by nineteenth-century romanticism, nor to the ethnic school. The

Japan of the Meiji era, indeed, needed a nationalistic type of law, one that had its roots in the philosophy of the historical school. But Honda's concerns were quite different. He had first been intent on isolating the essential principle behind all law, a principle which he felt must exist. And this was why the concept of natural law had fascinated him for a time. But now he was more concerned to define the outer limits of natural law, which were inadvertently pointed up by its claims to universality. He enjoyed giving his imagination free rein in this direction. If the law, he thought, was to do away with the restrictions that natural law and philosophy had imposed upon man's vision of the world since ancient times, and break through to a more universal principle (granted that such exists) would it not reach a stage where the law itself, as we know it, would cease to exist?

This was, of course, the kind of dangerous thinking that appealed to youth. And given Honda's circumstances, with the geometrical structure of Roman law towering so formidably in the background to cast its shadow over the modern operative law that he was now studying, it was no wonder that he found its orthodoxy rather tedious; from time to time, he therefore put aside the legal codes of Meiji Japan, so scrupulously based on Western models, and turned his eyes in another direction—to the broader and more ancient legal traditions of Asia.

In his present skeptical mood, a French translation by Delongchamps of the Laws of Manu, which had arrived from Maruzen at an opportune moment, contained much that he found strongly appealing.

The Laws of Manu, probably compiled over the period from 200 B.C. to 200 A.D., were the foundation of Indian law. And among faithful Hindus, it maintained its authority as a legal code right up to the present. Within its twelve chapters and 2,684 articles were gathered an immense body of precepts drawn from religion, custom, ethics, and law. It ranged from the origin of the cosmos to the penalties for robbery and the rules for dividing an inheritance. It was imbued with an Asian

philosophy in which all things were somehow one, in remarkable contrast to the natural law and world view of Christian-
ity, with its passion for making distinctions based on a neatly
corresponding macrocosm and microcosm.

However, the right of action in Roman law embodied a
principle that contradicted the modern concept of rights. Just
as Roman law held that rights lapse when there is no possibility of redress, so too the Laws of Manu, according to the pro-
cedural rules in force in the great courts of the rajahs and
Brahmins, restricted the suits that might be brought to trial
to cases of nonpayment of debts and some eighteen others.

Honda was fascinated by the uniquely vivid style of the
Laws. Even details as prosaic as court procedure were couched
in colorful metaphors and similes. During the conduct of a
trial, for example, the rajah was to determine the truth and
falsehood of the matter before him "just as the hunter searches
out the lair of the wounded deer by following the trail of
blood." And in the enumeration of his duties, the rajah was
admonished to dispense favors on his people "as Indra lets
fall the life-giving rain of April." Honda read right to the
very end, including the final chapter, which dealt with arcane
matters that defied classification either as laws or as proclama-
tions.

The imperative postulated in Western law was inevitably
based on man's power of reason. The Laws of Manu, however, were rooted in a cosmic law that was impervious to
reason—the doctrine of the transmigration of souls. This was
set out in the Laws as a matter of course:

"Deeds proceed from the body, speech, and the mind, and
result in either good or evil."

"In this world, the soul in conjunction with the body per-
forms three kinds of act: good, indifferent, and evil."

"That which proceeds from a man's soul shall shape his
soul; that which proceeds from his speech shall shape his
speech, and deeds that proceed from his body shall shape his
body."

"He who sins in body shall be a tree or grass in the next life, he who sins in speech shall be a bird or a beast, and he who sins in soul shall be reborn at the lowest level of caste."

"The man who retains a proper guard over his speech, his mind, and his body with regard to all living things—the man who bridles his lust and his anger—shall achieve fulfillment. Total liberation shall be his."

"It is fitting that every man should employ his inherent wisdom to discern how the fate of his soul depends on his adherence or nonadherence to the law and that he should exert himself wholeheartedly in the faithful observance of the law."

Here, just as in the natural law, to observe the law and to do good deeds were taken as being the same thing. But here the law was based upon the principle of the transmigration of souls, a doctrine that short-circuited normal rational inquiry. And rather than making an appeal to human reason, the Laws seemed to play on the threat of retribution. And thus as a doctrine of law, it placed somewhat less trust in human nature than did the Roman law with its reliance on the powers of reason.

Honda had no desire to spend his time mulling over the problem like this, or to steep himself in the wisdom of the ancients. Being a law student, he was inclined to support the establishment of law, but he was persistently troubled by doubts and misgivings about the operative system that was his subject. His struggles with its painfully intricate and tangled structure had taught him that a broader view was sometimes necessary; this was to be found not only in natural law, with its apotheosis of reason that was at the heart of operative law, but also in the seminal wisdom of the Laws of Manu. From this vantage point, he could enjoy two worlds— the clear blue of midday or the star-filled night.

The study of law was certainly a strange discipline. It was a net with mesh so fine as to catch the most trivial incidents of daily life, yet its vast extension in time and space encompassed even the eternal movements of the sun and stars. No fisherman seeking to increase his catch could be more greedy than the student of law.

Lost for so long in his reading and oblivious to the passage of time, Honda at last realized with some anxiety that he had better go to bed if he was not to look exhausted when he met Kiyoaki at the Imperial Theater the next night. When he thought of his friend, so handsome and so hard to fathom, and then considered how unlikely it was that his own future would be anything but ordinary and predictable, he could not suppress a slight shudder. He idly turned over in his mind the triumphs with which his classmates so proudly regaled him, such as using a rolled-up cushion to play rugby in a Gion teahouse with a flock of young geishas.

Then he thought of an episode in his own home this spring that would have been insignificant in a more worldly environment but which set off immense reverberations in the Honda household. A memorial service to commemorate the tenth anniversary of his grandmother's death had been held at the temple in Nippori where the family remains were buried, and afterwards the immediate family relatives had shared their hospitality. Shigekuni's second cousin Fusako was both the youngest of the guests, and the prettiest and most vivacious. In the staid Honda household, her loud peals of laughter caused a few raised eyebrows.

Despite the day's religious overtones, the awareness of death was not enough to hinder the contented babble of conversation among relatives who had not seen one another for so long. And so they talked, touching on the dead grandmother from time to time, perhaps, but much more concerned with telling one another about the children who were the pride of each family.

The thirty-odd guests wandered about the house from room to room, astonished at finding themselves confronted with books at every turn. A few of them asked to see Shigekuni's study and poked around his desk for a time, then they left one by one, until Fusako alone remained with him.

The two of them sat down on a leather couch by the wall. Shigekuni was wearing his school uniform, and Fusako a formal purple kimono. Once they became aware that they had been left alone, they became rather awkward with each other, and Fusako's peals of laughter ceased.

Shigekuni was wondering whether it would be the right thing to show Fusako a picture album or something like that, but unfortunately he had nothing of the sort at hand. To make matters worse, Fusako suddenly seemed displeased. Until now, he had not been particularly attracted to her, with her excess of physical energy, her loud, interminable laugh, her habit of teasing him although he was a year older than she, and her constant flurry of activity. Admittedly she had the warm bloom of a midsummer flower, but Shigekuni had already come to a private decision: he would rather not have a woman like her for his wife.

"I'm tired, you know. How about you, Shige, aren't you?"

Before he could reply, she seemed to fold at the waist and fall toward him in her wide obi, like a wall suddenly collapsing. An instant later, her head was snuggled in his lap, and he found himself contemplating the warm fragrant weight across his knees.

He was totally at a loss. He looked down at the supple burden settled in his lap and things remained that way for what seemed a very long time. He felt powerless to move even a muscle, and Fusako, too, once she had so contentedly buried her head in the blue serge of her cousin's uniform, gave no sign that she ever intended to remove it.

But then the door suddenly opened to reveal his mother and an aunt and uncle. His mother paled, and Shigekuni's heart gave a thump. Fusako, however, merely looked slowly in the direction of the newcomers, and then oh so languidly raised her head.

"I'm so very tired. And I have a headache too."

"My goodness, we can't have that. Shall I get you something for it?"

Not for nothing did his mother hold office in the Women's

Patriotic League, as she stepped into the breach as a volunteer nurse.

"No, thank you, I don't believe it's that serious."

This episode added considerable spice to his relatives' conversation, and although it fortunately did not reach his father's ears, his mother took him severely to task for it. And as for Fusako, despite being his cousin, she was never invited to the house again. Honda, however, would never forget those few brief moments when her warm weight lay heavy in his lap.

And although he had supported her whole upper body in its kimono and obi, it was the subtly complex beauty of her head and hair that had most attracted him. Its luxuriant mass had pressed against him with the clinging heaviness of smoldering incense. The blue serge of his trousers could not conceal its constant, penetrating warmth. It was like the heat of a distant fire—what caused it, he wondered. It had radiated from her as if from coals in a fine china vase. It implied that her affection for him was somehow excessive. And hadn't the pressure of her head been a stinging reproof as well?

And then there were Fusako's eyes. While her cheek was on his lap, he had been able to look down into her wide, dark eyes. They were small and vulnerable, as glistening as raindrops, like dancing butterflies momentarily at rest. The flutter of her long lashes was the flutter of their wings, which were as beautifully speckled as the pupils of her eyes.

So insincere, so close to him yet so indifferent, so ready to dart away—he had never seen such eyes that roamed ceaselessly in discontent. First focused, then vacant, they were as unsettled as the bubble in a spirit level.

But she was not flirting. Her look conveyed even less than it had when she was chattering gaily a few minutes before. Her eyes seemed to express nothing more significant than the headstrong passion that surged in her. The unnerving force of such sweetness and fragrance sprang from something far more elemental than a desire for flirtation.

What, then, was the pervasive mood of those moments of physical contact which had seemed to stretch into an eternity?

8

THE MAIN PRODUCTION at the Imperial Theater
from the middle of November to the tenth of December was
not a popular modern piece involving actresses, but two
Kabuki plays featuring such masters of the craft as Baiko and
Kojiro. Kiyoaki had picked the classical theater because he
felt that this kind of entertainment would have more appeal
for his foreign guests. But as he didn't know much about
Kabuki, he was unfamiliar with that evening's two offerings,
The Rise and Fall of the Taira and *Lion Dance*. And so he
persuaded Honda to spend his lunch hour in the library looking up the plays in order to explain them to the princes beforehand.

The two princes were inclined to bring no more than idle
curiosity to bear on foreign plays. Kiyoaki had introduced
them to Honda, who had come home from school with him.
And now, after dinner, he noticed that they were not paying
much attention to his friend's English summary of the evening's plays.

In such circumstances, Honda's loyalty and utter solemnity
moved Kiyoaki to both guilt and pity. Certainly none of the
theater party that night was much concerned with the plays
themselves. Kiyoaki, for one, was preoccupied; Satoko might
have read the letter after all and hence might break her
promise to come.

The butler came in to announce that the carriage was waiting. The horses neighed and their breath flared white from
their nostrils, to swirl up into the black, wintry sky. Kiyoaki
enjoyed seeing horses proudly displaying their strength in

winter, when their usual musky smell was fainter and their hooves rang clearly on the frozen ground. On a warm spring day, a galloping horse was only too clearly a sweating animal of flesh and blood. But a horse racing through a snowstorm became one with the very elements; wrapped in the whirling blast of the north wind, the beast embodied the icy breath of winter.

Kiyoaki liked riding in a carriage, especially when he was oppressed by some concern or other. For the bouncing would jolt him out of the dogged, steady rhythm of his worry. The tails arching away from bare rumps close to the carriage, the manes trailing wildly in the wind, the saliva falling in a gleaming ribbon from the gnashing teeth—Kiyoaki liked to savor the contrast between the animals' brute strength and the elegant fittings in the interior of the carriage.

Kiyoaki and Honda wore overcoats over their school uniforms. The princes, though they themselves were huddled in immense, fur-collared overcoats, shivered miserably.

"We're not used to the cold," said Prince Pattanadid, an unhappy look in his eye. "Some cousins of ours studied in Switzerland, and they warned us that it was cold. But no one said anything about how cold Japan was."

"But you'll get used to it in no time," said Honda to console them; they were already on good terms despite their short acquaintance.

Since it was December, the season for the traditional end-of-year sales, the streets were bright with advertising banners and crowded with shoppers in heavy cloaks, all of which prompted the princes to ask what festival was being celebrated.

For the past two days or more, the faces of both Prince Pattanadid and even the heedless and irrepressible Kridsada had become more and more downcast, an unmistakable proof of homesickness. Naturally they were careful not to be too open about this, as they did not wish to affront Kiyoaki's hospitality. Yet he knew that their thoughts were elsewhere, adrift on some broad ocean. But he was pleased by it, for to him the idea of human emotions remaining steadfast and inextricably anchored in the body, in the here-and-now, was unbearably oppressive.

As they were passing Hibiya Park and approaching the moat of the Imperial Palace, the three-storied white theater loomed up ahead in the early darkness of the winter evening.

When they entered the theater, the new play that came first on the program was already in progress. Kiyoaki picked out Satoko where she sat beside her old servant, Tadeshina. Their seats were two or three rows behind and somewhat to one side of the young men. Seeing her there and catching the hint of a flashing smile, Kiyoaki was ready to forgive her everything.

During the rest of the first play, while two rival generals of the Kamakura era marshaled their forces against each other on stage, Kiyoaki watched as though in a daze. Everything on stage paled before his self-esteem, now that he was delivered from any threat to it.

"Tonight Satoko is more beautiful than ever," he thought. "She has taken extra care over her toilette. She's come looking just as I hoped she would."

Kiyoaki was delighted with the way things had turned out. He congratulated himself over and over again as he sat there secure in his contentment, unable to turn and look in Satoko's direction but basking in the warmth of her beauty so close at hand. He could not wish for anything more.

What he had wanted of her tonight was a beautiful presence, a demand that he had never previously made on her. On reflection, he realized that he had not been accustomed to thinking of Satoko in terms of beauty. Though he had never exactly considered her as a confirmed enemy, she was nevertheless like fine silk disguising a sharp needle, or rich brocade that hid an abrasive underside. Above all, she was the woman who loved him without having bothered to consult him at all in the matter. This Kiyoaki could not bear. Not for him the meek acceptance of favors granted. He had always firmly shuttered his heart against the rising sun, for fear that a single ray of its harsh, overcritical brilliance might pierce through.

The intermission came. Everything went off naturally. First Kiyoaki turned to Honda and whispered to him that by a remarkable coincidence, Satoko was there. And although the look in his friend's eye, after a quick glance backward, left no doubt that he knew that something more than chance was at work, this, surprisingly enough, did not shake Kiyoaki's complacency in the least. For Honda's look was eloquent proof of Kiyoaki's concept of friendship, which never demanded an excess of honesty.

There was a bustle of talk and movement as everyone went out into the lobby. Kiyoaki and his friends strolled under the chandeliers to meet Satoko and her maid in front of a window that looked out over the castle moat and the ancient stone walls of the shogun's castle. His ears burning with unaccustomed excitement, he introduced Satoko to the two princes. Realizing how inappropriate cold formality would be, he observed all etiquette, but put on the same show of naïve enthusiasm he had displayed when he had first mentioned Satoko to the princes.

He knew that the expansive surge of emotion, the liberating power of his newly won sense of security, enabled him to adopt an alien maturity. Abandoning his characteristic melancholy, he reveled in his freedom. For Kiyoaki knew that he was not at all in love with Satoko.

Tadeshina had retired to the shelter of a pillar with all sorts of deprecating gestures. Judging from the tightness of the embroidered plum-colored collar of her kimono, one would gather that she had decided to treat these foreigners with circumspection. Her attitude pleased Kiyoaki, who was thus spared her high-pitched acknowledgment of his introduction.

Although the two princes were delighted to be in the company of such a beautiful woman, Chao P. was not too involved to notice the remarkable alteration in Kiyoaki's manner when he introduced Satoko. Never imagining that Kiyoaki was in fact modeling himself on his own boyish earnestness, the prince began to feel a real fondness for Kiyoaki, believing that for the first time he was seeing him behave as a young man should.

Honda, in the meantime, was lost in admiration for Satoko, who, although she did not speak a word of English, maintained exactly the right degree of poise before the two princes. Surrounded as she was with four young men, and wearing an elaborate formal kimono, she nevertheless carried herself without the least sign of constraint; her beauty and elegance were self-evident.

As Kiyoaki translated for the two princes, who were taking turns at plying Satoko with questions, she smiled at him as if to seek his approval. It was a smile that seemed to imply much more than the circumstances demanded. Kiyoaki became uneasy.

"She's read the letter," he thought. But no, if she had read the letter, she would not be behaving like this toward him tonight. In fact, she would not have come at all. Surely she could not have received the letter before he telephoned. But there was no way of knowing whether or not she had read it after his call. It would be pointless to confront her with a direct question because she would be quick to deny it. But still, he grew angry with himself for not daring to do it.

Trying to sound as casual as possible, he did his best to discover if there were not some note in her voice that differed from the cheerful warmth of two nights before, or some suggestive change in her expression. Once more the clarity of his self-possession was becoming blurred.

Her nose was as well molded as that of an ivory doll, without being so sharply defined as to give her a haughty profile. And her face seemed to glow and fall into soft shadow; alternating with the quick, vivacious movement of her eyes. Alertness of eye is usually considered a vulgar trait in women, but Satoko had a way of delivering her sidelong glances that was irresistibly charming. Her smile followed close upon her words, as her glance did upon her smile—the graceful sequence heightening the bewitching elegance of her expression. Her lips, although somewhat thin, concealed a subtle inner voluptuousness. When she laughed, she was always quick to hide the sparkle of her teeth with the slender, delicate fingers of one hand, but not before the young men had noticed a white brilliance that rivaled that of the chandeliers above.

As Kiyoaki translated the extravagant compliments of the princes for Satoko, he noticed a blush spreading to her earlobes. Almost hidden by her hair, they were shaped with the fluid grace of raindrops, and however hard he peered at them, he was unable to decide whether they owed their heightened color to some cosmetic or to embarrassment.

One thing about Satoko, however, transcended all artifice. This was the force of her bright eyes. It unnerved him as it always did. He felt pierced by its uncanny keenness; its power sprang from her very essence.

The bell rang to announce the beginning of *The Rise and Fall of the Taira*, and the audience began to file back to their seats.

"She's the most beautiful woman I've seen since my arrival in Japan. How lucky you are!" said Chao P. in a low voice as he and Kiyoaki walked down the aisle. Judging by the look in his eyes, one could gather that he had recovered from his attack of homesickness.

9

KIYOAKI'S TUTOR IINUMA had come to realize that the six years and more that he had spent in service to the Matsugae household had not only blighted the hopes of his youth but had dissipated the consequent indignation he had

felt at first. When he brooded over his frustrating circumstances, he did so with a chill resentment quite different from
the hot anger he had once felt. Of course the atmosphere of
the Matsugae household, so unfamiliar to him, had had much
to do with the changes in him. From the very beginning, however, the main source of contagion had been Kiyoaki, now
eighteen years old.

The boy would be nineteen this coming year. If Iinuma
could only see to it that he graduated from Peers with good
marks and then that he was entered in the law school of Tokyo
Imperial University when the autumn of his twenty-first year
came round, he would be able to feel that his own responsibility had been properly discharged. However, for some reason
that Iinuma could not fathom, Marquis Matsugae had never
seen fit to take his son to task over his school record. And as
things stood now, there seemed little chance of Kiyoaki's
studying law at Tokyo University. After graduating from
Peers, there seemed to be no other course open to him but to
take advantage of his privileges as a member of the nobility
and enter either Kyoto or Tohoku Imperial University without having to take an entrance examination. Kiyoaki's performance at school had been indifferent; he put no effort into
his studies, nor did he compensate for this at all by trying to
shine at athletics instead. Had he been an outstanding student,
Iinuma could have shared in the glory, giving his friends and
relatives in Kagoshima cause to be proud. But by now,
Iinuma could only dimly recall the fervent hopes he had once
entertained. And besides, he realized bitterly, no matter how
far short of the mark Kiyoaki fell, he was still assured of a
seat in the House of Peers.

The friendship between Kiyoaki and Honda was another
source of irritation. Honda was close to the top of his class,
but he made no attempt to influence his friend for the good,
despite Kiyoaki's regard for him; quite the reverse, in fact.
He behaved, in Iinuma's eyes, like an uncritical admirer, blind
to Kiyoaki's every shortcoming.

Jealousy, of course, played its part in Iinuma's resentment.

Being a friend and classmate, Honda was in a position to accept Kiyoaki as he was, whereas for Iinuma, he was an eternal monument to his own failure.

Kiyoaki's looks, his elegance, his diffidence, his complexity, his disinclination for any exertion, his languid dreaminess, his magnificent body, his delicate skin, his long lashes over those dreaming eyes—all of Kiyoaki's attributes conspired to betray Iinuma's hopes with a careless, elegant grace of their own. Iinuma saw his young master as a constant, mocking reproach.

So bitter a frustration, a sense of failure so gnawing in its intensity, can, over a long period, be transmuted into a kind of religious fervor directed at its cause. Iinuma became enraged at anyone who tried to slight Kiyoaki. By a sort of confused intuition of which he himself was unaware, he grasped something of the nature of Kiyoaki's almost impenetrable isolation. Kiyoaki's determination, in turn, to keep his distance from Iinuma, doubtless sprang from the fact that he perceived all too clearly the nature of his tutor's burning fanaticism.

Of all the retinue in the Matsugae household, only Iinuma was possessed by this fervor, something intangible yet quite apparent as soon as one looked into his eyes. One day, a guest asked: "Excuse me, but that houseboy of yours isn't a socialist, is he?" The Marquis and his wife could not help bursting into laughter at this, for they were well aware of Iinuma's background, his present behavior, and, above all, the zeal with which day in, day out, he performed his devotions at the "Omiyasama" shrine. It was customary for this taciturn young man, who had no words to waste on anyone, to go to the family shrine early each morning; there he poured out his heart to Marquis Matsugae's renowned father, whom he had never known in his lifetime. In the early days, his pleas were shot through with a radical anger, but as he grew older, they began to be shaped by a pervasive discontent that now had spread to envelop every aspect of his world.

He was the first to rise every morning. He washed his face and rinsed out his mouth, then putting on his indigo-striped

kimono and his *Okura hakama*, he set off in the direction of
the shrine.

He walked along the path that led past the maids' quarters
at the rear of the main house and through the grove of Japanese cypresses. In cold weather, like this morning's, the frost
tortured the dirt of the path into tiny spiral mounds; when
these were crushed by the blunt impact of Iinuma's wooden
clogs, they shattered into pure, glittering fragments. The
morning sun, lying bright and gauzy over the withered brown
and green leaves that still clung to the cypresses, shone on his
frosty breath rising in the winter air. He felt utterly purified.
Incessant birdsong filled the pale blue morning sky. However,
despite the stimulation of the cold air briskly striking his bare
skin under his open-necked kimono, something wrung his
heart with bitter regret: "If only the young master would
come with me, just once!"

He had never succeeded in communicating this vigorous,
masculine sense of well-being to Kiyoaki. No one could hold
him responsible for this failure. To force the boy to accompany him on these morning walks was out of the question,
yet Iinuma continued to blame himself. In six years he had
not been able to persuade Kiyoaki to participate even once in
this "virtuous practice."

On the flat crest of the small hill, trees gave way to a fairly
broad clearing of grass, now brown and dry, through which a
gravel path led to the shrine. As Iinuma gazed at it and the
full force of the morning sun struck the granite torii in front
of it and the two cannon shells to either side of its stone steps,
a feeling of self-possession came over him. Here in the dawn,
he found a bracing air of purity, free from the stifling luxury
penetrating the Matsugae household. He felt as if he were
breathing in a new coffin of fresh white wood. Since early
childhood, all that he had been taught to revere as honorable
and beautiful was to be found, as far as the Matsugaes were
concerned, in the proximity of death.

After Iinuma had climbed the steps and taken up his position before the shrine, he saw a small bird, a glimpse of dark red breast, as it hopped about the branches of a sakaki, rustling the gleaming leaves. Then, with a piercing cry, it flew away. A flycatcher, he thought.

He pressed his palms together and, as always, invoked Kiyoaki's grandfather as "Reverend Ancestor." Then in silence he began to pray: "Why is our era one of decadence? Why does the world despise vigor and youth and worthy ambitions and single-mindedness? You once cut men down with your sword, you were wounded by the swords of others, you endured the most terrible dangers—all to found a new Japan. And finally, having achieved high office and esteemed by everyone, you died, the greatest hero in a heroic age. Why can we not recapture the glory of your era? How long must this age of the effete and the contemptible endure? Or is the worst still to come? Men think only of money and women. Men have forgotten everything that should be becoming to a man. That great and shining age of gods and heroes passed away with the Meiji Emperor. Will we ever see its like again? A time when the strength of youth will unstintingly give of itself once more?

"In the present day—when places called cafés are springing up everywhere, drawing in thousands of idle people with money to squander, when male and female students behave so shockingly in streetcars that it has become necessary to segregate them—men have lost all trace of that fervor that drove their ancestors to accept the most frightening challenges. Now they are good for nothing but to flutter their effeminate hands like dry, fragile leaves shaken by the merest puff of air.

"Why all this? How did such an age come about, an age which has defiled everything that once was sacred. Alas, Reverend Ancestor, your own grandson, whom I serve, is in every way a child of this decadent era, and I am powerless to do anything about it. Should I die to atone for my failure? Or have things taken their course according to some great design of yours?"

Oblivious to the cold in the fervor of his devotions, Iinuma stood there, a virile figure with his matted chest showing through his open kimono. In truth, he secretly regretted that his body did not correspond to the purity of his zeal. On the other hand, Kiyoaki, whose body he saw as a sacred vessel, lacked the single-minded purity required of all true men.

Then suddenly, at the height of his ardent outpouring, as he was getting warmer and warmer despite the chill morning air swirling under the skirt of his *hakama*, he began to feel sexually aroused. He immediately snatched a broom from its place under the floor and began to sweep out the shrine in a frenzy of energy.

Shortly after the new year, Iinuma was called to Kiyoaki's room. There he found the old lady, Tadeshina, whom he knew to be Satoko's maid.

Satoko herself had already been to the Matsugae house to exchange New Year's greetings, and today, finding occasion to bring some traditional Kyoto bran mash as her own New Year's present, Tadeshina had made her way inconspicuously to Kiyoaki's room. Though Iinuma was aware who Tadeshina was, this was the first time he had ever been brought together with her intentionally, and the reason for it was not yet clear to him.

The New Year was always lavishly celebrated in the Matsugae household. Some twenty or more people came from Kagoshima, and after going to the residence of the traditional head of the clan to pay their respects, they were entertained at the Matsugaes'. The New Year's dinners, cooked in the

Hoshigaoka style and served in the black-beamed main hall, were famous, largely because of such desserts as ice cream and melon, which were delicacies almost never tasted by country people. This year, however, because the period of mourning for the Meiji Emperor was not yet over, no more than three guests came up from Kagoshima; among them, the principal of Iinuma's middle school, a gentleman who had the honor of having known Kiyoaki's grandfather.

Marquis Matsugae had established a certain ritual with the old teacher. As Iinuma waited on him at the banquet, the Marquis would speak graciously to the old man: "Iinuma has done well here." This year, too, the formula had been invoked, and the principal had murmured the usual politely deprecating words, as predictably as someone stamping his seal on a routine document. But this year, perhaps because there was only a handful of guests present, the ceremony struck Iinuma as being insincere, a perfunctory formality.

Of course Iinuma had never presented himself to any of the illustrious ladies who came to call on the Marquise, so he was taken aback at being confronted in his young master's study by a New Year's guest who happened to be a woman, however elderly.

Tadeshina wore a black kimono patterned with crests, and though she sat upright in her chair with extreme propriety, the whiskey that Kiyoaki had urged on her had evidently taken some effect. Beneath her graying hair, gathered neatly into a knot and still unruffled, the skin on her forehead glowed through the layer of white makeup with a shade of snow-covered plum blossom.

After acknowledging Iinuma with a brief glance, she returned to the story she had been telling about Prince Saionji.

"According to what everyone said, the Prince enjoyed tobacco and alcohol from the age of five onward. Samurai families are always so concerned to bring their children up impeccably. But in noble families—I think you know what I mean, young master—parents never discipline their children from the moment they're born; wouldn't you agree? For after all, their children receive the court rank of fifth degree at birth, which qualifies them to become retainers of His Imperial Majesty, and so out of reverence to the Emperor, their parents don't dare to be harsh with them. And in a court nobleman's house, nobody says anything about his Imperial Majesty that isn't absolutely prudent. Just as nobody belonging even to the household of a lord would ever dare to gossip openly about their master. And that's the way it is. And my mistress too has this same deep reverence for His Imperial Majesty. But of course it doesn't extend to foreign lords." This last was Tadeshina's ironic jab at the hospitality extended to the Siamese princes by the Matsugaes. Then she hastened to make some amends: "But then, thanks of course to your great kindness, I was privileged to see a play again after I don't know how long. I felt that it gave me a new lease on life."

Kiyoaki let Tadeshina ramble on as she liked. In asking her to come to his study, he had had something quite definite in mind. He wanted to be free of the nagging doubt that had pursued him ever since that night. And so now, after plying Tadeshina with more whiskey, he asked her abruptly if Satoko had in fact taken his letter and thrown it unopened into the fire as requested.

Her answer came more readily than he might have expected: "Oh that! The young lady spoke to me immediately after her telephone conversation with you. So when the letter came next day, I took it and burned it unopened. Everything was taken care of. You need not worry about it at all."

On hearing this, Kiyoaki felt like a man who has struggled for hours through tangled undergrowth and at last fights his way into the open. A multitude of delightful prospects unfolded before his eyes. Satoko's not having read the letter did two things: not only did it restore things to their former balance, but Kiyoaki was now happily confident that he had opened up a whole new perspective on life.

Satoko had already made an overture whose implications were dazzling. Her annual New Year's visit to exchange greetings fell on a day traditionally set aside by the Marquis for the children of his relatives. They would gather at his house, their ages ranging from three to twenty. And on this one day he would don the role of loving father, listening kindly to what each of them had to say and giving counsel when called upon to do so. This year, Satoko had brought some children out to see the horses.

Kiyoaki led them to the stable where the Matsugaes kept their four horses. It was decorated for the holidays with the twisted rope traditional in Shinto observance. The horses, with their powerful, smooth-muscled bodies, suddenly rearing back or kicking their hooves against the boards, struck Kiyoaki as having a pulsating life appropriate to the New Year. The children were enthralled. They asked the groom for each horse's name. Then, taking aim at the huge yellow teeth, they hurled salvos of squashed pieces of crumbling candy they had been clutching in their fists. The high-strung beasts glared sidelong at their tormentors with bloodshot eyes. This delighted the children even more since these baleful looks were proof that the horses regarded them as adults.

Satoko, however, was frightened by the saliva streaming from the horses' gaping mouths, and withdrew to the shelter of an evergreen some distance away. Kiyoaki walked over to join her, leaving the children to the groom.

Her eyes were showing the effects of the spiced saké that was traditional at New Year celebrations. What she said, therefore—to the accompaniment of the children's shouts of joy—might have been attributed to this stimulus. At any rate, as Kiyoaki came to her side, she looked at him far from demurely and began to speak with a lilt of excitement in her voice.

"I was so happy that night, you know. You introduced me as though I were your fiancée. I'm sure Their Highnesses were quite surprised that I should be so old. But do you know how I felt then? If I had had to die at that very moment, I would have had no regrets. My happiness lies in your hands. Be careful with it, won't you? I've never been so happy at a

New Year as I am now. I never looked forward so much to
what the year may bring."

Kiyoaki did not know what to say. "Why are you telling me
all this?" he asked finally, in a strained voice.

"Oh, Kiyo, when I'm very happy, my words come tumbling
out like the doves they release at a launching, flying up
through a burst of confetti. Kiyo, you'll understand soon
enough." To make matters worse, Satoko had ended on that
phrase calculated to irritate Kiyoaki: "You'll understand soon
enough."

"How proud and self-satisfied she is!" thought Kiyoaki.
"So much older and wiser."

All this had taken place some days before. And now today,
after Tadeshina's account of the fate of the letter, Kiyoaki lost
his lingering misgivings, now confident that he was embark-
ing on a New Year under the most favorable auspices. He
would be rid of the melancholy dreams that had plagued his
nights. He was determined that from now on his dreams
would be happy. His manner would never fail to be open, and
since he would be free of depression and worry, he would try
to communicate his own well-being to everyone. But dispensing goodwill to mankind is a hazardous business at best, and
one that demands a considerable degree of maturity and wisdom. Nevertheless, Kiyoaki was driven by an extraordinary
sense of urgency.

Whatever his sense of mission, however, he had not called
Iinuma to his room solely out of the warm desire to dispel
his tutor's gloom and see his face transformed with happiness.

The saké he had drunk combined with something else to
provoke Kiyoaki to rashness. Tadeshina, despite her self-
abashing manner and excruciating courtesy, had a certain
air about her that put one in mind of the proprietress of a
brothel, albeit one with an ancient and honorable reputation.
An unmistakable distilled sensuality seemed to cling to the
very wrinkles of her face. And having her so close at hand
aroused Kiyoaki's natural willfulness.

"As far as schoolwork goes, Iinuma has taught me all sorts of things," said Kiyoaki, deliberately directing his remarks exclusively at Tadeshina. "Still, there are a number of things he didn't teach me. Actually, the truth is that there are many things that Iinuma doesn't know. And it's just because of this that from now on you, Tadeshina, will have to become a teacher to Iinuma, you see."

"Really now, young master, whatever do you mean by behaving like this," said Tadeshina with heavy deference. "This gentleman here is already a university student. And an ignorant old soul like myself . . ."

"Exactly. Because what I am talking about has nothing to do with what's learned in school."

"Tch, tch, making such fun of an old woman!"

And so the exchange continued, still excluding Iinuma. Since Kiyoaki had not indicated that he might take a seat, he continued to stand, looking out over the pond. The day was overcast, and a flock of ducks swam near the island, from which the dark green crowns of the pines rose, cold and forbidding. The rough brown grass that covered the island reminded Iinuma of a farmer's straw raincoat.

Finally, at a word from Kiyoaki, Iinuma sat down stiffly in a chair. Until then, Kiyoaki had not appeared to notice him standing by the door, which seemed extremely odd to him. Perhaps, he thought, his master was making a show of his authority in front of Tadeshina. If so, it was something new in Kiyoaki, which pleased him.

"Well now, Iinuma, let's see. Tadeshina here has just been gossiping with our maids. And just by chance she happened to hear . . ."

"Young master, please! Don't." Waving her arms in a show of frantic distress, Tadeshina tried to stop him, but to no avail.

"She happened to hear that the maids are convinced that when you go to the shrine every morning, you have more on your mind than mere devotion."

"More on my mind, master?" Iinuma's face muscles

tightened and his clenched hands resting in his lap began to
tremble.

"Please, young master," wailed Tadeshina, "don't go into it
with him." She slumped back in her chair like a carelessly
dropped porcelain doll, but despite her manifestations of acute
distress, there was a faint but unmistakable gleam in her
deep-set eyes. And the lines around her mouth, with its badly
fitting false teeth, were slack, witnesses to past sensuality.

"To reach the shrine, you have to pass the rear wing of the
house, don't you? Which means, of course, that you walk
right past the windows of the maids' quarters. And on your
way every morning, you've also been exchanging looks with
Miné. And finally, just the other day, you slipped her a note
through the lattice. Or so they say. Is it true or isn't it?"

Before Kiyoaki had finished, Iinuma was on his feet. His
pale face was contorted in rigid desperation as he struggled
to control himself. It was as though a white heat were building within him, ready to explode into a terrible inferno.
Kiyoaki was delighted by the look on his face, which was
transformed from the dull phlegmatic expression he was used
to. Though Iinuma was obviously in agony, to Kiyoaki his
face, contorted into an ugly mask, was happy.

"If the master will be good enough to excuse me now
. . . ," said Iinuma, making a rapid turn toward the door. But
before he could take another step, Tadeshina lunged from her
chair to stop him with an alacrity that astounded Kiyoaki. In
an instant she had changed from a decrepit old woman to a
leopard making its kill.

"You mustn't go! Don't you see what will happen to me if
you do that? I've served the Ayakuras for forty years, but if
they find out that I'm to blame for somebody being dismissed
by the Matsugaes because of an indiscretion on my part, they'll
do the same to me. Please have a little pity on me. You've to
think what will happen. Do you understand what I'm saying?
Young people are so rash! But what can we do about it?
It's one of the attractions of youth."

And so Tadeshina clung to Iinuma's sleeve and spoke simply, and to the point, gently remonstrating, with the authority that comes with age.

Her manner of assured confidence had been perfected over the course of years, during which time she had convinced herself that she was indispensable to the running of the world. Her face was now composed again, and radiated the confidence of someone accustomed to supervising the smooth management of events from behind the scenes. In the middle of some solemn ceremony a kimono might tear at the seam with dismaying suddenness; someone might forget his copy of the speech of congratulation he had so painstakingly composed; Tadeshina's confidence was born of her proven ability to handle these and a thousand other crises with unflurried efficiency. Things that to most people were shattering bolts from the blue, to her were all in a day's work. And so, by her ready skill in warding off threats of sudden catastrophe, she had repeatedly vindicated her role in life. This tranquil old lady knew that nothing in human affairs could be counted on to turn out precisely as intended. A solitary swallow flitting across a cloudless blue sky might well be the harbinger of a surprise storm. Thus Tadeshina, with constant reserves of experience, need have no misgivings as to her worth.

Iinuma had plenty of time to reflect later, but very often a man's whole life alters course because of a moment's hesitation. That instant is like a fold made down the middle of a sheet of paper. In it, the underside becomes upmost, and what was once visible is hidden forever.

Standing there in the door of Kiyoaki's study, with Tadeshina clutching him, Iinuma experienced such a moment, and with it the matter was settled. Young and callow as he was, uncertainty cut into him the way a shark's fin cuts through the surface of the water. Had Miné laughed at his note and showed it to everyone? Or had it come to light some other way, causing her great shame? He desperately wanted to know.

Kiyoaki studied him as he sat down again. He had won a

victory that gave him little cause for pride. He gave up all
hope of extending his benevolence to Iinuma. There was
nothing else to do but to give free reign to his own sense of
happiness, he felt, and to work out the details as he went
along. He had a new sense of power, and felt able to behave
with the refinement of maturity.

"I didn't bring this matter up to cause you distress or to
subject you to ridicule. Don't you see that Tadeshina and I
are trying to work out the plan that is best for you? I'm not
going to say a word to my father, and I'll make sure that it
doesn't reach his ears from any other quarter. As for our
immediate course of action, I'm sure that Tadeshina's vast
knowledge and experience in these matters will be a great
help, won't it, Tadeshina? True, Miné is one of the prettiest
of the housemaids, and that presents a bit of a problem. But
you just leave things to me."

Iinuma's eyes glittered like those of a spy caught in a trap;
he hung on Kiyoaki's every word, afraid to utter a sound.
When he tried to penetrate the substance of Kiyoaki's words,
he seemed to release in himself a surging flood of anxieties.
On the other hand, when he sat there passively, Kiyoaki's
words seemed to bore into his very soul.

Iinuma had never seen so authoritative an expression on the
face of the younger man, who continued to speak with a
magnanimity that was quite out of character. His great hope,
of course, had been that Kiyoaki would some day acquire a
mature poise such as this. But he had never dreamed that this
would happen under circumstances like these. In losing to
Kiyoaki the way he had—was it not his own lust that had
defeated him, he wondered. And after his brief hesitation of
a moment ago—had he not felt that his shameful pursuit of
pleasure had now become inextricably bound up with loyalty
and service to his master? That was the trap that they had
laid for him so cleverly. However, even in his present depths
of unbearable humiliation, a small, golden door had been
opened for him in fulfillment of their unspoken bargain.

After Kiyoaki had finished, Tadeshina spoke up in tones as

smooth as a peeled scallion. "It's exactly the way the young master says it is. He has a wisdom far beyond his years."

Iinuma had always considered Kiyoaki's wisdom to be quite the opposite, but now he listened to Tadeshina without surprise.

"And now, in return, Iinuma," said Kiyoaki once again, "you must stop lecturing me and join forces with Tadeshina to give me some help. If you do, I'll do the same for your romance. We three could become quite friendly."

11

KIYOAKI TOOK UP the diary he kept of his dreams again, and wrote:

Even though I haven't known the Siamese princes very long, I dreamed about Siam recently. I was sitting on a splendid chair in the middle of a room. I seemed to be held there, unable to move. Throughout the dream, I felt as if I had a headache. And this was because I was wearing a tall, pointed gold crown set with all sorts of precious stones. Above my head, a huge flock of peacocks were perched on a maze of beams just under the roof. And from time to time white droppings fell on my crown.

Outside the sun was scorching. It was beating down in a desolate garden run wild. Everything was still, except for the faint droning of flies and the occasional thud of the peacocks' feet on the beams above or sometimes the rustling of their wings. The garden was surrounded by a high stone wall, but there were large openings like windows let into it. And through these I could see the trunks of palm trees and, behind them, piled-up white clouds, dazzling and unmoving.

Then I looked down at my hand and saw that I was wear-

ing an emerald ring. This, of course, was Chao P.'s, but somehow it had been placed on my finger. The design was certainly the same—the two weird faces of the guardian gods,
the yaksha, carved into the gold on either side of the stone.

I stared at the ring glinting in the sun pouring in from outside, my eyes held by a pure, flawless white light that sparkled
like frost crystals in the center of the emerald. And as I did so,
I became aware of the face of a woman, young and beautiful,
which had gradually formed within it. I turned around, thinking that it was the reflection of someone behind me, but there
was no one there. Now the face in the emerald moved slightly
and its expression changed. Where it had been serious, it was
now smiling. At that moment, the back of my hand began to
itch as one of the swarm of flies hovering above me settled on
it. Annoyed, I shook my hand to get rid of it and then looked
at the ring again. But the woman's face had vanished. And
then, as I began to feel an indescribable sense of bitterness
and loss, I woke up . . .

Kiyoaki never took the trouble to add a personal interpreta-
tion to these accounts of his dreams. He did his best to recall
exactly what had taken place, and he set it down as fully as
possible, recording happy dreams or ominous ones just as
they were. Perhaps this unwillingness to acknowledge specific meanings in dreams, and this compulsion for exact de-
scription pointed to some deep misgivings of Kiyoaki's concerning life itself. Compared to the emotional instability he
experienced when awake, his dream world seemed far more
authentic. He could never be certain that these day-to-day
emotions were part of his true self, but he knew that the
Kiyoaki of his dreams, at least, was real. The former resisted
all attempts at definition, whereas the latter had a recogniza-
ble form and character. Nor did Kiyoaki use his journal to
pour out his discontent with the irritations of the world
around him. Here, on the contrary, for the first time in his
life, immediate reality corresponded exactly to his wishes.

Iinuma, his resistance utterly crushed, had become blindly
obedient to his master. Together with Tadeshina, he frequently served as go-between to arrange meetings for Kiyoaki

and Satoko. This sort of devotion was enough to satisfy Ki-yoaki and, furthermore, made him wonder if such a thing as friendship was really so important. And in the meantime, without being wholly aware of it, he was growing apart from Honda. This saddened Honda, but he had always been keenly aware that he was only a marginal necessity in Kiyoaki's life. He thus knew that their relationship had lacked an element vital to friendship. The time he would have spent in idleness with Kiyoaki, therefore, he now spent on his books. Besides his study of law in German, French, and English, he read widely in literature and philosophy. And although he did not follow the great Christian leader, Kanzo Uchimura, he read and admired Carlyle's *Sartor Resartus*.

One snowy morning, as Kiyoaki was about to leave for school, Iinuma came to his study with conspicuous caution. His melancholy expression and bearing had not undergone any change, but his present obsequiousness robbed them of their power to annoy Kiyoaki.

He had, he said, just received a phone call from Tadeshina. The message was simply this: Satoko was so delighted by the snow that she would like Kiyoaki not to go to school, and come for a rickshaw ride through the snow with her instead.

No one had ever made so startlingly capricious a request of Kiyoaki. Ready for school, he stood with his book bag in his hand, appalled, and stared at Iinuma.

"What's this? Miss Satoko really suggested something like that?"

"Yes, sir. I heard it directly from Miss Tadeshina. There can be no mistake."

Curiously enough, as he confirmed this, Iinuma seemed more like his former independent self, and he looked ready to lecture Kiyoaki if challenged about it.

Kiyoaki gave a quick glance over his shoulder at the garden, where snow was falling. This time, Satoko's forceful methods did not wound his pride. On the contrary, he felt a sense of relief, as though her scalpel had skillfully cut out a malignant tumor of arrogance. Since the surgery was over be-

fore he knew it, this bypassing of his own wishes gave him a
kind of keen pleasure. "I'll do just as she wants," he said, gazing out thoughtfully at the thickly falling snow. Although it
was not yet deep, it had already turned the island and the
maple hill beyond to a shining white.

"All right, telephone the school for me. Tell them I've
caught a cold and will be absent today. Make certain that no
word of this reaches Mother or Father. Then go to the rickshaw stand and hire a large one pulled by two men. Make sure
the men can be trusted. I'll walk there."

"In this snow?"

Iinuma watched as his young master's face flushed crimson. Since Kiyoaki had his back to the window which looked
out onto the storm, his face was in shadow, but his blush was
no less apparent. This young man whom he had helped to
raise was not at all inclined to heroism, yet he was startled to
catch himself applauding the fiery glint in Kiyoaki's eyes,
whatever his purpose. Once, Iinuma had had nothing but contempt for his young master and his ways, but whatever Kiyoaki was up to now, and however self-indulgent he might be,
there seemed to be a hidden determination in him that had
never shown itself before.

12

THE AYAKURA RESIDENCE in Azabu was an old
feudal mansion, and on either side of the wide main gate, the
latticed windows of guard posts protruded from the wall.
Now a household with very few visitors, however, there was
no sign that the posts had been manned recently. The snow

had not blotted out the massed ridges of the roof tiles, but rather seemed to have molded itself faithfully to each of them as it fell.

A dark figure holding an umbrella, Tadeshina apparently, stood in front of the small door beside the gate, but as Kiyoaki's rickshaw approached, she vanished abruptly. As it drew up and he sat before the gate, Kiyoaki stared through it, seeing nothing in the garden through the snow.

Finally, protected by Tadeshina's half-open umbrella, Satoko appeared in the gateway wearing a purple robe, and as she bent her head before stepping out, her hands together at her breast, Kiyoaki felt his chest tighten at this sudden apparition of extravagant beauty, as though a billowing cloud of purple had burst out of the tiny gate into the falling snow.

Helped by Tadeshina and the rickshaw men, Satoko seemed to float up to meet Kiyoaki as he leaned over to push back the rickshaw hood, but when he suddenly faced her bright, warm smile and the whirl of snowflakes clinging to her hair and the collar of her robe, he was startled, as if he had been assailed by something nebulous in the torpor of his dreams. The sudden lurching of the light vehicle as Satoko climbed up doubtless strengthened this impression, as did the tumbled purple folds of her robe lying heaped beside him, and her heady perfume, whose fragrance seemed to draw the very snowflakes that swirled in, making them strike against his cold cheeks. As Satoko got into the rickshaw, her momentum carried her cheek close to Kiyoaki's for a second, and when she pulled her head back, disconcerted, to straighten up, Kiyoaki was caught by the supple strength of her neck. It made him think of the smooth, white neck of a swan.

"What's got into you all of a sudden?" he asked, trying desperately to keep his voice steady.

"Mother and Father took the train to Kyoto last night. One of our relatives is seriously ill. I was left all by myself, and I began to think how very much I would like to see you, Kiyo. After thinking about it all night, I saw the snow this morning, and then more than anything else in the world I

wanted to go riding through the snow with you. I've never
done anything so impulsive in all my life. You'll forgive me,
won't you, Kiyo?" Satoko spoke rather breathlessly in a
child's voice that was quite unlike her.

They had already started to move. Their ears rang with
the shouts of the two rickshaw men, one of whom was pushing, the other pulling. The snow had splashed into patterns
that turned from white to yellow in the confinement of the
tiny front window of the enclosed cab. In the interior, the
light flickered dimly in time to the constant swaying.

Kiyoaki had brought a green tartan blanket that now covered their legs. Since those forgotten days of childhood, this
was the first time that they had ever been so close together,
but Kiyoaki was distracted by the pale light flooding through
the cracks in the bonnet of the rickshaw that narrowed and
widened as a stream of snow filtered through them, by the
snow itself turning to water on the green blanket, by the loud
rustle of the snow pelting down on the hood as if onto dry
banana leaves.

"Go wherever you like. Take us anywhere you can go,"
said Kiyoaki in answer to the rickshaw man. He knew that
Satoko's mood was his own.

As the men raised the poles, ready to start, both of them
sat back in their seats, their bodies slightly tensed. As yet,
neither of them had even attempted to hold hands. Yet the
inevitable contact of their knees under the blanket was like
a spark flaring secretly under the snow.

Kiyoaki's gnawing doubt persisted: had Satoko really not
read the letter? "Tadeshina denied it so emphatically she
can't have," he thought. "But in that case, is Satoko just playing with me now, in the conviction that I am completely inexperienced with women? How could I tolerate such an insult?
I was so anxious for her not to read the letter, but now I wish
she had, because then to meet me in this insane way on such
a snowy morning could mean only one thing: she'd be throwing down the gauntlet to a man of the world. And there'd be
advantages for me in that. The only problem is that I am in

fact inexperienced and I suppose there's no way to hide it."

Kiyoaki's thoughts twisted and turned as he sat in the small, dark, square confines of the swaying rickshaw. Since he would not look at Satoko, there was nothing else to do but stare out at the snow, flashing brightly through the narrow window of yellow celluloid. Finally, however, he put his hand under the blanket, where Satoko's was waiting, already in possession of the one warm, narrow refuge available.

One of the snowflakes blew in and lodged itself on Kiyoaki's eyebrow. It made Satoko cry out, and without thinking, Kiyoaki turned toward her as he felt a cold trickle on his eyelid. She closed her eyes abruptly. Kiyoaki stared at the face with its closed lids; only the subdued crimson of her lips glowed in the shadows, and because of the swaying of the rickshaw, her features, like a flower held between trembling fingertips, were softly blurred.

Kiyoaki's heart thumped violently. He felt as if he were being choked by the high, tight collar of his uniform jacket. Never had he been confronted with anything as inscrutable as Satoko's white face, eyes closed, quietly waiting. Beneath the blanket, he felt her grip on his hand tighten slightly. He realized that she was telling him something, and so, despite his terrible sense of vulnerability, he felt that something gentle but irresistible was drawing him on. He pressed a kiss on her lips.

A moment later, the shaking of the rickshaw was about to force their lips apart, but Kiyoaki instinctively resisted the movement, until his whole body seemed to balance on that kiss, and he had the sensation that a huge, invisible, perfumed fan was slowly unfolding where their lips met.

At that instant, although totally engrossed, he was still keenly aware of his own good looks. Satoko's beauty and his: he saw that it was precisely this fine correspondence between the two that dissolved all constraint and allowed them to flow together, merging as easily as measures of quicksilver. All that was divisive and frustrating sprang from something alien to beauty. Kiyoaki now realized that a fanatical insistence on total independence was a disease, not of the flesh but of the mind.

Once his anxiety had been erased and he felt increasingly sure of the girl who was the source of his happiness, their kiss became increasingly, passionately intense; Satoko's lips were growing more pliant, and then just as he began to fear that his very essence might be melted and drawn into the sweet fragrance of her mouth, his fingertips stirred with the desire to touch her flesh. He pulled his hand out from under the blanket and passed it around her shoulders to hold her chin. He felt the small, fragile bones of a woman's jaw with his fingertips and so gained a renewed awareness of a physical presence quite outside his own. This realization, however, only intensified the passion of his kiss.

Satoko had begun to cry, as he realized when her tears wet his own cheeks. He felt a surge of pride, which owed nothing to his recent mood of altruism, the complacent desire to benefit mankind that had seized him; and in the same way, Satoko's manner had lost all trace of her former condescension, so like that of a critical older sister. As he moved his hands over her body, touching first her earlobe, then her breast, the softness under his fingers excited him. This must be the true nature of caresses, he thought. At last his sensuality, given to drifting away like a rising mist, had settled upon something tangible. His mind was now filled with nothing but his own joy. And this, for Kiyoaki, was the height of abandon.

The moment when a kiss ends—it was like awakening reluctantly from sleep, struggling drowsily against the glare of the morning sun as it struck their eyelids, as they yearned to hold on to the fragment of unconsciousness left to them. That is the moment when sleep is sweetest.

When their lips parted, an ominous silence seemed to fall, as though the birds had suddenly stopped their attractive song. They looked away from each other and stared fixedly into space. The movement of the rickshaw, however, saved the silence from becoming too oppressive. At least they could feel part of some other activity.

Kiyoaki dropped his eyes. Beneath the bottom of the green blanket, the toe of a woman's white *tabi* edged out timidly, like a nervous white mouse peeping out of its grassy burrow. It was already covered with a light dusting of snow. He felt his cheeks burning, and so he reached over as spontaneously as a child to touch her cheek, pleased to discover the same warmth in her. It was like a tiny promise of summer.

"I'll open it up."

She nodded. He reached out and unfastened the front flap of the cab. The layer of snow that had collected on it to form a momentary square of solid white crumbled away without a sound.

The rickshaw men, noticing movement inside the cab, suddenly stooped.

"No, no! Keep going!" Kiyoaki shouted. Spurred on by the young man's tone, they broke into a trot again.

"Keep going! And as fast as you can!"

The cab glided through the snow, the rickshaw men giving cries of encouragement to each other.

"Somebody might see," said Satoko, sitting back in the seat, unwilling to show her eyes still wet with tears.

"It doesn't matter."

The decisive ring in his own voice took Kiyoaki by surprise. Suddenly he understood. What he really wanted to do was to challenge the world.

As he looked up, the sky above seemed to be a fury of boiling white. The snow was now lashing down right on their faces. If they opened their mouths, it lay on their tongues. To be buried in such a drift . . . it seemed like heaven.

"Now there's snow in here," she said dreamily. Apparently, she meant that it had melted in a trickle from her neck to her breast. There was nothing anarchic in the falling snow, however: it fell with the steady solemnity of an ordered ritual. He felt his cheeks grow cold, and gradually became aware that his heart was fading within him.

By now the rickshaw had climbed to the top of a hill in the fashionable Kasumi section of Azabu. The edge of the slope

was skirted by a field that allowed a clear view of the parade
ground and barracks of the Azabu Third Regiment below. On
the white expanse of parade ground, there was not one soldier
to be seen. Suddenly Kiyoaki had the illusion of seeing a
huge mass of troops drawn up, just as in the familiar picture
of the memorial ceremony near Tokuri Temple for the fallen
of the Russo-Japanese War. With bowed heads, thousands
of soldiers stood in groups around a white wood cenotaph
and an altar covered with white cloths that were blowing in
the wind. This scene differed from the photo only insofar as
the soldiers' shoulders were covered with snow and the visors
of their caps had turned white. The moment he saw these
phantoms, Kiyoaki understood that they had all died in battle. The thousands of troops below had massed not only to
pray for fallen comrades, but to mourn their own lives as well.

In a moment, the phantoms were gone. Behind a curtain of
snow, scene after scene swept past them. The thick straw-
colored ropes that supported the pines on the steep side of the
Outer Moat bore a dangerous weight of snow. And behind
the tight-shut windows of the small houses, the lamps were
burning faintly although it was mid-morning.

"Close it," said Satoko.

Kiyoaki shut the front flap, and they found themselves once
more in the familiar half-light. The mood of ecstasy, however, was not to be so easily recaptured. Kiyoaki as usual was
prey to misgivings. "I wonder how she felt when I was kiss-
ing her," he thought. "She's probably angry about the way I
did it. She knows that I get too carried away, that I was all
wrapped up in myself—just like a child. And it's true. I
couldn't think about anything except how wonderful it felt
to me."

Then Satoko's voice broke into his thoughts.

"Shouldn't we go home?" she said, her voice altogether too
composed.

"There she goes," he thought, "leading me by the nose
again." But even as he grumbled to himself, he knew that he
was letting pass by the moment when he had the chance to

change things. He could say: "No, let's not go back." But to do that was to reach out and pick up the dice. And his unskilled hand would have frozen at the very touch of them. He was not ready.

 13

HE WENT HOME and concocted a story about leaving school early because of a sudden chill. His mother rushed up to his room to take his temperature. In the midst of this commotion, Iinuma appeared to say that Honda was on the phone. Kiyoaki had the greatest difficulty in persuading his mother not to take the call in his place, and when he had finally won his point and had gone downstairs to the phone, he was wrapped in a cashmere blanket, at his mother's insistence.

"It's all very simple: the story is that I did go to school today but came home early. No one here knows anything different. My cold?" Made uneasy by the glass door at his back, he continued in a low, muffled voice. "Don't worry about that. I'll be at school tomorrow, and we can talk about it then. Don't start telephoning just because I wasn't at school—you do exaggerate!"

When Honda rang off, he was shaking with anger at Kiyoaki's icy response to his expressions of concern, but there was more to it than his unfriendly tone or his rudeness. Honda had never once put Kiyoaki in the position of having to share a secret.

Once he had recovered himself, however, he began to think: "To telephone just because he wasn't at school today— that's not very like me." And indeed, something more than friendly concern had driven him to telephone so hurriedly. When rushing across the snow-covered schoolyard to the administration office at recess to make the call, he had been driven by a feeling of foreboding that he could not pin down.

Kiyoaki's desk had been empty all morning. Looking at it, Honda experienced the sense of dread of a man whose worst fears are confirmed. The old desk, with its scars under the new varnish, reflected the direct glare of the snow through the window. It made him think of an upright coffin draped in white, the kind used to bury ancient warriors in a sitting position.

His gloom persisted even after he had got home. Then there was a phone call; it was Iinuma with a message from Kiyoaki: he was sorry about the way he had spoken to Honda. If he sent a rickshaw to Honda's house tonight, would he please come to visit him? Iinuma's heavy, sepulchral tone depressed him still further. He curtly refused, saying that they could discuss things when Kiyoaki was well enough to go back to school.

When Iinuma delivered this message, Kiyoaki felt the discomfort of real sickness. Afterwards, he called Iinuma to his room late that night, but instead of ordering him to do something, he surprised Iinuma by unburdening himself of his vexations.

"Satoko causes nothing but trouble. It's true what they say, isn't it? A woman will destroy the friendship of men. If Satoko hadn't behaved so willfully this morning, I wouldn't have given Honda such cause for anger."

During the night it stopped snowing, and the next day was clear and pleasant. Prevailing over his mother and the rest of the household, Kiyoaki left for school. He intended to get there before Honda and be the first to say good morning. But as the sun rose in the sky, the dazzling splendor of this winter morning worked a change of mood. He was affected by a deep, insuppressible happiness that transformed him. Later, when Honda came into the classroom and returned his smile with a nonchalant one of his own, Kiyoaki in a sudden about-face abandoned his intention to tell him everything about the day before.

Honda had managed a smile, but no words. After putting his book bag down on his desk, he leaned on the windowsill for a few moments and looked out at the snow. Then after a quick glance at his watch that presumably told him there were still thirty minutes to spare before class, he turned without a word and walked out. Kiyoaki felt impelled to follow him.

A number of small flowerbeds were laid out geometrically along the side of the school, a two-story wooden structure. In their midst was an arbor. Not far beyond the edge of the beds the ground dropped away sharply, and a small path led down the slope to a pond surrounded by a grove of trees. Kiyoaki was reasonably sure that Honda would not go down to the pond, since the melting snow would make walking extremely difficult. Just as he had guessed, Honda stopped in the arbor, brushed the snow off one of the benches and sat down. Kiyoaki, threading his way through the drifts in the flower garden, walked up to him.

"Why are you following me?" asked Honda, squinting into the brilliant light as he looked up.

"I behaved very badly yesterday," Kiyoaki apologized smoothly.

"Never mind. Your cold was just an excuse, wasn't it?"

"Yes."

Copying Honda, Kiyoaki brushed some snow off the bench and then sat down beside him. Because of the glare, the two of them had to squint painfully to look at each other, which greatly reduced the emotional charge in the atmosphere. The pond below was hidden from view, although they only had to stand up to see it through the snow-laden tree branches. They were surrounded by the sound of trickling water, proof that the mounds of snow on the school roof, on the arbor, and on the trees were now melting. The frozen crust that covered the

flowerbeds had collapsed here and there, leaving coarse, lay-
ered chips of ice that glittered like split granite.

Honda expected Kiyoaki to divulge some portentous secret
and yet he didn't want to admit to himself that he was curious,
which almost made him hope that Kiyoaki would say nothing
at all. Any confidence that smacked even remotely of condescension would be bitterly distasteful.

It was Honda, then, who spoke first, wishing only to find
a subject that had no bearing on the issue between them.

"You know, I've been thinking a lot about personality
lately. Take the times we live in, this school, this society—
I feel alien to them all. At least I would like to think I did.
And the same can be said for you too."

"Yes, of course," Kiyoaki replied, his tone as uninterested
and aloof as ever, yet with a sweetness that was very much in
character.

"But let me ask you this: what happens after a hundred
years? Without us having any say in the matter, all our ideas
will be lumped together under the heading, 'The Thought of
the Age.' Take the history of art, for example: it proves my
point irrefutably, whether you like it or not. Each period has
its own style, and no artist living in a particular era can completely transcend that era's style, whatever his individual outlook."

"Does our age have its style too?"

"I think I'd be more inclined to say that the style of the
Meiji era is still dying. But how would I know? To live in
the midst of an era is to be oblivious to its style. You and I,
you see, must be immersed in some style of living or other,
but we're like goldfish swimming around in a bowl without
ever noticing it. Take yourself: yours is a world of feeling.
You appear different from most people. And you yourself are
quite sure that you have never allowed your personality to be
compromised. However, there is absolutely no way of proving
that. The testimony of your contemporaries has no value
whatever. Who knows? It may just be that your world of

feeling represents the style of this era in its purest form. But then again, there's no way of knowing."

"Well, then, who does decide?"

"Time. Time is what matters. As time goes by, you and I will be carried inexorably into the mainstream of our period, even though we're unaware of what it is. And later, when they say that young men in the early Taisho era thought, dressed, talked, in such and such a way, they'll be talking about you and me. We'll all be lumped together. You detest that bunch on the *kendo* team, don't you? You despise them?"

"Yes," Kiyoaki said, uncomfortably aware that the cold was beginning to penetrate the seat of his trousers, but gazing nevertheless at some green camellia leaves beside the frame of the arbor. Freshly bared by the melting snow, they were gleaming brightly. "Yes, I not only dislike them, I despise them."

Taking his perfunctory reply in his stride, Honda went on: "All right, then, just imagine this if you can. In a few decades, people will see you and the people you despise as one and the same, a single entity. Your slow-witted friends—with their sentimentality, their vicious narrow-mindedness that con- demns as effeminate anyone who' is not like themselves, their harassment of the underclassmen, their fanatical worship of General Nogi, the frame of mind that lets them draw such in- credible satisfaction from sweeping the ground every morn- ing around the sakaki planted by the Meiji Emperor—you with all your sensitivity will be seen cheek-by-jowl with these people when they stop to think about our times in years to come. You see, this is the easiest way to establish the essence of our era—to take the lowest common denominator. Once the churning water has settled to a calm surface, you can see the rainbow oil slick floating there. And that's the way it will be. After we're all dead, it will be easy to analyze us and isolate our basic elements for everyone to see. And of course this es- sence, the thought that is the foundation of our era, will be considered quite benighted a hundred years from now. And you and I have no way of escaping the verdict, no way to

prove that we didn't share the discredited views of our contemporaries. And what standard will history apply to that outlook? What do you think? The thoughts of the geniuses of
our age? Of great men? Not at all. Those who come after us
and decide what was in our minds will adopt the criterion of
the uncritical thought patterns of your friends on the *kendo*
team. In other words, they'll seize upon the most primitive
and popular credos of our day. You see every era has always
been characterized solely in terms of such idiocies."

Kiyoaki was not sure where this was taking Honda, but as
he listened, a germ of thought began to grow in his mind. By
now several of their classmates were to be seen at the open
windows of their second-floor classroom. The windows of the
other rooms were shut, reflecting the glare of the morning
sun and the brilliant blue of the sky. A familiar morning
scene. When he thought of the events of the previous day,
the morning of the snowstorm, he felt as if he had been
drawn unwillingly from a dark world of sensuous excitement
into the clear, bright courts of reason.

"Well, that's history," he said. He was embarrassed by the
immaturity of his remarks in contrast to Honda's, but he was
finally making an effort to come to grips with the other's
thought. "In other words, no matter what we think, or hope
for, or feel—all that has not the slightest bearing on the
course of history? Is that what you mean?"

"That's it exactly. Europeans believe that a man like Na-
poleon can impose his will on history. We Japanese think the
same of the men like your grandfather and his contemporaries
who brought about the Meiji Restoration. But is that really
true? Does history ever obey the will of men? Looking at you
always makes me ponder that question. You're not a great
man and you're not a genius either. But, nonetheless, you have
one characteristic that sets you quite apart: you have no trace
whatever of willpower. And so I am always fascinated to
think of you in relation to history."

"Are you being sarcastic?"

"No, not a bit. I'm thinking in terms of unconscious

participation in history. For example, let's say that I have will-power—"

"You certainly have."

"Say that I want to alter the course of history. I devote all my energies and resources to this end. I use every ounce of strength I possess to bend history to my will. Say I possess the prestige and authority so necessary to bring this about. None of this would ensure that history proceeded according to my wishes. Then, on the other hand, perhaps a hundred, two hundred, even three hundred years later, history might veer abruptly to take a course that was consonant with my vision and ideals—and this without my having had anything whatever to do with it. Perhaps society would assume a form that was the exact replica of my dreams of a hundred or two hundred years before; history, enjoying the new glory that had been my vision, would smile at me with cool condescension and mock my ambition. And people would say: 'Well, that's history.' "

"But there is such a thing as the time being ripe for everything, isn't there?" asked Kiyoaki. "Your vision's time would finally have come, that's all. Maybe it wouldn't even take as long as a hundred years; maybe thirty or fifty. That sort of thing often happens. And perhaps even after your death, your will would serve as an invisible guideline, unknown to anyone, that would help bring about what you wanted to accomplish in your lifetime. Maybe if someone like you had never lived, history would never have taken such a turn, no matter how long it lasted."

Even though such cold, uncongenial abstractions were a struggle for him, Kiyoaki felt stirred by a certain warmth, an excitement that he knew he had Honda to thank for. He was reluctant to acknowledge satisfaction from such a source. But as he looked around the white-carpeted school grounds, with the bare branches of the trees casting shadows over the snow-covered flowerbeds, and the clear sound of trickling water in his ears, he knew he was happy that Honda had started this discussion. Even though he must have known that he was still engrossed in the memory of the happiness and fascination of the day before, Honda had chosen to ignore it, a decision that seemed appropriate to the purity of the snow around them. At that moment, some of it slid off the roof, baring a few square feet of wet tile, gleaming black.

"And so," continued Honda, "if society turned out as I wanted it to after a hundred years, you'd call that an accomplishment?"

"It must be."

"Whose accomplishment?"

"That of your will."

"You're joking. I'd be dead. As I just told you, all this came about without my having had anything to do with it."

"Well, can't you say that it's the accomplishment of the will of history then?"

"So history has a will, eh? It's always dangerous to try to personify history. As far as I'm concerned, history has no will of its own and, furthermore, it hasn't the least concern for mine either. So if there is no will whatever involved in the process, you can't talk about accomplishments. And all the so-called accomplishments of history prove it. They're no sooner achieved than they begin to crumble away. History is a record of destruction. One must always make room for the next ephemeral crystal. For history, to build and to destroy are one and the same thing.

"I am fully aware of all this. Although I understand it, I cannot be like you and stop being a man of determination. I suppose it's probably a compulsion in my character. No one can say for certain, but I will say this much: any will has as its essence the desire to influence history. I'm not saying that human desires affect history, only that they try to. Then, too, some forms of will are bound up with destiny, even though this concept is anathema to the will.

"But in the long run, all human will is doomed to frustration. It's a matter of course that things turn out contrary to your intentions. And what conclusion does a Westerner draw from this? He says: 'My will was the sole rational force involved. Failure came about by chance.'

"To speak of chance is to negate the possibility of any law of cause and effect. Chance is the one final irrationality acceptable to the free will.

"Without the concept of chance, you see, the Western philosophy of free will could never have arisen. Chance is the crucial refuge of the will. And without it the very thought of gambling would be inconceivable, just as the Westerner has no other way of rationalizing the repeated setbacks and frustrations that he must endure. I think that this concept of chance, of a gamble, is the very substance of the God of Europeans, and so they have a deity whose characteristics are derived from that refuge so vital to free will, namely chance —the only sort of God who would inspire the freedom of human will.

"But what would happen if we were to deny the existence of chance completely? What would happen if—no matter what the victory or the defeat—you had to exclude utterly all possible role of chance in it? In that case, you'd be destroying all refuge of free will. Do away with chance and you undermine the props under the concept of the will.

"Picture a scene like this: it's a square at midday. The will is standing there all alone. He pretends that he is remaining upright by virtue of his own strength, and hence he goes on deceiving himself. The sun beats down. No trees, no grass. Nothing whatever in the huge square to keep him company but his own shadow. At that moment, a thundering voice comes down from the cloudless sky above: 'Chance is dead. There's no such thing as chance. Hear me, Will: you have lost your advocate forever.' And with that, the Will feels his substance begin to crumble and dissolve. His flesh rots and falls away. In an instant his skeleton is laid bare, a thin liquid spurts from it, and the bones themselves lose their solidity and begin to disintegrate. The Will still stands with his feet planted firmly on the ground, but this final effort is futile. For at that very moment, the bright, glaring sky is rent apart with a terrible roar, and the God of Inevitability stares down through the chasm.

"But I cannot help trying to conjure up an odious face for this dreadful God, and this weakness is doubtless due to my own bent toward voluntarism. For if Chance ceases to exist, then Will becomes meaningless—no more significant than a speck of rust on the huge chain of cause and effect that we only glimpse from time to time. Then there's only one way to participate in history, and that's to have no will at all—to function solely as a shining, beautiful atom, eternal and unchanging. No one should look for any other meaning in human existence.

"You are not likely to see things this way. I wouldn't expect you to subscribe to such a philosophy. The only things you do put any faith in—and that without much thought—are your own good looks, your changing moods, your individuality and—not your fixed character, but on the contrary, your very lack of it. Am I right?"

Kiyoaki could not manage an answer. For want of anything better, he smiled, knowing that Honda was not trying to insult him.

"And that for me is the greatest riddle," said Honda, sighing so earnestly that it seemed almost comical. His breath became a frosty cloud that hovered for a second in the clear morning air, and seemed to Kiyoaki to be a secret manifestation of Honda's concern for him. Deep down inside him, his sense of happiness intensified.

The bell rang to announce the beginning of classes, and the two young men stood up. Just then, someone scooped up some of the snow piled on the second floor window ledges and threw down a snowball. It struck the path at their feet, in a burst of sparkling fragments.

14

KIYOAKI'S FATHER had entrusted him with the key to the library. This was in a corner of the north side of the main house, and it was one room of the Matsugaes that received scant attention. The Marquis was not the man to devote much time to books. But here were gathered the Chinese classics that had belonged to Kiyoaki's grandfather, the Western books that the Marquis had ordered from Maruzen out of the desire to appear intellectual, and many others received as gifts. When Kiyoaki started high school, his father had handed over the key with the pomposity of one conferring the guardianship of a treasure trove of wisdom. Thus he alone was privileged to go there whenever he liked. Among the books in the library least likely to excite the Marquis's interest were many collections of Japanese classics and children's books. Prior to publication, each of their publishers had requested a brief recommendation from the Marquis together with a photograph of him in formal dress, and then in exchange for this privilege to print "Recommended by His Excellency Marquis Matsugae" in gilt letters on the binding of each book, they presented him with the collections.

Kiyoaki himself was not inclined to make frequent use of the library. He preferred his own reveries to books. For Iinuma, however, who was given the key once a month by Kiyoaki so that he could clean the room, the library was the most hallowed place in the house, sanctified as it was by the Chinese classics dear to Kiyoaki's grandfather. When he spoke of it, he never referred to it merely as the library. It was always "His Late Excellency's Library," and when he pronounced those words, his voice was choked with emotion.

On the evening after Kiyoaki had become reconciled with
Honda, he called his tutor to his room just as Iinuma was
about to leave for his night classes, and dropped the library
key into his hand without a word. There was a set day for the
monthly cleaning. Furthermore, this was a job that Iinuma
never did at night. What, he wondered, was the reason for
giving him the key now, on the wrong day and in the evening
at that? It lay on the palm of his thick, blunt hand, blue and
metallic like a dragonfly with its wings torn off.

Afterwards Iinuma would recall this moment time and
again. How torn and naked the key seemed, like a ravaged
body as it lay in his palm. He stood for some time trying to
decide what it meant, but he could not. When Kiyoaki finally
did explain, he seethed with anger directed not so much at
his master as at himself for being at his mercy.

"Yesterday morning I didn't go to school and you stood by
me. Tonight it's my turn to help you. Go out just as if you
were leaving for school. Then go round to the back and come
in by the door opposite the library. That key will open the
room and you can wait inside. But don't turn on the light.
And the safest course would be to lock the door from the inside.

"Tadeshina has given Miné full instructions. She'll telephone here with a message for her, asking when Miss Satoko's sachet will be finished. That will be the signal. Miné
is skilled at such delicate work and people are always asking
her to do something like this. Miss Satoko herself asked her
to make a gold brocade sachet. So such a phone call won't
arouse the least suspicion.

"Once Miné receives the message, she'll wait for the time
when you're supposed to leave for school and then she'll go to
the library and knock lightly on the door, hoping that you'll
open it for her. And since it'll be just after dinner, when
everyone is bustling around, no one will miss her for thirty
or forty minutes.

"Tadeshina believes that for you two to meet outside

instead would be too dangerous and hard to arrange. There would have to be all sorts of pretexts for a maid to go out alone without everyone having something to say about it.

"At any rate, I took the liberty of deciding the matter without consulting you. Tadeshina is going to call Miné tonight. And so you must go to the library. If you don't, Miné will be terribly upset."

As he stood listening, a bear at bay, Iinuma's hand shook so violently that he almost dropped the key.

*

The library was very cold. The heavy curtains of gold thread let in a little light from the lanterns burning in the garden behind the house, but not enough to allow one to decipher the titles of the books. The room was filled with the smell of mildew, like the odor hanging over the banks of a clogged canal in winter.

The darkness was no obstacle to Iinuma. He had memorized the place of almost every book in the library. Works such as the writings of Han Fei-tzu, *The Testimony of Seiken*, and *The Eighteen Histories* lined the shelves, including a Japanese-bound edition of the *Commentaries on the Four Classics* which had lost its protective cover. This was a book that Kiyoaki's grandfather had thumbed so often that its binding was worn out.

One day when Iinuma was turning over the pages of one of the books he was dusting, a poem by Kayo Honen had caught his eye. It was in a collection of famous Japanese and Chinese works, and Iinuma had carefully memorized the place. The title was "Song of a Noble Heart." One verse of it was particularly consoling as he performed his duties of cleaning the library:

> Though now I sweep a little room
> I will not do so forever
> Can Kyushu hold my ambition?
> Can flocks of chattering sparrows
> Share the eagle's solitary path?

Iinuma now understood. Knowing his deep reverence for
"His Late Excellency's Library," Kiyoaki had deliberately
chosen it for this tryst. There could be no doubt about it.
When he had been explaining the plan that he had so con-
siderately arranged, the cold satisfaction in his manner was
proof enough that he grasped all its implications. He wanted
events to take their course so that Iinuma himself would commit sacrilege in the place he worshipped.

When he thought about it, there had been a silent menace
in Kiyoaki ever since he had been a beautiful child. A delight
in sacrilege. And when Iinuma had thus defiled what was so
precious to him, Kiyoaki would be as delighted as if he had
taken a piece of raw meat and rolled it up in a sacred Shinto
pendant. In legendary times, the savage god Susano, the
brother of the Sun Goddess, had found satisfaction in the
same way.

Ever since Iinuma had lost himself to a woman, Kiyoaki's
power over him had grown immensely. Furthermore—and to
Iinuma the injustice of it was baffling—the world would always accept Kiyoaki's pleasures as charming and natural,
whereas it would condemn his own with unflagging severity
as sordid, not to say sinful. As he brooded over this, Iinuma's
self-loathing steadily deepened.

From the ceiling of the library came the rustle of scurrying
rats, and an occasional muffled squeal. When he had done
the cleaning the previous month, he had spread plenty of poi-
soned chestnuts up there, but apparently to no avail. Suddenly he shuddered, remembering what he most wanted to
forget.

Every time he saw Miné's face, no matter how he tried to
suppress it, the same evil thought stirred in his mind. Even
now, as her warm body was coming to meet him in the evening darkness, this thought stood between them. It concerned
something that Kiyoaki probably knew already, but since he
had never mentioned it to him, Iinuma himself, without forgetting about it for a moment, had kept quiet about it. Actually, it was a rather open secret, which made Iinuma's dis-

tress increasingly hard to bear. He was tormented by it, as if
a pack of rats were swarming over him in all their filth. The
Marquis had slept with Miné and still occasionally did. His
imagination was triggered by the rats above—their bloodshot
eyes, their loathsome bodies. . . .

The cold was biting. No matter how brave a figure Iinuma
cut when he went out to perform his daily devotions, he shook
now as the cold struck his back and crept through him until
it covered his skin like an icy compress. Miné had probably
been delayed until there was an opportunity to leave the table
without attracting attention.

As he waited, his desire grew, sharp and insistent. Then a
mass of disagreeable feelings combined with the piercing chill
and the smell of decay to assault his already taut nerves. He
had a sinking sensation as though the foul waters of a drain-
age ditch were rising against his legs, soiling his fine silk
hakama. "Is this my way of finding pleasure?" he thought—a
man of twenty-four, capable of great bravery and ripe for the
highest honors.

There was a light knock at the door. Iinuma reacted with
such speed that he crashed painfully into a bookcase. Finally,
however, he managed to turn the key in the lock. Miné turned
slightly and slipped through the doorway. When Iinuma had
turned the lock behind her, he took her by the shoulders and
propelled her unceremoniously toward the back of the library.
Whatever the reason, his mind was fixed on the dirty gray
snow he had seen shoveled into piles along the outside wall of
the library on his way there. Though he had no time or inclination to speculate about this, he was consumed with the need
to violate Miné in the corner that was closest to the dirty
snow.

Driven to savagery by his fantasies, he was brutal with the
girl. The more he pitied her, the crueler he became. And when
in the midst of it all he realized that his viciousness was a
passion to revenge himself on Kiyoaki, he was overcome by
an indescribable misery. Since time was short and silence imperative, Miné let Iinuma have his way without offering any

resistance. But the meekness of her submission only tormented Iinuma the more, for her gentle manner bespoke a
quiet understanding of himself as someone very similar to
her.

Still, this was by no means the only reason for her gentle
compliance. Miné was cheerfully promiscuous. And for her
the total awkwardness of his manner—his attempt to intimi-
date her by his silence, his clumsy, fumbling hands—proved
the reality of his desire. She never dreamed that he might be
pitying her.

Lying there in the dark, Miné suddenly felt the cold like a
sword thrust under the spread skirt of her kimono. Looking
up through the gloom, she saw shelves laden with books, each
tucked into its case, the gold of its title dulled by the passage
of time. They seemed to be pressing in on her from all sides.
Speed was essential. Tadeshina had briefed her down to the
last detail so that she would be clear on every point, and all
that was required of her in this brief moment was to act without hesitation. She saw her role in life as that of someone who
was ready to give her body freely to soothe and comfort. This
was enough for her. And her small ripe body, with its firm
flesh and smooth, flawless skin, was pleased to give satisfaction.

It would be no exaggeration to say that she was fond of
Iinuma. Whenever she was desired, Miné had a wonderful
knack of discovering the good points in her suitor. She had
never joined the other maids in their contemptuous mockery
of Iinuma, and so his virility, so long harassed and ridiculed,
at last received its due in her woman's heart.

She suddenly had a vision of a temple holiday in all its
gaudy festivity: the acetylene lights with their glare and
acrid smell, the balloons and pinwheels, the gaily-colored
candies. . . .

She opened her eyes in the darkness.

"What are you staring at?" asked Iinuma in irritation.

The rats were scurrying around in the ceiling again. Their
movements were almost soundless, and yet they held a note

of desperate urgency. They seemed to be rushing frantically
through their dark domain in a frenzy that dashed them from
one end of it to the other.

15

ALL THE MAIL that was delivered to the Matsugae
household was handled according to a fixed ritual: the steward Yamada took charge of it and stacked it neatly on a gold-
lacquered tray engraved with the family crest. This was then
borne into the presence of the Marquis and Marquise. Since
Satoko was aware of this procedure, she had taken the pre-
caution of entrusting her note to Tadeshina, who, in turn,
was to give it to Iinuma.

So it was that Iinuma, in the middle of studying for his
final examinations, took the time first to meet Tadeshina and
then to hand over Satoko's love letter to Kiyoaki.

> Though the morning after that snowstorm was clear and
> bright, I just couldn't help thinking about what had happened
> the day before. In my heart it seemed as if the snow had not
> stopped, but was falling still. And the snowflakes seemed to
> merge into the form of Kiyo's face. How I wished that I could
> live somewhere where the snow fell every day of the year so
> that I would never stop thinking of you, Kiyo.
>
> If we were living in Heian times, you would have composed
> a poem for me, wouldn't you? And I would have had to offer
> one of my own in reply. I am shocked to think that although I
> have been learning *waka* since my childhood, at a time like
> this I can't set down a single poem to express my feelings. Is
> it because I lack the talent?
>
> Why do you believe that I'm so happy? Just because I have

found someone who is kind enough not to be upset by whatever I say or do, no matter how capricious? That would be the same as thinking that I enjoy treating Kiyo however I choose —and nothing could cause me greater pain than to know that you believe this.

No, what really makes me happy is your gentleness. You were able to see through that whim of mine the other day. You could see how desperate I secretly felt. And without a word of reproach you came with me on that ride through the snow and you fulfilled the dream that I had buried deep inside me with so much embarrassment. That is what I mean by your gentleness.

Kiyo, even now, remembering what happened, I feel my body tremble with joy and shame. Here in Japan, we think of the spirit of snow as a woman—the snow fairy. But I remember that in Western fairy tales I read it's always a handsome young man. And so I think of Kiyo as the spirit of snow, so masculine in your uniform. I think of you as overwhelming me. To feel myself dissolve into your beauty and freeze to death in the snow—no fate could be sweeter.

At the end, Satoko had written: "Please be kind enough not to forget to throw this letter into the fire."

Up to this final line, the style was smooth and graceful, for Satoko never expressed herself other than with elegance. Nevertheless, Kiyoaki was startled by the sensuous vigor that seemed to flare up here and there.

After he had read it, his immediate reaction was that it was the kind of letter that ought to transport a man into ecstasy. On reflection, however, it seemed more of a textbook exercise from Satoko's classes in the art of elegance. He felt she wanted to teach him that elegance overrides any question of indecency.

If the two of them had really fallen in love that snowy morning, how could they bear to let a day pass without meeting, if only for a moment or two? What could be more natural? Yet Kiyoaki was not inclined to follow his impulses in such a way. Oddly enough, living only for one's emotions, like a flag obedient to the breeze, demands a way of life that makes one balk at the natural course of events, for this implies being altogether subservient to nature. The life of the emotions detests all constraints, whatever their origin, and thus, ironically enough, is apt eventually to fetter its own instinctive sense of freedom.

Kiyoaki delayed seeing Satoko again, though not to practice self-denial. Still less was he guided by a profound knowledge of the subtleties of emotion which are only open to those already experienced in love. His behavior was simply the result of his imperfect grasp of the art of elegance, and was still so immature, almost bordering on vanity, that he envied Satoko her serene freedom, wantonness even, and was made to feel inferior.

Just as a stream returns to its normal course after a flood, Kiyoaki's predilection for suffering began to reassert itself. His dreamy nature could be as demanding as it was capricious, so much so, in fact, that he was angered and frustrated at the lack of obstacles to his love. The meddlesome assistance of Tadeshina and Iinuma provided a ready target, and he came to view their maneuvers as inimical to the purity of his feelings.

His pride was hurt when he realized that this was all he had to rely on as the fierce pain and agony of love spun their coil. Such pain ought to be fit material for weaving a magnificent tapestry, but Kiyoaki had only a tiny domestic loom with nothing but pure white thread at his disposal.

"Where are they leading me," he wondered, "at this very moment when I am gradually, genuinely, falling in love?"

But even as he decided that what he felt was love, his contrary nature was asserting itself once more.

For any ordinary young man, the memory of Satoko's kiss would have been enough to lift him into ecstasies of joy and satisfaction. But for this young man, for whom complacency was already too common a condition, it was a memory that caused greater heartache with every passing day.

No matter what else might be true, the happiness he had felt at that moment had the brilliant fire of a rich jewel. There was no doubt about that. It was engraved on his memory. In the midst of a formless, colorless snowy desert, with his emotions in turmoil, not knowing how he had embarked on this journey or how it should end, the warm glow of that jewel had been like a compass point.

His sense of discrepancy between the memory of that happiness and his present heartache grew steadily, and its effect on him deepened; he finally lapsed into the black melancholy that had been so congenial before. The kiss ceased to be anything more than another reminder of Satoko's humiliating mockery.

He decided to write a reply to her letter as chill as he could make it. He tore up several sheets of stationery in the attempt, making a fresh start each time. When he had finally composed what he thought was the ultimate in unfeeling billets-doux and put down his writing brush, he suddenly became aware of the extent of his achievement. Without intending to, he had hit upon the style of a man of great worldly experience, having built on the letter of accusation he had once sent her. This time the very thought of such outright deception was so painful that he began yet another letter. In it, without any attempt at qualification, he conveyed the joy of experiencing a kiss for the first time. It was filled with boyish passion. He closed his eyes as he slipped it into an envelope and ran the tip of his tongue over the flap. The glue tasted vaguely sweet, like medicine.

16

THE MATSUGAE ESTATE was most famous for its autumn display of maple leaves, but its cherry blossoms were also the object of much admiration. Cherry trees were scattered among the pines in the long rows of trees that flanked the drive to the main gate for more than half a mile. The best view was from the second-floor balcony of the Western-style house. Standing there, one could take in all the cherry blossoms on the Matsugae estate in a single sweeping glance; some bloomed along the drive, several trees stood among the huge gingko trees in the front garden, some ringed the small grassy knoll where Kiyoaki's Otachimachi ritual had taken place, and a few grew on the maple hill beyond the pond. Many discriminating viewers preferred this arrangement to an overwhelming display of massed blossoms in the middle of a garden.

From spring to early summer, the three principal events in the Matsugae household were the Doll Festival in March, the cherry blossom viewing in April, and the Shinto festival in May. But since the prescribed year of mourning following the death of His Imperial Highness had not yet elapsed, it was decided that this year the March and April festivals would be curtailed to strictly family observances—much to the disappointment of the women in the house. For throughout the winter, as happened every year, all sorts of rumors had been filtering down from the quarters of the senior staff about plans for the Doll Festival and the blossom viewing— such as the story that a troupe of professional entertainers would be brought in. The house was always full of such tales, the kind of speculation that gave a thrill to simple souls, accustomed to making a great deal out of the arrival of spring-time. To have their expectations blighted in this way seemed like a blight on spring itself.

The full Kagoshima-style celebration of the Doll Festival at the Matsugaes' was renowned; thanks to appreciative foreign visitors invited in years gone by, it was now famous abroad as well, so much so in fact that every year, a large number of Americans and Europeans who were in Japan at the festival time would use whatever influence they had to try to obtain invitations.

The pale cheeks of the two ivory dolls representing the Emperor and Empress shone cold in the early spring light, despite the gleam of the surrounding candles and the reflection from the scarlet carpet beneath. The Emperor doll was dressed in the splendid ceremonial robes of a Shinto high priest, and the Empress in the extravagantly rich Heian court costume. Despite the bulk of their countless skirts, their gowns dipped gracefully at the back to reveal the pale translucence of the napes of their necks. The scarlet carpet covered the entire floor of the huge main reception room. Countless wooden balls inside richly embroidered cloth hung down from the beamed ceiling, and bas-relief pictures of various kinds of popular dolls covered the walls. An old woman named Tsuru, famed for her skill at this sort of picture, came to Tokyo every February to throw herself wholeheartedly into the preparations; her pet refrain was a mumbled "as madam wishes."

Even though this year's Doll Festival lacked the usual gaiety, the women were nevertheless cheered by the prospect of the cherry blossom season; it would not be observed publicly, but it would still be celebrated with considerably more festivity than they had first been led to believe. This hope was warranted by a communication from His Highness Prince Toin announcing that he would deign to be present, though in a private capacity.

This had also cheered the Marquis immensely. He was

happiest in the midst of extravagance and ostentation, and the restraints of polite society weighed heavily on his outgoing nature. If the Emperor's cousin himself saw fit to take a lax view of the observation of mourning, then no one would dare cast aspersions on the Marquis's own sense of what morality required.

Since His Highness Haruhisa Toin had been the Emperor's personal representative at the coronation of Rahma VI and so was personally known to the royal family of Siam, the Marquis decided that it would be proper to include the two young princes in the invitations.

Years before in Paris, during the Olympic Games of 1900, the Marquis had become rather intimate with the Prince while rendering him valued service as a guide to the night life of the city. Even now the Prince was fond of recalling those days with references that only the Marquis understood. "Matsugae," he would say, "remember that place with the fountain that gushed champagne? That was a night to remember!"

April the sixth was the day set for the formal viewing of the cherry blossoms, and as soon as the rather subdued observance of the Doll Festival was over, the tempo of life in the household quickened as preparations got underway.

Kiyoaki, however, did nothing at all during his spring vacation. His parents urged him to take a trip somewhere, but even though he did not see Satoko very often, he was not in the mood to leave Tokyo while she was there.

As spring came gradually, day by day, despite the sharp cold, Kiyoaki struggled with a series of unsettling premonitions. Finally, when his ennui became overpowering, he decided to do something he did only rarely; he paid a visit to his grandmother's house on the estate. She seemed unable to shake off a lifetime's habit of treating him like an infant, and this, together with her fondness for cataloguing his mother's faults, was reason enough for his reluctance to visit her. Ever since the death of his grandfather, his grandmother, with her masculine shoulders and no-nonsense face, had turned her back on the world completely, and ate little but a handful of

rice a day, as though living in anticipation of the death she
hoped was soon to come. As it turned out, however, she
thrived on this diet.

When people came from Kagoshima to visit her, she talked
to them in the dialect of her home region, indifferent to what
others might think. With Kiyoaki and his mother, though,
she spoke in the Tokyo manner, however stiffly and awkwardly. Furthermore, since she had none of the nasal tone of
Tokyo speech, the strong parade-ground quality of her voice
was all the more apparent. He was convinced that she carefully preserved her Kagoshima accent as an implicit condem-
nation of the easy fluency of his own Tokyo inflections.

"So, Prince Toin is coming to see the blossoms, eh?" she
said without preamble as he entered; she was warming her
legs in the *kotatsu.*

"Yes, that's what they say."

"I'm not going. Your mother asked me, but I prefer being
here out of everybody's way."

Then, showing concern over his idleness, she went on to
ask him if he didn't feel inclined to take up judo or fencing.
There had once been an exercise hall on the estate, but it had
been torn down to make way for the Western house. She
made the sarcastic comment that its destruction had marked
the beginning of the decline of the family. This was one
opinion, however, that was congenial to his own way of thinking. He liked the word "decline."

"If your two uncles were alive, your father wouldn't be
carrying on the way he does. As far as I'm concerned, this being on familiar terms with the Imperial Family and pouring
out money on entertainment is just a big show. Whenever I
think of my two sons dead in the war without ever having
known what luxury was, I feel I don't want to have anything
more to do with your father and the rest of them—floating
through life and thinking of nothing but having a good time.
And as for the pension I receive for my two boys, that's why I
put it up there on the shelf beside the household altar without
ever touching it. It seems to me that His Imperial Majesty

gave it to me for the sake of my sons and the blood they shed so gallantly. It would be wrong ever to use it."

His grandmother enjoyed delivering herself of little sermons like this, but the truth was that the Marquis was unstintingly generous in granting whatever she wished, be it clothes, food, spending money, or servants. Kiyoaki often wondered if perhaps she was acutely ashamed of her rural origins and so was trying to avoid any kind of Western social life.

Still, whenever he visited her and only then, he felt that he was escaping from himself and from the artificial environment that suffocated him. He enjoyed the contact with a person who was so close to him but who still retained the earthy vigor of his ancestors. It was a pleasure of a rather ironic sort.

Everything about his grandmother was in physical harmony with his image of her character: her hands were large and her fingers blunt; the lines of her face seemed to have been laid there with the firm, sure strokes of a writing brush, and her lips were set with firm resolution. Once in a while, however, she was willing to allow a lighter note to creep into her conversations with him. Now, for example, she tapped her grandson's knee under the low table that covered the foot-warmer and teased him: "Whenever you come here, you know, my women get flustered and I don't know what to do with them. To me, I'm afraid, you're still a little boy with a wet nose, but I suppose that these girls see things differently."

Kiyoaki looked up at the faded photograph of his two uncles in uniform on the wall. Their military dress seemed to him to preclude any possible bond between them and himself. The war had ended a mere eight years before, yet the gap between them seemed immeasurable.

"I'll never shed real blood. I'll never wound anything but hearts," he boasted to himself, although not without a slight sense of misgiving.

Outside, the sun shone on the shoji screen. The small room bathed him in cozy warmth, making him feel as if he were wrapped in a huge, opaque cocoon of glowing white. He felt as if he were basking luxuriously in the direct sunlight. His grandmother began to doze. In the silence of the room, he became aware of the ticking of the huge old-fashioned clock. His grandmother's head tipped forward slightly. Her forehead jutted out sharply under the line of her short hair which she wore bound and sprinkled with a black powder dye. He noticed the healthy sheen of her skin. More than half a century ago, he thought, the hot Kagoshima sun must have burned her brown each summer of her youth, and even now she seemed to have retained its mark.

He was daydreaming, and his thoughts, moving like the sea, gradually turned from the rhythm of the waves to that of the long, slow passage of time, and hence to the inevitability of growing old—and he suddenly caught his breath. He had never looked forward to the wisdom and other vaunted benefits of old age. Would he be able to die young—and if possible free of all pain? A graceful death—as a richly patterned kimono, thrown carelessly across a polished table, slides unobtrusively down into the darkness of the floor beneath. A death marked by elegance.

The thought of dying suddenly spurred him with a desire to see Satoko, if only for a moment.

He telephoned Tadeshina and then hurriedly left the house. There was no doubt that Satoko was full of life and beauty, as he himself was—these two facts seemed to be a strange twist of fortune, something to seize and cling to in time of danger.

Following Tadeshina's scheme, Satoko pretended to go out for a stroll and met Kiyoaki at a small Shinto shrine not far from her home. The first thing she did was to thank him for the invitation to the cherry blossom festival. She obviously thought that he had persuaded the Marquis to issue it. This was, in fact, the first he had heard of the matter, but with his usual deviousness, he did not disabuse her of the idea, and accepted her thanks in a vague, noncommittal way.

17

AFTER A PROLONGED STRUGGLE, Marquis Mat-
sugae succeeded in compiling a severely curtailed guest list
for the blossom festival. His criterion was to invite the number of suitable guests most appropriate to the occasion, as the
banquet that concluded it would be graced by the august presence of the Imperial Prince and his wife. Besides Satoko and
her parents, Count and Countess Ayakura, he therefore included only the two Siamese princes and Baron Shinkawa and
his wife, who were frequent visitors and great friends of the
Matsugaes. The Baron was the head of the Shinkawa *zai-
batsu*. His whole way of life was modeled on that of the complete English gentleman, whom he copied with scrupulous attention to detail. The Baroness, for her part, was on intimate
terms with such people as the noted feminist Raicho Hiratsuka and her circle, and was also a patron of the Women
of Tomorow. She could thus be relied upon to add a touch of
color to the gathering.

Prince Toin and his wife were to arrive at three in the afternoon and be shown around the garden after a short rest in one
of the reception rooms of the main house. They would then be
entertained until five o'clock at a garden party by some geishas, who would go on to perform a selection of cherry blossom dances from the Genroku era.

Just before sunset, the imperial couple were to retire to the
Western-style house for aperitifs. After the banquet itself,
there would be a final entertainment: a projectionist had been
hired to show a new foreign film. Such was the program

devised by the Marquis with the help of Yamada, his steward, after pondering the varied tastes of his guests.

Trying to settle the choice of films gave the Marquis some agonizing moments. There was the one from Pathé featuring Gabrielle Robin, the famous star of the Comédie Française, that was indisputably a masterpiece. The Marquis rejected it, however, fearing that it might destroy the mood of the blossom viewing, created with such care. At the beginning of March the Electric Theater in Asakusa had begun to show films made in the West, the first of which, *Paradise Lost*, had already become wildly popular. But it would hardly do to present a film that was readily available in a place like that. Then there was another film, a German melodrama filled with violent action, but that could hardly be expected to score a success with the Princess and the other ladies in waiting. The Marquis finally decided that the choice most likely to please his guests was an English five-reeler based on a Dickens novel. The film might be rather gloomy, but it did have a certain refinement, its appeal was fairly wide, and the English captions would help all his guests.

But what if it rained? In that case, the large reception room in the main house would not offer a sufficiently varied array of blossoms, and the only suitable alternative would be to hold the viewing on the second floor of the Western-style house. Afterwards, the geishas could also perform their dances there, and the aperitifs and the formal banquet would follow as planned.

The preparations got underway with the construction of a temporary stage at a spot near the pond, just at the foot of the grassy hill. If the weather turned out to be fine, the Prince and his party would undoubtedly make a full tour of the estate in order not to miss any of the blossoms. The traditional red and white curtains that must be extended along his route were far larger than those required by more ordinary events. The work of decking the interior of the Western-style house with cherry blossoms and decorating its banqueting table to suggest a rural spring scene demanded all the attentions of a large group of helpers. Finally, on the day before the party, the hairdressers and their assistants were driven into a frenzy of activity.

Happily, April 6 was clear, even if the sunshine left something to be desired. It came and went, and there was even a chill in the morning air.

An unused room in the main house was set aside as a changing room for the geishas and was filled with all the available mirrors. His curiosity aroused, Kiyoaki went there to take a look for himself, but the maid in charge quickly chased him away. His imagination, however, was caught by the room, scoured and swept in preparation for the women who were soon to come. Screens were set up, pillows scattered everywhere, and mirrors glinted through their brightly colored covers of printed Yuzen muslin. At the moment there wasn't the faintest hint of the scent of cosmetics in the air. But within no more than half an hour, there would be a transformation; the place would be filled with lovely voices as the women gathered about the mirrors, donning and shedding their costumes with unflurried self-possession. Kiyoaki found the prospect fascinating. He was caught up by the seductive magic of the occasion, which did not emanate from the rough stage that had just been built in the garden, but rather was concentrated here in this room with its promise of intoxicating fragrance soon to come.

As the Siamese princes had very little concept of time, Kiyoaki had asked them to come as soon as lunch was over. They arrived at about one thirty. He invited them up to his study for the moment, startled to see that they were wearing their school uniforms.

"Is that beautiful girl of yours coming?" Prince Kridsada asked loudly in English before they were through the door.

Prince Pattanadid, always gently reserved, was affronted; he scolded his cousin for his unthinking rudeness and apologized to Kiyoaki in halting Japanese.

Kiyoaki assured them that she would come, but he caused surprised glances by asking that they refrain from speaking about him and Satoko in front of either the imperial guests or the Matsugaes and Ayakuras. The princes had apparently assumed that the relationship was common knowledge.

By now the two princes were showing no sign of their former homesickness, and they seemed to have settled into the rhythm of life in Japan. In their school uniforms, they struck Kiyoaki as being almost indistinguishable from his other classmates. Prince Kridsada, who was a gifted mimic, did an imitation of the dean that was good enough to make Chao P. and Kiyoaki laugh out loud.

Chao P. walked over to the window and looked out over the grounds of the estate at a scene quite different from what one saw on ordinary days. The red and white curtain that wound through it was waving in the wind.

"From now on it must surely get warmer," he said forlornly, his voice filled with longing for the hot summer sun.

Kiyoaki was quite taken with this touch of melancholy. He stood up and was about to walk over to the window himself, but as he rose, Chao P. gave a sudden, boyish cry that aroused his cousin and brought him out of his chair.

"There she is!" he exclaimed, slipping into English. "There's the beautiful lady we mustn't mention today."

And indeed it was Satoko, unmistakable in her long-sleeved kimono as she came along the path beside the pond toward the main house with her parents beside her. Even at a distance, Kiyoaki could see that the kimono was a beautiful cherry-blossom pink, its pattern reminiscent of the fresh green profusion of a spring meadow. As she turned her head momentarily, pointing out the island, he caught a glimpse of her profile, the delicate pallor of her cheek set off by her shining black hair.

No red and white curtains had been hung on the island. It was still too early to see the first tinges of spring green, but the curtains that marked the twisting path up the maple hill beyond cast wavering reflections on the surface of the water, their colors putting Kiyoaki in mind of striped cookies. Although the window was shut, he felt that he could hear Satoko's warm, bright voice.

Two young Siamese and a Japanese . . . they stood in a trio at the window, each catching his breath. How strange, thought Kiyoaki. When he was with the two young princes, was it that he found their passionate natures so infectious that he could believe himself to be the same, and feel able to show it openly? At this moment he could tell himself without a qualm: "I love her. I'm madly in love with her."

Six years before, he had had all too brief a glimpse of the Imperial Princess Kasuga's beautiful profile as she turned to glance back at him; it had filled his heart with a hopeless and lingering yearning, but now as Satoko left the pond, she turned her face toward the main house with a graceful movement of the head, and although she was not looking directly at his window, Kiyoaki suddenly felt liberated from that former obsession. In one moment, he had experienced something that surpassed it. Six years later, he now felt that he had recaptured a fragment of time, sparkling and crystalline, from a different perspective. As he watched Satoko walking in the pale watery spring sunshine, she suddenly laughed, and as she did so, he saw her raise her arm in a fluid movement, hiding her mouth behind the graceful curve of her white hand. Her slim body seemed to vibrate like a superb stringed instrument.

18

BARON SHINKAWA and his wife were uniquely matched as a couple: absentminded detachment was here quite literally wedded to frenzy. The Baron took not the slightest notice of anything his wife said or did, while the Baroness, oblivious to her effect on others, kept up a ceaseless outpouring of words. This was their customary behavior, whether at home or in public. Despite his abstracted manner, the Baron was perfectly capable on occasion of mercilessly nailing a person's character with a single, incisive, pithy observation, on which, however, he never deigned to elaborate. His wife, on the other hand, no matter what torrent of words she might expend on that same individual, never succeeded in bringing him to life.

They owned a Rolls Royce, the second ever purchased in Japan; it was a distinction they treasured as evidence of their social position. It was the Baron's custom to don a silk smoking jacket after dinner and, thus attired, to spend the rest of the evening ignoring his wife's inexhaustible flood of chatter.

At the Baroness's invitation, Raicho Hiratsuka's circle met at the Shinkawa residence once a month, calling themselves the Heavenly Fire Group after a famous poem by Lady Sanunochigami. However, since it invariably rained on the appointed day, the newspapers amused themselves by referring to them as the Rainy Day Club. Any sort of serious thought was beyond the Baroness, who was amazed at the intellectual awakening among Japanese women. She observed it with the same excited curiosity that might have been aroused in her by hens laying eggs of some novel shape—pyramids, for instance.

The Shinkawas were both irritated and flattered by the Matsugaes' invitation to the blossom viewing. Irritated because they realized how bored they would be. Flattered because it would give them an opportunity to display their authentically European manners in public. The Shinkawas were an old and wealthy merchant family, and while it was, of course, essential to maintain the mutually profitable relationship established with the men from Satsuma and Choshu who had risen to such power within the government, the Baron and his wife held them in secret contempt because of their peasant origins. This was an attitude inherited from their parents, and one that was at the very heart of their newly acquired but unshakable elegance.

"Well, now that the Marquis has invited Prince Toin to his house," the Baron remarked, "perhaps he'll organize a brass band to greet him. That family views the visit of an imperial prince as a sort of theatrical event."

"We just have to keep our enlightened views to ourselves, I'm afraid," was his wife's reply. "I think that it's rather chic to remain au courant as we do without seeming to, don't you think so? In fact it's rather amusing, don't you agree, to mix unobtrusively with old-fashioned people like them. For example, I think it's frightfully amusing the way Marquis Matsugae is so obsequious in front of Prince Toin at one moment and then tries to behave as though they were old friends the next. But I wonder what I should wear? We'll be leaving early in the afternoon, so I imagine it wouldn't quite do to go in formal evening dress. When all is said and done, I suppose a kimono would be the wisest. Perhaps I should hurry and put in an order at Kitaide in Kyoto and have something made up, perhaps in that lovely blossoms-by-firelight pattern? But for some reason I never look well in a Suso pattern. I'm never sure if it's just me who thinks that the Suso pattern looks frightful on me and that it's really just the thing, or whether other people also think it looks frightful. So I just don't know what to do—but what do you think I should do?"

On the day itself, the Shinkawas received a note from the

Matsugaes. They were respectfully requested to arrive some time before the time set for the imperial couple's arrival, and although they chose with cool deliberation to make their appearance five or six minutes after the time the Toinnomiyas were expected, they were chagrined to discover that they were still early. The Marquis had apparently allowed for such maneuvers. This display of country manners ruffled the Baron.

"Perhaps His Imperial Highness's horses had a stroke on the way," he observed by way of a greeting. But no matter how biting the Baron's sarcasm, his speech was mumbled and his expression blank in true English fashion, so that no one heard him.

A dispatch from the distant main gate announced the appearance of the imperial carriage, and the host and his party immediately took up their positions at the entrance of the main house to welcome the Prince.

His carriage was splattered here and there with spring mud as the horses, the gravel spurting under their hooves, trotted up under the pine tree that stood in the drive in front of the house. They snorted irritably and tossed their heads, and for a moment their flying gray manes made Kiyoaki think of the seething crest of a huge wave about to break on the shore. At the same instant, the imperial chrysanthemum on the door blurred in a whirlpool of gold and then was still as the carriage came to a halt.

Prince Toin's fine gray moustache was well set off by a black derby. The Princess, following her husband, walked into the entranceway, crossing the threshold onto the white carpeting that had been spread over the floors of the main house that morning to obviate the necessity of changing into slippers. The imperial couple naturally gave a brief nod before entering the house, but the formal ritual of welcome was to be enacted in the reception room.

As the Princess passed him, Kiyoaki's eye was caught by the black tips of her shoes flashing beneath the frilly white material of her skirt. They were like pods of seaweed, he thought, bobbing in a rippling eddy. The elegance of it so fascinated him that he was even more reluctant to look up at her face, which was beginning to show signs of age.

In the reception room, Marquis Matsugae presented the other guests to the Toinnomiyas. The only person who was new to them was Satoko.

"What have you been up to, Ayakura," the Prince chided her father, "hiding such a beautiful young lady from me?"

Kiyoaki, standing to one side, was seized by a slight shudder that he could not explain. He felt that Satoko had suddenly been transformed into a rare work of art on public display.

Since the Prince was so close to the court of Siam, the two princes had been presented to him immediately on arrival in Japan. He now chatted with them familiarly, asking whether or not they liked their fellow students at Peers. Chao P. smiled brightly, his reply the very model of dutiful courtesy: "They all help to make things easier for us in every way; it's as if we'd been friends for years. We lack for nothing."

Since the princes had hardly ever appeared at school until now and apparently had no friends at all there, except for himself, Kiyoaki found this enthusiastic testimony very funny.

Baron Shinkawa liked to think of his sensibility as being of polished silver. Its luster shone unmarred in the congenial atmosphere of his own home, but no sooner was he plunged into the vulgar intercourse of the outside world than its carefully burnished surface began to tarnish. To suffer a single encounter such as this was enough to cast a light film over it.

Under the direction of the Marquis, the guests now went outside, on the heels of the Prince and Princess, to see the blossoms. Being Japanese, however, the couples did not permit themselves to mingle freely; each wife remained behind her husband. Baron Shinkawa had already fallen into a fit of abstraction that was noticeable to the others. Nevertheless, as soon as he and his wife had put a suitable distance between themselves and the other guests, he roused himself to remark to her: "When the Marquis was studying in Europe, he took to foreign ways. Before that he kept his mistress in the same house as his wife, but afterwards he installed her in a rented house just outside the front gate, which is about half a mile from the house. That amounts to, say, one half-mile of Westernization. It's what I believe is called six of one, half a dozen of the other."

"To be enlightened at all," replied his wife, launching out, "one must be enlightened all the way. Half measures just won't do. If the household is really to be run on European lines, then whether it's a matter of replying to a formal invitation or merely going out for a short evening stroll, husband and wife should do it together as we do, regardless of what others say. Oh, look over there! See how the hill's reflected in the pond, with two or three cherry trees and the red and white curtain? Isn't it pretty? And do you like my kimono? Looking at what the other ladies are wearing, I'd say that mine has the most elaborate, the boldest, the most enlightened pattern here. And so how gorgeous it would look to someone on the other side who saw it reflected in the water, don't you think? Oh, how frustrating! Why can't I be on both sides of the pond at once? One is so frightfully limited, isn't one, don't you think?"

Pairing each husband with his own wife was an exquisitely refined torture that the Baron endured with cheerful equanimity. It was, after all, one that he preferred and had, in fact, pioneered. He looked on it as the kind of ordeal that might well become general practice in advanced civilization a hundred years hence. The Baron was not the kind of man to desire a passionate rapport with life, and he was ready to welcome any form of behavior that precluded this, however unendurable or tedious it might be to lesser men; he accepted his lot with the noblesse oblige of an English sophistication.

When the guests finally reached the top of the hill, from which they were to view the entertainment, they were greeted by the Yanagibashi geishas, already disguised as the traditional characters of the Genroku cherry blossom dances. Thus they found themselves mingling with the samurai in his padded costume, the female Robin Hood, the clown, the blind minstrel, the flower seller, the carpenter, the seller of wood-cuts, the young hero, the town and the village maidens, the haiku master, and all the others. Prince Toin was gracious enough to be amused, letting the Marquis at his side see his smile of pleasure, and the Siamese princes gleefully thumped Kiyoaki on the shoulder.

Since his father and mother were busy entertaining the Prince and Princess respectively, Kiyoaki was left more or less alone with the two Siamese boys; he had enough to do fending off the geishas who clustered around him while he looked after the princes, who were still awkward in Japanese, and had little chance to worry about Satoko.

"Young master," said the old geisha who played the poet, "won't you please come and visit us soon? So many of the girls have fallen head over heels in love with you today; must they go unrequited?"

The young geishas and even the ones who took masculine roles wore a light touch of rouge around the eyes, which gave their laughing faces a slightly drunken cast. Though the growing chill in the air told Kiyoaki that evening was drawing on, he nevertheless had the feeling of being sheltered from the real night wind, surrounded by a folding screen of silk, embroidery, and white powdered skin.

He wondered how these women could laugh and play as happily as if they were bathing in water warmed to their lik-ing. He observed them closely—the way they gestured as they told stories, the way they all nodded alike, as though each had a finely wrought gold hinge in her smooth white neck, the way they allowed themselves to be teased, letting mock anger flash for an instant in their eyes without ceasing to smile, the way they instantly assumed a grave expression to complement a guest's sudden sententious turn, their fleeting air of cold detachment as they adjusted their hair with a touch of the hand—and of all these many devices, the one that interested him most was their manner of letting their eyes rove incessantly. Without being aware of what he was doing, he was comparing it with Satoko's characteristic habit of casting sidelong glances. The geishas' eyes were certainly cheerful and alive, their only expression of independence, but Kiyoaki found them distasteful nevertheless. They darted here and there as aimlessly as buzzing flies, quite in contrast with their expressions. They had none of Satoko's delicate coordination, a gift that comes only with a sure sense of elegance.

Now as she stood talking with the Prince, Kiyoaki watched her profile. Her face was lit with a faint glow from the setting sun, and as he looked on from the other side of the group, he thought of a crystal sparkling far away, the faint note of a koto, a distant mountain valley—all alike imbued with that peculiar charm of the inaccessible. As the background of trees and sky gradually darkened, moreover, her profile became still more brightly etched, like Mount Fuji's silhouette, caught by the setting sun.

In the meantime, Baron Shinkawa and Count Ayakura were exchanging laconic observations quite unhindered by the attendant geisha whose ministrations they accepted with cool indifference. The lawn beneath their feet was thickly scattered with blossoms, and one of these petals, to the fascination of the Baron, was clinging to the polished toe of one of the Count's shoes as they gleamed in the rays of the setting sun. They were small enough to be women's shoes, he thought. And indeed, as the Count stood there holding a glass of saké, his hand seemed so small and white as to be doll-like. The Baron, faced with such manifest evidence of noble breeding in elegant decline, experienced a pang of jealousy. However, the Baron was convinced that the interplay of his own carefully nurtured "English" absentmindedness with what was a natural condition of beaming abstraction in the Count imparted a quality to their conversation that no other pair could possibly match.

"As to animals," said the Count unexpectedly, "whatever one says, I maintain that the rodent family has a certain charm about it."

"The rodent family . . .?" replied the Baron, not getting the drift at all.

"Rabbits, marmots, squirrels, and the like."

"You have pets of that sort, sir?"

"No, sir, not at all. Too much of an odor. It would be all over the house."

"Ah, I see. Very charming, but you wouldn't have them in the house, is that it?"

"Well, sir, in the first place, they seem to have been ignored by the poets, d'you see. And what has no place in a poem has no place in my house. That's my family rule."

"I see."

"No, I don't keep them as pets. But they're such fuzzy, timid little creatures that I can't help thinking there's no more charming animal."

"Yes, Count, I quite agree."

"Actually, sir, every charming creature, no matter what sort, seems to have a strong odor."

"Yes, indeed, sir. I believe one might say so."

"They tell me, Baron, that you spent a good deal of time in London."

"Yes, and in London at tea time the hostess makes a great point of asking everyone: 'Milk or tea first?' Though it all comes to the same in the end, tea and milk mixed together in the cup, the English place enormous importance on one's preference as to which should be poured in first. With them it seems to be an affair of greater gravity than the latest government crisis."

"Very interesting. Very interesting indeed, sir."

They gave the geisha no chance to contribute a single word, nor, despite the day's theme, did they seem to have the slightest interest in cherry blossoms.

Marquise Matsugae was talking with Princess Toin, who was extremely fond of *nagauta* and also played the samisen with great skill. Beside them stood the old geisha who was the best singer in Yanagibashi, contributing her share to the conversation. The Marquise was telling them how, some time before, at a relative's engagement party, she had played "The Green of the Pines" on the piano to the accompaniment of a koto and samisen, an ensemble, she said, that all the guests found charming. The Princess followed the story with keen interest and exclaimed how much she regretted not having been there to take part herself.

Marquis Matsugae's loud laugh rang out frequently. Prince Toin, on the other hand, was pleased to laugh now and then, but he did so with due moderation, putting a hand to his handsomely trimmed moustache. The old geisha who played the blind minstrel whispered something in the Marquis's ear, and he immediately called out to his guests in his hearty voice. "Well now, it's time for the cherry blossom dances. Will you please be kind enough to move over close to the stage."

This sort of announcement, in fact, belonged to the steward Yamada's sphere of authority. Shocked at having his master snatch his role from him without warning, the old man now blinked rapidly behind his spectacles. This reaction, which he concealed from everyone, was customary when he had to put up with the unexpected.

Yamada would never lay a finger on anything belonging to the Marquis, and he expected his master to show a like discretion toward him in return. There was, for example, an incident that had occurred the previous fall. The children of the foreigners who lived in the houses outside the gate had gathered some acorns while playing on the grounds of the estate. Yamada's children had come out to join them, but when the foreign children had offered them a share of the acorns, they had refused in horror. Their father had warned them severely against touching anything that belonged to the master. The foreign children misunderstood their reaction, however, and later the father of one of them came to Yamada to complain. When he thus learned what had happened, he summoned his solemn, pinch-faced children with their mouths turned down in perpetual obsequious respect and praised them highly for their behavior.

As he thought about this, he rushed forward with pathetic determination into the midst of the guests, the skirts of his *hakama* flapping about his unsteady legs, and directed them feverishly toward the stage.

Just at this moment, from behind the red and white curtain that was stretched in a semicircle at the back of the stage, there came the sharp crack of the two sounding sticks that announced the start of the program; the report cut through the evening air and seemed to make the fresh sawdust that was scattered over the boards dance for an instant.

 19

Kɪyoaki and Satoko had no chance to be alone until there was a brief interval after the dance, just as darkness was finally beginning to settle. This was the time allotted for the guests to move toward the Western-style house where the banquet was to be held. The geishas mingled with the guests once more to hear high praise for their performance while everyone drank freely. It was that strange moment, poised on the edge of evening, when lights are still unnecessary, when even in the midst of a convivial gathering, one may be caught by a vague intimation of precariousness.

Kiyoaki deliberately glanced back in Satoko's direction and saw that she was being careful to follow him at a discreet distance. At a point where the path leading down from the hill came to a fork—one branch leading toward the pond, the other toward the front gate—there was an opening in the red and white curtain. A big cherry tree stood here, its trunk thick enough to give some protection from prying eyes. Kiyoaki stepped through the curtain and waited behind the tree. Before Satoko could join him, however, she was caught up in a group of court ladies, Princess Toin's attendants, as they came from the pond on their way back from a tour of the maple hill. Since Kiyoaki could not come out of hiding at this moment, there was nothing for him to do but wait in the shelter of the tree until Satoko was able to find a pretext for escape.

Left to himself, Kiyoaki looked up at the tree above him and for the first time that day gave some thought to the cherry blossoms. They hung in huge clusters from the black austerity of the branches like a mass of white seashells spread over a reef. The evening wind made the curtains billow along the path, and when it caught the tips of the branches, they bent gracefully in a rustle of blossoms. Then the great, widespread branches themselves began to sway with an easy grandeur under their weight of white. The pallor of the flowers was tinged here and there by pink clusters of buds. And with almost invisible subtlety, the star-shaped center of each blossom was marked with pink in tiny, sharp strokes, like the stitches holding a button in place.

The sky had darkened, and the outline of the clouds began to blur as they merged into it, and the blossoms themselves, already turned into a single mass, began to lose their distinctive coloring for a shade that was almost indistinguishable from that of the evening sky. As he watched, the black of the tree trunk and branches seemed to grow steadily heavier and more somber.

With every minute, every second that passed, the cherry blossoms sank into deeper, darker intimacy with the evening sky. Kiyoaki was plunged into feelings of foreboding.

Out of the corner of his eye, he thought he saw the curtain swell once more in the wind, but it was Satoko brushing against it as she slipped through the opening. He took her hand, cold to his touch from the chill of the night breeze.

She resisted him and glanced anxiously about when he tried to kiss her, but since she was also trying to protect her kimono from the dust-streaked moss on the tree trunk, he was able to embrace her with ease.

"This is breaking my heart. Please let me go, Kiyo."

Satoko kept her voice low, afraid that others might hear. Kiyoaki was angered by her self-control, for he had set his heart on nothing less than an ecstatic, supreme consummation at that moment, there beneath the blossoms. The rising moan of the night wind had made him more and more uneasy, and now he was driven in desperation to seize one sure moment of happiness for them both, to the exclusion of all else. Hence his frustration when he discovered that her thoughts were obviously turned elsewhere. He was like a husband so jealous that he insists his wife have the very dreams he has.

Satoko had never looked more beautiful than now as she closed her eyes, still struggling in his arms. But although there was no feature, no contour that marred the delicacy of her face, it was nonetheless imprinted with a subtle, fleeting cast of willfulness. The corners of her lips were slightly up-turned. He anxiously tried to make out whether she was smiling or crying, but her face was already deep in shadow, an omen of the darkness almost upon them. He looked down at her ear, half-hidden by her hair. With its tinge of pink and its fine curve, the wonder of it made him think of a delicate coral recess that might appear in a dream, containing a tiny, beautifully carved Buddha. There was something mysterious about the hollow of her ear, now fading in the darkness. Was it there that her heart was hidden, he wondered, or was it concealed behind her slightly thin lips and sparkling teeth.

With a sense of nagging frustration, he wondered how he could ever penetrate Satoko's defenses. Then suddenly, as though she could no longer bear his look, she thrust her face forward and kissed him. One of his arms was around her waist. He felt a warmth that insinuated itself through his fingertips resting on her hip and that reminded him somehow of the sweet, sultry atmosphere of a greenhouse whose flowers were dying.

There was a scent to it that struck his nostrils and gave him a delightful sensation of being smothered in it. Although she had not said a word, he was in the grip of his own images, and was quite convinced that he was on the verge of a moment of peerless beauty.

She pulled her mouth away, but this left the huge mass of her hair pressed against the front of his uniform jacket. Gazing over her head at the cherry trees some distance beyond the curtain as they became edged with silver, his head reeled from the perfume of her hair oil, which became indistinguishable from the scent of the blossoms themselves; they stood out against the last light of the sun like thick, shaggy white wool, but their powdery color, shading almost to silver-gray, could not altogether blot out a faint, and to Kiyoaki ill-omened, pink. It made him think of an undertaker's cosmetics.

In the midst of this, he suddenly realized that tears were pouring down her cheeks. Afflicted by the spirit of pure research, he was prompted to try to identify these as tears either of joy or of grief, but she was too quick for him.

She shook herself free, and then without even pausing to wipe her eyes, she glared at him, her manner completely changed, and lashed out with stinging words that held no trace of compassion: "You're just a child, Kiyo! A mere child! You don't understand a thing. You don't even try to understand. Why did I hold back so much? How I wish I had taught you what you know about love. You've got such a high opinion of yourself, don't you? But the truth is, Kiyo, you're no more than a baby. Oh, if only I had realized it! If only I had tried harder to help you! Now it's too late."

After this outburst, she vanished back through the curtain, leaving the young man, utterly shattered, to his own devices.

What had happened? With unerring accuracy, she had marshaled just those words that were calculated to wound him most deeply, like arrows aimed at his weakest points. She had

tipped them with a poison distilled from the misgivings that
preyed on him most. He should have stopped to reflect on the
extraordinary efficacy of this poison. He should have tried to
decide just why such a crystallization of pure malice had occurred.

But his heart was thumping in his chest, and his hands
shook. Bitter anger so overwhelmed him that he was close to
tears. He could not be objective and coolly analyze the emotion that wracked him. Worse yet, he had to rejoin the guests.
And later in the evening there would be no escape; he would
have to make pleasant conversation as though nothing were
troubling him. He could imagine no task that he felt less fit to
perform.

 20

As for the banquet, everything went off as
planned and was brought to a successful conclusion without
any slips being apparent to the guests. The Marquis's rude
optimism was proof against all subtleties of misgiving. He
himself was well satisfied, and he never dreamed that any of
his guests might possibly feel otherwise. It was at such
moments that his wife's dazzling worth was brought home
to him, as their subsequent conversation revealed.

"The Prince and Princess seem to have had a good time
from beginning to end, wouldn't you say?" the Marquis began.
"I think they went home quite happy, don't you?"

"That goes without saying," replied the Marquise. "Didn't
His Highness the Prince deign to remark that he had not
spent so delightful a day since the Emperor died?"

"That's not the best way he could have phrased it, but I

know what he meant. But still—to go from mid-afternoon until late at night—don't you think it might have been too tiring for some of them?"

"No, no, not at all. You arranged things so cleverly, with a variety of diversions following one after the other, that it all flowed wonderfully well. I don't believe that our guests had a moment to spare in which they could have become weary."

"There wasn't anybody asleep during the film?"

"Oh, no. They were all watching wide-eyed from beginning to end and following with the keenest interest."

"But, you know, that Satoko is a tenderhearted girl. I did think the pictures were quite emotional, but she was the only one sufficiently moved to cry."

Satoko had, in fact, been crying uncontrollably throughout the show. The Marquis had noticed her tears when the lights were lit.

Kiyoaki made his way up to his room, worn out. He was wide awake, and sleep became impossible. He opened the window and imagined that the snapping turtles were gathering together just at that moment, lifting their metallic green heads above the dark surface of the pond to peer in his direction. Finally he rang the bell that summoned Iinuma, who since graduating from night school was always home in the evening.

On stepping into the room, Iinuma needed no more than a single glance to realize that anger and frustration were contorting the face of the young master. In recent weeks he had gradually developed a certain skill in reading facial expressions, a talent that until recently had been totally beyond him. He had become especially adept with Kiyoaki, with whom he had daily contact and whose expressions reminded him of the whirling fragments of colored glass that settled into continually changing patterns within a kaleidoscope.

As a result, his disposition and outlook began to alter. Not so long ago, the sight of his young master's face drawn in this way by anxiety and grief would have filled him with loathing for what he would have judged to be Kiyoaki's sluggish indolence. But now he was able to see it as a refinement.

Joy and exuberance did not, in fact, suit Kiyoaki. His beauty had a melancholy cast and so appeared most attractive when he was under the stress of anger or grief, and together with these there was always a forlorn suggestion of the spoiled child as a kind of shadow image. At times like this his pale cheeks became still whiter, his beautiful eyes bloodshot, his finely arched eyebrows were twisted into a frown, and his whole spirit seemed to waver as though his inner world were shattered. He seemed desperately to need something to cling to. And so the hint of sweetness lingered in the midst of his desolation, like the echo of a song over a barren waste.

Since Kiyoaki said nothing, Iinuma sat down on the chair he had made a habit of using recently even when Kiyoaki did not offer it to him. Then he reached out and began to read the banquet menu, which Kiyoaki had thrown down on the table. The dishes listed constituted a feast such as Iinuma knew he would never taste, no matter how many decades he might serve the Matsugaes.

The Evening Banquet of the Cherry Blossom Festival

April 6, 1913
The Second Year of the Taisho Era

SOUP

Turtle Soup   *Finely chopped turtle meat floating in broth*
Chicken Soup   *Broth with thin slices of chicken*

ENTREES

Poached Trout   *Prepared in white wine and milk*
Roast Fillet of Beef   *Prepared with steamed mushrooms*
Roast Quail   *Stuffed with mushrooms*
Broiled Fillet of Mutton   *Garnished with celery*
Pâté de Foie Gras   *Served with assortment of cold fowl
and sliced pineapple in iced wine*
Roast Gamecock   *Stuffed with mushrooms*

INDIVIDUAL SALADS

VEGETABLES
Asparagus   Green Beans
Prepared with Cheese

DESSERTS
French Custard   Petits Fours
Ice Cream   *A choice of flavors*

While Iinuma read the menu, Kiyoaki kept staring at him, one expression succeeding another on his face. One moment his eyes seemed full of contempt, the next brimming with pathetic appeal. He was irritated that Iinuma should sit there with insensitive deference just waiting for him to break the silence. If only Iinuma had been capable of forgetting the master–retainer relationship at that moment, and had put his hand on Kiyoaki's shoulder like an elder brother, how easily he could have started to talk.

He had no idea that the young man who sat in front of him was different from the Iinuma to whom he was accustomed. What he did not realize was that the Iinuma who had once been obsessed with the rough suppression of his own passions had now developed a gentle forbearance toward him, and, inexperienced as he was, had taken his first tentative steps into the world of subtle emotions.

"I can hardly imagine that you have the least idea what's on my mind," Kiyoaki said at last. "Miss Satoko insulted me terribly. She spoke to me as if I were a mere child. And she as much as said that in everything up to now I've behaved like a foolish little boy. No, in fact she said it in so many words. She came at me with everything that would hurt me most, as though she had had it all carefully planned. I just don't understand how she could have brought herself to do it. Now I realize that the ride that snowy morning—which was her idea—now I know that I was nothing more than a toy she felt like playing with." Kiyoaki paused for a moment. "But you had no inkling at all of how things really stood? Tadeshina, for example, didn't say anything at all that sounded suspicious?"

Iinuma thought for a while before answering.

"Well, no, sir. I haven't heard anything." But his awkward pause clung to Kiyoaki's nerves like a vine.

"You're lying. You do know something."

"No, sir, I don't."

Finally, however, under the pressure of Kiyoaki's questions, Iinuma poured out what he had been determined not to reveal. Being able to sense a man's mood is one thing, but to gauge his probable reaction is quite another. He did not realize that his words would strike Kiyoaki with the force of an axe.

"This is what Miné told me, sir. I'm the only one she told, and I promised faithfully not to breathe a word of it to anyone else. But since it concerns the young master, I think it's best that I tell it. It was on the day of the New Year's family party, when Miss Ayakura was here at the house. It's the day your father the Marquis is kind enough to invite all your relatives' children here to entertain them, talk to them and listen to their problems, as you know. And so it came about that your father the Marquis asked Miss Ayakura in a joking way if she didn't have any problems she wanted to discuss with him.

"She answered, also apparently as a joke: 'Yes, as a matter of fact I have a very serious matter I want to discuss with you, Marquis Matsugae. I wonder if I might inquire about your views on education.'

"At this point I must tell you, sir, that this entire incident was related to Miné by the Marquis as—well, a so-called bedtime story"—these two words cost Iinuma inexpressible pain—"and so he told it to her in detail, like a bedtime story, laughing a great deal as he did so. And so she told it to me just as he said it happened. At any rate, Miss Ayakura had caught the interest of your father the Marquis, and he asked: 'My views on education, you say?'

"And then Miss Ayakura said: 'Well, according to what I've heard from Kiyo, his father seems to be a great advocate of the empirical approach. He told me that you treated him to a guided tour of the world of geishas so that he could learn how best to conduct himself there. And Kiyo seems to be very happy with the results, feeling that he's now quite a man. But really, Marquis Matsugae, is it true that you champion the empirical method even at the expense of morality?'

"I understand that the lady asked this awkward question with her usual effortless ease. He himself burst out laughing and then answered: 'What a difficult question! That's just the sort of thing these moral reform groups ask in their petitions to the Diet. Well, if what Kiyoaki said were true, I could muster something in my defense. But the truth is this: Kiyo himself rejected just that very educational opportunity. As you know, he's a late bloomer—he's so fastidious, it's hard to believe he's my son. Certainly I asked him to come with me, but I hardly had time to open my mouth before he bristled and stalked off in a high dudgeon. But how amusing! Even though that's what actually happened, he's made up a story so as to have something to boast to you about. However, I'm pained to think that I've raised a boy who would mention the red-light district to an aristocrat, no matter how close friends they are. I'll call him in now and let him know how proud I am of his behavior. It might persuade him to go out and have a fling at a geisha house.'

"But Miss Ayakura pleaded with your father the Marquis and finally convinced him to give up such a rash idea. And she also made him promise to forget what she had told him. And so he refrained from mentioning it to anyone else out of respect for his word. But he finally told Miné, laughing all the time and obviously very amused by the whole thing. But he gave her a strict warning not to say a word to anyone. Miné is a woman, of course, and so she couldn't keep it to herself; she finally told just me. I realized that the young master's honor was involved, so I threatened her in no uncertain terms, saying that if this story went any further, I would break off with her at once. She was so shaken by the way I said this that I don't think there's any danger of the tale spreading."

As he listened to this account, Kiyoaki became even paler. He was like a man who has been groping wildly in thick fog, striking his head on one obstacle after another, until the fog suddenly lifts about him to reveal a line of white marble columns. The amorphous worry that had enveloped him now assumed a shape that was perfectly clear.

Despite her denial, Satoko had read his letter after all. It had of course dismayed her somewhat, but when she found out at the New Year's family party from the Marquis himself that it was a lie, she became ecstatic and exhilarated over her "happiest New Year." Now he understood why she had opened her heart to him so passionately and so suddenly at the stable that day. And finally, her confidence at its highest, she had thus been sufficiently emboldened to invite him to go for that ride through the February snow.

This revelation did not explain Satoko's tears today nor the severe tongue-lashing she had given him. But it was abundantly clear to him that she was a liar from first to last, that she'd been laughing at him secretly from beginning to end. No matter how one might try to defend her, it was undeniable that she had taken a sadistic pleasure in his discomfiture.

"On the one hand," he thought bitterly, "she accuses me of behaving like a child and on the other, how obvious it is that she has been behaving as though she wants me to remain that way forever. How shrewd she is! She gives the appearance of being a woman who needs to be dependent at the very moment when she's up to one of her unscrupulous tricks. She pretended to worship me, but she was really baby-nursing."

Overcome as he was by resentment, he did not pause to reflect that it was his letter that had begun everything, that it was his lie that had initiated the train of events. All he could see was that his every misfortune sprang from Satoko's treachery.

She had wounded his pride at a stage in his life—the painful transition between boyhood and manhood—when nothing was more precious to him. Though the affair itself would seem trifling to an adult—as his father's laughter had so clearly demonstrated—it was a trifle that nevertheless bore upon his self-esteem, and for Kiyoaki at nineteen, nothing was more delicate nor more vulnerable. Whether she realized this or not, she had trampled on it with an incredible lack of sensitivity. He felt sick with disgrace.

Iinuma watched his white face in the lengthening silence with compassion, but he didn't realize how punishing a blow he had just delivered. This handsome boy had never missed an opportunity to discomfit him, and now, without the least trace of revenge in his intentions, he had crushed Kiyoaki. Furthermore, he had never felt anything so close to affection for him as at this moment, watching him sitting with his head bowed.

His thoughts took a still gentler, more affectionate turn: he would help Kiyoaki up and over to his bed. If the boy began to cry, he too would cry in sympathy. But when Kiyoaki raised his head, his features were hard and set. There was no trace of tears. His cold, piercing glance banished all Iinuma's fantasies.

"All right," he said. "You may go now. I'm going to bed."

He got to his feet by himself and pushed Iinuma toward the door.

21

THE NEXT DAY Tadeshina telephoned repeatedly, but Kiyoaki would not go to the phone. She then asked to speak to Iinuma and told him that Miss Satoko wanted at all costs to speak directly with the young master and would Iinuma please convey this to him. Kiyoaki, however, had given him strict instructions, and so he could not act as a mediator.

Finally, after a number of calls, Satoko herself telephoned Iinuma. The result, however, was the same: his unqualified refusal.

The calls kept up for some days, causing no little stir among the housemaids. Kiyoaki's response did not vary. At last Tadeshina came in person.

Iinuma received her at a dark side entrance. He sat on his heels on the entrance platform, every fold of his cotton *hakama* in place, determined not to let Tadeshina one step into the house.

"The young master is absent and so is unable to welcome you."

"I don't believe that's altogether true. However, if you insist that it is, would you please call Mr. Yamada."

"Even if you were to see Mr. Yamada, I'm afraid that it would make no difference. The young master will not see you."

"All right then, if that's the way you feel. I'll just take the liberty of coming in uninvited and I'll discuss the matter directly with the young master himself."

"You are, of course, quite free to enter as you like. But he has locked himself in his room, and there is no way of gaining access to him. And then, I presume that your errand is of a rather confidential nature. If you were to disclose it to Yamada, it might give rise to some talk within the house and eventually come to the ears of His Excellency the Marquis. However, if that prospect does not unduly concern you . . ."

Tadeshina said nothing. As she glared with loathing at Iinuma, she noticed how clearly his pimples stood out, even in the gloom of the entranceway. She herself stood against the background of a bright spring day, the pale green tips of the pine branches flashing in the sunlight. Her old face, its wrinkles barely subdued by their covering layer of white powder, reminded him of a figure painted on crepe. Malice glinted sharply from her eyes sunk deep in their nests of folded skin.

"Thank you very much. I presume that even though you are only following the orders of the young master himself, you must be prepared to take the consequences of addressing yourself to me in such a fashion. Up until now, I have been exercising my ingenuity to some considerable extent on your behalf as well. It would not be wise to depend on it too much from now on. Please be kind enough to convey my respects to the young master."

Some four or five days later, a thick letter came from Satoko. Usually Tadeshina gave letters for Kiyoaki directly to Iinuma, so as to circumvent Yamada; but this time the letter was placed upon a gold lacquer tray with the family crest and delivered openly by Yamada to Kiyoaki's room.

Kiyoaki was at pains to call Iinuma to his room and show him the unopened letter. Then he told him to open the window. In his presence he put the letter into the fire of his hibachi. Iinuma watched his white hand darting about in the hibachi contained in paulownia wood, avoiding the small tongues of flame that flared up from time to time, stirring up the fire whenever the weight of the letter threatened to choke it. Iinuma had the feeling that a refined form of crime was being committed before his eyes. Had he helped, he was sure that the thing could have been done more efficiently, but he did not offer to, fearing a refusal. Kiyoaki had called him there to be a witness.

Kiyoaki could not avoid the smoke that rose from the smoldering paper, and a tear rolled down his cheek. Iinuma had once hoped that hard discipline and tears would help Kiyoaki to achieve a suitable attitude to life. Now he sat looking at the tears that graced Kiyoaki's cheeks, reddened by the fire, tears that owed nothing whatever to any efforts of his. Why was it, he wondered, that he always felt helpless in Kiyoaki's presence?

*

One day about a week later, when his father came home unusually early, Kiyoaki dined for the first time in several weeks with both his parents in the Japanese reception room of the main house.

"How time passes!" the Marquis said exuberantly. "Next year you will receive the fifth degree, junior grade. And once you have it, I'll have all the servants address you that way."

Kiyoaki dreaded his majority, which was looming over him in the coming year. Possibly Satoko's faint influence was at the heart of his weary disinterest at the age of nineteen in the prospect of achieving adult status. He had left behind the childhood disposition that makes a boy count the time remaining to New Year on his fingertips and burn with impatience to grow to manhood. He heard his father's words in a cold and somber mood.

The meal proceeded according to fixed ritual: his mother with her mask of classic melancholy and her never-failing gentility, his father with his red face and deliberately cheerful scorn for the niceties. Still, being perceptive, he was quick to notice something that surprised him: his parents' eyes met once, though not so that anyone could say they were exchanging glances. There seemed to be nothing more afoot than the usual silent conspiracy between the couple. As Kiyoaki looked into his mother's face, her expression wavered slightly, and she stumbled for a second over her words.

"Now . . . Kiyoaki . . . there's something I'd like to ask you which may not be altogether pleasant. Though it would be making far too much of things to call it unpleasant. But I would like to know how you feel about it."

"What is it?"

"Well, the fact is that Miss Satoko has received another wedding proposal. And this time the circumstances are extremely complex and delicate. If it proceeds much further, there can be no question of a free and easy refusal being permissible. As always, Miss Satoko is disinclined to let anyone know how she really feels, but this time I doubt if she would feel like giving an outright refusal as she has done in the past. And then her parents are also disposed in favor. So now let's say something about you. You and Miss Satoko have been fond of each other ever since you were babies. About her getting married, you have nothing to say against it? All you

have to do now is just to tell us how you feel. For if you have
an objection, I think it would be most helpful if your father
knew the exact reason."

Kiyoaki answered expressionlessly and without hesitation,
without even pausing in the use of his chopsticks. "I have no
objection at all. It's something that doesn't concern me in the
least."

A brief silence followed, after which the Marquis spoke in
a tone that indicated how unruffled his good mood was. "Well
now, at this point it's still possible to go back. If just for the
sake of argument we were to suppose that you might feel
yourself involved somehow, even to the smallest degree, what
would you say to that?"

"I feel no involvement whatever."

"I said it was for the sake of argument, didn't I? But if
that's the case, well and good. We have a long-standing obligation to that family, and therefore I intend to do all I can
to help in this matter and to spare no expense in bringing it
to a suitably happy conclusion. Well, at any rate, that's the
way things stand. Next month is the Omiyasama festival, but
if things keep progressing at this rate, I imagine that Satoko
is going to find herself rather busy and won't be able to take
part in it this year."

"In that case, perhaps it would be a good idea not to go to
the trouble of inviting her."

"Well, this is a surprise," the Marquis exclaimed with a
loud laugh. "I had no idea that you were at each others'
throats."

And the laugh was the end of the discussion.

In the final analysis Kiyoaki was a mystery to his parents.
His emotional reactions were quite different from theirs. As
often as they had tried to fathom what he was thinking, they
had always been frustrated in their efforts. And so they eventually gave up. With regard to the present matter, they even
bore the Ayakuras some resentment for having educated their
son, although they themselves had entrusted them with him.
They wondered if the courtly elegance that they had both

yearned for did not, after all, consist in precisely the kind of fluctuating moods that made their son so difficult to understand. From a distance, such elegance had an undeniable attraction, but when they were confronted with it in the person of their own son, the effect was an enigma.

The Marquis and Marquise, whatever their intrigues, wore their emotions like clothes that were dyed in the vivid primary colors of the tropics. Kiyoaki's emotions, however, were as subtly complex as the layer upon layer of color in the dresses of the court ladies; they were constantly merging—the drab brown of an autumn leaf shading into crimson, the crimson dissolving into the green of bambo grass. His father was exhausted by the mere attempt at solving the riddle of his son's moods. He was exhausted by the mere sight of his handsome son's bored indifference and his cold silences. He searched the memories of his own youth, but he could not recall any torment that had given rise to the kind of instability that ruled his son. Kiyoaki was like a lake whose clear waters reveal the very pebbles on its bed at one moment, only to cloud over the next in a sudden squall.

After a few moments, the Marquis spoke to Kiyoaki again: "By the way, I've been thinking of letting Iinuma go fairly soon."

"Why's that?" Kiyoaki asked, looking genuinely surprised for the first time that evening. This really was unexpected.

"Well, he's been very faithful to you for a long time now, but you'll be grown up next year. And then he's graduated from college, so I think this is a good time. There's also a more specific reason. A rather unpleasant rumor about him has come to my attention."

"What sort of rumor?"

"That his conduct within the house has been a bit irregular. Not to mince words, it seems that he's been carrying on with one of the maids, Miné. In the old days it would have been a matter of my having to cut him down with my own sword."

As she listened to her husband's words, the Marquise's

calm reserve was admirable. In every aspect of this matter, she would be her husband's staunch ally.

"From whom did you hear this rumor, Father?" Kiyoaki persisted.

"That's irrelevant."

Kiyoaki had an immediate vision of Tadeshina's face.

"Yes, in the old days I would have had to cut him down. But times have changed. And then he came here with a fine recommendation from the people in Kagoshima, and I know his old middle-school principal, who comes up here to give us New Year greetings. It's best to let him go without creating any kind of stir that would damage his future prospects. Not only that, but I want to handle it tactfully, so as to make things easy for him. I'll send Miné off on her own too. And then if they're both still in the mood and want to marry, well and good. I'm willing to find work for him. The main thing is to get him out of the house, so it would be best to handle it in a way that will give him no cause for resentment. That's the best thing. After all, he served you faithfully for such a long time, and we have no complaints about him in that regard."

"How compassionate you are! And so generous!" the Marquise exclaimed.

Kiyoaki passed Iinuma in the corridor that night but said nothing to him.

As he lay with his head on his pillow, his head was a whirling mass of images. He was faced with the stark realization that from now on he would be alone. He had no friend but Honda, and he had told Honda nothing about his immediate problem.

He had a dream, and in the midst of it, the thought came to him that he would never be able to record it in his journal. The events were far too complex and irrational for that.

All sorts of faces appeared in it. The snow-covered parade ground of the Third Regiment seemed to be spread out before him. There stood Honda, dressed as an officer. Then he thought he saw a flock of peacocks settle suddenly on the snow. He saw Satoko. She wore a jeweled necklace, and on either side of her stood the two Siamese princes holding a golden crown that they were about to place on her head. In another corner, Iinuma and Tadeshina were having a heated argument. Then he saw their entangled bodies go rolling over the edge and down into a vast, gaping chasm. Miné came riding up in a carriage and his mother and father came out to meet her with obsequious smiles. Then he himself seemed to be sailing on a pitching raft over a vast ocean. "I'm too involved in my dream-world," he thought while still in the middle of this one. "They've spilled over into reality. They're a flood that's sweeping me away."

 22

PRINCE HARUNORI, the third son of His Imperial Highness Prince Toin, had recently attained his twenty-fifth birthday and a generalcy in the Imperial Horse Guards. He had a magnanimous, sturdy nature, and on him rested most of his father's hopes. To select a bride for such a paragon, his father did not require anyone's mediation, and so a vast array of candidates had been brought directly to the young man's attention. None of these, however, had struck his imperial fancy. Thus the years went by, and just when his imperial parents were at their wits' end, Marquis Matsugae took a chance and invited them to the cherry blossom celebration at his estate. There Satoko Ayakura was casually presented to them. The imperial couple were quite taken with her, and when the Ayakuras later received a confidential request for a photograph, they hastily obeyed by sending a picture of her in a formal kimono. When Prince Harunori's parents showed it to him, he did not make his usual derogatory remarks, but stared at it for some considerable time. Satoko's advanced age of twenty-one became a matter of no consequence.

Marquis Matsugae was well aware of the debt he owed the Ayakuras for having taken care of Kiyoaki as a child and he had long been anxious to do something to help the Count's family regain something of its former grandeur. The best way to achieve this, short of a marriage into the Emperor's immediate family, would be a marriage that united the Ayakuras with one of the princes, and the flawless lineage of the Ayakuras as a noble Urin family precluded any question of status being an obstacle. What the Ayakuras did lack, however, was the financial means for the incredible expenses they would incur in their new position. These ranged from a huge dowry to the money that would have to be disbursed regularly for the traditional seasonal gifts to all the retainers of the imperial household, an appalling sum to consider. The Marquis, nevertheless, was prepared to underwrite the cost in all particulars.

With cool composure, Satoko watched the bustle as these events went on around her. There was very little sun in April that year, and as one dark day gave way to another beneath the overcast sky, the fresh imprint of spring faded, to be replaced by the signs of approaching summer. Satoko looked out over the wide, neglected garden from a bay window of her austere room in the handsome, old-fashioned mansion that now retained its pretensions only in its imposing gate. She saw how the camellia blossoms had already fallen and new buds were pushing out from the thick dark clusters of leaves. The intricate tracery of branches and pointed leaves of the pomegranate, bristling with thorns, also showed reddish buds that were straining to burst. All the new buds grew vertical, so that the entire garden seemed to be standing on tiptoe and stretching upward to reach the sky. Indeed, every day seemed to bring it closer to its goal.

Tadeshina was deeply concerned that Satoko had become so subdued and that she should so often appear lost in thought. On the other hand, she listened attentively to all her mother and father had to say and followed their wishes as a quiet brook its banks. She now accepted everything with a faint smile, and there was no trace of her former willfulness. But behind the screen of gentle compliance, Satoko was hiding an indifference as vast as the gray April sky.

One day early in May, Satoko was invited to tea at the summer villa of Their Imperial Highnesses, Prince and Princess Toin. Ordinarily, an invitation should have come from the Matsugaes by this time of year to attend their Omiyasama festival, but although all her hopes were now centered on it, it did not come. In its place, an official of the Prince's household appeared bearing the invitation to tea, handed it casually to a steward of the Ayakuras, and departed.

Despite the semblance of complete naturalness that attended this and similar incidents, they were in fact carefully plotted in the deepest secrecy, and though her parents said little, they were supporting the conspirators in their attempt to ensnare Satoko in the complex spell that was stealthily being woven around her.

The Count and Countess, of course, were also invited to tea at the Toinnomiya villa. Since it seemed that to go in a carriage sent by the Prince with all its appropriate trappings would be to create too much of a spectacle, the Ayakuras decided they would rather ride in one kindly lent by Marquis Matsugae. The villa, built just a few years before, toward the end of the Meiji era, stood on the outskirts of Yokohama. Had their purpose been different, a trip of this sort would have had the happy, carefree spirit of an all-too-infrequent family outing in the country.

For the first time in many days, the weather was pleasant, a good omen cheerfully noted by the Count and his wife. Since Boys' Day was approaching, nearly every house they passed along the way had hoisted its cloth or paper carps, one for each son, and they were flapping vigorously in the stiff south breeze. They ranged in size from huge black carp to tiny red ones that looked like goldfish. If five or more were hanging from the same staff, they seemed to bunch awkwardly to-

gether, unable to swim freely in the wind's powerful current.
When the carriage passed one farmhouse on the edge of the
mountains, the school of carp above the roof was so vast that
the Count was moved to raise a white forefinger to count them
from the window. There were ten in all.

"My, what a vigorous sort of fellow!" said the Count with
a smile. To Satoko, this remark smacked of a vulgar humor
uncharacteristic of her father.

The trees along the way bore evidence of a remarkable
surge of growth with their clusters of new leaves and
branches. The mountains were a mass of green that ranged
from a near yellow to a dark tone verging on black. The
bright young maple leaves stood out especially against the
general outpouring of green that made the whole countryside
glitter.

"Oh, a bit of dust . . . ," the Countess exclaimed, gazing
at Satoko's cheek. But just as she reached out with her handkerchief to wipe it off, Satoko drew quickly away and the
speck of dust vanished. It was then that her mother realized
that the dust on her daughter's cheek had been no more than
a shadow cast by a spot on the window. Satoko gave a wan
smile; she didn't find her mother's mistake particularly amusing. She disliked being given a special inspection today, as if
she were a bolt of silk intended as a gift.

The windows had been kept shut in case the breeze rumpled Satoko's hair, and the interior of the carriage had become
unpleasantly hot as a result. As it rocked unceasingly and the
green of the mountains flashed up in reflections from the
flooded rice paddies beside the road, Satoko could not remember what she was looking forward to with such yearning. On
the one hand, she was letting a rash caprice sweep her with
appalling boldness into a course of action from which there
would be no turning back. On the other, she was waiting for
something to intervene. For the moment there was still time.
There was still time. Up until the very last instant, a letter
of pardon might come—or so she hoped. And then again, she
despised the very thought of hope.

The Toinnomiya villa, a palatial Western-style house, stood on a high cliff overlooking the sea. Stairs carved out of marble led up to its front entrance. As a groom took charge of the horses, the Ayakuras descended from the carriage and exchanged admiring remarks about the view of the harbor below, which was filled with all sorts of ships. Tea was served on a wide porch that faced south, looking down over the water. It was decorated with a number of luxuriant tropical plants, and on either side of the door that opened onto it hung a pair of giant curving tusks, a gift from the royal court of Siam.

Here the imperial couple welcomed their guests and cordially offered them chairs. The tea was, of course, in the English manner, complete with small, thin sandwiches, some cookies and biscuits—all neatly arranged on a tea table furnished with silverware engraved with the imperial chrysanthemum.

The Princess remarked how delightful the recent cherry blossom festival at the Matsugaes had been and then, by and by, her conversation turned to mahjong and *nagauta*.

"At home we still think of Satoko as a child, and we haven't let her play mahjong yet," said the Count, wanting to save his silent daughter embarrassment.

"Oh, don't tell me!" the Princess laughed graciously. "We sometimes spend a whole day playing nothing else, when we have time."

Satoko could no longer bring up a topic such as the old-fashioned *sugoroku* and its set of twelve black and white pieces, with which they often played.

Prince Toin was relaxed and informal today in a European suit. Calling the Count over to the window beside him, he pointed down to the ships below and displayed his knowledge of things nautical as if he were instructing a child: that was an English freighter, that was a ship with a flush deck, that one was a French freighter, see the shelter deck on the one over there, and so on.

Judging by the atmosphere, one might well conclude that

the imperial couple were making rather anxious efforts to hit
upon some topic congenial to their guests. Anything at all
that sparked a mutual interest—be it sports or wine or anything else—would suffice. Count Ayakura, however, received
whatever subject came up with earnest but benign passivity.
As for Satoko, she had never been so conscious as she was
this afternoon of the uselessness of the elegance bred in her
by her father's example. Sometimes the Count had a way of
foolishly coming out with a stylish joke that had nothing to
do with the conversation at hand, but today he was obviously
restraining himself.

After some time, Prince Toin glanced at the clock and
made a casual remark, as if something had just occurred
to him.

"By a happy coincidence, Harunori will be coming home on
leave from his regiment today. Though he's my own son, he
has the look about him of a rough sort of fellow. But please
don't be upset by it. He's truly quite gentle beneath it all."

Soon after he said this, the sound of servants scurrying
about at the front entrance heralded the arrival of the young
prince.

A few moments later, sword clattering, boots squeaking,
the martial figure of His Imperial Highness Prince Harunori
appeared on the porch. He greeted his father with a military
salute, and the immediate impression he gave Satoko was one
of empty dignity. But how obvious the paternal pride of
Prince Toin was in this display of military pomp, and how
evident the young prince's conviction that he was fulfilling
every detail of his father's projected image of him. The truth
was that his two older brothers were, in fact, quite different.
Unusually effeminate and sickly, they had been the despair
of their imperial father.

Today, however, a touch of embarrassment at being confronted for the first time with Satoko's beauty may perhaps
have had some effect on Prince Harunori's subsequent behavior. At any rate, neither when she was presented to him
nor at any time thereafter did he look at her directly.

Though the young prince was not particularly tall, he had an impressive physique. He moved briskly at all times, with an air of importance and decision that lent him a gravity extraordinary in one so young—all of which his father watched, complacent and happy, his eyes narrowed with pleasure. This paternal satisfaction, however, was giving rise to a growing impression among many that Prince Toin himself concealed a certain weakness of will beneath that grand and impressive exterior.

As for hobbies, His Imperial Highness Prince Harunori was devoted to his record collection of Western music. This seemed to be the one subject on which he had opinions of his own. When his mother asked: "Would you play something for us, Harunori?" he was quick to agree and to turn toward the reception room, where the phonograph stood.

As he did so, Satoko could not resist raising her eyes to watch him. He covered the distance to the door with long strides, his brilliantly polished black boots sparkling in the sunshine that was pouring in through the porch windows. They were so dazzling that she imagined she could even see patches of the sky itself reflected in them like fragments of blue porcelain. She closed her eyes and waited for the music to begin. She felt the first stirrings of ominous premonition, and the faint sound of the phonograph needle falling into place echoed like thunder in her ears.

Afterwards, the young prince contributed little to the casual conversation that followed the musical interlude. As evening approached, the Ayakuras took leave of their hosts.

A week later, the steward of Prince Toin's household came to the Ayakura residence and had a long, detailed discussion with the Count. The upshot was a decision to begin the formal proceedings for obtaining the Emperor's permission for the wedding. Satoko herself was shown the document, which read:

To His Excellency the Minister of the Imperial Household:
Herein is a humble plea with reference to negotiations concerning a marriage between:

His Imperial Highness Prince Harunori Toin and Satoko, the daughter of His Excellency Count Korebumi
Ayakura, Second Degree, Junior Grade; Bearer of the
Order of Merit, Third Class;
That a petition as to whether such negotiations may proceed
in accordance with the Imperial Pleasure may be vouchsafed
to be brought before the Imperial Throne.

Offered upon this 12th Day of the Fifth Month of the Era
of Taisho.

> Saburo Yamauchi
> Steward of the Household of
> His Imperial Highness Prince Toin

Three days later a response came from the Minister of the
Imperial Household:

To the Steward of the Household of
His Imperial Highness Prince Toin:

Relative to the disposition presented to the Officials of
the Imperial Household concerning the marriage of
His Imperial Highness Prince Harunori Toin and Satoko, the daughter of His Excellency Count Korebumi
Ayakura, Second Degree, Junior Grade; Bearer of the
Order of Merit, Third Class;
it is herein acknowledged that a petition destined for presentation to the Imperial Throne whereby such negotiations
may proceed with the Imperial Pleasure has been duly and
properly entered.

Given this 15th Day of the Fifth Month of the Era of
Taisho.

> The Minister of the Imperial Household

And so with the preliminary formalities observed, the petition for imperial sanction could be presented to the Emperor
at any time.

23

KIYOAKI WAS NOW in his senior year at Peers. He
was to begin his university studies in the coming fall, and
there were those in his class who had been busy preparing
for the entrance examinations for more than eighteen months.
Honda, however, betrayed no such concern, a fact which
pleased Kiyoaki.

The spirit of General Nogi lived on in the compulsory dormitory regime at Peers, but its harsh rules did, nonetheless,
contain allowances for those whose health was not up to the
demands made on them. Students such as Honda and Kiyoaki,
whose families kept them out of the dormitories as a matter of
policy, were provided with suitable medical certificates from
their doctors. Honda's convenient ailment was put down as
valvular heart disease and Kiyoaki's as chronic bronchial ca-
tarrh. Their nonexistent illnesses were the source of much
amusement, with Honda pretending to be choking for breath
and Kiyoaki putting on a hacking cough.

There was no real need for pretense, because no one believed they were sick. However, the noncommissioned officers
in the military science department, all veterans of the Russo-
Japanese War, vented their hostility by making a point of
treating them like invalids. Then during drill period, the
sergeants were fond of interspersing their rhetoric with
oblique digs at the shirkers, asking what use they would
be in the service of their country if they were too feeble
to live under the dormitory regime, and other such questions.

Kiyoaki felt deep sympathy for the Siamese princes when

he heard that they were to be put in the dormitory. He often visited them in their quarters and brought small presents. They felt very close to him, and so they took turns pouring out their complaints, lamenting in particular the restrictions on their freedom of movement. The other dormitory students, moreover, being rowdy and insensitive, were not the sort to make friends with them.

Though Honda had been neglected by Kiyoaki for quite some time, he welcomed him nonchalantly when he came dancing back to him, bold as a sparrow. It was as if he had completely forgotten his recent disregard of Honda. With the start of the new school term, he seemed to have changed character, now full of forced gaiety, or so it appeared to Honda. Naturally, he made no comment on this, and Kiyoaki himself, just as naturally, provided no explanation.

Kiyoaki was able to congratulate himself for at least one piece of wisdom—he had never let his friend know his innermost feelings. This now spared him any worry that he might appear to have let a woman manipulate him like a foolish child. He realized that this made him feel secure enough to behave with carefree good humor toward Honda. To him, the ultimate proof of his friendship was his desire to avoid disillusioning Honda and to feel easy and unconcerned in his presence—and this desire should more than make up for his countless moments of reserve.

He was so cheerful, in fact, that he surprised even himself. At about this time, his parents had begun to talk quite openly and matter-of-factly about the course of negotiations between the Ayakuras and Toinnomiyas. They seemed to take great amusement in recounting incidents such as how "even that headstrong girl" became so tense that she could not say a word during the carefully arranged meeting with the young prince. Kiyoaki, of course, had no reason to suspect what grief the incident had caused Satoko. Those who lack imagination have no choice but to base their conclusions on the reality they see around them. But on the other hand, those who are imaginative have a tendency to build fortified castles they have designed themselves, and to seal off every window in them. And so it was with Kiyoaki.

"Well, once the imperial sanction is received, that should settle everything," said his mother.

Somehow he was moved by her words, especially the phrase "imperial sanction." It made him think of a darkened corridor, long and wide, and at the end a door fastened with a small but impregnable padlock of solid gold. And suddenly, with a noise like the grinding of teeth, it opened of its own accord, a metallic rasp echoing clearly in his ears.

He was full of self-satisfaction that he could remain so calm while his mother and father discussed such matters. He had triumphed over his own rage and despair and so was relishing a sense of immortality. "I never dreamed that I could be so resilient," he thought, never more confident in his life.

Once he had been convinced that his parents' unfeeling coarseness was something totally alien to him, but now he took pleasure in the thought that he had not escaped his origins after all. He belonged not among the victims but among the victors.

He drew an exquisite pleasure from the thought that day by day Satoko's existence would recede further and further from his mind until it would finally pass beyond recall. Those who set a votive lantern afloat on the evening tide stand on the shore and watch its light growing fainter over the dark surface of the water as they pray that their offering may travel as far as possible and so attain the maximum grace for the dead. In the same way, Kiyoaki looked upon the receding memory of Satoko as the surest vindication of his own strength.

Now there was nobody left in the world who was privy to his innermost feelings. No further obstacle would prevent him from disguising his emotions. The devoted servants, ever at his elbow, with their customary words: "Please leave everything to us. We know just how the young master feels," had been removed. Not only was he happy to be free of that master conspirator, Tadeshina, but also of Iinuma, whose loyalty had become so intense as to threaten him with suffocation. The last of his irritants was gone.

As for his father's dismissal of Iinuma, however kindly done, he rationalized his own indifference with the argument that Iinuma had brought it upon himself. He made his self-satisfaction complete with the vow, faithfully kept, thanks to Tadeshina, never to mention to his father what had happened. And so he had brought everything to a successful conclusion out of his acuity and coldness of heart.

The day came for Iinuma's departure. When he went to Kiyoaki's room for his formal farewell, he was crying. Kiyoaki could not accept even such grief for what it was. The thought that Iinuma was emphasizing his fervently exclusive loyalty to him gave him no pleasure.

Inarticulate as ever, Iinuma merely stood there crying. By his very silence he was trying to tell Kiyoaki something. Their relationship had lasted some seven years, beginning in the spring when Kiyoaki was twelve. Since his recollection of his thoughts and feelings at that age were rather vague, he had the general impression that Iinuma had always been there beside him. If his boyhood and youth cast a shadow, that shadow was Iinuma, in his sweaty, dark blue, splashed-patterned kimono. The relentlessness of his discontent, his rancor, his negative attitude to life, had all weighed heavily on Kiyoaki, try as he might to feign immunity. On the other hand, however, the dark woe in Iinuma's eyes had served to warn him against those very same attitudes in himself, although they were normal enough in youth. Iinuma's particular demons had tormented him with manifest violence, and the more he wanted his young master to emulate him, the more Kiyoaki had shied off in the opposite direction, a predictable turn of events.

Psychologically, Kiyoaki had probably taken the first step toward today's parting when he had broken the power that had dominated him for so long and turned Iinuma into his confidant. Their mutual understanding was probably too deep for master and retainer.

As Iinuma stood before him with bowed head, the chest hair escaping from the neck of his blue kimono glistened faintly, caught in a ray of the evening sun. Kiyoaki stared gloomily at this matted tangle, depressed at the realization of what a distastefully coarse and heavy vessel Iinuma's flesh made for his overpowering spirit of loyalty. It was, in fact, a direct physical affront. Even the glow on Iinuma's rough-skinned, pimpled cheeks, mottled and unhealthy as it was, had something shameless about it that seemed to taunt Kiyoaki with Miné's devotion—Miné who was leaving with Iinuma, ready to share his fate. Nothing could be more insulting: the young master betrayed by a woman and left to grieve; the retainer believing in a woman's fidelity and going off triumphant. Iinuma, moreover, was quite secure in the conviction that today's farewell had come about in the line of duty—a presumption that Kiyoaki found galling.

However, deciding that noblesse oblige was the best course, he spoke humanely, if curtly.

"So then, once you're on your own, I presume you'll marry Miné?"

"Yes, sir. Since your father was gracious enough to suggest it, that's exactly what I shall do."

"Well, let me know the date. I must send you a present."

"Thank you very much, sir."

"Once you have a permanent home, send me a note with your address. Who knows, perhaps I might come and see you some time."

"I cannot imagine anything that would give me greater pleasure than a visit from the young master. But wherever I live, it will be too small and dirty to be a fit place to receive you."

"Don't worry about that."

"How gracious of you to say so . . ."

And Iinuma began to cry again. He pulled a piece of

coarse tissue paper from his kimono and blew his nose.

During this exchange Kiyoaki had chosen his every word with care and an eye to its suitability for the occasion before smoothly giving voice to it. He made it patently clear that in a situation such as this, the emptiest words were those that aroused the strongest emotions. He professed to live for sentiment alone, but circumstances now compelled him to learn the politics of the intellect. This was an education that he would apply to his own life with profit from time to time. He was learning to use sentiment as a protective armor and how best to polish it.

Devoid of worry or annoyance, free of all anxiety, Kiyoaki at nineteen liked to see himself as a cold and supremely capable young man. He felt that he was now past some watershed in the course of his life.

After Iinuma had gone, he stood at the open window gazing down at the beautiful reflection of the maple hill, with its fresh green mantle of new leaves, as it floated on the water of the pond. Close to the window itself, the foliage of the zelkova was so thick that he had to lean out in order to see the place at the bottom of the hill where the last of the nine waterfalls plunged into its pool. All around the edge of the pond, the surface was covered with clusters of pale green water shields. The yellow water lilies had not yet flowered, but in the angles of the stone bridge that zigzagged a path close to the main reception room, irises were pushing their purple and white blossoms out from sharp-pointed clusters of green leaves.

His eye was caught by the iridescent back of a beetle that had been standing on the windowsill but was now advancing steadily into his room. Two reddish purple stripes ran the length of its brilliant oval shell of green and gold. Now it waved its antennae cautiously as it began to inch its way forward on its tiny hacksaw legs, which reminded Kiyoaki of minuscule jeweler's blades. In the midst of time's dissolving whirlpool, how absurd that this tiny dot of richly concentrated brilliance should endure in a secure world of its own. As he watched, he gradually became fascinated. Little by little the beetle kept edging its glittering body closer to him as if its pointless progress were a lesson that when traversing a world of unceasing flux, the only thing of importance was to radiate beauty. Suppose he were to assess his protective armor of sentiment in such terms. Was it aesthetically as naturally striking as that of this beetle? And was it tough enough to be as good a shield as the beetle's?

At that moment, he almost persuaded himself that all its surroundings—leafy trees, blue sky, clouds, tiled roofs—were there purely to serve this beetle which in itself was the very hub, the very nucleus of the universe.

*

The atmosphere of the Omiyasama festival was not the same as in previous years. For one thing, Iinuma was gone; every year, long before the day of the festival, he had thrown himself into the task of cleaning up and had done the arranging of the altar and chairs all by himself. Now it had all fallen to Yamada, and was the more unwelcome for being without precedent. Furthermore, it was work more befitting a younger man.

In addition, Satoko had not been invited. There was thus the sense that someone was missing from the group of relatives customarily present, but more significant than that—for Satoko was not really a relative after all—none of the women there was remotely as beautiful as she.

The gods themselves seemed to view the altered circumstances with displeasure. Midway through the ceremony, the sky darkened and thunder rumbled in the distance. The women, who had been following the priest's prayers, were thrown into a fluster, worried that they might be caught in a shower. Fortunately, however, when the time came for the young priestesses in their scarlet *hakama* to distribute the sacred offerings of wine to everyone, the sky lightened again. As the women bowed their heads, the bright sunshine on the napes of their necks drew beads of sweat despite the heavy coating of white powder. At that moment, the clusters of wisteria blossoms on the trellis cast deep shadows that fell like a benediction on those in the back rows.

Had Iinuma been present, the atmosphere of this year's festival would doubtless have angered him, since each year brought less reverence and mourning for Kiyoaki's grandfather. He now seemed to have been relegated to a vanished era, especially since the death of the Meiji Emperor himself. And so he had become a distant god who had no connection at all with the modern world. True, his widow, Kiyoaki's grandmother, took part in the ceremony, as did a number of other old people; their tears, however, seemed to have dried up long ago.

Each year as the painfully long ceremony went on, the women's whispering grew steadily louder. The Marquis did not go out of his way to manifest disapproval. He himself was finding the observance more tedious year by year, and he was hopeful of finding some way of making it a bit more cheerful and less depressing for himself. During the ritual, his eye was drawn to a young priestess whose pronounced Okinawan features were all the more striking under her heavy white makeup. As she held the earthenware vessel filled with sacred wine, he was fascinated by the reflection of her bold dark eyes on the surface of the liquid. As soon as the ceremony was over, he rushed over to his cousin, who was not only an admiral but also a drinker of no small fame, and apparently made a vulgar joke about the priestess, for the admiral's laugh was so loud and crude that it drew a number of stares. The Marquise, however, knowing how appropriate her mask of classic melancholy was to today's affair, did not alter her expression in the slightest.

Kiyoaki meanwhile was otherwise occupied. The women of the household, the whole vast array of them, many of whom he did not even know by name, were crowded together in the luxuriant shade of the late spring wisteria. They were whispering among themselves, their air of reverence vanishing with each passing moment. Their faces were expressionless, empty even of sadness as they stood dutifully grouped according to their instructions, waiting until they could disband once more, and full of heavy, sluggish reluctance. The sultry atmosphere that surrounded these women with white faces as blank as the moon at midday had a profound effect on Kiyoaki. Beyond a doubt, much of it had to do with their scent, from which there was no excluding Satoko herself. And this was something that even the Shinto priest, armed with the sacred sakaki branch with its weight of glossy dark green leaves and its string of white paper pendants, would have been hard put to exorcise.

 24

KIYOAKI DREW COMFORT from the peace of mind that comes with loss. In his heart, he always preferred the actuality of loss to the fear of it.

He had lost Satoko. And with that he was content. For by now he had learned how to quiet even his subsequent resentment. Every show of feeling was now governed with a marvelous economy. If a candle has burned brilliantly but now stands alone in the dark with its flame extinguished, it need no longer fear that its substance will dissolve into hot wax. For the first time in his life, Kiyoaki came to realize the healing powers of solitude.

*

The rainy season had begun. Kiyoaki, like a recuperating invalid who cannot resist endangering his health despite his fears, began to test his emotional stability by deliberately provoking memories of Satoko. He would open his album to look at the old pictures. He saw himself as an infant, standing next to Satoko beneath the pagoda tree on the Ayakura estate. Both of them were wrapped in children's white pinafores, but he took satisfaction in having been taller than she even at that early age. Count Ayakura, who was a superb calligrapher, had taken great pains to instruct the two children according to Tadamichi Fujuwara's Hossho Temple school of writing. Sometimes, when they tired of their usual exercises, he had rekindled their interest by letting them take turns copying verses from the Okura One Hundred Poets card game onto a scroll.

Kiyoaki had written a verse by Shigeyuki Minamoto:

> I feel the wind's keen force
> As waves break over rocks
> Worn down by loneliness
> I dream of days gone by.

Below it Satoko had written a verse by Yoshinobu Onakatomi:

> When day gives way to night
> And guards kindle fires
> The thoughts of other times
> Come alive within me.

The childishness of his handwriting was apparent at a glance. But Satoko's was flowing and precise, so much so that the brush hardly seemed to have been wielded by a little girl. In fact he rarely opened this scroll simply because he did not relish being confronted with the unhappy evidence of how much Satoko, two years older than he, had surpassed him even then. Now, however, as he studied the writing with a measure of objectivity, he felt that his own scrawl had a boyish vigor that made a pleasing contrast with the refined elegance of Satoko's smooth, flowing script.

But there was more to it than that. The very thought of himself that day boldly setting down the tips of his writing brushes, heavy with ink, against the fine, gold-flecked paper of the scroll, was enough to evoke the entire scene with the force of vivid immediacy. At that time, Satoko's long, thick black hair was cut straight across at the brow. As she bent over the scroll, she kept the handle of the writing brush tight in her slim, delicate fingers, concentrating with such passion that she was oblivious to the mass of hair that poured down her shoulders in a jet-black cascade, nearly flooding the scroll itself. Her small, white teeth bit ruthlessly into her lower lip, and although she was just a little girl, her nose was already well formed in her profile that stood out with sweet determination against the torrent of falling hair. Kiyoaki watched as if in a dream. Then there was the ink that smelled dark and solemn, and the sound made by the tip of the brush as it raced over the surface of the scroll, like the wind rustling through bamboo grass. And finally, there was the sea—the well of the inkstone was the sea, and above it rose the hill with the strange name. This sea fell away so sharply from its shore that it gave not so much as a glimpse of its shallow bed. The still black sea, without a single wave, a sea spangled with gold powder fallen from the ink stick, always made him think of the rays of the moon fragmented on the night sea of eternity.

"I can even enjoy memories of my past and it doesn't bother me at all," he thought in silent boast.

Satoko did not even appear in his dreams. If he caught a glimpse of a figure in his sleep that seemed to resemble her, the woman quickly turned her back and disappeared. But then the scene was most often a broad crossroads at midday, totally deserted.

*

One day at school, Prince Pattanadid asked Kiyoaki a favor. Would he please return the ring that Marquis Matsugae had put in a deposit box for him?

General rumor had it that the two princes had not made a very favorable impression at school. The language barrier presented an understandable obstacle to their studies, but more than that, there could be nothing resembling friendly banter between them and their fellow students, who became impatient with the princes and as a result kept them at a respectful distance. Furthermore, being simple and boorish, their classmates were apparently quite put off by the smiles that the princes produced on all occasions.

It had been the foreign minister's idea that they live in the student dormitory, a decision, Kiyoaki heard, that had created considerable anxiety for the dormitory prefect since his was the responsibility for deciding upon the specific arrangements made for them. He gave them their own room, furnished with the best beds available, as befitted royalty. Then he made every effort to promote good relations between them and the other students, but as the days went by, the princes tended to isolate themselves more and more in their own little castle, frequently missing exercises like reveille and group calisthenics. The estrangement between them and the others thus grew still more pronounced.

There was good reason for this. The preparatory period of less than six months following their arrival was inadequate for the princes to have learned Japanese, even if they had applied themselves far more seriously than they had done. And then, even in the English classes, where their ability should have shown to advantage, the system of translating from English into Japanese and from Japanese into English thoroughly confused them.

Since Marquis Matsugae had arranged to have Pattanadid's ring placed in his personal vault at the Itsu Bank, Kiyoaki had to return home to get his father's seal before going to the bank to reclaim the ring. It was nearly evening before he returned to Peers and went to the princes' room.

It was a typical "dry" day in the midst of the rainy season, overcast and humid, a day that was perfectly attuned to the frustration of the two princes, who were longing for the sparkling summer weather that was still beyond reach, though it seemed close enough. The dormitory itself, a rough-frame one-story building surrounded by trees, seemed to be sealed in a gloom all its own.

The shouts coming from the direction of the athletics field indicated that rugby practice was still in full swing. Kiyoaki hated the idealistic cries that rose from those young throats. His classmates' rough-and-ready relationships, their untried humanism, their constant jokes and puns, their never-faltering reverence for the talent of Rodin and the perfection of Cézanne—they were no more than the modern equivalent of the old traditional shouts of *kendo*. And so, hoarse in voice and reeking of youth like green paulownia leaves, they went about wearing their arrogance much as the ancient courtiers wore their tall caps.

Life for the two princes was extremely difficult, having to swim in the midst of this riptide of old and new. When Kiyoaki thought about this, he rose above his own preoccupations and now was able, out of a new generosity, to sympathize with them. He walked down a dark, rough-finished corridor of the dormitory toward the princes' room at the end of it, selected with such care. Stopping in front of a battered old door, on which hung a wooden rectangle with their names on it, he knocked lightly.

The princes were overjoyed to see him, as though he had come as a savior. He had always felt much closer to the serious and somewhat dreamy Pattanadid—Chao P.—but in recent months Kridsada too, once so frivolous and carefree, had become subdued. The two of them now spent much of their time here in their room, whispering to each other in their native language.

The room, bare of all decoration, was furnished austerely with two beds, two desks, and two cupboards for their clothing. The building itself was redolent of the barracks atmosphere so prized by General Nogi. The blank white expanse of wall above the paneling, however, was relieved by a small shelf holding a golden Buddha, before which the princes performed their worship morning and evening. The altar lent a hint of the exotic to the room. Wrinkled, rain-spotted muslin curtains hung at the window.

Now with the approach of darkness, the smiling princes'

teeth gleamed white against their dark skin and deep tans. They offered Kiyoaki a seat on the edge of one of the beds and then eagerly asked to see the ring.

Its brilliant green emerald, guarded on either side by the fierce beasts' heads of the yaksha, glowed richly in complete contrast to the atmosphere of the room.

With an exclamation of happiness, Chao P. took the ring and slipped it onto his dark, slender finger. Thin and supple, on a hand that seemed created for caresses, it made Kiyoaki think of a warm tropical moonbeam stretching a slender finger through a crack in the door and striking a mosaic floor.

"Now Ying Chan has finally returned to my touch," Chao P. said, heaving a melancholy sigh.

In months gone by, such a reaction would have provoked Prince Kridsada to make fun of his cousin, but now he searched through the drawer of his clothes cupboard and took out a picture of his sister which he had carefully hidden between layers of shirts.

"In this school," he said, nearly in tears, "even if you tell them it's a picture of your own sister, they make jokes about you if you put it out on your desk. That's why we hide Ying Chan's picture in here."

Chao P. was soon able to explain to Kiyoaki that no letter from Princess Ying Chan had come for more than two months. He had made inquiries about this at the Siamese legation but had not yet received a satisfactory answer. Moreover, the princess's brother Prince Kridsada himself had had no word about her. If something had happened to her, if she had fallen ill, he would normally have been informed by telegram. Chao P.'s imagination was exacerbated by the thought of what her family might be hiding even from her brother. It might well be that she was being pushed into another marriage, one that held greater political advantage. The very idea was enough to plunge him into gloom. Tomorrow, he thought, there might be a letter, but even if there were, what unhappiness might it not contain? With such thoughts preying on his mind, he was in no state to study. Since he had no other consolation, all he could think of was the return of the ring that had been a parting present from the princess, and all his intensity of longing became focused on its emerald, which shone with the brilliant green of the jungle at first light.

It now seemed that Choa P. had become oblivious to Kiyoaki as he stretched out his finger that bore the emerald ring and rested it on the desk beside the picture of Ying Chan that Prince Kridsada had placed there. He seemed to be about to make an effort of will that would not only dissolve the barriers of time and space but merge two separate lives into one.

When Prince Kridsada turned on the light that hung from the ceiling, the picture glass caught the reflection of the emerald on Chao P.'s finger, and a square of vivid green glowed on the white lace of the princess's bodice.

"Look at that—how does it strike you?" Chao P. asked in English, in a bemused tone of voice. "Doesn't it seem as though her heart were a green flame? Perhaps it's the cold green heart of a small green snake, with a minute flaw in it, the kind of small green snake that slithers from branch to branch in the jungle, passing itself off as a vine. What's more, perhaps when she gave me the ring with such a gentle, loving expression, she wanted me to draw such a meaning from it some day."

"No, Chao P. That's utter nonsense," Prince Kridsada cut in sharply.

"Don't be angry, Kri. I don't mean to insult your sister for a moment. All I'm trying to do is find words for the strangeness of a lover's existence. Let me put it this way: although she is here in this picture, it shows her only as she was at a certain moment in the past. But I feel that here in this emerald she gave me when we parted is her soul, just as she is now at this moment. In my mind, the emerald and the picture—her body and her soul—were separated. But look now: the two are reunited.

"Even when we're with someone we love, we're foolish enough to think of her body and soul as being separate. Although I am apart from her now, I may be in a much better position than I was to appreciate the structure of the single crystal that is Ying Chan. Separation is painful, but so is its opposite. And if being together brings joy, then it is only proper that separation should do the same in its own way.

"But what do you think, Matsugae? As for me, I've always wanted to know the secret that enables love to evade the bonds of time and space as if by magic. To stand before the person we love is not the same as loving her true self, for we are only apt to regard her physical beauty as the indispensable mode of her existence. When time and space intervene, it is possible to be deceived by both, but on the other hand, it is equally possible to draw twice as close to her real self. "

Kiyoaki had no idea how profound the prince's philosophizing was intended to be, but he listened intently. Many of his words did, in fact, strike home. As for Satoko, Kiyoaki believed that he had now indeed drawn that much closer to her real self. He saw quite clearly that what he had loved had not been the real Satoko. But what proof did he have of that? Wasn't he liable to be deceived twice over? And wasn't the Satoko he loved once again the real Satoko after all? He shook his head slightly, almost unconsciously. Then suddenly he remembered the dream in which the face of a strangely beautiful girl had suddenly appeared in Chao P.'s emerald ring. Who was that woman? Satoko? Ying Chan, whom he had never seen? Someone else perhaps?

"Well anyway, will it ever be summer?" Prince Kridsada said sadly, gazing out of the window at the grove of trees surrounding the dormitory.

The three boys could see the lights burning in the other dormitory buildings as they flickered through the trees, and they also heard shouting and loud conversation coming from various directions. It was time for the dining room to open for the evening meal. One student making his way along the path through the grove was burlesquing an ancient song, to the raucous laughter of his companions. The princes' eyes widened as though in fear that at any moment monsters of the mountains or rivers would appear out of the darkness.

Kiyoaki's return of the ring on this occasion was to lead to an unpleasant incident.

*

A few days later, there was a telephone call from Tade-shina. The maid informed Kiyoaki, but he did not go to the phone. Another call came next day. He did not accept that one either.

The calls unsettled him to some extent, but he fell back on his established rule: he put Satoko out of his mind and concentrated on the anger Tadeshina's rudeness provoked in him. All he had to do was to think about the cunning, lying old woman who had deceived him outrageously time and time again, and his consequent fury was strong enough to outweigh any slight misgivings he might have had about not going to the phone.

Three days passed. It was well into the rainy season, and it poured without let-up. When Kiyoaki came back from school, Yamada came up to him carrying a lacquered tray and respectfully presented a letter that lay face down upon it. Glancing at it, he was startled to see that Tadeshina had brazenly put her own name on it. The thick, oversized envelope had been carefully sealed, and to go by the feel of it, so was the letter inside. He felt afraid that if left to himself he might not be able to restrain himself from opening the letter. So, steeling himself to act deliberately, he tore it to shreds intentionally in front of Yamada and then ordered him to dispose of what was left of it. He knew that if he threw it into the wastebasket in his own room, he would be tempted to take it out and reassemble the fragments. Yamada's eyes flickered with surprise behind his glasses, but he said not a word.

A few more days passed. The matter of the torn-up letter began to weigh on Kiyoaki and his reaction took the form of anger. This was more than mere irritation that a supposedly trivial letter should have such power to unsettle him. What was agonizing was the realization, impossible to ignore, that he now regretted the decision not to open it. At first he had been able to regard the letter's destruction as proof of his strength of will, but in retrospect he was now beset by the feeling that on the contrary he had acted out of sheer cowardice.

When he had torn up that thick, plain white envelope, his fingers had encountered stiff resistance, as though the letter had perhaps been written on paper reinforced with tough linen fiber. But it was not the paper's composition that mattered. He now realized that had it not been for his burst of willpower, it would have been impossible for him to tear it up. Why should he have been afraid? He had no desire to become painfully involved with Satoko again. He hated the very thought of being re-enveloped in that fragrant haze of anxiety that she could conjure at will, especially now that he had finally achieved command over himself again. But despite all this, when he had been ripping up that thick letter, he had had the feeling that he was tearing a gash in Satoko's skin with its soft white glow.

On his way back from school one torrid Saturday afternoon during an unseasonal break in the wet weather, he noticed a hum of activity at the entrance of the main house. The grooms had prepared one of the carriages and were now loading it with a bulky package whose purple silk wrapping immediately identified it as a present. The horses were twitching their ears, and bright streams of saliva dropped from their mouth as they gaped to reveal yellowed teeth. In the hot sunlight their dark coats glistened as if smeared with grease, and their throbbing veins stood out on their necks beneath the fine, thick coats.

Just as he was about to go up the steps into the house, his mother appeared dressed in bulky ceremonial robes marked with the family crest.

"Hello," he said.

"Oh, welcome home. I'm just on my way to the Ayakuras to extend our congratulations."

"Congratulations for what?"

Since his mother disliked discussing important matters in front of the servants, she did not answer at once but drew Kiyoaki over to a dark corner of the wide entrance next to an umbrella stand before beginning to speak in a low voice.

"This morning the imperial sanction was graciously granted at last. Would you like to go with me?"

Before her son replied, the Marquise noticed that her words had caused a flash of grim pleasure in his eyes. Naturally she did not have time to reflect what it meant. Furthermore, her next words there by the doorway were eloquent proof of how little she had derived from that moment.

"After all, a joyful event is a joyful event," she said, her mask of classic melancholy on her face. "So no matter how badly you are at odds with her, the only correct thing to do on such an occasion is to be polite and offer your congratulations."

"Please send my regards. I'm not going to go."

He stood at the entrance and watched his mother leave. The horses' hooves scattered the gravel with a noise like a sudden squall, and the gold crest of the Matsugaes on the carriage seemed to quiver in the air as it flashed through the pines that stood in front of the house as the vehicle disappeared. Their mistress had gone, and Kiyoaki could sense the consequent relaxation of the servants. The tension in their muscles dissolved with a fall like a noiseless snowslide.

He turned back toward the house, so empty without either master or mistress. The servants, their eyes cast down, stood waiting for him to enter. At that moment, he was certain that he was holding the seeds of a problem immense enough to fill the vast emptiness of the building. Without bothering to glance at the servants, he went inside and hurried down the corridor, anxious not to waste a single moment reaching his room where he could seal himself off from the rest of the world.

His heart was beating with a strange excitement, and he was feverishly hot. The solemn words "imperial sanction" seemed suspended before his eyes. The imperial sanction had been graciously granted. Tadeshina's repeated phone calls, the bulky letter—they must have represented a last, desperate flurry before it came. Their object had clearly been to obtain his forgiveness, to be relieved of a feeling of guilt.

All that day, he let his imagination run loose. He was oblivious of the outside world. The clear, calm mirror of his soul had now been shattered. There was a turmoil in his heart that churned with the force of a tropical storm. He was now shaken by a violent passion that bore no trace of the melancholy that had been such a part of its feeble precursors. But what emotion now had him in its grip? It must be called delight. But it was a delight so irrational, so passionate, that it was almost unearthly.

If one were to ask what was its cause, the only possible answer would be that it sprang from an impossibility, a sheer impossibility. Just as the string of a koto cut by a sharp blade yields with an abrupt, poignant note, so the tie that bound him to Satoko had been cut by the shining blade of the imperial sanction. In the midst of his wavering inconsistency, this was something that he had dreamed of and hoped for in secret ever since he had begun to grow out of boyhood.

To be more precise, the dream had begun to form in the moment when he had looked up from Princess Kasuga's train and had been dazzled by the nape of her white neck with its peerless beauty, forever unattainable. That instant certainly foreshadowed today's fulfillment of his hopes. Absolute impossibility—Kiyoaki himself had helped to bring it about by single-mindedly shaping events to the pattern of his every caprice, his every twist of feeling.

But what kind of joy was it? Something in it obsessed him; there was something sinister, ominously threatening about it. Long ago he had resolved to recognize his emotions as his only guiding truth and to live his life accordingly, even if this meant a deliberate aimlessness. That principle had now brought him to his present sinister feelings of joy, which seemed to be the brink of a racing, plunging whirlpool. There seemed to be nothing left but to throw himself into it.

He thought back once again to himself and Satoko all those years before, copying verses from the Hundred Poets during their writing exercises. He bent over the scroll trying to inhale a trace of Satoko's fragrance that might have remained from that day fourteen years earlier. As he did so, he caught a scent of incense that was not far removed from mildew, something faint and so distant that still evoked such a powerful nostalgia that he felt he had laid bare the very source of all his emotion, so aimless and at the same time so impetuous.

Each piece of the Empress's confection, the prize for winning at *sugoroku*, had been molded in the form of the imperial crest. Whenever his small teeth had bitten into a crimson chrysanthemum, the color of its petals had intensified before melting away, and at the touch of his tongue, the delicately etched lines of a cool white chrysanthemum had blurred and dissolved into a sweet liquid. Everything came back to him —the dark rooms of the Ayakura mansion, the court screens brought from Kyoto with their pattern of autumn flowers, the solemn stillness of the nights, Satoko's mouth opening in a slight yawn half-hidden behind her sweep of black hair— everything came back just as he had experienced it then, in all its lonely elegance. But he realized that he was now slowly admitting one idea that he had never dared entertain before.

 25

SOMETHING SOUNDED within Kiyoaki like a trumpet call: *I love Satoko.* And no matter how he viewed this feeling he was unable to fault its validity, even though he had never experienced anything like it before.

Then a further revelation released the flood of desire he

had pent up for so long: elegance disregards prohibitions, even the most severe. His sexual impulses, so diffident until now, had been lacking just such a powerful impulse. It had taken so much time and effort to find his role in life.

"Now at last, I'm sure that I do love Satoko," he told himself. And the impossibility of fulfilling that love was proof enough that he was right in his conviction.

He could not stay still. He rose from his chair and then sat down again. His thoughts had always been preponderantly melancholy and anxious, but now he was swept by a surge of youthful energy. He felt that everything previous had been mere delusion. He had allowed his sensitivity and melancholy to dominate, smother him.

Opening the window, he took a deep breath as he stood looking out at the pond, whose surface glinted in the bright sunshine. He smelled the strong fresh odor of the zelkovas. In the midst of the clouds that were massed to one side of the maple hill, he noticed a hint of brightness that told him summer had come at last. His cheeks were hot and his eyes bright. He had become a new person. Whatever this might hold in store, he was at least nineteen years old.

 26

HE GAVE HIMSELF over to passionate daydreams while he waited impatiently for his mother to return from the Ayakuras. Her presence there did not fit in with his plans at all. Finally he could wait no longer, and took off his school uniform, dressing in a Satsuma splashed-pattern kimono and *hakama*. Then he called one of the servants and told him to have a rickshaw waiting for him.

Following his plan, he left the rickshaw at Aoyama, 6-chome, which was the terminus for the streetcar that went to Roppongi. He boarded it and rode to the end of the line. Around the corner from Roppongi, at the turn to Toriizaka, were three huge zelkova trees, the remainder of the six that had given the Roppongi or Six Trees district its name. Beneath them, just as in old times before there were streetcars in Tokyo, a big placard with "Rickshaw Stand" scrawled on it was fastened to a post, and rickshaw men in conical wicker hats, short jackets, and blue trousers were gathered waiting for customers.

Kiyoaki called one of them, immediately handed him an exorbitant tip and told him to take him at once to the Ayakura mansion, which was no more than a few minutes away on foot. The old-fashioned Ayakura gate would not admit the Matsugaes' English carriage, and so if it were still waiting outside with the gate open, he would know that his mother was still there. However, if it were gone and the gate closed, he could safely assume that she had already fulfilled her ceremonial obligations and left.

When the rickshaw passed the gate, he saw that it was shut and in the road in front he recognized the marks left by a carriage.

He instructed the rickshaw man to take him back to the top of Toriizaka. Once there he sent him back on foot for Tadeshina while he himself remained behind, making use of the cover provided by the rickshaw.

As it turned out, he had a long wait. Through an opening in the side of the rickshaw, he watched the setting rays of summer sun flood the new leaves clustered at the tips of the branches. It seemed to be slowly submerging them in liquid brilliance. A giant horse chestnut towered above the red brick wall that ran along the edge of the slope of Toriizaka. Its very topmost leaves made him think of a white bird's nest decorated with a loosely woven crown of white flowers tipped with pink. Then all at once he was thinking of that snowy morning in February, and for no obvious reason he was shaken by a vio-

lent wave of excitement. But nevertheless, his intention was
not to force an immediate meeting with Satoko, for since passion had now found a definite course, he was no longer vulnerable to each new onrush of emotion.

Tadeshina came out of a side entrance, followed by the
rickshaw man. When she reached the rickshaw, Kiyoaki
pushed back its top to reveal his face and so startled her that
she could only stand there gaping up at him. He reached
down, seized her hand and jerked her up into the rickshaw.

"I've something to tell you. Let's go somewhere we can talk
safely."

"But, master . . . this is such a shock! The Marquise
your mother took her leave just a few minutes ago. Then tonight we're preparing for an informal celebration . . . I'm
really so busy."

"Never mind. Hurry up and tell the boy where to go."

Since Kiyoaki kept a firm grip on her hand, she had no
choice but to comply.

"Go toward Kasumicho," she told the rickshaw man. "Near
Number Three there's a road going downhill that turns toward the main gate of the Third Regiment barracks. Please
take us just to the bottom of the slope."

The rickshaw lurched forward and Tadeshina stared
straight ahead with desperate concentration, nervously
smoothing back a stray hair. This was the first time he had
been so close to this old woman with her thick mask of white
powder, and the experience was far from pleasant. Yet he
could not help but notice that she was even tinier than he had
imagined, hardly more than a dwarf in fact. Buffeted by the
shaking rickshaw, she kept up a mumbled stream of protest
that he could only barely understand.

"It's too late, too late . . . no matter what, it's just too
late." And then: "If only you'd sent one word of answer . . .
before this happened. Oh why . . . ?"

Kiyoaki said nothing and so she finally said something
about their destination just before they got there: "A distant
relative of mine runs an inn for soldiers near here. It's not a

very presentable place but an annex is always available, and it will permit me to hear whatever the young master wishes to say in confidence."

Tomorrow was Sunday, when Roppongi would be transformed suddenly into a bustling garrison district, its streets full of khaki-uniformed soldiers, many out strolling with their visiting families. But it was still Saturday afternoon, and this transformation was yet to take place. As the rickshaw carried him along through the streets toward Tadeshina's destination, he had the feeling that on that snowy morning too, he and Satoko had passed first this spot, then another. Just as he became convinced that he remembered the slope they were following, Tadeshina told the man to stop.

They were in front of an inn at the foot of the slope. Its main wing was two stories high, and although it had neither gate nor entranceway, it was surrounded by a good-sized garden enclosed by a broad fence.

Standing outside this fence, Tadeshina glanced up at the second floor of the rough wooden structure. It showed no sign of life. The six glass doors facing the front were shut, and none of the interior was visible. The low-quality panes in the latticed doors mirrored the evening sky in their own warped fashion, even catching the reflection of a carpenter working on an adjacent roof and distorting his image as though it were lying across water. The sky itself bore a watery image as seen there, tinged with the melancholy of a lake at evening time.

"It would of course be awkward if the soldiers were back—but only officers take rooms here," Tadeshina said as she pushed open a close-worked lattice door beside which there hung a plaque of the Goddess of Children. She then called out to announce their presence.

A tall, white-haired man who was on the verge of old age appeared.

"Ah, Miss Tadeshina! Please come in," he said in a somewhat squeaky voice.

"Is the annex available?"

"Yes, yes, of course."

The three of them went down the back hallway to the rear
of the inn and entered a small room perhaps ten feet square,
the kind often used for assignations.

"I can't stay very long, though," said Tadeshina. "Besides,
being alone like this with such a handsome young man, I don't
know what people would say." Suddenly she was speaking
casually and coquettishly, addressing herself to both Kiyoaki
and the old innkeeper.

The room was suspiciously tidy. A small scroll suitable for
a tea ceremony room hung in a little alcove, and there was
even a sliding Genji screen. The atmosphere was quite different from what one would have expected from the exterior,
that of a cheap inn frequented by the army.

"What then do you so kindly wish to communicate to me?"
Tadeshina asked as soon as the innkeeper withdrew. When
Kiyoaki did not answer, she repeated her question, making no
further effort to hide her irritation.

"What is this all about? And why choose today of all
days . . . ?"

"Because it's so appropriate. I want you to arrange a meeting between me and Satoko."

"What do you mean, young master? It's too late. After
what's happened, how can you ask such a thing? From now
on, there's nothing more to be done. Everything must be sub-
ordinated to the Emperor's pleasure. And now this—after all
those phone calls and the letters I sent! You didn't see fit to
give us any reply whatever. And today you make a request
like this! It's not a joking matter."

"Just remember this: everything that happened was your
fault," said Kiyoaki with as much dignity as he could muster,
staring at the veins that throbbed under the white powder
caking Tadeshina's forehead. Angrily he accused her of having allowed Satoko to read his letter and then to lie about it
brazenly, and also of having spread malicious gossip that had
lost him his faithful retainer Iinuma. Tadeshina finally con-
trived to burst into tears, and apologized abjectly on her knees.

She then pulled some tissue paper from the sleeve of her

kimono and began to wipe her eyes, rubbing away the white powder around them to reveal the pink web of wrinkles over her cheekbones, unmistakable proof of mortality. There was hardly any difference in texture between that wrinkled skin and the crumpled, rouge-smeared piece of tissue. Finally, staring into thin air, she began to talk.

"It's true. It's all my fault. I know that no amount of apology can make up for what I have done. But I should apologize more to my mistress than to you. Tadeshina's grievous failure was not communicating to the young master exactly how Miss Satoko felt. Everything that I had planned so carefully, thinking it for the best, has failed terribly. Please be kind enough to bear with me for a moment, young master. Imagine Miss Satoko's distress when she read your letter. And think what effort of courage it cost her not to show any sign of it when she met you. And then, after she had decided to take my advice and put a direct question to His Excellency your father, imagine how profoundly relieved she was to learn the truth from him at the family New Year's party. And after that, morning, noon, and night, she thought of nothing but the young master, until finally she went so far as to issue that invitation to ride through the snow that morning, whatever embarrassment it cost her as a woman. For some time after that, she was happy every day and even whispered your name at night in her sleep. But then she realized that through the kindness of His Excellency the Marquis, she was going to receive a proposal from the Imperial Family itself, and though she was counting on your courageous decision and had staked all her hopes on it, you didn't say a word, young master, and just let things go on. Miss Satoko's anxiety and suffering became unspeakable. Finally, when the granting of the imperial sanction was becoming imminent, she said that as a last hope, she wanted to tell the young master how she felt. Despite all my pleas, she decided to write a letter under my name. But now that hope too is dead. Miss Satoko was just coming to consider it all as a thing of the past. And so your demand today is a piece of cruelty. As you know, my mistress was brought up since childhood to revere the wishes of His Imperial Majesty the Emperor. We cannot expect her to go back on her word now. It's too late . . . simply too late. If your anger is unappeased, hit Tadeshina, kick her—do whatever is necessary to quiet your heart. But there's no other solution—it's just too late."

Listening to Tadeshina's speech, a thrill of joy went through him like a knife. Yet at the same time he felt somehow that he knew it all already, that he was hearing things repeated that were quite clear to him in his heart. He was now finding himself possessed of an acute wisdom he had never suspected before. Thus armed, he felt strong enough to overcome all that the world had to offer in the way of obstacles. His eyes were full of the fire of youth. "She read the letter I begged her to destroy," he said to himself, "so why shouldn't I resurrect the letter of hers that I destroyed?"

He stared wordlessly and fixedly at the little old lady with the white-powdered face. Once more she dabbed her reddened eyes with a piece of tissue paper. The room was growing steadily darker with the onset of evening. Her hunched shoulders seemed so frail that he was sure that if he grasped them suddenly, the bones would give way with a hollow crack.

"It's not too late."

"But it is."

"No it isn't. I wonder what would happen if I were to show Miss Satoko's last letter to the Prince's family? Especially when one considers that it was written after the formal request for imperial sanction."

At these words the blood suddenly drained from Tadeshina's face.

Neither said anything for a long time. It was no longer the rays of the setting sun but light from the second-floor rooms of the main wing that lit up the window. The lodgers were returning and there was an occasional flash of khaki uniform at a window. Outside the fence a beancurd-seller sounded his bugle. The evening air was characterized by the mild warmth, like flannel, of the few summer days that come before the final end to the rainy season.

From time to time, Tadeshina whispered something to herself which Kiyoaki heard only in snatches: "This is why I tried to stop her . . . this is why I said not to do it." She was evidently muttering about having opposed Satoko's writing of that final letter.

He maintained his silence, with increasing confidence that he held the winning hand. A wild animal seemed to be gradually if invisibly rearing its head within him.

"Very well then," said Tadeshina. "I will arrange just one meeting. And now the young master will, I trust, be kind enough to return the letter."

"Splendid. But a meeting of itself is not enough," he answered. "I want the two of us to be alone together—without your being there. And as for the letter, I'll return that afterwards."

 27

THREE DAYS WENT BY. The rain did not cease. After class, Kiyoaki went to the boarding house in Kasumicho, hiding his school uniform under a raincoat. He had received a message from Tadeshina that today would be Satoko's sole opportunity to escape from the house, since both her parents would be away.

Even after being shown to the back room in the boarding house by the innkeeper, Kiyoaki felt hesitant about removing his raincoat. Noticing this as he poured out his tea, the old owner reassured him: "Please feel quite comfortable, sir.

There's no cause for concern with someone like me who has renounced the world."

The innkeeper left him. He looked around the room and noticed that a bamboo blind was now covering the window through which he had looked up at the second floor of the main wing last time. The windows had been shut to keep out the rain, and a damp, oppressive heat filled the room. When he idly opened a lacquered box on the desk, its inside was covered with drops of moisture.

He knew that Satoko had arrived when he heard the rustle of clothing and the sound of whispers coming from the other side of the Genji sliding door.

The panel opened and Tadeshina made him a deep bow. Then without saying a word, she let Satoko into the room and quickly shut the panel again. Before it slid back into place, her upturned eyes momentarily flashed white in the sultry midday gloom of the hallway like a squid.

Satoko sat down on the tatami floor in front of Kiyoaki, her knees primly together. Her head was bent and she hid her face with a handkerchief, letting the other hand rest on the floor. Her body was turned sideways, so that the nape of her neck shone white like a small lake that one sometimes comes upon in the mountains.

He sat facing her in silence, feeling as though they were both submerged in the rain falling on the roof. He could hardly believe that the moment had finally come.

Satoko was bereft of words, and he himself had brought her to this. It had been his most fervent hope to see her reduced to this state, robbed of the power given her by her greater age to drop those little homilies she had been so fond of, capable of nothing but silent tears. At this moment she held an irresistible attraction for him, in her kimono the color of white wisteria, but it was not merely that of a rich prize finally within his grasp; it was the lure of the forbidden, the utterly unattainable, the proscribed. He wanted her this way and no other. And she herself, on the other hand, had always wanted to keep him off balance by playing games. How things

had changed now! She could have chosen this beautiful, sacred, inviolable position at any time, but she had always preferred the false role of elder sister, cherishing him with that
affectionate condescension he so hated.

Now he realized why he had objected so strongly when his
father had proposed to give him an introduction to the pleasures that the women of Yoshiwara had to offer. Just as one
can discern the stirrings of a dark green chrysalis inside a
cocoon, he had always foreseen the gradual distillation of
some ineffably sacred essence in Satoko. And he could give
his purity to that essence alone. From that moment on, a dawn
of unimaginable brilliance would begin to flood the world of
black, inchoate melancholy in which he had imprisoned himself.

The elegance he had absorbed from his infancy under
Count Ayakura's tutelage now became a silken cord in his
hands, a noose for his innocence and Satoko's sanctity. Now
at last he had found a valid use for the shining rope whose purpose had puzzled him for so long.

He was sure that he loved Satoko. And so he edged forward
on his knees and grasped her by the shoulders. He felt them
tense in resistance. This firm rebuff to his fingers delighted
him. It was resistance on the grand scale, a ritual of resistance
with cosmic significance. The soft shoulders that aroused such
desire in him were opposing him with a force that drew on the
weight of imperial sanction. For this very reason it had the
remarkable power to drive him mad, making his fingertips
ache with feverish desire. Her fragrant, jet-black hair, carefully dressed and piled lightly above her forehead, had a full-
bodied gloss; glimpsed so briefly at close range, it made him
think of being lost in a forest on a bright, moonlit night.

He put his face close to one wet cheek that had escaped the
protection of her handkerchief. Still wordless, she began to
shake her head in an attempt to ward him off, but her struggles were so mechanical that he knew they were not heartfelt,
but imposed from outside. He pushed aside the handkerchief

and tried to kiss her, but whereas her lips had been willing on
that snowy February morning, they resisted fiercely now, and
finally she ducked her head and, like a sleeping fledgling,
froze with her chin burrowed in the neck of her kimono.

The drumming of the rain grew louder. Maintaining his
grip on her, he paused to assess the strength of her defenses.
Her kimono, its neckband embroidered with a design of summer thistles, was chastely gathered at the throat, revealing a
tiny triangle of skin. Her wide, tight-wrapped obi was cold
and hard to the touch, like the door barring entrance to a
sanctuary, and in the center there gleamed a golden clip like
the ornamented head of a spike in a pillar of a temple courtyard. Nevertheless, her body gave off the warm scent of flesh.
Passing through the inner sleeve openings at her shoulders,
it escaped from the wide kimono sleeves, a warm breeze
against his cheek.

He took one hand away from her back and gripped her chin
firmly. It fitted there as smoothly as a small, rounded ivory
chessman. Her nose was wet with tears, and her delicate nostrils flared. He was thus able to kiss her properly.

Suddenly she seemed consumed by a mysterious fire, much
as the flame in a stove burns more fiercely when the door is
open. Both her hands were now free, and she pressed them
against Kiyoaki's cheeks, pushing hard against him, but her
lips remained on his, even though she tried to thrust him
away. As a result of her resistance, however, her lips, with an
incredible, liquid smoothness that intoxicated him, kept twisting one way, then the other against his own. The firm edge of
her resolve was melting away like a lump of sugar in hot tea,
and now a wonderfully sweet dissolution had begun.

He had no idea whatever of how to unfasten a woman's obi.
Its tightly fastened flared bow at her back defied the efforts of
his fingers. But as he groped blindly, trying to undo it by
force, she reached behind her and while giving every sign that
she was trying desperately to check his fumbling efforts, she
subtly guided them in a more profitable direction. Their fin-

gers lay tangled for a few moments in its folds, and then as its clip suddenly fell away, the obi uncoiled in a rustle of silk and sprang away from her body as though it had a life of its own. It was the beginning of a confused riot of uncontrollable movements. Her entire kimono swirled in revolt as he tore frantically at the folds of silk that bound her breasts, rebuffed at every turn by a whole network of straps that tightened as others came loose. But then right before his eyes, he saw the tiny, well-guarded triangle of white below her throat spread into a rich and fragrant expanse of skin.

She did not actually utter a word of protest. There was nothing to prove whether it was silent resistance or silent seduction. She seemed to be drawing him on at the same time as she was fighting him off. He sensed, however, that the strength underlying his assault upon her sacred inviolability was not wholly his own.

What was its source, then? As he looked at her face, it gradually flooded crimson, and her desire was unmistakable. He had one hand under her back to support her, and felt her lean on it more strongly, though with shy subtlety, until, as if giving up all hope of resistance, she fell back on the floor.

He parted the skirts of her kimono and began pushing aside the printed silk of her Yuzen underskirts in a dazzling tangle of fretted patterns and brilliant phoenixes soaring above stylized cloud formations. A distant vision of her thighs wrapped in fold after fold of silk drew him on as he fought his way through more and more layers of the clouds. Some secret hidden core was cunningly maintaining the complex arrangements with which he was struggling, and the key to it kept eluding him as his breath grew harsher and more irregular.

Finally, however, he was drawing closer to her body, slowly lowering himself onto her thighs, which had the faint sheen of a pale dawn horizon, when she raised her hands and gently helped him; this intended kindness ruined the moment, for at the instant when he merged with the dawn, whether he was touching her or not, it all ended abruptly.

*

The two lay side by side on the tatami floor staring up at the ceiling. The rain had become torrential again and was beating on the roof. The pounding of their hearts had scarcely subsided. Kiyoaki felt an exaltation that overrode not only his momentary exhaustion but even the realization that something had come to an end. However, a lingering sense of shared regret still hung over them, as palpable as the shadows now gradually forming in the darkening room. He thought he heard the faint sound of an old woman clearing her throat on the other side of the Genji panel. As he was about to sit up, however, Satoko reached over to stop him with a gentle grasp of his shoulder.

And then, without a word, she dispelled every vestige of regret. He was delighted to follow her lead. From that moment on, there was nothing he could not forgive her.

He was young; his desire quickly revived, and this time she was receptive and everything went smoothly. Under her sure, feminine guidance, he sensed that for the first time every barrier was gone and that he had found himself in a rich new world. In the heat of the room he had already stripped off the last of his clothes and now he felt the immediacy of flesh on flesh, firm but yielding, with the resistance of water and clinging plants to the advancing prow of a boat. He saw that there was no trace of distress in her face. She was even smiling faintly but this gave him no misgivings now. His heart was completely at rest.

*

Afterwards, he took her, rumpled, in his arms and pressed his cheek against hers, feeling the wetness of fresh tears. He knew that they were tears of joy, but still, nothing could better convey in silence their mutual consciousness of having committed unpardonable sin than her tears quietly rolling down his cheek as well as her own. For Kiyoaki, however, this sense of sin increased his already rising courage.

"Here," she said, picking up his shirt, "it won't do for you to catch cold."

Just as he was about to snatch it roughly from her, she checked him for a moment, and pressed the shirt to her face with a deep breath. When she handed it to him, it was wet with tears.

When he had put on his school uniform and finished dressing, he was startled by the sudden sound of her clapping her hands. Then, after a significant pause, the Genji panel slid open a fraction and Tadeshina's head appeared.

"Did you call me, Miss Satoko?"

Satoko nodded and with a quick glance indicated her obi, which lay on the floor in a tangle around her. Tadeshina slid the door shut behind her and edged across the tatami floor to Satoko without looking in Kiyoaki's direction. She helped her mistress to dress and fastened her obi. Then she brought over the mirror from a corner of the room and began to arrange Satoko's hair. Meanwhile Kiyoaki was in acute embarrassment, at a loss as to what he should do; so while the two women performed their long-drawn-out ritual in the now-lighted room, he felt quite superfluous.

When everything was finally in order, Satoko, more beautiful than ever, sat with drooping head.

"I'm afraid, young master, that we have to go now," the old woman began. "The promise I made has been kept. From now on, please, I beg you, try to forget Miss Satoko. And now if you would be so kind, would you please return the letter as you promised?"

Kiyoaki sat cross-legged in silence. He did not answer.

"As you promised, would you please return the letter?" Tadeshina asked again.

Kiyoaki remained silent, as if he were deaf. He was staring at Satoko, who sat calmly without a single hair out of place and her beautiful kimono in perfect order. All at once she raised her eyes. They met Kiyoaki's. A brilliant piercing flash passed between them and in that instant he knew just how she felt.

"I'm not returning the letter. Because I want to meet her again, just like this," he said, drawing on his newfound courage.

"Young master!" Tadeshina made no attempt to hide her anger. "What do you think will happen? Only a spoiled child would say such a thing! You know what terrible things will come about, don't you? It's not just Tadeshina who will be destroyed."

Then Satoko stopped her, her voice so composed, so other-worldly, that the sound of it sent a chill down his spine.

"It's all right, Tadeshina. Until Master Kiyo wishes to return the letter, there's nothing we can do but agree to keep meeting him. There's no other way to save both you and me—that is, if you intend to save me too."

 28
KIYOAKI'S VISIT to his house to confide in him in such detail was so rare an event that Honda not only asked his mother to invite his guest to stay for dinner but even went so far as to forego the work for the entrance examinations that normally occupied his entire evening. The mere prospect of Kiyoaki's arrival somehow charged the sedate atmosphere of the house with expectancy.

Throughout the day the sun, engulfed in cloud, had shone like white gold and now in the evening the sultry heat it had left behind was not appreciably diminished. As they sat talking, the two young men wore light summer kimonos with a Kasuri pattern.

Honda had had some sort of premonition about Kiyoaki's visit, but it had by no means prepared him for what was to come. As soon as Kiyoaki began to speak, Honda was startled to realize that the young man sitting beside him on the old leather couch along the wall of the reception room was someone radically different from the Kiyoaki he had known before. He had never seen eyes flash so openly. They were unmistakably the eyes of a worldly adult, but Honda had a lingering regret for the melancholy look and the downcast eyes that he had grown used to in his friend.

Despite this, however, he was delighted that Kiyoaki had chosen to confide in him without reservation what was a secret of the gravest consequence. Honda had been hoping for a gesture like this for a long time, and it had come about without the slightest urging on his part. On reflection, he realized that Kiyoaki had kept his secrets even from his friend, as long as they had concerned nothing but his own inner struggles, but now that it was a matter of reputation and serious wrongdoing, he had poured it all out in an impetuous flood of words. Considering the gravity of the confession and the limitless trust it implied, Kiyoaki could hardly have given him greater cause for happiness. As he studied his friend, he found Kiyoaki noticeably matured, and some of the beauty that had belonged to the face of an irresolute young boy was gone from his features. They now shone with the determination of the passionate young lover, and his words and gestures were free of any hint of reluctance and uncertainty.

He was the very image of a man proud of his conquest. As he told his story to Honda, his cheeks glowed with color, his teeth gleamed, and his voice was firm and clear, although he paused shyly at times and there was a new gallantry evident even in the set of his eyebrows. Almost nothing seemed more alien to him than introspection, or so it struck Honda, whether because the tale came so abruptly to an end or because of the incoherence of his outpourings.

"Listening to you, the oddest thing came to my mind—why, I don't know," said Honda. "One day, when we were talking—I'm not sure when it was—you asked me if I remembered anything about the Russo-Japanese War. And then afterwards, when we were at your house, you showed me a collection of war photographs. And I remember you telling me that the one you liked best had written under it 'Vicinity of Tokuri Temple: Memorial Services for the War Dead' —a strange picture, in which all the soldiers looked as if they had been assembled like actors in a huge pageant. At the time it struck me as being an odd preference for you since you had so little taste for anything that smacked of military life.

"But at any rate, as I was listening just now, the memory of that dusty plain in the picture came to my mind and somehow seemed to fuse with your beautiful love story."

Honda had managed to surprise himself. He was startled not only by the obscurity of what he had said and the fervor with which he had said it, but also by the admiration he felt for Kiyoaki's wanton disregard of commandment and precept —he, Honda, who had long ago decided to become a man of the law!

Two servants entered with small tables on which their dinners had been placed. His mother had arranged things like this so that the two could eat and talk as friends without any constraint. A saké bottle stood on either table, and Honda offered him some.

"Mother was rather worried. She didn't know how well you'd take to the food we serve, seeing as you're accustomed to such luxuries," he remarked, turning the conversation to something more commonplace.

He was happy to see Kiyoaki starting to eat as though, in fact, he found the food much to his liking. So for a little while the two young men stopped talking and gave themselves over to the healthy pleasures of eating.

*

Enjoying the further brief silence that usually follows a good meal, Honda asked himself why, after hearing his classmate confess to so romantic an exploit, he had felt so happy about it, without a twinge of jealousy or envy. He was refreshed by it the way a lakeside garden is imperceptibly steeped in moisture during the rainy season.

"Well then, what do you intend to do?" he asked, breaking the silence.

"I don't have the least idea. I'm slow off the mark, but once I get started, I'm not the type to stop halfway."

Honda stared at him wide-eyed. He had never dreamed that he would ever hear Kiyoaki say something like this.

"You mean you want to marry Miss Satoko?"

"That's out of the question. The sanction has already been granted."

"But you've already violated the sanction. Why can't you marry her then? Couldn't the two of you run away—go abroad and get married there?"

"You just don't understand," he answered. Then he lapsed into silence, and for the very first time that day, Honda noticed a trace of the old melancholy in the lines that suddenly appeared between his eyebrows.

Perhaps he had been expecting as much, but now that he had seen it, he felt a slight uneasiness cast a shadow over his own mood of exhilaration. As he sat staring at his friend's handsome profile, whose fine and delicate lines would defeat all but the most skilled artist, he wondered just what it was that Kiyoaki hoped to get from life. He felt a shudder pass through him.

Kiyoaki picked up his strawberries, got up from the couch and sat down in front of the scrupulously tidy desk where Honda worked. He propped his elbows on its austere surface and casually began to swing the swivel chair from side to side. As he did so, he put his weight on his elbows and restlessly eased the posture of his head and torso, his bare chest showing at the neck of his loose-fitting kimono. Then, after arming himself with a toothpick, he began lightly spearing the strawberries one by one and popping them into his mouth. It was a display of relaxed bad manners that showed how glad he was to escape the strict decorum of his own home. He spilled some sugar, which dropped down onto his light-skinned chest, but he brushed it off with no sign of embarrassment.

"You're going to attract ants, you know," said Honda, laughing through a mouthful of strawberries.

Kiyoaki's delicate eyelids, usually too pale, were now diffused with color, thanks to the saké he had drunk. As he kept turning the swivel chair from side to side, his bare flushed forearms still propped on the desk, he happened to move too far in one direction, and his body was oddly twisted. It was just as if he had suddenly been stricken by some vague pain of which he himself was unaware.

There was no mistaking the faraway look in those eyes beneath their fine, graceful brows, but Honda was well aware that their flashing glance was not directed toward the future. Unlike his usual self, he had a cruel desire to inflict his growing uneasiness on his friend—an urgent impulse to pretend to raise his own hand to destroy Kiyoaki's all-too-recent sense of happiness.

"Well, what *are* you going to do? Have you even thought about what will come of this?"

Kiyoaki raised his eyes and looked at him steadily. Honda had never seen a gaze of such burning eagerness and yet such gloom.

"Why must I think about it?"

"Because all those people around you and Miss Satoko are moving slowly but inexorably toward a dénouement. You don't think the two of you can hover forever in mid-air like two dragonflies making love?"

"I know we can't," Kiyoaki replied, breaking off the exchange and casually glancing elsewhere. He gave himself over to an examination of the shadows in the various nooks and crannies of the room, such as the intricate patterns beneath the bookcases and the ones beside the wicker wastepaper basket—those elusive little shadows that crept into Honda's plain and functional study night after night, insidious as human emotions, to lurk wherever they could find cover.

As Honda watched him, he was struck by the prominence of his graceful eyebrows. They were like shadows themselves, bent into elegant bows. They seemed to be an embodiment of an emotion, yet nevertheless had force enough to check its expression. He imagined them guarding the dark, brooding eyes beneath, loyally following their master's glance wherever it went, like zealous servants with impeccable training.

Honda decided to come out directly with something that had been taking form in a corner of his mind.

"A bit earlier," he began, "I said something very odd. I mean about thinking of the picture from the Russo-Japanese War while you were telling me about you and Miss Satoko. I wondered why that came to me, and now that I've given it a little more thought, I have an answer. The age of glorious wars ended with the Meiji era. Today, all the stories of past wars have sunk to the level of those edifying accounts we hear from middle-aged noncoms in the military science department or the boasts of farmers around a hot stove. There isn't much chance now to die on the battlefield.

"But now that old wars are finished, a new kind of war has just begun; this is the era for the war of emotion. The kind of war no one can see, only feel—a war, therefore, that the dull and insensitive won't even notice. But it's begun in earnest. The young men who have been chosen to wage it have already begun to fight. And you're one of them—there's no doubt about that.

"And just as in the old wars, there will be casualties in the war of emotion, I think. It's the fate of our age—and you're one of our representatives. So what about it then? You're fully resolved to die in this new war—am I right?"

Kiyoaki's only answer was a flickering smile. At that moment a strong breeze, heavy with the rain's dampness, found its way in through the window and, in passing, cooled their foreheads, which were covered with a light film of sweat. Honda was perplexed at Kiyoaki's silence. Was his answer so obvious that no reply was necessary? Or had his words really struck a responsive chord in his friend, while his way of

putting them had been so extravagant that there was no way
for him to answer frankly? He thought that it had to be one
or the other.

 29

THREE DAYS LATER, when two canceled classes
gave Honda a free afternoon, he went to watch the district
court in session, accompanied by a law student who was one
of the family houseboys. It had been raining since morning.

Honda's father was a justice of the Supreme Court and,
even within his own family, was a strict observer of principles.
He was greatly pleased by the promise shown by his nineteen-
year-old son, who had applied himself to the law even before
entering college. His father thus felt confident enough to conclude that his son would eventually succeed him. Up to this
year, the office of judge had been for life, but the previous
April a large-scale reform of the juridical system had been
put into effect. As a result, more than two hundred judges had
been laid off or requested to hand in their resignations. Justice
Honda, wanting to show his solidarity with his unfortunate
old friends, had offered his own resignation, but it had not
been accepted.

The experience, however, seemed to have marked a turning
point in his views on life, which, in their turn, affected what
had been a rather formal relationship with his son. From then
on, he brought to it a warmth of generosity that resembled the
affection shown by a high official to the subordinate he has
selected to succeed him. Honda himself was determined to
work harder than ever at his studies to try to be worthy of
such unprecedented favor.

One result of his father's changed views was that he permitted his son to attend court sessions even though he was not yet an adult. He did not, of course, go so far as to let him come into his own court, but he gave him permission to watch whatever civil or criminal cases he liked, as long as he was accompanied by the young retainer who was also a law student.

His father explained to Shigekuni that since all his familiarity with the law came from books, it would be extremely valuable for him to come in contact with the actual process of law in Japan and to experience it at a practical level. Justice Honda had more than this in mind, however. Truth to tell, his main concern was to expose his still sensitive, nineteen-year-old son to those elements of human existence that were dredged up in all their shockingly sordid reality in criminal court. He wanted to see what Shigekuni was able to draw from such experience.

It was a dangerous sort of education. Still, when the Justice considered the greater danger of allowing a young man to form his character out of an assimilation from careless popular behavior, cheap entertainment and so on, from whatever might please or appeal to his immature taste, he felt confident of the advantages of this educational experiment. There was a good chance that it would at least make Shigekuni acutely aware of the stern and watchful eye of the law. He would see all the amorphous, steaming, filthy detritus of human passions processed right then and there according to the impersonal recipes of the law. Standing by in such a kitchen should teach Shigekuni a great deal about technique.

Honda hurried through the dark corridors of the courthouse on his way to the 8th District Criminal Court, a route lit only by the faint light that filtered through the rain soaking the ravaged grass of the quadrangle. The pervasive atmosphere of this building had absorbed the raw essence of the criminal spirit; the place struck him as being altogether too sinister for the palace of reason it was supposed to be.

His depression still clung to him after he and his companion had taken their seats in the courtroom. He glanced at the

highly strung law student who had conducted him here with
such anxious haste and was now engrossed in the case book
he had brought with him, as though he had completely forgotten his master's son. Then he turned the same listless gaze
on the still empty judge's bench, the public prosecutor's desk,
the witness stand, the defense attorney's desk, and so on. Such
universal emptiness struck him as being expressive of his own
spiritual state on this damp, humid afternoon.

So young and so lethargic! As though he had been born to
sit and stare like this. Ever since Kiyoaki had confided in him,
Shigekuni, who would have been bright and confident, as befitted such an able young man, had undergone a change. Or
rather, the friendship between him and Kiyoaki had undergone a strange reversal. For years, each of them had been extremely careful to intrude in no way on the personal life of the
other. But now, just three days before, Kiyoaki had suddenly
come to him and, like a newly cured patient transmitting his
disease to someone else, had passed on to his friend the virus
of introspection. It had taken hold so readily that Honda's
disposition now seemed a far better host to it than Kiyoaki's.
The first major symptom of the disease was a vague sense of
apprehension.

What was Kiyoaki to do, he wondered. Was it right for
himself, as Kiyoaki's friend, to do nothing more than sit by
idly and let things take their course?

While he waited for the court session to begin at one thirty,
he sat engrossed in the reflections provoked by his anxiety,
his mind far from the hearings that he had come to attend.

"If I were really to act as a true friend," he thought,
"wouldn't it be best to persuade him to try and forget Miss
Satoko? Up until now I thought it best as his friend to pretend
not to notice even if he were in his death agonies, out of respect
for that elegance of his. But now that he's told me everything
as he did the other day, shouldn't I interfere, as I have the
right to do in an ordinary friendship, and do my best to save
him from the clear danger that's threatening him? Moreover,
I shouldn't hold back even if it makes him so resentful that he

breaks our friendship. In ten or twenty years, he'll understand why I did it. And even if he never understands, it should make no difference to me.

"There's no doubt that he's heading straight for tragedy. It will be beautiful, of course, but should he throw his whole life away as a sacrificial offering to such a fleeting beauty—like a bird in flight glimpsed from a window?

"I know what I have to do. From now on I've got to put aside all the niceties and behave like an insensitive and imperceptive friend. And whether he likes it or not, I've got to do something to pour cold water on that raging passion of his. I've got to use every ounce of my strength to prevent him from fulfilling his destiny."

*

This feverish rush of thoughts made Honda's head ache with the effort they cost. He no longer felt able to sit there patiently and wait for the start of the hearings, in which he had lost all interest. He wanted to leave at once, rush to Kiyoaki's house and pour out every argument at his command to persuade him to change his mind. And the frustration of realizing that this was impossible caused a new upsurge of anxiety that increased his discomfiture.

He glanced around and noticed that all the seats had been filled. Now he understood why the houseboy had brought him here so early. Among those present were young men who looked like law students, drab middle-aged men and women, and newspaper reporters with armbands who were coming and going with a great show of urgency. He watched as those who had been drawn by nothing more than base curiosity hid their interest behind masks of sober propriety, stroking their moustaches and passing the time with a genteel wave of a fan or using the long nails of their little fingers to dig sulfur-colored deposits out of their ears. It was an instructive sight, and one that, more than anything seen previously, opened his eyes to the moral ugliness of the belief that "Oh, I'm in no danger of ever committing a sin." Whatever the future might hold, he was determined never to fall prey to that kind of attitude.

The windows were shut against the rain, and they admitted a dull, flat light that lay over all the spectators indifferently like a coat of gray dust; only the shiny black visors of the guards' caps were exempt from it.

The entrance of the defendant set up a flurry of comment. Flanked by two guards and dressed in a blue prison uniform, she made her way to the dock. He tried to get a look at her as she passed, but there was so much jostling and neck-craning going on among the spectators that he could do little more than catch a glimpse of plump white cheeks with conspicuous dimples. Then after she had entered the dock, all he could see was that her hair was pulled back in the cylindrical bun worn by female prisoners. Although she hunched forward respectfully, he noticed that there was a little sign of nervous strain in the way her plump shoulders were set beneath her uniform.

The defense lawyer had already come in, and now everyone was waiting for the public prosecutor and the judge himself.

"Just take a look at her, young master. Would you think she's a murderess?" said the young law student, whispering in his ear. "It's true what they say about not being able to tell a book by its cover."

*

The court ritual began with the presiding judge putting the usual questions to the accused about name, address, age, and social status. The courtroom was so hushed that Honda imagined he could hear the busy swish of the recorder's writing brush.

"Two-five, Nihonbashi Ward, Tokyo City. A commoner. Tomi Masuda," the woman replied in a voice that was clear and steady but so low that the crowd of spectators pricked up their ears and leaned forward as one, afraid of missing something when the testimony reached matters that were crucial. The responses came smoothly enough until the accused came to her age, and there, whether intentionally or not, she hesitated. Then, after the urgings of her lawyer, she shook herself and said in a louder voice: "I'm thirty-one."

At that moment, she turned her head toward her lawyer and Honda caught a glimpse of her profile, her eyes wide and clear and a few stray hairs brushing her cheek.

The spectators stared at this small woman in fascination, as if she might perhaps have the translucent body of a silkworm that had somehow excreted a thread of inconceivable complexity and evil. Her slightest movement made them imagine the sweatmarks on the armpits of her uniform, her nipples tight with fear, the line of her buttocks, rather too full, dull, and a little cold. This body had spun threads without number until they were finally wrapping her in a sinister cocoon. For the spectators, there had to be a peculiarly intimate correspondence between her body and her crime. They would be dissatisfied with anything less. For the average man, driven as he is by lurid fantasies, there is almost nothing more deliciously titillating than the contemplation, from a safe distance, of evil laid out in its cause and effect. Had the woman been thin, her very thinness would have embodied this for them. But since she was plump, her plumpness served just as well. And so, satisfied that she was nothing less than evil incarnate, they eagerly exercised their harmless powers of imagination, fastening with delight on every detail down to the very beads of sweat that they were sure covered her breasts.

Honda's scruples would not let him follow the thoughts of the crowd, although these were quite clear to him, despite his youth; he focused his entire attention on the testimony of the defendant as she answered the judge's questions. Her account was now getting to the matter at issue.

Her way of telling things was tedious and confused, but it was clear enough that the chain of events leading up to this crime of passion had unfolded relentlessly in a manner that must lead inevitably to tragedy.

"When did you start living with Matsukichi Hijikata?"

"I . . . it was last year, Your Honor. I remember it very well. June the fifth."

Her retentive memory made the spectators laugh, but the guards quieted them at once.

Tomi Masuda was a waitress who had become enamored of a cook named Matsukichi Hijikata, who worked at the same restaurant. The man was a widower who had only recently lost his wife. Spurred by affection, she had begun to take care of him, and the previous year they had started to live together. Hijikata, however, gave no sign that he wanted to make the arrangement official, and in fact after they had set up house-keeping, he became more and more energetic in his pursuit of other women. Then toward the end of the previous year, he had taken up with a maid who worked at an inn called Kishimoto in the same Hama district. Though Hidé, the maid, was only twenty, there was little she did not know about men. As a result, Hijikata's nights away from home became more and more frequent. Finally, this spring, Tomi had gone to confront Hidé and plead with her to leave her man alone. Hidé had treated her with contempt, and Tomi unable to control her rage, had killed her.

It was, in brief, a triangle that ended in violence, a common affair of the streets with no particularly distinguishing feature. Yet under the close scrutiny of the court hearing, many undoubtedly authentic and totally unpredictable elements came to light.

The woman had found herself with a fatherless child, now eight years old, who had been left in the care of relatives in her home village, but she had asked them to send him to Tokyo so that he would have the benefit of a better school system. But although she had hoped to use the boy as an inducement to Hijikata to settle down, Tomi, even as a mother, had already embarked on the course that would force her to become a murderess.

And now her testimony came to the events of that night.

"No, Your Honor. If only Hidé had not been there that night, everything would have been all right. I know that this whole thing just wouldn't have happened. If only she had had a cold or something that night and had been in bed when I went to the Kishimoto to see her, everything would have been all right too.

"The knife I used was the one Matsukichi uses to cut *sashimi*. He's a man who takes real pride in his work and he has all kinds of good knives. 'To me these are like a samurai's sword,' he keeps saying, and he never lets any of the women at work touch them but always sharpens them carefully himself. But about the time I started to get jealous of Hidé, he hid them all away somewhere, thinking it was dangerous.

"When I realized the way his mind was working, it made me angry. After that I used to make jokes about it, pretending to threaten him. I'd say: 'I don't need any of your knives. There're plenty of others around I can lay my hands on, you know.' Then one day after Matsukichi hadn't been home for a long time, I was cleaning out a closet, and all of a sudden I came across a package with all his knives in it in a place you'd never expect. And what surprised me most, Your Honor, was that almost all of them were covered with rust. When I saw that rust, I just knew how much he'd got himself involved with Hidé, and I started to shake with one of the knives right there in my hand. But just then my boy came home from school, and I gradually calmed down. Then I thought to myself that maybe if I took his favorite knife, the one he uses to cut *sashimi*, to be sharpened, Matsukichi would appreciate it —trying to make myself think I was a real wife. I wrapped it up in a cloth, and then when I was going out, my boy asked me where I was off to and I told him I had a little errand to run and I'd be right back and he should be a good boy and watch the house. And then he said: 'I don't care if you never come back. Then I can go back to my school back home.' This gave me such a shock and when I stopped to ask him what he meant, I found out the children in the neighborhood were making fun of him and saying: 'Your old man couldn't stand your mother's nagging, and he ran out on her.' This is something the children probably picked up from hearing their parents gossiping about us. And so now here was my boy wanting to get away from a mother who's been turned into a

laughing stock and go back to his foster parents in the country. Suddenly I got so angry and before I knew it, I'd hit him
across the face. As I rushed out of the house, I could hear him
crying behind me."

According to the testimony that followed, Tomi was not
thinking about Hidé at this moment, but was hurrying through
the streets with one thing only on her mind: to get the knife
sharpened so that she would feel better. The knife sharpener
had a great deal of other work to do, but she would not be
turned away. After she had waited for over an hour, he finally
sharpened it for her. When she left his shop, she had not
felt at all like going back home, and finally had turned almost
involuntarily in the direction of the Kishimoto Inn.

Shortly beforehand, Hidé had returned to the Kishimoto
after enjoying a wild night with Matsukichi and had been
lectured by the innkeeper's wife for leaving work. She had
gone to the woman and apologized tearfully, just as Matsukichi had instructed. It was only a few minutes after this
was over that Tomi arrived at the inn and asked to speak to
Hidé for a moment outside. Hidé came out to see her and
was surprisingly cordial. She had just changed into a stylish
working kimono, and as she walked along the street with
Tomi, her loose clogs scraped languidly along the ground in
the manner affected by affluent prostitutes.

"I made a promise to the boss just now. From now on I'm
going to have nothing more to do with men, I told her," she
said.

Tomi felt a rush of happiness when she heard this, but
next moment Hidé, smiling brightly, robbed her words of all
significance with a further remark: "But I don't know if I
can hold out even for three days."

Making a great effort at self-control, Tomi then offered to
treat her to a drink at a nearby *sushi* shop on the bank of the
Sumida River. Once they had begun to drink, Tomi did her
best to talk to her as though she were addressing her elder
sister, but Hidé refused to be drawn; her only reaction was
an ironic smile. And finally, when she was probably driven

to melodramatic extremes by the saké, Tomi lowered her head in supplication, but the younger woman turned away in brusque contempt. They had been there for over an hour by this time, and it was dark outside. Hidé got up to go, saying that the manager would be angry at her again unless she returned immediately.

After they left the *sushi* shop, Tomi claimed that she did not know why they wandered into a badly lit vacant lot in Hama that lay by the river. She said that perhaps when she tugged at Hidé's kimono, trying to get her to stay and talk, Hidé had happened to begin walking in this direction as she pulled herself free. At any rate, Tomi denied any intention of having led her that way in order to kill her.

After walking for a short time, Tomi began to argue again, but Hidé only laughed. As she did so, her even teeth flashed white, although there was no more than a glint of light on the surface of the Sumida to relieve the darkness that engulfed the two of them.

"It's no use you keeping on like this," Hidé replied at last. "No wonder Matsukichi got so fed up with you."

This, according to Tomi, was the decisive moment, as she went on to describe her reactions.

"When I heard that, the blood rushed to my head. I don't know how to describe it exactly . . . right then I felt like a baby crying desperately in the dark, waving its arms and legs because it had no words to say it wanted something—or because it was hurting somewhere. And then I started to swing my own arms about, and somehow they loosened the cloth, got hold of the knife, and while they were still waving it around, Hidé's body bumped into it in the dark—that's the only way I can say it."

Her words had been so intense that the crowd in the courtroom, and Honda with them, could clearly see the phantom baby miserably waving its arms and legs.

After she had finished, Tomi Masuda covered her face with her hands and sobbed. Her shoulders under the prison uniform seemed the more pathetic for being plump. The mood of the spectators now seemed to be shifting gradually from undisguised curiosity to something else.

The rain was still falling outside the windows and veiled the courtroom in a bleak light which seemed to focus on Tomi Masuda. She stood there as though she were the sole representative of all the complex passions of man, living, breathing, grieving, and crying out in pain. She alone was endowed with the privilege of emotion. Until a few moments before, the spectators had seen nothing but a plump, perspiring thirty-one-year-old woman. But now with bated breath and staring eyes, they were looking at a human being wracked by her feelings, writhing like a fish carved up alive for the dinner table.

She had absolutely no protection from their gaze. The crime that she had once committed in darkness had now taken possession of her to reveal itself before the eyes of them all. For it was the vivid character of the crime itself, rather than any consideration of good intentions or moral scruples, that she had impressed with such cogent force upon the spectators. Tomi Masuda's self-revelation far surpassed the possible accomplishment of even the most skilled of actresses, who, after all, would have revealed no more than she had intended. It amounted to facing the whole world and turning it into one giant audience. Her lawyer, who stood beside her, seemed too shabby to have any capacity to help. She stood there, a short, plump figure, with nothing to mitigate her drabness—no combs in her hair, no jewelry, no fine kimono to catch a man's eye—but the fact of being a criminal was enough to make them see her as a woman.

"If we had the jury system here in Japan, this is the kind of case where they might let her get away with it," said the law student, whispering in Shigekuni's ear again. "What can you do with a glib woman like that?"

Shigekuni sat thinking. Once passion was set in motion according to its own laws, then it was irresistible. This was a theory that would never be accepted by modern law, which took it as self-evident that conscience and reason ruled man.

Then his thoughts turned to more personal things. Although
he had come to watch this trial as a thoroughly disinterested
spectator, he was now fascinated. At the same time, however,
it had made him realize something else: he would never
plunge into the kind of molten red-hot passion that had come
gushing out of Tomi Masuda.

Outside, the overcast sky had brightened further and the
rain had slackened into brief, scattered showers. The raindrops coating the window shone eerily in the sunshine.

He hoped that his reason would always be like that sunlight. But a part of him was drawn irresistibly to the darkness
of human passion. This blackness was a fascination, no more.
And Kiyoaki, too, was a fascination that seemed to come
surging up to shake the very fabric of life, but that instead
of being life-giving, carried the seeds of a fateful end.

It was in this mood, then, that Honda decided not to interfere with Kiyoaki for the time being.

 30

AS THE SUMMER VACATION grew closer, something
happened that disturbed the atmosphere at Peers. Prince Pattanadid lost his emerald ring. The affair became very serious
when it became generally known that Prince Kridsada had
protested in anger that the ring had been stolen. More than
anything else, Prince Pattanadid wanted the matter to be
settled as quietly as possible, and he rebuked his cousin for
his rudeness. Nevertheless, it was evident that in his heart,
he, too, believed it to have been stolen.

Prince Kridsada's angry charge provoked a predictable
response from the school administration. They said that such

a thing as theft was unthinkable at Peers. The ensuing turmoil was eventually to reach such proportions that the princes, more and more homesick, were finally to decide that they wanted to return to Siam. The chain of events that was to put them on a collision course with the school began when the dormitory prefect, trying to be as helpful as possible, asked them to give him an account of the events immediately preceding the disappearance of the ring.

As he continued to question them, their stories began to differ. They both agreed that they had gone for a walk on campus in the early evening, returned to the dormitory for dinner, and then discovered the loss of the ring when they went back to their room afterwards. Prince Kridsada claimed that his cousin had worn the ring during the walk and then left it in the room before dinner, contending, therefore, that it must have been stolen during dinner. But Prince Pattandid himself was not so sure on this point, as was evident from the vagueness of his testimony. He was sure that had worn the ring when he went out for the walk but confessed that he could not remember whether or not he had left it in his room during the meal.

This, of course, was crucial to deciding whether the ring had been stolen or lost. Then, when the prefect asked about where they had been on their walk, he discovered that the two princes, drawn by the pleasant evening, had gone through the fence surrounding the Reviewing Mound and had lain down for a while on the grass at the top, an act forbidden by school rules. It was not until the next day, a muggy afternoon with intermittent showers, that the prefect heard their account of what had happened. Nevertheless, he decided that there was only one thing to be done, and he asked the princes to come with him at once so that all three of them could make a thorough search of the top of the mound.

The Reviewing Mound was in a corner of the drill field. Though it was small and undistinguished, the Emperor Meiji had once deigned to review a student parade from its flat, grassy top. And so it had afterwards been made into a memorial of the event, with several of the sakaki trees sacred to Shintoism planted at the top, one of them by the Emperor himself. It was considered the most venerable place at Peers, second only to the sanctuary where Emperor Meiji had planted a sakaki.

Accompanied by the prefect, the two princes passed through the fence again, this time in broad daylight, and climbed to the top of the mound. The grass had been soaked by the drizzle, and the task they faced of searching roughly two hundred square yards of the mound's surface was obviously not going to be an easy one. Since it did not seem adequate to search merely the spot where they had lain down, the prefect decided that they should divide the area into three, with each of them scouring a section. And so with the rain, now increasing somewhat, falling on their backs, they picked through the grass, blade by blade.

Prince Kridsada made little effort to hide his reluctance, and carried out his task with a certain amount of grumbling. Prince Pattanadid, however, being good-natured, began his search more willingly, recognizing that it did, after all, concern his own ring. He started at the bottom of the slope in his section and worked his way upwards with great precision.

He had never taken so close a look at each blade of grass. For nothing less than the most painstaking care would do, because despite the ring's gold setting, its large emerald would be next to invisible in the grass. The drizzle became raindrops on the back of his neck, finally slid under his tight collar and rolled down his back, a sensation that aroused a yearning for the warm monsoons of Siam. The light green at the roots of the grass gave the illusion that a ray of sunshine had broken through, but the sky remained overcast. Here and there, there were small white wildflowers in the grass, their heads drooping under the weight of the rain, but the powdery whiteness of their petals remained as bright as ever. Once Prince Pattanadid's eye was caught by a bright glittering spot under a sawtooth leaf of a tall weed. Sure that his ring could not have lodged there, he nevertheless turned the leaf over to

find a small, brilliantly colored beetle clinging to the underside to escape the rain.

Peering at the grass at such close range made it loom up
under his nose, immense and green, reminding him of the
jungles of his homeland in the rainy season. With his eyes
thus fixed on the grass, he could imagine the gathering
cumulus clouds shining with such white intensity, the sky a
deep azure blue in one quarter but dark and threatening in
another, and he could even hear the violent rumble of thunder.

It was not really the ring that made him willing to expend
such painful effort. He wore himself out searching through
the grass that defied his exertions for the sake of recovering
the image of Princess Chan, however slight the hope of success. He was near to tears.

A group of students on their way to the gymnasium walked
by carrying umbrellas and wearing their sweaters draped over
the shoulders of their gym uniforms. Seeing the activity on
the mound, they stopped to watch.

A rumor about the lost ring had already spread through the
school, but since the students considered it effeminate for a
man to wear a ring, there were few who felt the least sympathy or concern for its loss or for the frantic search. They
grasped its purpose, of course, as soon as they saw the two
princes working their way through the wet grass on hands
and knees. Prince Kridsada's charge of theft had obviously
reached their ears and now they seized the chance to express
their resentment by hurling bitter taunts at the two princes.
But when they caught sight of the prefect getting to his feet
to look in their direction, they were taken aback. When he
requested them quietly to join the hunt, they fell silent,
turned their backs, and scattered in all directions.

The two princes and the prefect, each working from a different direction, had almost met up in the center of the mound,
and so there was no escaping the realization that all their
efforts were likely to prove in vain. The showers were now
over, and some late afternoon sunshine had broken through
the clouds. The wet grass sparkled as it caught the low-slant-

ing rays, and the shadows cast by the leaves made complex patterns on its surface.

Prince Pattanadid thought he saw the unmistakable glint of an emerald in one clump of grass, but when he plunged his wet hands into it, he found nothing but a faint, unsteady gleam, blurred by the dirt, no more than a tangle of wet grass, glowing golden at the roots, with no resemblance at all to the ring.

*

Afterwards, Kiyoaki heard the story of the futile hunt. The prefect had certainly given evidence of goodwill by helping as much as he could, but there was no denying that the search had been an unnecessary humiliation for the two princes. Not too surprisingly, they chose to make an issue of it and so furnished themselves with a good excuse to pack their bags and move to the Imperial Hotel. They confessed to Kiyoaki that they had decided to return to Siam as soon as they could.

When he heard this news from his son, Marquis Matsugae was most distressed. He realized that to allow the two princes to return home in their present mood was to leave them permanently scarred. For the rest of their lives their attitude to Japan would be tinged by bitter memories. At first he tried to mitigate the antagonism that existed between them and the school, but he found that the princes' attitude had hardened to such an extent that there was little hope of any successful mediation at present. He therefore bided his time for the moment, having decided that the first thing was to persuade the princes not to go home, and then to work out the best plan for softening their hostility.

Meanwhile the summer vacation was almost on them. After conferring with Kiyoaki, the Marquis decided to invite the princes to the family villa on the seashore once the vacation had begun. Kiyoaki was to go with them.

31

THE MARQUIS HAD ALREADY given Kiyoaki permission to invite Honda to the villa, and so, on the first day after school ended, the four young men boarded a train at Tokyo station.

Whenever the Marquis himself went to the Kamakura villa, there had to be a huge delegation, led by the major and the chief of police, at the station to greet him with the appropriate honors. Moreover, white sand was hauled up from the beach and scattered along the road from Kamakura station to the villa at Hasé. However, since the Marquis had told the town council that he wanted the four young men to be treated as mere students without any welcome committee whatever, despite the princes' status, they were able to get into rickshaws at the station and enjoy the ride to the villa in privacy.

The narrow winding road was overhung with branches heavy with greenery. As they neared the top of a steep hill, they saw the stone gate of the villa come into view, its name carved in Chinese characters on the right-hand pillar. It was called Chung-nan, from the title of a poem by the Tang poet Wang Wei.

The estate attached to this Japanese Chung-nan covered more than eight acres, taking up an entire wooded ravine that opened onto the beach. Kiyoaki's grandfather had once built a simple reed-thatched cottage there, but after it was destroyed by fire some years previously, his father had immediately seized the opportunity to put up a substantial summer home with twelve guest rooms, of combined Japanese and Western design. The garden, however, which spread out from the terrace on the south side of the house, had been landscaped entirely in the Western style. From this same terrace, one could see the island of Oshima, its volcano glowing at night like a distant bonfire. A walk of no more than five or six minutes through the garden brought one to the Yuigahama beach. In fact the Marquis, with the aid of binoculars, could sit on the terrace and watch the Marquise frolicking in the surf, an incidental diversion that amused him greatly. There was a narrow field of vegetables between the garden and the beach, however, and in order to suppress this element of discord, a line of pines had been planted along the southern edge of the garden. Once these trees were fully grown, they would destroy the uninterrupted view from the garden to the sea, and the Marquis would no longer be able to amuse himself with his binoculars.

On clear summer days, the beauty of the villa's setting was at its peak. The ravine spread out like a fan with the house at its apex, its two ridges bounding the garden on either side: the right-hand one ended in a promontory called Cape Inamuragazaki, and the left-hand one pointed to the island of Iijima.

The sweeping view was unobstructed and made one feel that all it encompassed—sky, land, and the sea embraced by the capes—was part of the Matsugae domain. No images obtruded on its sovereignty save those of the fantastically billowing clouds, the occasional bird, and the ships that passed by far out in the offing. In summer, when the cloud formations were at their peak, the whole thing seemed to be transformed into a huge theater, with the villa for the spectators and the smooth expanse of the bay becoming the vast stage on which the clouds performed their extravagant ballets.

The outside terrace was floored in heavy teak, laid out in checkers. The architect had been against exposing a wooden floor to the ravages of the weather, but he yielded when the Marquis reminded him sharply that the decks of ships were made of wood. From the vantage point of this terrace, Kiyoaki had spent whole days last summer carefully observing each subtle nuance of the shifting clouds. The sunlight became awsome as it shone on the cumulus clouds, towering up over the offing like huge masses of whipped cream, and penetrated their deep, curving hollows. While the areas that lay in shadow resisted the probing sun, its bright rays threw the rugged force of their sculptured outlines into relief. In his imagination, the parts cut off from direct light were totally different in character from those that were dazzlingly exposed. They slumbered on uneventfully, while in contrast their brilliant counterparts fiercely enacted a swiftly unfolding drama of tragic proportions. But there was no place for the human element, and so both slumber and tragedy came to the same thing, an idle game at best.

If he gazed fixedly at the clouds, he noticed no alteration, but if he looked away for a moment, he found that they had changed. Without his realizing it, their heroic mane became ruffled like hair disheveled in sleep. And as long as he kept his eyes on it, this new disorder persisted in just the same slow-moving way.

What had disintegrated? One moment their brilliant white shapes dominated the sky, and the next, they dissolved into something trivial, an enervated banality. Yet their dissolution was a kind of liberation. For as he watched, their scattered remnants gradually reformed and as they did so, they cast strange shadows over the garden as if an army were marshaling its forces in the sky above. Its might first overshadowed the beach and the vegetable field, and then, moving up toward the house, it overran the southern border of the garden. The vivid colors of the leaves and flowers that covered the garden slope, laid out in imitation of Shugakuin Palace, glowed like a mosaic in the dazzling sunlight—maples, sakakis, tea shrubs, dwarf cedars, daphnes, azaleas, camellias, pines, box trees, Chinese black pines, and all the others—and then suddenly it was all in shadow; even the cicada's song was hushed, as though in mourning.

The sunsets were especially beautiful. He imagined that as each one approached, every cloud knew in advance what color

it would take on—scarlet, purple, orange, light green, or something else—and then, under the strain of the moment, that it
paled just before turning to its new shade.

*

"What a beautiful garden! I had no idea that summer
in Japan could be so glorious," Chao P. said, bright-eyed.

As the two brown-skinned princes stood on the terrace
flooded with sunlight, Kiyoaki could not imagine anyone
seeming more at home there. Today, their bleak mood was
clearly gone.

Although he and Honda both thought the sunshine excessive for their taste, to the princes it was no more than pleas-
antly warm and exactly as they liked it. They stood on the
terrace soaking it up as though they could not get enough of
its heat.

"After you have washed and rested a little," Kiyoaki said
to them, "I'll show you around the garden."

"Why bother to rest? Aren't we all four young and energetic?" Kridsada replied.

More than anything else, Kiyoaki thought, more than Princess Chan, the emerald ring, their friends, their school, perhaps what the princes had needed had been sunshine. It
seemed that summer had the power to heal all frustrations,
soothe every grief, restore their lost happiness.

As he was ruminating in this way about the torrid heat of
Siam which he had never experienced, he noticed in himself
too a certain intoxication with the summer that had burst on
them so suddenly. He heard the cicadas singing in the garden.
The coolness of reason had evaporated like cool sweat from
his brow.

The four of them stepped down from the terrace and
gathered around an old sundial that stood in the middle of
the wide lawn around it.

The legend "1716 Passing Shades" was carved in English
on its face. Its upright bronze needle was a fantastic arabesque
of a bird with its outstretched neck pointing directly at the

Roman numeral twelve, just between the markers that desig-
nated northwest and northeast. The shadow it cast was drawing close to three o'clock.

As Honda rubbed his finger against the letter S in the inscription, he thought of asking the princes in which direction
was Siam, but he decided not to take the needless risk of
arousing their homesickness again. At the same time, without meaning to, he shifted his position slightly and blocked
out the sun so that his own shadow overwhelmed the one that
was about to mark three o'clock.

"That's it. That's the secret," said Chao P. when he saw
what Honda had done. "If you did that all day, time would
have to stop. When I get back home, I'm going to have a
sundial set up in the garden. And then on days when I'm
very, very happy, I'll have a servant stand next to it from
morning to night and cover it with his shadow. I'll stop time
passing."

"But he'll die of sunstroke," said Honda, stepping aside to
let the fierce sunlight restore the hour to the dial.

"No, no," replied Kridsada, "our servants can stand all day
in the sun, and it doesn't trouble them in the least. And the
sun at home is probably at least three times as strong as this."

The princes' skin, so richly brown and warm in the sunlight, captured Kiyoaki's imagination. He felt that such skin
must surely seal within itself a cool darkness that constantly
refreshed these young men, like a luxuriant shade tree.

*

He had only to make a casual reference to the enjoyment
to be had from the walking trails in the mountains behind the
villa; and immediately nothing would do but for all four of
them to set out at once to explore, before Honda could wipe
away the sweat brought on by the heat of the garden. Honda,
moreover, was amazed at the sight of the once-indolent
Kiyoaki taking the lead in this enterprise with such energy.

Despite his misgivings, however, when they had made
their way up as far as the ridge, they were met by a delight-

fully cool sea breeze blowing through the shady pine forest, which made them forget the sweat of the climb as they enjoyed a panoramic view of the Yuigahama beach.

Kiyoaki led them along the narrow trail that followed the line of the ridge, and as they tramped energetically over last year's fallen leaves and crashed through the ferns and bamboo grass that nearly choked the path, they felt all the energy of youth. Then all at once, Kiyoaki stopped and pointed to the northwest.

"Look over there," he called to them. "This is the only place from which you can see it."

A collection of shabby, nondescript houses stood in a valley that stretched out below, but towering above and beyond them, the four young men caught sight of the figure of the Great Buddha of Kamakura.

Everything about the image of this Buddha, from his rounded shoulders to the very folds of his robe, was on a grand scale. The face was in profile, and the chest partially visible as it protruded somewhat beyond the graceful lines of the sleeve that flowed smoothly down from the shoulder. The bright sunlight beat upon the glinting bronze of the rounded shoulder and struck brilliant lights from the broad bronze chest. It was already approaching sunset, and the rays caught the bronze snails coiled like hair on the Lord Buddha's head, and each stood out in relief. The long earlobe seemed to hang like dried fruit on a tropical tree.

The princes startled Honda and Kiyoaki by falling to their knees as soon as they saw the statue. With no thought for their freshly creased white linen trousers, they knelt unhesitatingly on the wet, moldering leaves that covered the path and pressed their palms together in reverence toward the distant figure bathed in summer sunlight.

The other two were irreverent enough to exchange a quick glance. Faith such as this was so removed from their experience that they had never even thought of it ever touching their lives. Not that they felt the least inclination to mock the princes' exemplary devotion. But they felt that these two young men, whom they had come to regard as students much like themselves, had suddenly flown away into a world whose ideals and faith were quite alien to them.

 32

THE WALK IN THE MOUNTAINS behind the house was followed by a complete tour of the garden. All this exertion taxed their energy, so that the four of them were finally quite happy to rest for a while in the living room of the villa. There they enjoyed the sea breeze from the terrace while they sipped lemonade brought from Yokohama and cooled in the villa's well. They were soon ready to set off again, however. This time they gave in to the impulse for a quick swim before sunset and hurried to their rooms to dress for the occasion according to their individual taste. Kiyoaki and Honda put on the red loincloths used for swimming at Peers, and over them they threw the thin cotton tunics decorated with feather-stitching that completed the uniform. Then they put on straw hats and would have been on their way to the beach if they had not been delayed by the two princes. When these two finally appeared, they were dressed in striped English bathing suits that showed their brown shoulders to advantage.

Kiyoaki and Honda had been friends for a long time, but Kiyoaki had never before invited him to the family villa during the summer, though he came once in the fall to gather chestnuts. This was therefore the first time that he had gone swimming with Kiyoaki since they both were boys together at the school villa at Katasé beach, when their present intimacy had hardly begun.

The four of them plunged impetuously down the garden

slope, broke through the border of young pines, and dashed across the narrow vegetable field onto the beach.

Here Honda and Kiyoaki paused to perform the prescribed pre-swimming calisthenics, a formality that made the two princes double up with laughter. Perhaps this was a mild form of retaliation against the two Japanese for not having joined them in kneeling to the distant Great Buddha. In the eyes of the princes, this modern, totally self-centered penance was the funniest thing in the world.

However, the very nature of their laughter showed that they were feeling more at ease than ever before; not for a long time had they looked so cheerful. After they had enjoyed themselves in the water to their hearts' content, Kiyoaki felt that he could forget about playing host for a while; the princes paired off to talk in their own language, and he and Honda talked Japanese until all four fell asleep on the beach.

The setting sun was blurred by a thin film of cloud. It had lost much of its earlier heat, but this was a pleasant time to lie in it, especially for someone whose skin was as white as Kiyoaki's. Dressed only in his red loincloth, he threw his wet body down on the sand and lay face up, his eyes shut.

To his left, Honda sat cross-legged in the sand staring out at the waters of the bay. Though the sea was calm, its rolling waves fascinated him. As he watched, the crest of the sea seemed to be level with his eyes. How strange, he thought, that it should come to an abrupt end and give way to the land right in front of him.

He kept pouring dry sand from one palm to the other. When he had spilled a good part of it in the process, he reached down automatically and began again with a fresh handful, his thoughts completely taken up with the sea.

It ended a few feet from where he sat. The sea, broad and vast, with all its mighty force, ended right there before his eyes. Be it the edge of time or space, there is nothing so awe-inspiring as a border. To be here at this place with his three companions, at this marvelous border between land and sea, struck him as being very similar to being alive as one age was ending and another beginning, like being part of a great moment in history. And then too the tide of their own era, in which he and Kiyoaki lived, also had to have an appointed time to ebb, a shore on which to break, a limit beyond which it could not go.

The sea ended right there before his eyes. As he watched the final surge of each wave as it drained into the sand, the final thrust of mighty power that had come down through countless centuries, he was struck by the pathos of it all. At that very point, a grand pan-oceanic enterprise that spanned the world went awry and ended in annihilation.

But still, he thought, this final frustration was a gentle, soothing one. A small, lacy frill, the wave's last farewell, escaped from disintegration at the last moment before merging into the glistening wet sand as the wave itself withdrew, and vanished into the sea.

Starting a good way out in the offing at a point where the whitecaps thinned out, the incoming waves went through four or five stages, each of which was visible at any given moment—a swelling, a cresting, a breaking, the dissolution of its force and an ebbing—a constantly recurring process.

The breaking wave let out an angry roar as it showed its smooth, dark green belly. The roar tailed off to a cry and the cry to a whisper. The charging line of huge white stallions yielded place to a line of smaller ones until the furious horses gradually disappeared altogether, leaving nothing but those last imprints of pounding hooves on the beach.

Two remnants, streaming in from left and right, collided roughly, spread like a fan, and sank into the bright mirror of the sand's surface. At that moment, the reflection in the mirror came to life, catching the next white-crested wave just as it was about to come crashing down, a sharp vertical image that sparkled like a row of icicles.

Beyond the ebb, where other waves kept rolling in one after the other, none of them formed smooth white crests.

They charged at full power again and again, aiming for their goal with determination. But when Honda looked out to sea in the distance he could not escape the feeling that the apparent strength of these waves that beat upon the shore was really no more than a diluted, weakened, final dispersion.

The farther out one looked, the darker the color of the water, until it finally became a deep blue-green. It was as if the innocuous ingredients of the offshore water became more and more condensed by the increasing pressure of the water as it got deeper, its green intensified over and over again to produce an eternal blue-green substance, pure and impenetrable as fine jade, that extended to the horizon. Though the sea might seem vast and deep, this substance was the very stuff of the ocean. Something that was crystallized into blue beyond the shallow, frivolous overlapping of the waves—that was the sea.

*

His staring and his thoughts were at length enough to tire both his eyes and his mind, and he turned to look at Kiyoaki, who was assuredly sound asleep by now. The light skin on his handsome graceful body seemed all the whiter in contrast to the red loincloth that was all he had on. Just above the loincloth, on his pale stomach that rose and fell lightly with his breathing, there had lodged some sand, now dry, and some tiny fragments of seashell. Since he had raised his left arm to put it behind his head, his left side, that ordinarily was hidden, lay revealed to Honda, and behind the left nipple, which made him think of a tiny cherry-blossom bud, a cluster of three small black moles caught his eyes. There was something odd about them, he felt. Why should Kiyoaki's flesh be marked like that? Though they had been friends for so long, he had never seen them before, and now they embarrassed him too much for him to keep looking at them, as though Kiyoaki had abruptly confessed to a secret better left untold. But when he closed his eyes, he saw the three black moles come into focus against his eyelids, as clear as the shapes of three distant birds flying across the evening sky, so brilliantly lit up by the setting sun. In his imagination he saw them draw closer, turn into birds with flapping wings, and then pass overhead.

When he opened his eyes again, a light sound was coming from Kiyoaki's well-formed nose, and his teeth glistened wet and pure white through his slightly parted lips. Despite himself, Honda's eyes fell on the moles on Kiyoaki's side again. This time he thought that they looked like some grains of sand that had embedded themselves in his white skin.

The dry area of the beach ended right at their feet, and here and there the waves had splashed up beyond their usual limit and left contracted patterns of wet sand behind them, a sort of bas-relief that preserved the trace of the wave. Stones, shells, and withered leaves were embedded here too, for all the world like ancient fossils, and the smallest pebble among them was backed by its own rivulet of wet sand to prove how it had fought the receding wave.

And there were more than stones, shells, and withered leaves. Tangles of brown algae, fragments of wood, pieces of straw, and even orange peelings had been cast up and lay fixed in the sand. He thought it possible that some fine wet grains might also have worked their way up into the white skin that stretched taut over Kiyoaki's side.

Since he found this idea very disturbing, he tried to think of some way to brush the grains away without waking Kiyoaki. But as he continued to watch, he realized that the black marks were moving in such a free and natural way with the rise and fall of his chest that they could not be foreign matter. They were part of him and so could be nothing other than the black moles he had first taken them to be.

He felt that they were a kind of betrayal of Kiyoaki's physical elegance.

Perhaps Kiyoaki sensed the intensity of his gaze, because he suddenly opened his eyes, catching Honda's stare directly. And then he raised his head and began to speak abruptly, as if to prevent his flustered friend from escaping him.

"Would you do something for me?"

"Yes."

"I didn't really come here to play nursemaid to the princes. That's a good excuse, but actually I want to give everyone the impression that I'm not in Tokyo. Do you see what I mean?"

"I had guessed that you were thinking something of the sort."

"What I want to do is to leave you and the princes here sometimes and go back there without anyone knowing. I can't go for as much as three days without her. So it will be up to you to smooth things over with the princes while I'm gone and also to have a good story ready just on the off chance that someone telephones from Tokyo. Tonight I'm going to go third-class on the last train and I'll be back on the first one tomorrow morning. So will you do it for me?"

"I'll do it," said Honda emphatically.

Delighted at his friend's firm agreement, Kiyoaki reached up to shake his hand before he spoke again.

"I suppose your father will be attending the state funeral for Prince Arisugawa."

"Yes, I think so."

"It was good of the Prince to die when he did. As I heard just yesterday, the Toinnomiyas have no choice but to postpone the betrothal ceremony for a while."

This remark reminded Honda that Kiyoaki's love for Satoko was inextricably bound up with the interests of the nation as a whole, and the danger of it sent a shiver through him.

At this point their conversation was interrupted by the two princes who came running over in such enthusiastic haste that they almost fell over each other. Kridsada spoke first, struggling both to regain his breath and to express himself in his scanty Japanese.

"Do you know what Chao P. and I were talking about just now?" he asked. "We were discussing the transmigration of souls."

33

WHEN THEY HEARD THIS, the two young Japanese spontaneously glanced at each other, an instinctive reaction whose significance was lost on Kridsada, who was an impetuous sort, not given to gauging his listeners' expressions. Chao P., on the other hand, had learned a great deal from six months of dealing with the tensions brought on by living in a foreign environment. And now, although his skin was too dark to betray anything as obvious as a blush, he was clearly hesitant about continuing such a conversation. Nevertheless, he did so, using his fluent English, perhaps because he wished to appear sophisticated.

"You see, when Kri and I were children, we used to hear all sorts of stories from the *Jataka Sutra*. Our nurses would tell us how even the Lord Buddha underwent many rebirths while he was still a bodhisattva—as a golden swan, a quail, a monkey, a great stag, and so on. So we were speculating just now as to what we might have been in our previous existences. However, I'm afraid that we didn't agree at all. He maintained that he had been a deer and I a monkey. And I insisted that it was just the other way around: he was the monkey and I the deer. But what do you say? We'll leave it to you."

Whichever way they answered, they ran the risk of offending somebody, so they just smiled, hoping that would serve as a reply. Then Kiyoaki, wanting to turn the conversation to other matters, said that he knew nothing about the *Jataka Sutra* and he wondered if the princes would be kind enough to tell him and Honda one of the stories from it.

"We'd be glad to," said Chao P. "There's the one about

the golden swan, for example. It took place when the Lord Gautama was a bodhisattva, during his second reincarnation. As you know, a bodhisattva is someone who voluntarily travels the road of mortification and suffering before entering into the full enlightenment of buddhahood. And in his previous existence the Lord Gautama himself was a bodhisattva. The austerities they practice are the works of *paramita*, one's good deeds to others, by means of which one crosses from this sphere to the sphere of total enlightenment. As a bodhisattva, Buddha is said to have lavished abundant grace on mankind. He was reincarnated in many guises and there are all sorts of stories about the good works he performed.

"For example, in very ancient times, he was born to a Brahmin family. He married a woman of another Brahmin family and after having three daughters by her, he died, forcing his bereaved wife and daughters to make their home with strangers.

"But after his death as a Brahmin, the bodhisattva took on another life in the womb of a golden swan. And he carried within him the knowledge that would in due course make him fully aware of his previous existence. And so the bodhisattva grew into an adult swan, covered in gold feathers and unrivaled in beauty. When he glided over the water, he glowed like the rising full moon. And when he flew through the forest, the very leaves that he brushed looked like a golden basket. And when he rested on a branch, it seemed as though the tree had borne some fabulous golden fruit.

"The swan came to realize that he had been a man in his previous existence and also that his wife and children were compelled to live with strangers, eking out their existence by doing whatever work they could find.

" 'Any one of my feathers,' he said to himself one day, 'could be hammered out into a sheet of gold and sold. And so, from time to time, I'll give a feather to my poor companions whom I've left behind to lead such hard lives in the world of men.'

"And so the swan appeared at the window of the house where his wife and daughters of times gone by were living.

And when he saw how wretched their condition was, he was overcome with pity.

"Meanwhile, his wife and daughters were amazed at the sight of the glittering figure of the swan on their window ledge.

" 'What a beautiful bird!' they cried. 'Where have you come from?'

" 'I was once your husband and father. After I died, I came to life again in the womb of a golden swan. And now I have come to change your poor lives into ones of happiness and plenty.'

"So saying, the swan dropped one of its feathers and flew off. Afterwards he came back at regular intervals and left a feather in the same way, and soon life had greatly improved for the mother and her three daughters.

"One day, however, the mother spoke to the girls.

" 'We can't trust that swan,' she said to them. 'Even if he's really your father, who knows if he might stop coming here one day? So next time he comes, let's pluck every one of his feathers.'

" 'Mother, how cruel!' said the girls, very much opposed to this.

"Nevertheless, the next time the swan appeared at the window, the greedy woman pounced on him, took him in both hands, and plucked out every single one of his feathers. But strangely enough, each gold feather turned as white as a heron feather as she pulled it out. Still undaunted, his former wife then took the helpless swan and thrust him into a large empty container and fed him while she waited doggedly for his golden feathers to grow again. But when the feathers did appear, they were ordinary white ones. And once they had grown, he flew off and his shape grew smaller and smaller in the sky until it became a white dot lost in the clouds, never to be seen again.

"And that was one of the stories that our nurses used to tell us from the *Jataka Sutra*."

Honda and Kiyoaki were surprised to find that many of the

fairy tales that had been told to them were very similar to the prince's story. The conversation then turned into a discussion of reincarnation itself and whether or not it was credible as a doctrine.

Since Kiyoaki and Honda had never talked about anything like this before, they were naturally somewhat perplexed. Kiyoaki glanced at Honda with a questioning look in his eyes. Usually headstrong, he always began to look forlorn whenever abstract discussions took place. His look now urged Honda to do something, as if he were prodding him lightly with silver spurs.

"If there is such a thing as reincarnation," Honda began, betraying a certain eagerness, "I'd be very much in favor of it if it were the kind in your story, with the man himself being aware of his previous existence. But if it's a case of a man's personality coming to an end and his self-awareness being lost so that there's absolutely no trace of them in his next life, and if a completely new personality and a totally different self-awareness come into being, well, in that case I think that various reincarnations extending over a period of time are no more significantly linked to one another than the lives of all the individuals who happen to be alive at the same given moment. In other words, I feel that in such a case the concept of reincarnation would be practically meaningless. Something has to be passed on in transmigration, but I don't see how we can take any number of separate and distinct existences, each with its own self-awareness, and bracket them together as one, claiming that a single consciousness unites them. Right now, each one of us has no memory at all of even a single previous existence. And so it's obvious that it would be pointless to try to produce any proof of transmigration. There's only one way that it could be proved: if we had a self-awareness so independent that it could stand aside from both this life and previous lives and view them objectively. But as it is, each man's consciousness is limited to the past, the present, or the future of that single life. In the midst of the turmoil of history, each one of us builds his own little shelter of self-awareness

and we can never leave it. Buddhism seems to hold out a
middle way, but I have my doubts: is this middle way an
organic concept which a human being is capable of grasping?

"But to go back just a bit. . . . Granted that all human
concepts are mere illusion, in order to distinguish the various
illusions arising from other reincarnations from the illusion
of the present reincarnation of that same life, you must nevertheless be able to observe them all from a thoroughly independent viewpoint. It's only when one stands aside in this
way that the reality of reincarnation would be apparent. But
when one is in the midst of a reincarnated existence oneself,
the whole must remain an eternal riddle. Moreover, since this
independent standpoint is probably what is called full enlightenment, only the man who has transcended reincarnation can
grasp its reality. And wouldn't it then be a case of finally
understanding it at a time when it was no longer relevant?

"There is an abundance of death in our lives. We never
lack reminders—funerals, cemeteries, withered commemora-
tive bouquets, memories of the dead, deaths of friends, and
then the anticipation of our own death. Who knows? Perhaps
in their own way the dead make a great deal of life. Perhaps
they're always looking in our direction from their own land—
at our towns, our schools, the smokestacks of our factories, at
each of us who has passed one by one back from death into
the land of the living.

"What I want to say is that perhaps reincarnation is nothing more than a concept that reverses the way that we, the
living, ordinarily view death, a concept that expresses life
as seen from the viewpoint of the dead. Do you see?"

"But how is it," replied Chao P. quietly, "that certain
thoughts and ideals are transmitted to the world after a man's
death?"

"That's a different problem from reincarnation," Honda said
emphatically, with a trace of the impatience to which intel-
ligent young men are susceptible showing in his voice.

"Why is it different?" asked Chao P. in the same gentle
tone. "It seems that you are willing to admit that the same

sense of self-awareness might inhabit various bodies successively over a period of time. Why then do you object so strongly to differing senses of self-awareness inhabiting the same body over a similar period of time?"

"The same body for a cat and a human being? According to what you said before, it was a matter of becoming a man, a swan, a quail, a deer, and so on."

"Yes, according to the concept of reincarnation, the same body. Even though the flesh itself might differ. As long as the same illusion persists, there is no difficulty in calling it the same body. However, rather than do that, perhaps it would be better to call it the same vital current.

"I lost that emerald ring that was so rich in memories for me. It wasn't a living thing, of course, and so it won't be reborn. But still, the loss of something is significant, and I think that loss is the necessary source of a new manifestation. Some night I might see my emerald ring appear as a green star somewhere in the sky."

The prince abruptly abandoned the problem, apparently overcome with sadness.

"Chao P., maybe the ring was actually a living thing that underwent a secret transformation," Kridsada responded with earnest naïveté, "and then it ran off somewhere on legs of its own."

"Then, round about now it might be reborn as someone as beautiful as Princess Chan," Chao P. said, now completely absorbed in thinking about his loved one. "People keep telling me in their letters that she's well, but why don't I hear anything at all from her herself? Perhaps they're all trying to protect me from something."

Honda, meantime, had ignored the prince's last words, as he was lost in thought about the strange paradox that Chao P. had brought up a few minutes earlier. One could certainly think of a man not in terms of a body but as a single vital current. And this would allow one to grasp the concept of existence as dynamic and on-going, rather than as static. Just as he had said, there was no difference between a single consciousness possessing various vital currents in succession, and a single vital current animating various consciousnesses in succession. For life and self-awareness would fuse into a whole. And if one were then to extrapolate this theory of the unity of life and self-awareness, the whole sea of life with its infinity of currents—the whole vast process of transmigration called *Samsara* in Sanskrit—would be possessed by a single consciousness.

While Honda organized his ideas, the beach had gradually been growing darker, and Kiyoaki became absorbed in building a sand temple with Kridsada. The sand did not lend itself to molding the tall pointed towers and the upswept roof-corner tiling that distinguished Siamese temples. Nevertheless Kridsada skillfully added wet sand and built up the slender peaks, and carefully molded up the corners of the roof as if he were drawing a woman's dark, slender fingers from her sleeve. They curved out into the air for an instant, and then as soon as they dried out, the black sand-fingers twisted convulsively, crumbled, and fell down.

Honda and Chao P. stopped talking to watch the others playing with the sand in childlike glee. Their sand temple needed lanterns. All the care they had lavished on the fine detail of the facade and the tall windows now went for nothing, for darkness had already reduced the temple to a small, dim outline silhouetted against the white foam of the breakers, which seemed to reflect what lingering light there was, much as the last flickers of life show in the eyes of a dying man.

Unnoticed, the sky over their heads had become filled with stars, dominated by the brilliance of the Milky Way. Honda did not know much about them, but even he could make out the Weaver Maid and her lover the Herd Boy, separated by the broad stream of the Milky Way, and also the Northern Cross of the Swan constellation, which stretched its huge wings in flight as it acted as go-between for the two lovers.

The roar of the waves seemed to have grown much louder than it had been during the day. The beach and the water had each been part of their own sphere in daylight, but now they seemed to have merged under cover of darkness. The inconceivable array of stars above overwhelmed the four young men. To be surrounded by such majestic massive power was like being shut up within a vast koto.

Indeed, it was precisely that. They themselves were like four grains of sand that had somehow found their way into its base, an enormous world of darkness, outside which all was light. Above them were stretched thirteen strings from one end to the other. And fingers of a whiteness that was beyond words were touching these strings, making the koto come alive with the grand and solemn music of the spheres, its immense vibrations shaking the four grains of sand within.

A breeze came in off the night sea. The salty fragrance of the tide and the smell of seaweed thrown up on the beach made their bodies tingle with emotion, bare to the cool night air. The sea breeze, heavy with the smell of salt, coiled against their naked flesh, but made them burn rather than shiver.

"Well, it's time we went back," said Kiyoaki abruptly.

It was meant, of course, as a reminder that it was time for them to get ready for dinner. Honda, however, knew that Kiyoaki's mind was fixed on the departure of the last train for Tokyo.

 34

KIYOAKI MADE SECRET TRIPS to Tokyo at least once every three days, and on his return, he would give Honda all the details of what had gone on. The Toinnomiyas had indeed postponed the betrothal ceremony, but that by no means meant that there was any significant obstacle to Satoko's mar-

riage to the young prince. She was, in fact, often invited to
their home, and the Prince's father, His Imperial Highness
himself, had started treating her with cordial affection.

Kiyoaki was not at all satisfied with the way things stood.
Now he was thinking of having Satoko down to Kamakura to
spend the night at the villa, and he asked Honda if he had any
idea about how to carry out such a dangerous plan. But on
even the most cursory reflection, one grave difficulty after another was brought to light.

One hot sultry night, as Kiyoaki was settling into an uneasy sleep, he began to dream. It was quite unlike his previous
experiences. If one flounders in the shallows of sleep, wading
where the water is tepid and full of all sorts of flotsam that
has come in from deeper water to pile up with the land debris
in a tangled heap, one is liable to slash one's feet.

Kiyoaki was standing in the middle of a road that led
through open fields. For some reason he was wearing a white
cotton kimono and matching *hakama*, a costume he had never
worn, and he was armed with a hunting rifle. The land around
him was rolling country, but it was not deserted. He could
see a cluster of farmhouses up ahead, and a cyclist passed
him on the road. A strange, somber light permeated the entire scene. It was no brighter than the final traces of daylight,
and was so diffuse that it could more easily have sprung from
the ground rather than the sky, for the grass in the rolling
fields gave off a green glow from its very roots and bathed the
bicycle in a hazy silver gleam as it vanished into the distance.
He looked down and saw that even the thick thongs of his
clogs and the veins of his bare feet stood out with brilliant,
uncanny clarity.

At that moment, the light filmed over and a huge flight of
birds appeared in the sky. When they reached a point above
his head, filling the air with their squawking cries, he aimed
his rifle upward and pulled the trigger. He did not fire in
cold blood. It was rather that he was seized by an unfathomable anger and grief, and he fired, aiming not so much at the
birds as at the great blue eye of the sky itself.

The whole flock plummeted earthward in a single mass, a tornado of screams and blood that linked heaven and earth. Countless shrieking birds, their blood spurting out, tumbled down in an unending stream, gathered into one thick column that formed the cone of the whirlwind. The cascade of blood and fury never slackened.

As he watched, the whirlwind suddenly solidified before his eyes and became a giant tree that stretched to the heavens. Its trunk was a forbidding rust color, devoid of leaves or branches. As soon as this giant tree took shape and the screaming died away, the same somber glow that had lit up the fields before the storm spread out over them once more. Down the road appeared a new silver bicycle without a rider and made its way unsteadily toward him.

He was proud to have been the one to sweep away the obstacle that had blocked the light of the sun.

But then in the distance he saw a group coming his way along the road. They were all dressed in white just as he was. They checked their solemn, measured advance a few yards away. He saw that each of them carried a shining sakaki branch in his hand.

They pointed their branches toward him and began to wave them in the rite of purification, the rustle of leaves echoing clearly in his ears. As they did so, he was startled to recognize the face of his former retainer Iinuma in their midst. Iinuma himself spoke to him.

"You are heedless and intractable. You have proved it beyond all question."

He looked down at his chest when Iinuma spoke. A necklace of crescent-shaped stones, dark maroon and purple, now hung around his neck. The stones were cold and as they touched his skin they sent a chill through his body. His chest felt like a flat, heavy rock.

Then the white-clad group pointed to the tree, and when he looked at it, he saw that the massive trunk of dead birds was now covered with branches, all of which were laden with glossy green leaves. The whole tree was a vivid green, down to its lowest branches.

Then he woke up.

Since the dream had been so extraordinary, he reached out to open his dream journal, which he had neglected for some time now. He began to write, trying to record the events as accurately and as objectively as he could. Even now that he was awake, however, he was torn by the fierceness and antagonism of the dream. He felt as if he had just returned from battle.

*

Kiyoaki's problem was to bring Satoko from Tokyo in the dead of night and get her home again by dawn. A carriage was no good. Nor was the train. A rickshaw would be quite out of the question. Somehow he had to get the use of a car.

Obviously it could not be one belonging to anyone who knew the Matsugaes. And, even more important, anyone in the Ayakuras' circle had to be ruled out. And the car would have to be driven by someone completely ignorant of the situation and the people involved.

The villa area was large enough, but precautions still had to be taken to avoid a chance meeting between Satoko and the princes. Kiyoaki and Honda had no idea whether or not the princes were aware of the circumstances of her engagement, but even if they were not, a meeting could only lead to disaster.

Without the least experience in such things, Honda had to find a way through these difficulties somehow. For he had promised Kiyoaki to see to it that Satoko would be able to come down from Tokyo and return in safety.

As he began to size up the problem, he thought of a friend of his named Itsui, the eldest son of a wealthy commercial family. Since Itsui was the only one in his class at Peers who had his own car to use as he liked, Honda had no choice but to go up to Tokyo to visit him in Kojimachi and ask if he would lend him the Ford and a driver for a night.

High-living Itsui, whose career at Peers continually veered toward the shoals of academic shipwreck, was astounded. That the class genius, who was notorious for his sobriety and application moreover, should come to him with such a request! When he had recovered a little, he decided to make the most of the opportunity, and so with no more arrogance than befitted the occasion, he said that if Honda would tell him honestly why he wanted the car, he might be willing to lend it to him.

With that, Honda began to stutter through the confession he had concocted for the loutish Itsui's benefit, and as he did so, was conscious of an unaccustomed and pleasurable sensation. This was provoked by the rapt expression of total belief on Itsui's face; he obviously took Honda's stumbling manner not as an indication of an outright lie, but as testimony to his classmate's brooding sense of shame.

A man may be hard to persuade by rational argument while he is easily swayed by a display of passion, even if it is feigned. Honda was amused at the spectacle, but his amusement was tinged with disgust. He wondered if Kiyoaki had used him in much the same way as he was using Itsui.

"Well, you are turning out to be altogether different from what I imagined. I never thought I'd see this side of you. But you're still being secretive. Won't you at least tell me her name?"

"Fusako," said Honda, spontaneously coming up with the name of the second cousin he hadn't seen in months.

"I see. So Matsugae is going to provide a place to spend the night and I'm going to provide the car. And in return, when the exams come round, you'll remember old Itsui, won't you?" he said, bowing his head in mock supplication that was still meant in earnest.

The light of friendship shone in his eyes. Despite Honda's awesome brain, Itsui now felt on a par with him in many respects. He was vindicated in his unimaginative view of human nature.

"After all, people are all alike," he said, summing it up, his voice expressing the fact that he felt at one with the world, which was exactly the state of mind Honda had been intent on inducing from the beginning.

And so, thanks to Kiyoaki, Honda could soon expect to enjoy a romantic reputation that any boy of nineteen would envy. All in all, this transaction would benefit each of them: Kiyoaki, Honda, and also Itsui.

Itsui's car was a 1912 Ford, the newest model. It was one of the first equipped with a self-starter, the recent invention that had eliminated the nuisance of the chauffeur having to get out each time it happened to stall. It was the ordinary Model T, with a two-speed transmission, painted black with a crimson line around the doors. The driver's seat was open and the rear enclosed, an arrangement that seemed to preserve something of the air of a carriage. A speaking tube in the back seat led to a trumpet-shaped device next to the driver's ear. A rack fastened onto the roof, besides holding a spare tire, could also carry baggage. The car seemed altogether capable of making a long journey.

Mori, the driver, had been the Itsuis' coachman and had learned his new trade from a master driver. He had pointedly arranged for the man to accompany him to the police station to get his license. Every time Mori ran into a difficult question on the written examination, he went into the lobby to consult with his master before returning to the examination room to continue.

Honda went to Itsui's house very late at night to borrow the car. In order to conceal Satoko's background from Mori as much as he could, he had him park the car near a boarding house for military officers where they waited until Satoko and Tadeshina appeared according to plan, arriving inconspicuously in a rickshaw. Kiyoaki had hoped that Tadeshina would not make the trip to Kamakura, but she could not possibly come even if she wanted to, for it was up to her to stay behind and pretend that Satoko spent the night fast asleep in her room, a task of crucial importance. Her face betrayed her worry. She cautioned Satoko at great length before finally surrendering her to Honda's care.

"I'll call you Fusako in front of the chauffeur," he whispered in her ear.

Mori started the Ford with a blast that shattered the midnight silence of the residential neighborhood.

Satoko's calm and resolution surprised Honda. She was in Western clothes, and the white dress she had chosen seemed to enhance her air of quiet determination.

*

Riding through the night like this in the company of the woman claimed by a friend was an odd experience for Honda. There he sat as the car bounced over the rough road, friendship personified, while the scent of Satoko's perfume wafted around him in the summer night.

She belonged to another man. Her very femininity, moreover, seemed to be mocking him. The unprecedented trust that Kiyoaki had shown in him made him more sharply aware than ever before of the cold, subtle poison that permeated their relationship. His friend's contempt and trust were as closely linked as a fine leather glove and the hand inside it. But Kiyoaki had an aura about him that made Honda forgive him.

The only way he could cope with contempt of this sort was to hold onto a belief in his own nobility, and this he did with moderation rather than with the blind traditionalism of so many young men. This meant that he would never come to think of himself as ugly, as Iinuma did. For if this ever happened, there would be nothing left but for him to become Kiyoaki's slave.

Although the breeze blowing in through the window naturally ruffled her hair, Satoko maintained her poise throughout the trip. Kiyoaki's name had become a sort of taboo word between them, quite of its own accord. And the name "Fusako" served as a mild, fictional term of endearment.

*

The return trip was quite different. "Oh, there's something I forgot to tell Kiyo," she said soon after they had left
the villa. But if they turned back, there would be no hope of
her getting home before the early summer dawn.

"Could I tell him for you?" Honda asked.

"Well . . ." Satoko hesitated. Then she seemed to make
up her mind, and gave him the message: "Please tell him this:
Tadeshina talked with Yamada, the Matsugaes' steward,
some time ago, and she's found out that Kiyo was telling a lie.
She discovered that he actually tore up the letter he was pretending still to have a long time ago in Yamada's presence.
But . . . tell him not to worry about it. Tadeshina has re-
signed herself to everything. She said she would keep her
eyes shut. Would you please pass that on to Kiyo?"

Honda memorized it as she spoke, and didn't ask any questions about its cryptic meaning. From then on, impressed perhaps by his good manners, she became very talkative.

"You've done all this for his sake, haven't you, Mr. Honda?
Kiyo should think himself the luckiest man in the world to
have a friend like you. You see, we women have no real friends
at all."

Satoko's eyes still burned with passion, but her coiffure
was in perfect order, with not a hair out of place. When he
did not reply, she bent her head, and after a time, spoke in a
subdued voice.

"But Mr. Honda . . . I know what you must think of me
. . . What else am I but a slut?"

"Don't talk like that," he replied with considerable force.
He certainly had not been thinking of her with such contempt,
but even so, her words had accidentally hit a nerve with uncanny accuracy.

He had gone without a night's sleep to be loyal and fulfill
the duty with which he had been entrusted, of bringing Satoko down from Tokyo, turning her over to Kiyoaki, and now

taking charge of her again to get her back. But his real source of pride was in keeping himself emotionally uninvolved. Nothing good would come of that sort of thing. It was a gravely dangerous situation, for which he was sufficiently responsible already.

When he had stood watching Kiyoaki take Satoko by the hand and run down through the shadows of the moonlit garden to the beach, he had felt that he too was sinning by helping them. But if it was sin, it was also indescribably beautiful; a recurrent image of loveliness running away from him and disappearing.

"You're right," said Satoko. "I shouldn't talk like that at all. I can't think of what I've done as being something nasty. Why is that? Kiyo and I have committed a terrible sin, but I still don't feel defiled in any way. In fact I feel as if I'd been purified. You know, when I saw those pines by the beach tonight, I knew that I'd never see them again no matter how long I lived. And when I heard the sound of the breeze that blew through them, I knew that I'd never hear that again as long as I lived. But every moment I was there felt so pure that now I have no regrets about anything at all."

As she spoke, she tried to convey something to Honda, some essence of everything that happened between her and her lover during their meetings, each of which had felt like the final one—she longed to throw discretion aside and try to make Honda understand by telling him how on this last night, in the midst of such a tranquil, natural setting, she and Kiyoaki had soared to dazzling heights that were almost terrifying. But it was the kind of experience—like death, like the glow of a jewel, like the beauty of a sunset—that is almost impossible to convey to others.

*

Kiyoaki and Satoko wandered over the beach, trying to avoid the uncomfortably dazzling brightness of the moon. Now, in the middle of the night, there was no trace of human life along the deserted shore, apart from a beached fishing

boat, whose tall prow cast a black shadow on the sand. Because of the brilliant moonlight all around, it seemed to offer
a reassuring darkness. The moon's rays washed over the boat,
making its planks glisten like bleached bones. When Kiyoaki
rested his hand against the side for a moment, his skin seemed
to become translucent in the moonlight.

They embraced immediately in the shadow of the boat as
the sea breeze swirled around them. She hardly ever wore
Western clothes, and now hated the glaring white of her
dress. Forgetting the whiteness of her skin, she had only one
thought: to tear the dress off as quickly as possible and hide
herself in the darkness.

No one was likely to see them, but the rays of moonlight,
infinitely fragmented over the surface of the sea, were like
millions of eyes. She gazed up at the clouds suspended in the
sky and the stars that seemed to graze their edges. She could
feel Kiyoaki's small, firm nipples touching hers, brushing
against them playfully, then finally pressing against them,
pushing down into the rich abundance of her breasts. It was
a touch far more intimate than a kiss, something like the playful caress of a young animal. An intense sweetness hovered
on the edge of her awareness. The unexpected familiarity
when the very edges, the extremities of their bodies brushed
together made her think of the stars sparkling among the
clouds, even though her eyes were closed.

From there it was a direct path to a joy as profound as the
sea. But even as she felt herself dissolving gradually into the
darkness, she felt afraid that this was nothing more than a
shadow that was dependent in turn on the fishing boat beside
them. They were not lying in the protection of a solid structure or a rocky ridge, but of something fortuitous, that in a
few brief hours might be far out to sea. Had the boat not happened to be beached there at that moment, its heavy shadow
would have been no more real than a ghost. She was afraid
that this huge old fishing boat might begin to slide noiselessly
across the sand even now and plunge into the water and sail
away. To follow its shadow, to remain forever within it, she

herself would have to become the sea. And at that moment, in a single great surge, she did.

Everything that framed the two of them—the moonlit sky, the sparkling water, the breeze that blew across the sandy beach to rustle the pines at its edge—all these boded destruction. Just beyond the merest flicker of time there boomed a monstrous roar of negation. Its message was carried in the sound of the pines. She felt that she and Kiyoaki were hemmed in, observed, guarded by an unforgiving spirit, just as a single drop of balm that has fallen into a bowl of water has nothing to sustain it but the water itself. This water was black, vast, silent, and the single drop of balm floated in a world of total isolation.

That "No!" was all-embracing. Was it a creature of the night—or the approaching dawn? To them it seemed incomprehensible. But even though it hovered threateningly over them from moment to moment, it had not yet struck at them directly.

They both sat up. Their heads were just out of the shadow now and the sinking moon shone directly into their faces. She felt that it was somehow the emblem of their transgression, fixed there so bright and full and conspicuous in the sky.

The beach was still deserted. They stood up to fetch their clothes, which they had placed in the bottom of the boat. Each of them stared at the other, at the remnant of darkness that was the black area just below their white bellies so brilliantly lit by the moon. Although it lasted only for a moment, they gazed with intense concentration.

When they had dressed, Kiyoaki sat dangling his legs over the edge of the boat.

"You know," he said, "if we had everyone's blessing, we would probably never dare to do what we've done."

"You are awful, Kiyo. So that's what you really want!" she replied in mock affront. Their banter was affectionate enough, but it had an indefinably gritty taste. They sensed that the irrevocable end of their happiness was not far away. She was still sitting in the sand, hiding in the shadow of the boat. His

foot, shining in the moonlight, hung in the air in front of her.
She reached out, took it in her hand, and kissed his toes.

*

"I suppose it's un-called-for—my telling you all this. But
you see, there's no one else I could even think of telling. I
know that I'm doing something terrible. But please don't say
anything against it, because I do realize that it will come to
an end sometime. But until then, I want to live each day as it
comes. Because there's nothing else to be done."

"Then you are quite prepared for whatever may happen?"
Honda asked, his voice unable to conceal the deep pity he felt.

"Yes, I'm quite ready."

"Matsugae is too, I think."

"That's why it's not at all right for him to involve you so
deeply in our problems."

Honda suddenly felt an unaccountable desire to understand
this woman. It was his subtle form of revenge. If she intended to assign him the role of truly understanding friend,
rather than one of mere compassionate supporter, then he
would have the right to know everything. But it was a formidable challenge to try to understand her—this graceful
woman overflowing with love, who was sitting by his side
with her heart elsewhere. Nevertheless, his bent for logical
inquiry began to gain the upper hand.

The car jounced a great deal, and tended to throw the two
of them together, but she protected herself so skillfully that
their knees never so much as brushed, a display of agility that
reminded him of a pet squirrel making its exercise wheel
whir. He was slightly annoyed. If Kiyoaki were beside her, he
thought, she would not be so nimble.

"You just said that you were prepared for anything, didn't
you?" he asked, not looking at her. "Well then, I wonder
how that acceptance of the consequences squares with the realization that it will have to end some day. When it does end,
won't it be too late to make a decision about the consequences?
Or alternatively, will your acceptance of the consequences

somehow gradually bring about the end, of itself? I know I'm asking you a cruel question."

"I'm glad you did," she replied calmly.

Despite himself, he glanced at her earnestly. Her profile was beautifully composed, and showed no sign of distress. While he was looking at her, she suddenly shut her eyes, and the long lashes of her left eye cast a still longer shadow over her cheek in the dim light of the roof lamp. The trees and shrubbery glided past in the pre-dawn darkness like black clouds swirling about the car.

Mori, the driver, kept his reliable back to them, wholly intent on his driving. The thick sliding glass behind him was shut. Unless they went out of their way to put their mouths close to the speaking tube, there was no chance that he would overhear.

"You say that I'm the one who should be able to end it some day. And as you're Kiyo's best friend, you have the right to say it. If I can't end it and stay alive, then dying . . ."

She might have wanted to startle Honda into interrupting with a command to stop saying such things, but he doggedly kept silence and waited for her to continue.

". . . but the moment will come sometime—and that time is not too far off. And when it does—I can promise you right now—I shan't shrink from it. I've known supreme happiness, and I'm not greedy enough to want what I have to go on forever. Every dream ends. Wouldn't it be foolish, knowing that nothing lasts forever, to insist that one has a right to do something that does? I've nothing in common with these 'new women.' But . . . if eternity existed, it would be this moment. And perhaps you, Mr. Honda, will come round to seeing it this way some day."

Honda was at last beginning to understand why Kiyoaki had once been so terribly in awe of Satoko.

"You said that it wasn't right of Matsugae to involve me in your problems. Why not?"

"You're a young man who set himself worthwhile goals.

It's wrong to get you entangled with us. Kiyo has no right at all to do it."

"I wish you wouldn't think of me as such a saint. You're unlikely to find a more grimly moral family than mine. But despite that, I have already done something that makes me an accomplice in sin."

"Don't say that. It's not true," she broke in angrily. "This is our sin, Kiyo's and mine . . . and nobody else's."

Of course she only meant to convey that she wanted to protect him, but her words had a cold, proud glitter that could not tolerate the intrusion of a third party. In her own mind, she had fashioned their sin into a tiny, brilliant, crystal palace in which she and Kiyoaki could live free from the world around them. A crystal palace so tiny that it would balance on the palm of one's hand, so tiny that no one else could fit in. Transformed for a fleetingly brief instant, she and Kiyoaki had been able to enter it and now they were spending their last few moments there, observed with extraordinary clarity in all their minute detail by someone standing just outside.

She suddenly leaned forward with bent head. He reached over to support her and his hand brushed against her hair.

"Excuse me," she apologized, "but I think I just felt some sand in my shoe, even though I was so careful. Tadeshina doesn't look after my shoes, and so if I took them off at home with sand left in them that I didn't notice, I'd be afraid of what some startled maid might blurt out."

He had no idea how to behave while a woman was inspecting her shoes, so he turned away and began to look out of the window with intense concentration.

They had already reached the outskirts of Tokyo. The night sky had turned to a vivid dark blue. The dawn showed the clouds spread low over the roofs of the houses. Though he wanted to get her home as soon as possible, he still felt regret that the morning light would put an end to what was probably the most extraordinary night of his life. Behind him he heard the sound—so faint that he thought he must be imagining it at first—of Satoko pouring the sand from the shoe she had taken off. To Honda, it sounded like the most enchanting hourglass in the world.

 35

THE SIAMESE PRINCES were thoroughly enjoying themselves at Chung-nan Villa. One evening shortly before dinner the four young men had rattan chairs brought out and placed on the lawn so that they could enjoy the cool evening breeze before eating. The princes chatted in their native language, Kiyoaki was lost in his own thoughts, and Honda had a book open on his lap.

"Would you like some twist?" asked Kridsada in Japanese, walking over to Honda and Kiyoaki holding out a pack of gold-tipped Westminster cigarettes. The princes had been quick enough in picking up "twist," the slang word for cigarettes at Peers. The school rules forbade smoking, but the authorities allowed the upperclassmen a certain amount of laxity, provided they did not go so far as to smoke openly. The boiler room in the basement had thus become a haven for smokers and was known as "the Twist Room."

Even now, as the four of them puffed on their cigarettes beneath the open sky without fear of being observed, they sensed the lingering, secret pleasure that went with smoking in the Twist Room. The smell of coal dust that filled the boiler room, eyes flashing white in the gloom as their classmates kept careful watch, the deep, luxurious puffs of smoke, the recurring restless glow of the red tips—these and many other impressions now enriched the fine flavor of their English cigarettes.

Kiyoaki turned away from the others, and as he watched
the smoke trailing away into the sky, he saw how the cloud
formations out over the ocean were beginning to dissolve,
their clear outlines now blurred and tinged with a pale gold.
At once he thought of Satoko. Her image, her scent, were
mingled with so many things. There was no alteration of nature, however slight, that did not bring her to mind. If the
breeze suddenly dropped and the warm atmosphere of the
summer evening pressed in on him, he felt Satoko brush
naked against his own nakedness. Even the gradually deep-
ening shadow cast on the lawn by the dense green foliage of
the silk tree held a hint of her.

As for Honda, he could never be quite at ease unless there
were books within easy reach. Among those now at hand was
a book he had been lent in secret by one of the student houseboys, a book proscribed by the government. Entitled *Nationalism and Authentic Socialism*, it had been written by a
young man named Terujiro Kita, who at twenty-three was
looked upon as the Japanese Otto Weininger. However, it
was rather too colorful in its presentation of an extremist position, and this aroused caution in Honda's calm and reasonable
mind. It was not that he had any particular dislike of radical
political thought. But never having been really angry himself,
he tended to view violent anger in others as some terrible, infectious disease. To encounter it in their books was intellec-
tually stimulating, but this kind of pleasure gave him a guilty
conscience.

In order to be prepared for any further discussions on reincarnation with the princes, he had stopped off at his own
home that morning after accompanying Satoko back to Tokyo
and had borrowed a book from his father's library, *A Summary of Buddhist Thought* by Tadanobu Saito. Here for the
first time he was treated to a fascinating account of the varied
origins of the doctrine of Karma, and he was reminded of the
Laws of Manu which had so absorbed him at the beginning
of the winter. But at that time his examination ambitions had
forced him to postpone a more thorough study of Saito's book.

This and several others were spread out on the arms of his
rattan chair. After dipping at random into one or another of
them, Honda looked up at last from the one that was now open
on his lap, his slightly short-sighted eyes narrowed a little.
He turned to look at the sharp slope that marked the western
border of the garden. Though the sky was still bright, the
slope was in deep shadow, and the heavy growth of trees and
shrubbery on the ridge stood out blackly against the white
glare of the sky. However, the light was breaking through
here and there like silver thread skillfully woven into an
otherwise dark tapestry. Behind the trees, the western sky
was like a sheet of isinglass. The bright summer day had
been a gaudy scroll which was tapering off into blankness.

The young men savored the delicious hint of guilt that
added spice to their cigarettes, as a swarm of mosquitos towered up in one corner of the sunset garden. They felt the
golden heaviness that comes from a day of swimming, their
skin still warm from the midday sun. . . . Though Honda
sat there in silence, he felt that the day would be counted as
one of the happiest of their youth.

The princes seemed to feel similarly content. They were obviously pretending to take no notice of Kiyoaki's amorous
pursuits. On the other hand, Kiyoaki and Honda both chose
to ignore the princes' lighthearted forays among the fisher-
men's daughters along the beach, though Kiyoaki was careful
to follow them up with suitable sums of compensation to the
girls' fathers. And so, under the protective eye of the Great
Buddha, whom the princes worshipped every morning on top
of the ridge, summer waned in languorous beauty.

*

Kridsada was the first to notice the servant who came
down onto the lawn from the terrace bearing a letter on the
gleaming silver tray that he doubtless spent most of his free
time polishing, lamenting the while that he had so few occasions to use it at the villa, compared with the house in Shibuya.

Kridsada jumped up to meet him and took the letter. Then, when he saw that it was a personal letter to Chao P. from his mother the Queen Dowager, he walked over to where Chao P. was sitting and presented it to him facetiously with a deferential flourish.

Kiyoaki and Honda had, of course, noticed this piece of by-play, but they restrained their curiosity and sat waiting for the princes to come over to them in a rush of nostalgic happiness. As Chao P. took the thick letter from its envelope, they heard the crinkle of paper, and white stationery flashed like the feathers of an arrow winging through the darkness. Then suddenly they were on their feet staring at Chao P., who had let out an agonized cry and collapsed in a faint.

Kridsada stood looking down at his cousin with astonishment on his face as Kiyoaki and Honda rushed over to help. Then he bent over to pick up the letter, which had fallen on the grass, and had just started to read when he burst into tears, throwing himself to the ground. The two young Japanese could understand nothing of what Kridsada was sobbing to himself in a rush of Siamese, and since the letter, which Honda now picked up, was in the same language, it furnished no clues either, apart from the glittering golden seal of the royal family of Siam at the top, with its intricate design of pagodas, fabulous beasts, roses, swords, scepters and other devices grouped around three white elephants.

Chao P. regained consciousness while he was being carried back to his bedroom by servants, but he was obviously still dazed. Kridsada trailed after him, still moaning.

Though they were ignorant of the facts, it was obvious to Kiyoaki and Honda that some terrible news had arrived. Chao P. lay silent, his head on his pillow and his eyes, as cloudy as two pearls, staring up at the ceiling. The expression on his swarthy face grew less and less discernible by the minute as the room grew rapidly darker. After some time, it was Kridsada who was finally able to explain in English.

"Princess Chan is dead. Chao P.'s love, my sister. . . . If I had been told first, I could have watched for a chance to tell him in a way that would spare him such a shock, but I suppose his mother, the Queen Dowager, was more afraid of upsetting me and so wrote to Chao P. If so, she miscalculated. But then she may have had a deeper concern . . . to strengthen his courage by making him confront his sorrow head-on."

This was more judicious than anything they usually heard from Kridsada. The princes' violent grief, as powerful as a tropical cloudburst, affected Kiyoaki and Honda profoundly. But they sensed that after the thunder, the lightning, and the rain, their grief would be a wet and glistening jungle that would recover all the more quickly and luxuriantly.

Dinner that evening was brought to the princes' room, but they did not touch their food. Some time later, however, Kridsada evidently recalled the duties of politeness to one's host, and called Kiyoaki and Honda back to their room to translate the entire letter into English.

Princess Chan had, in fact, fallen ill in the spring, and though she was too sick to write, she had pleaded with everyone not to tell her brother and cousin. Her lovely white hand grew more and more emaciated until she could no longer move it. It lay there as cold and still as a single moonbeam coming in through a window.

The English doctor in charge tried everything he knew, but he could not prevent the relentless paralysis of her whole body. Finally it became a great strain for her even to speak. But in order perhaps to leave Chao P. with the image of her in full health as she was when they parted, she repeatedly insisted to everyone that nothing should be said about her illness. It reduced them to tears.

The Queen Dowager went to see her very often, and she could never help crying when she saw the young princess. When Her Majesty was informed of Chan's death, she restrained the others and said immediately: "I myself will tell Pattanadid."

"What I have to tell you is very sad," the letter began.

Please bear it as bravely as you can. Your beloved Chantrapa has died. Later I will tell you just how much her thoughts were of you at the end. As your mother, what I most want to convey to you right away is that you must resign yourself to all this as the will of the Lord Buddha. I pray that you will always be mindful of your princely dignity and accept this tragic news with good bearing. How well I know what your feelings must be on learning of this away in a foreign land, and how I regret that I am not at your side to comfort you as a mother should. But now where Kridsada is concerned, please behave as an elder brother and tell him of his sister's death with the deepest solicitude. I have given you the tragic news like this without warning only because I believe that you have sufficient fortitude not to give way to grief. And then do please take consolation at least that the Princess had thoughts for you alone until she breathed her last. No doubt you regret not having been there when she died, but you must make every effort to appreciate how she felt in wanting you to preserve forever in your heart the image you had of her as a girl in the bloom of youth . . .

Chao P. lay listening intently until Kridsada had translated the very last word. Then he sat up in bed and turned to Kiyoaki.

"I'm rather embarrassed," he began. "I neglected my mother's admonition, and just collapsed. But do please try to understand.

"What I've been struggling with these past few hours is not the riddle of Princess Chan's death. In the period that began with her illness and lasted until her death—no, that lasted in these twenty days since the moment of her death—I have of course been in constant anxiety. But even so, having no idea of the truth, I lived calmly enough in a false world through all that time. That's the riddle.

"I clearly saw the bright sea and the shining beach just as they were. Why wasn't I able to see the subtle change that had occurred deep in the substance of the universe? The world was constantly and imperceptibly changing, just like wine inside a bottle. And I'm like a man who sees no farther than the dark red liquid glowing warmly inside the glass. Why did it never occur to me to taste it, if only once a day, and try to gauge if some small change had taken place. The soft morning breeze, the rustling trees, the flutter of birds' wings and the sound of their calls—all these were constantly in my eyes and ears. But I merely took them all to be an embodiment of the joy of being alive, the beautiful essence of life itself. It never occurred to me that under the surface something was changing day by day. If I had stopped one morning to taste the world and so discovered that it had subtly altered on my tongue . . . oh, if only I had done that, then it couldn't have escaped me that this world had suddenly become a world without Princess Chan."

As he said this, his voice gradually became choked and his words were muffled in tears.

Leaving him in Kridsada's care, they returned to their own room. They found, however, that they were in no mood for sleep.

"The princes will want to go back to Siam as soon as they can. Whatever the others may say, they certainly won't feel like going on studying here," Honda said as soon as the two of them were alone.

"Yes, I'm sure they'll go home," Kiyoaki answered gloomily. The prince's grief had evidently had a deep effect on him, and he was sunk in a mood of vague foreboding. "And after they've gone, you and I won't have any good reason to stay here just by ourselves," he went on, almost to himself. "Or perhaps Mother and Father will be coming down, and then it'll be a matter of spending the summer with them. Whatever happens, our happy summer is over."

Although Honda was well aware that a man in love has no room in his heart for anything but his feelings and loses even his ability to sympathize with the sorrows of others, he could imagine no heart more naturally suited than Kiyoaki's to be such a vessel of pure passion, cold and tough as tempered glass.

*

A week later, the two princes began their homeward journey on an English ship, and Kiyoaki and Honda went to Yokohama to see them off. Since it was in the middle of the summer vacation, none of the princes' other classmates were on hand. In deference to his close ties with Siam, however, Prince Toin sent his steward to represent him. Kiyoaki greeted the man coolly, exchanging no more than a word or two.

As the huge cargo-passenger liner pulled away from the pier, the trailing streamers parted and were carried away by the wind. The two princes stood on the fantail to one side of the Union Jack snapping in the breeze, and waved their handkerchiefs unceasingly.

Long after the ship was far out into the channel and all the other well-wishers had gone, Kiyoaki stayed on, despite the torrid heat of the afternoon sun that beat down on the pier, until Honda could not help urging him to leave. Kiyoaki was not parting with the two princes from Siam. He felt, rather, that it was his youth, or the most glorious part of it, that was about to vanish below the horizon.

36

WHEN AUTUMN CAME, classes started once more, and meetings between Kiyoaki and Satoko became more and more restricted. Tadeshina had to take the most extreme precautions to enable them to go walking together in the early evening without being discovered.

They had to be careful to avoid even the lamplighters who

still made their rounds in that one part of Toriizaka. With their tight-collared uniforms they carried long poles which they thrust under the protective mantle of each streetlight into the gas jet below. By the time this hurried ceremony was completed daily at dusk, the streets of the neighborhood were emptied of passersby. It was therefore a time when Kiyoaki and Satoko could walk through the crooked back lanes in comparative security. The chorus of insects grew louder at this hour, but the lights in the windows were not unduly bright. Many houses had no gates to separate them from the street, and the two of them could even hear the footsteps of a returning husband and then the noise of a door being shut.

"Everything will be over in a month or two. The Toin-nomiyas will certainly not be willing to delay the betrothal ceremony longer than that," Satoko said rather mildly, as if she were talking about someone else. "Every night when I go to bed, I think: it will end tomorrow, something irrevocable will happen tomorrow. And then, strangely enough, I sleep peacefully. That's just what we're doing now—something that can't be undone."

"Well, suppose even after the engagement ceremony . . ."

"Kiyo, what are you saying? If we increase our sins any more than we have, your gentle spirit will be crushed. Instead of thinking of things like that, I would rather keep counting how many times I will still be able to see you."

"You've made up your mind, haven't you? In due course, you're going to forget everything, aren't you?"

"Yes. Though I don't yet know just how I'll be able to do it. The path we're taking is not a road, Kiyo, it's a pier, and it ends someplace where the sea begins. It can't be helped."

That was indeed the first time they had talked about the end. And confronted by it, they felt no more responsibility than a pair of children. They had no plans in mind, nothing to fall back on, no solution, no plan of action—and they felt that all this testified to the purity of their intentions. Still, once they had mentioned the final separation, the idea clung to their minds like rust.

Had they embarked on all this without considering the end? Or had they begun their affair precisely because they had thought about its end? Kiyoaki did not know. He thought that if the two of them were suddenly charred to ashes by a bolt of lightning, well and good. But what was he to do if no dreadful punishment fell from the skies and things remained as they were? It made him uneasy. "If that were the case," he wondered, "would I be able to go on loving Satoko just as passionately as I do now?"

It was the first time that he had experienced an anxiety of this sort. It made him take Satoko by the hand. But when she linked her fingers with his in response, he was irritated and tightened his grip with almost paralyzing force. She did not let out the smallest cry of pain. He maintained his hold with the same force, and when the light of a stray beam from a distant second-story window showed him a trace of tears in her eyes, he felt a black satisfaction.

This, he knew, was further proof of the hidden, savage essence of the elegance he had cultivated for so long. Surely the simplest solution was for them to die together, but he felt that something far more agonizing was called for. The taboo that they were violating even now with every fleeting moment of this secret meeting, and that was growing more formidable with each violation, fascinated Kiyoaki and drove him on, like the peal of a distant, forever unattainable golden bell. The more he sinned, the more the sense of sin eluded him. And the end? How could things end otherwise than in a gross deception, he thought with a shudder.

"It seems that you don't much enjoy walking with me like this," she said in her usual clear and untroubled tones. "I am drinking in every passing moment of happiness, but . . . you seem to have had enough of it."

"It's just that I've come to love you too much. And happiness is something I've left far behind me," he answered gravely. Even as he uttered this rationalization, he realized that he need no longer worry about any trace of childishness in the way he spoke.

The lane they were in was now approaching Roppongi and its clustered shops. A faded flag bearing the character for ice hung in front of an ice house with closed shutters, a forlorn sight on this street echoing with the cries of insects. When they had gone a little farther, they came to a window that spilled light into their path. The shop belonged to a dealer in musical instruments named Tabé, who, according to his sign, was accredited to the band of the Azabu Regiment. He was apparently working late on some sort of urgent order.

They skirted the pool of light, but even so a dazzling glare of brass from the window lit up the corners of their eyes for a moment. A line of new bugles hung there, and they flashed with a brilliance more suited to a midsummer parade ground under the extravagance of the lights above them. From inside the shop came the sudden, melancholy note of a bugle, a single, experimental blast that ceased as soon as it was heard. It struck Kiyoaki's ears like the prelude of doom.

"Please turn back. There'll be too many people up ahead," Tadeshina whispered to Kiyoaki. She had slipped up close behind them unnoticed.

37

THE TOINNOMIYAS made no attempt to intrude on the course of Satoko's life. Prince Harunori was taken up with his military duties, and no one else among those concerned troubled to arrange a meeting between the Prince and Satoko, nor did Prince Harunori himself give any sign that he wanted one. All this, however, by no means implied that the Toinnomiyas were treating her coolly. In terms of the progression of such betrothals, everything was going smoothly. Those around the Prince believed that frequent meetings between the two young people whose marriage was a foregone conclusion could yield no profit and might well engender some mishap.

In the meantime, there were those accomplishments expected of a young lady who was about to become a princess. Had she been the daughter of a family whose quality might be even slightly in question, she would have had to undergo a varied course of training that conceded little to any previous education. But the tradition of good breeding maintained in Count Ayakura's household was so strong that a daughter of his could rise with ease to the status of princess. Such elegance had become so much a part of Satoko that she could, whenever she wished, compose poems worthy of a princess, write in a hand suitable for a princess, arrange flowers as befitted a princess. There would have been no obstacle to her becoming a princess at any time after her twelfth birthday.

Count Ayakura and his wife, however, were both concerned about three accomplishments that so far had not been featured in her education. They were therefore anxious that she should familiarize herself with them as soon as possible. These were singing *nagauta* and playing mahjong, of which Princess Toin was so fond, and listening to European records, the favorite diversion of Prince Harunori himself. After the Count had explained the situation to him, Marquis Matsugae immediately arranged to have a *nagauta* master come and give lessons to Satoko, and he also had a German gramophone delivered to the Ayakuras, together with all the available records. Finding an instructor for something like mahjong, however, presented him with a harder task. Though he himself was an avid player of English-style billiards, he was nevertheless scandalized that a noble family of such exalted rank could take pleasure in so plebeian a game as mahjong.

It so happened that the proprietress of the geisha house in Yanagibashi and her oldest geisha were both skilled mahjong players. And so the Marquis arranged for them to pay frequent visits to the Ayakura residence and make a foursome with Tadeshina to introduce Satoko to the game. He himself, of course, paid the extra fee for the trips they made.

One would expect that this foursome, including two professionals, would have brought an unaccustomed touch of frivolity to the austere atmosphere of the Ayakura household. Tadeshina, however, was immovable in her opposition. She pretended that it was an affront to her dignity, but she was in fact terrified that the keen eyes of these two women of the world would uncover Satoko's secret. And even if this did not happen, these mahjong games would nevertheless offer the occasion for Marquis Matsugae to plant paid spies in the Ayakura residence.

The proprietress and the old geisha lost no time in interpreting Tadeshina's unyielding arrogance as a calculated insult, and their reaction took less than three days to reach the ears of the Marquis. He bided his time, and at the first favorable opportunity, gently reproved Count Ayakura.

"Indeed it's most admirable that a faithful old servant of yours should value your family dignity so highly, but surely in this case the whole object is to cater to the pleasure of the Prince's family, so some degree of forbearance may be in order. And then these Yanagibashi women look upon this as a glorious opportunity to be of service, and so, busy as they are, they're willing to take the time to come."

The Count conveyed all this to Tadeshina, putting her in an extremely awkward position.

Satoko and the two women had in fact met before. On the day of the cherry blossom garden party, the proprietress had been in charge behind the scenes and the old geisha had played the part of the haiku master. When they had come for the first mahjong session, the proprietress had delivered a speech of congratulation to the Count and Countess on the engagement and had also brought an extravagant present:

"What a beautiful lady your daughter is! And as she is possessed of the gracious dignity of a born princess, how pleased you must be at this betrothal. The memory of your permitting us to be associated with it will remain with us for-

ever, and we will pass it on from generation to generation—
in the utmost secrecy of course."

After this commendable expression of their esteem, however, the proprietress and her companion had not been quite
up to maintaining the proper veneer when they retired to another room and sat down at the mahjong table with Tadeshina and Satoko. The eyes so overflowing with damp devotion to Satoko would, from time to time, run dry, exposing
the shoals of criticism beneath. Tadeshina was distastefully
conscious of the same look turned upon her and her old-
fashioned silver obi clip. But still more disturbing than that
was an incident that occurred at the very beginning.

"I wonder how Marquis Matsugae's young son is?" the old
geisha remarked offhandedly as she shuffled the mahjong
tiles. "I don't believe I ever saw a better-looking young gentleman."

Thereupon, with remarkable skill the proprietress casually
turned the conversation to other things. She might have done
this merely to chide her companion for introducing an un-
suitable topic, but the exchange had set Tadeshina's nerves
on edge.

In accordance with her advice, Satoko tried to say as little
as possible. But overconcentration on guarding her inner
thoughts in front of these two women, who were unsurpassed
in their skill at interpreting the subtleties of a woman's out-
ward behavior, gave rise to another danger. If she showed
herself to be too subdued, this might start a scandalous rumor
that she seemed unhappy about her coming marriage. To
conceal her feelings was to risk betrayal by her behavior, and
to dissemble in her behavior was to risk revealing her feelings.

As a result, Tadeshina was compelled to draw on all of her
considerable tactical ability to put an end once and for all to
the mahjong sessions.

"I'm simply astounded," she said to the Count, "that His
Excellency Marquis Matsugae should deign to accept the
slanders of these two women at face value. They say that I'm
to blame for Miss Satoko's lack of enthusiasm. If they did not

do so, her indifference would otherwise be blamed on them. I'm sure that was why they said I was haughty with them. However much it conforms with the wishes of His Excellency the Marquis, having women of that profession coming and going here in the master's house is a disgrace. Furthermore, Miss Satoko has already learned the rudiments of mahjong. And so if she only plays after her marriage to be sociable, and always loses, it will make her very appealing. I would therefore be very opposed to any further lessons, and if Marquis Matsugae will not desist, then I will request that Tadeshina be dismissed from the master's service."

Count Ayakura had little choice but to bow to an ultimatum delivered with such force.

The moment she had learned from the steward Yamada that Kiyoaki had lied about Satoko's letter, Tadeshina had found herself at a fork in the road. She had the choice either of becoming Kiyoaki's enemy or of doing whatever he and Satoko wanted her to do, in full awareness of the consequences. And she had chosen the latter course.

Although her main motive in this was a genuine affection for Satoko, she was at the same time afraid that keeping the lovers apart could drive Satoko to suicide. She had decided that the best course was to guard their secret and let them do as they liked, waiting until the affair ended of its own accord. And in the meantime, she would exert herself to the utmost to maintain secrecy.

She prided herself on knowing all there was to know about the workings of passion. A firm advocate, moreover, of the philosophy that what is unknown does not exist, she did not think of herself as betraying either her master the Count or the Toinnomiyas or anyone at all. She was able to help along this love affair and be the lovers' ally, just as if she were conducting an experiment in chemistry, and at the same time she could deny its existence by covering up any betraying details. She knew very well that she had charted a dangerous course, but she believed that she had been born into this world to fulfill the role of savior of every critical situation. And she could

thus lay a wealth of obligations on others that would eventually force them in turn to do exactly as she wished.

She was intent on making the meetings as frequent as possible to hasten the wane of their passion, but she failed to
perceive that her own passions had become involved. This
had nothing to do with revenge on Kiyoaki for his cruel behavior. True enough, she was waiting for the day when he
would tell her that he wanted to leave Satoko and would she
please gently read the funeral rites for him. And when that
happened, she would remind him forcefully of how ardent his
now cooled desires had once been. But she already only half-
believed in this dream. And if it did come true, how agonizing for Satoko.

Why was it that this self-possessed old woman, who should
have followed her philosophy that nothing in this world was
safe by putting her own self-preservation first, let it prompt
her instead to throw aside all thoughts of safety? How could
she have brought herself to use this very philosophy as a pretext for adventure? In some unguarded moment, she had, in
fact, submitted to a joy that defied rational analysis. To be
the means of uniting two young people of such beauty, to
watch their hopeless love burn more and more passionately
—bit by bit she gave way to an agony of delight that ignored
every single danger.

Thus possessed, she felt that there was something so sacred
about the physical union of two beautiful young people that
it could be judged only by extraordinary criteria. The way
their eyes flashed when they met, the way they throbbed as
they drew close—this was a fire to warm Tadeshina's frozen
heart. For her own sake, she wanted to keep its glow from
dying. Each time before they met, their cheeks were pale and
sunken with melancholy, but as soon as they saw each other,
their faces began to shine as brightly as glossy heads of bar-
ley in a June field. For Tadeshina that moment was a miracle,
no less than the lame walking or the blind restored to sight.

Her actual role, of course, was to protect Satoko from all
evil. But something that flamed like this was not evil; some-

thing that was transformed into poetry was not evil—surely this tenet subtly permeated the ancient tradition of elegance in the Ayakura family?

And yet Tadeshina was waiting patiently for something to happen. In some ways she was like a woman who has let her pet bird fly free to forage and now waits for a chance to recapture it and return it to its cage, but there was something in that expectation that reeked of blood and doom. Every day she scrupulously applied the thick white makeup affected by the court ladies of long ago. She hid the nests of wrinkles under her eyes with white powder and those around her lips with vivid Kyoto rouge. And while she was doing this, she avoided studying her face in the mirror, and stared somberly, questioningly, into space instead. The brilliance of the high autumn sky seemed to condense into clear, bright drops in her eyes, but in their depths one could see a desperate thirst for the future. Then, in order to give her makeup a final inspection, she would pick up a pair of old-fashioned spectacles, which she ordinarily avoided wearing, and put them on, hooking the slender metal side pieces over her ears. As she did so, their pointed ends pricked her earlobes, white with makeup, making them burn.

*

At the beginning of October the Toinnomiyas sent the prescribed notification that the betrothal ceremony was to take place in December, and attached to this was an informal listing of the presents: five rolls of dress material, two barrels of refined saké, and one carton of fresh sea bream. The last two items were, of course, readily available, but as for the dress material, Marquis Matsugae himself had undertaken to arrange for that. He sent a long telegram to the Itsui Corporation's London office to have the finest English cloth specially ordered and sent at once.

One morning when Tadeshina went to wake Satoko, she noticed that her face was drained of color when she roused her. Then Satoko pushed her hand aside, got out of bed and rushed into the hallway. She had barely reached the wash-room before she vomited, slightly soiling the sleeve of her nightgown. Tadeshina helped her back into the bedroom and made certain that the door was shut.

Some ten or more chickens were kept in the back yard of the house, and their clucking and crowing pierced the shoji screens as they began to lighten each morning, announcing the beginning of a new day to the Ayakura household. Nor did the chorus cease once the sun was high. In the midst of this crowing, Satoko laid her face back on her pillow and shut her eyes.

"Please listen," said Tadeshina, her mouth close to Satoko's ear. "It wouldn't do to mention this to anyone. Please don't give your nightgown to the maid to wash under any circumstances. I'll take care of it myself, so that nobody will know. And from now on, I'll make all the arrangements for your food. I'll see to it that you eat only what agrees with you so that your maid won't suspect a thing. What I'm telling you is only for your own good. So it will be best to do exactly as I say."

Satoko agreed uncertainly as a single tear rolled down her lovely face.

Tadeshina was filled with delight. First of all, she was the only one to have received this initial sign. And then, the moment it occurred, something had dawned on her: this was just what she had been waiting for. Now Satoko was in her hands!

All things considered, Tadeshina was far more at home in the area of life represented by Satoko's present condition than in the realm of passion. Just as she had been prompt to notice and advise Satoko years before when she began to menstruate, so now she showed herself a practiced specialist in all things physical. By contrast, Countess Ayakura, who maintained only a nodding acquaintance with the everyday, learned that her daughter had begun to menstruate a full two years later, and only then from Tadeshina.

Tadeshina, who had never failed to note Satoko's every physical sign, intensified her vigilance after that first morning sickness. And once she recognized the signs one by one—the way Satoko put on her makeup, the way she frowned as though anticipating another bout of nausea from a distance, her capricious appetite, the vague heaviness in her movements—she unhesitatingly made her decision.

"It's not healthy to stay indoors all the time like this. Let's go for a walk," she said to Satoko.

This was usually the hint that a meeting with Kiyoaki had been arranged, but since the sun was still high in the sky, Satoko was somewhat puzzled and looked up questioningly. Tadeshina's customary expression was gone, replaced by a look of stern aloofness. She was well aware that she held a matter of honor in her hands that was of national concern.

As they went out through the rear yard, Countess Ayakura was standing there, her arms clasped to her breast, watching one of the maids feeding the chickens. The bright autumn sun picked out the shiny feathers of the clustering birds and struck the wash hanging out to dry, turning it into a pageant of whiteness. As Satoko walked along, trusting Tadeshina to clear a path through the chickens, she nodded politely to her mother. She noticed the strutting legs thrusting out so abruptly from their feathers, and for the first time in her life she thought of these creatures as being hostile—a natural enmity born of the antagonism of species. It was a dire feeling. A few loose, white feathers floated toward the ground. Tadeshina greeted Satoko's mother.

"I'm just taking Miss Satoko for a little walk."

"A walk? Well, thank you for your trouble," the Countess answered. But since her daughter's wedding was drawing closer by the day, she seemed, naturally enough, to be feeling rather nervous. On the other hand, she was becoming more and more polite and reserved toward her daughter. As was customary in the families of court nobles, she never uttered a single word of criticism to her, as she was already like a member of the Imperial Family.

*

The two of them walked through the streets of Ryudo until they came to a small shrine surrounded by a granite wall and dedicated to the Sun Goddess. They entered its narrow precincts, deserted now that the autumn festivals were over, and after bowing before the inner shrine draped with purple curtains, Tadeshina led the way to the rear of the little pavilion used for sacred dances.

"Is Kiyo coming here?" Satoko asked hesitantly. For some reason, she found herself intimidated by Tadeshina's manner today.

"No, he won't be coming. Today there's something I'd like to ask you, Miss Satoko, and that's why we've come here. We needn't worry that anyone will overhear us."

Three or four huge rocks had been placed to one side of the pavilion for the convenience of anyone who might want to sit down and watch the ritual dances. Tadeshina now took off her *haori*, folded it, and placed it on the moss-covered surface of one of them.

"Here, now you won't catch a chill," she said, as Satoko sat down.

"Well now, young mistress," she said formally, "I know that I have no need to remind you now, but you are, of course, well aware that loyalty to the Emperor must take absolute precedence. It's a foolish kind of sermon for someone like Tadeshina to make to Miss Satoko Ayakura, whose family has been blessed down the centuries with the imperial favor for twenty-seven generations. But even leaving all that aside, once a marriage is proposed and ratified by imperial sanction, there is no question of having second thoughts. And to spurn it is to spurn the beneficence of His Imperial Majesty. In all the world, there is no sin more terrible than this."

Tadeshina went on to a detailed explanation. Despite what she had to say, she was by no means blaming her for anything that had already occurred. For she herself had been equally guilty. Furthermore, whatever escaped the notice of the public need not be agonized over and considered as a sin. However, she insisted, there had to be a limit somewhere, and now that Satoko had become pregnant, the time had come to put an end to it. She had been a silent observer up to now, but with matters in their present state, she felt that it would not do to let things slide and permit this love affair to go on and on. So now was the time to muster her determination. She had to make it clear to Kiyoaki that they must part. And she was to do everything according to Tadeshina's instructions. And thus, making each of her points in their proper sequence, and deliberately excluding every emotional consideration, she said what she had to say.

Thinking that this was enough to convince Satoko and that she would obey, Tadeshina cut short her lecture and, with a neatly folded handkerchief, dabbed lightly at the sweat that had gathered on her brow.

Rational as her argument had been, she had spoken with a sadly sympathetic expression and a hint of tears in her voice. This girl was dearer to her than a daughter, but she was aware that her sorrow was not genuine. She was conscious of a barrier between her sorrow and her love. Since her affection for Satoko was so great, she hoped that the girl would share the unfathomable and frightening joy that lurked in her own terrible resolve. To wash oneself clean of one sin that was so permeated with sacrilege, one must commit another. In the end, the two would cancel each other out, as if neither had ever existed. One must merge one form of darkness with another, and then wait for the darkness to be tinged with the rosiness of the fateful dawn to come. And above all, maintain secrecy.

Since Satoko was still silent, Tadeshina began to feel uneasy and asked: "You'll do everything just as I say, won't you? How do you feel about it?"

Satoko's expression was blank. She gave no sign that Tadeshina's words had startled her. The truth was that her stilted remarks had held no meaning for her whatsoever.

"But what am I to do?" she replied. "You must be specific."

Tadeshina looked around her before replying, satisfying

herself that the faint sound of the gong that hung before the shrine had been caused by a gust of wind and not by a chance worshipper. The halfhearted chirping of a cricket came from beneath the wooden floor of the pavilion.

"You must get rid of the baby—as soon as possible."

Satoko caught her breath.

"What do you mean? They'll send me to prison."

"Don't talk like that. Please leave it to me. Even supposing that it did somehow leak out, it would be impossible for the police to punish either you or me. Your wedding has already been arranged. Once the betrothal gift is presented in December, things will be all the safer. Because in matters like this, the police understand. However, Miss Satoko, this is what I want you to realize: if you dillydally and everyone can see that you're pregnant, of course His Imperial Highness and the rest of the world as well would never be able to forgive you. The engagement would be broken off without delay, His Excellency your father would have to hide himself from the eyes of the world, and Master Kiyoaki would also be in a terrible situation. To put it frankly, his future hopes as well as those of the Matsugae family would be so threatened that there would be no course for them but to pretend that he was in no way involved. And so everything would then be lost where you are concerned. Would you want that to happen? There's only one thing you can do now."

"If it did come out somehow, even supposing that the police said nothing, the Toinnomiyas might still hear something about it. Then how would I be able to show myself at the wedding? And afterwards, how would I dare go on serving the Prince? Tell me that?"

"There is absolutely no need to get upset over what's only a rumor. As for what the Toinnomiyas think, that will depend entirely on you. So if you behave at all times like a chaste and beautiful princess, that's what they'll take you for. The rumors and the rest—they'll be forgotten in no time."

"Then you can assure me that there's no chance I'll be punished, that I'd go to prison?"

"Let me try to explain it this way, so that you will under-stand. First of all, the police have the greatest reverence for the nobility. And so there is not the slightest possibility of their allowing something like this to become public. If you're still worried, we could always ask Marquis Matsugae for his kind assistance. His Excellency has a great deal of influence and he can accomplish anything. After all, it would be to cover up for the young master."

Satoko cried out sharply: "No! You're not to do that. That's something I shall not allow. You're not under any circum-stances to ask either the Marquis or Kiyo for help. I'd be com-pletely disgraced if you did."

"Well . . . I only mentioned it as a mere possibility. But secondly, even in strictly legal terms, I am determined to shield you. We would make it a matter of you having done as I said without any idea of what scheme I had in mind, of breathing in the anesthetic without realizing what it was, and so becoming helpless. And if we did that, no matter how pub-lic a matter it became, it would end with me bearing the pun-ishment."

"So you say that whatever happens, then, I shan't go to prison?"

"You can rest assured about that."

However, her reply brought no look of relief to Satoko's face. "I want to go to prison," she said.

Tadeshina's tenseness dissolved as she burst out laughing. "You sound like a little girl. Why do you say that?"

"I wonder how women prisoners have to dress. What would Kiyo do if he saw me like that . . . would he still love me or not? I'd like to know."

As she made this absurd remark, her eyes, far from being filled with tears, flashed with such fierce satisfaction that Tadeshina shivered.

However great the difference in status between these two women, there was no denying that they shared the same strength and courage. Whether for deception or for truth's

sake, there could never be a more severe demand on their
joint bravery than now.

Tadeshina felt that she and Satoko were matched like a
boat advancing against the current and the current itself, so
well matched that the boat was held immobile for a time,
bound together with it from moment to moment in impatient
intimacy. At this instant, moreover, the two of them felt the
same joy. It had the sound of the beating wings of a flock of
birds fleeing overhead before an approaching storm. Their
violent emotion, though it had something of sorrow, of fear,
of anxiety, was different from all of these and could be called
by no other name than joy.

"Well, at any rate, you'll do as I say, won't you?" Tadeshina
asked, watching Satoko's pale cheeks flush under the autumn
sun.

"I want you to say nothing at all about this to Kiyo," Satoko
replied. "About my condition, I mean. Whether or not I do
just as you say, don't worry. Without bringing anyone else
into it, I'll talk everything over with you, and eventually I'll
decide what's best."

Her words already held the dignity of a princess.

 38

KIYOAKI WAS HAVING DINNER with his father and
mother in early October when he learned that the betrothal
ceremony would at last take place in December. His parents
displayed the keenest interest in the etiquette for this occasion
and vied with each other to show how much they knew about
ancient court rites and observances.

"Count Ayakura will have to prepare a chamber of state for the Prince's steward when he comes," his mother remarked. "Which room do you suppose it will be?"

"Well, since everyone will stand for the ceremony, a grand Western-style room would be nice, if they had one. As it is, they'll have to spread cloth on the floor of the drawing room and in the corridor leading to it from the entrance, to receive the steward. He will come in a carriage with two attendants, and Ayakura will have to be ready with the letter of acceptance, written on fine, thick crepe paper, in an envelope of the same paper and tied with two ropes of twisted paper knotted together. The steward will be dressed in ceremonial robes and so when Ayakura makes the acceptance speech, he too will have to wear the uniform of a count. But he's an expert on all these little details and there's no need for me to say anything. Only when money becomes a problem, that's when I can be of help."

Kiyoaki was deeply shaken, and spent a restless night. He imagined that he could hear the dull clank of chains dragging across the floor, coming closer and closer to imprison his love. Now he felt none of the exhilarating energy that had fired him when the imperial sanction was granted. What had so aroused him then, the idea of utter impossibility, had appeared to him like an exquisite piece of white porcelain. But now it was covered with a network of hair-fine cracks. And so in place of the wild joy that had flowed from his sense of resolution at that time, he now felt the sadness of a man who watches the dying of a season.

Had he given up, then, he asked himself. No, he had not. But nevertheless he felt that while the force of the imperial sanction had served to throw him and Satoko wildly into each other's arms, this official announcement of the betrothal ceremony had the power to tear them apart, despite the fact that it was no more than the extension of the first. Dealing with the other had been extremely simple: he had had to do no more than follow his desires. But how was he to cope with this new force? He had no idea.

The next day, using his customary method of contacting Tadeshina, he phoned the owner of the officers' boarding house and told him to tell Tadeshina that he wanted to see Satoko as soon as possible. Since he could not expect any answer before evening, he dutifully went to school, but the lectures he heard that day made no impression on him. After classes were over and he was able to phone the inn from a place close to the school, the innkeeper conveyed Tadeshina's answer. The situation being what it was, Kiyoaki must surely realize that for the present there seemed to be no possibility of arranging a meeting for at least ten days. As soon as an opportunity arose, however, Tadeshina would inform him at once. And so would he please wait until then?

Those ten days were spent in an agony of impatience. He felt that he was now suffering for his behavior in the past, especially for the time when he had showed such coldness to Satoko.

Autumn became more and more evident. It was still a little early for the maples to have reached their full color, though the leaves of the cherry trees had already turned a smoldering scarlet and begun to fall. He was in no mood to seek out the company of friends, but to spend the days alone was trying. Sundays were especially difficult, the thought, as he stood looking out over the pond, whose surface reflected the moving clouds. Then he gazed blankly toward the distant waterfall and wondered why the water that flowed unceasingly down its nine levels never ran dry. How strange that this smooth continuity should never be broken! He felt it to be like an image of his emotions.

He was oppressed by a mood of empty frustration that made him feel both feverish and chilled. It was as though he were afflicted with a disease that turned his movements sluggish and heavy, but nevertheless made him feel restless. He roamed alone through the huge family estate, and turned onto the path that led through the grove of Japanese cypresses to the back of the house. He passed by the old gardener hard at work digging up wild potatoes with yellowed leaves.

Blue sky was showing through the cypress branches, and a drop of yesterday's rain fell from them to strike his forehead. He suddenly felt that he had received a message of devastating clarity, as if this raindrop were gouging a furrow down his brow. It rescued him from the anxiety he thought he had left behind him, forgotten. He was only waiting, and nothing was happening. It seemed as if he were standing at a crossroads, where his doubts and misgivings were parading to the hollow beat of a multitude of footsteps. He was so tense that he became oblivious to even his own beauty.

The ten days passed. Tadeshina kept her promise. But the meeting was hedged about with so many restrictions that it tore his heart.

Satoko was going to the Mitsukoshi department store to order new kimonos for the wedding. Her mother was to have gone with her, but since she was in bed with a slight cold, Tadeshina would accompany her alone. They were to meet at the store, but not under the eyes of the salesclerks, which wouldn't do. So Kiyoaki was to be waiting at the entrance decorated with the lion's statue at three o'clock. When Satoko and Tadeshina came out, he was to pretend to ignore them, but follow them at a distance. Finally, when they had entered a small bean-soup restaurant nearby, where they were unlikely to be seen, he could follow and speak to her for a short time. In the meantime, their rickshaw man, waiting at the front entrance of Mitsukoshi's, would think they were still inside.

He left school early, and at three o'clock he was waiting in the crowd of shoppers at the entrance of Mitsukoshi's, wearing a raincoat over his uniform so that it concealed even his collar insignia. He had put his cap inside his bag. Satoko came out, cast an unhappy but burning glance at him, and walked down the street with Tadeshina. Doing as he was directed, he followed and sat down with them in a corner of the almost deserted restaurant.

Satoko and Tadeshina seemed to be somewhat vexed with one another. He noticed that Satoko's makeup was not as becoming as usual, and he realized that she was using it to make herself look healthy at all costs. Her voice, moreover, sounded dulled, and her hair had lost its luster. He felt that he was looking at a fine painting whose colors, once brilliant, were fading horribly before his very eyes. What he had spent ten days praying to see in an agony of expectation had undergone a subtle change.

"Can we meet tonight?" he asked impetuously, but even as he did so, he sensed that the answer would be no.

"Please don't be so unreasonable."

"Why am I being unreasonable?"

His words were aggressive enough, but his heart was empty. Her head was drooping and her eyes were now filled with tears. Tadeshina, fearful that the other customers would notice, took out a white handkerchief and shook Satoko by the shoulder. Her gesture struck Kiyoaki as harsh, and he glared at her angrily.

"Why are you looking at me like that?" she retorted, her words full of rudeness. "Don't you realize, young master, that I've been driving myself frantic for you and Miss Satoko? And not just you, young master—Miss Satoko, you don't understand what I've been through either. It would be better if old people like me had already departed this earth."

A waiter had placed three bowls of red bean soup on the table in front of them, but nobody touched them. A bit of hot bean paste clung to the edge of the small lacquer cover on one of them like a daub of slowly hardening mud.

Their time together was short. The two parted with no more than a vague promise to meet again in ten days.

That night his agony of mind raged unchecked. He wondered if Satoko would ever agree to meet him at night again, and felt rejected by the whole world. Now that he was plunged in despair, he could no longer doubt his love for her.

When he had seen her tears today, he saw that she belonged to him wholeheartedly. But at the same time he understood that a mere rapport no longer had the strength to sustain them.

What he was experiencing now was genuine emotion.

When he compared this to the various sentiments of love that had once occupied his imagination, he knew that this was something crude and blunt, violent and sinister, an emotion that was altogether far removed from elegance. It was hardly the stuff that poems are made of. For the first time in his life, he accepted raw ugliness as indeed being part of him.

After a sleepless night, he went to school next day with his face pale and haggard. Honda noticed this at once and questioned him; his eyes filled with tears in response to his friend's shy kind-heartedness.

"This is what's the matter: Satoko's not going to sleep with me any more, I think."

Honda's face flushed with virginal consternation.

"What do you mean?"

"It's because the betrothal ceremony's finally been arranged for December."

"And so she feels she can no longer . . . ?"

"That seems to be it precisely."

Honda could think of nothing to say to console his friend. This was a situation outside his range of experience, and he was saddened to think that he had nothing to offer but his usual generalizations. Even if it were futile, he would have to climb to a vantage point in place of his friend, survey the lay of the land, and then offer a psychological analysis.

"That time when she was with you at Kamakura, didn't you say that you happened to get a feeling that you might tire of her someday?"

"But that was only for an instant."

"Perhaps she's only putting you off like this because she wants you to love her more fiercely and more deeply."

For once, however, Honda had miscalculated in attempting to make use of Kiyoaki's delusions of vanity as a means to console him. For he had not the slightest interest in his own attractiveness any more, nor even in Satoko's love for him.

He was only concerned with when and where the two of them could meet without anxiety, as freely as they liked, regardless of anyone else. And he feared that by now it could only happen in some place beyond this world, and only when this world had been destroyed. The vital issue was not feeling but circumstance. In his weary, desperate, bloodshot eyes there was a vision of a world thrown into chaos for their sake.

"If only there were a great earthquake! If so, then I could rescue her. Or a major war would do just as well. If it broke out, what couldn't I do then! . . . But no, what I'm after is something that will shake the whole country to its foundations."

"And who is going to bring about this great event of yours?" asked Honda, looking at this elegant young man with pity in his eyes. He knew that irony and a touch of scorn were now the best means of strengthening his friend. "Why don't you give it a try yourself?"

Kiyoaki made no attempt to hide his distress. A young man obsessed with love had no time for such things. But there was more than that in his expression. Honda felt a shiver of fascination when he saw the destructive gleam momentarily kindled in Kiyoaki's eyes by his taunt.

It was as if a pack of wolves went raging through the darkness of a sacred precinct. The malevolence fell short of realization: it escaped the notice of Kiyoaki himself: it was born and died in his eyes—but for an instant they flashed with the image of a savage destroyer.

"How am I going to break out?" Kiyoaki muttered as if to himself. "Would power do it? Or money?"

Honda thought it more than a little ridiculous for the son of Marquis Matsugae to be talking in these terms.

"Well, as far as power goes, what are your prospects?" he asked coldly.

"I'll do everything I can to acquire some. But still, that takes time."

"There has never been the slightest chance that either power or money would be of any use. You're not forgetting, are you? From the very beginning you've been bewitched by *impossibility*—something which is outside the scope of authority and money. You were drawn in precisely because the whole thing was impossible. Am I wrong? And if it were to become possible now, would it have any value for you?"

"But it did once become possible."

"You saw an illusion of possibility. You saw the rainbow. What else do you want now?"

"What else . . . ?"

Kiyoaki faltered and his words came to a stop. Beyond this interruption spread a vast great void, unfathomable to Honda. He shuddered.

"These words we exchange," he thought, "they're like a mass of building blocks lying scattered over a construction site in the dead of the night. With the immense, starry sky spread out about them and its awful pressure of silence, what else can they do but be mute?"

The two of them were talking at the end of the first period of the school day as they walked along the path that led through the grove surrounding Chiarai Pond. Since the second period was almost upon them, they now turned and retraced their steps. A vast variety of objects had come to rest on the path underfoot as it wound its way through the autumn woods—tangled heaps of wet, brown leaves, their skeletons conspicuous, acorns, green chestnuts, split open and rotting, cigarette butts. Then in the midst of all this, Honda saw something that made him stop and stare at the ground. It was a whitish, crumpled lump of fur, sickly white. By the time he had recognized it as the body of a young mole, Kiyoaki had also stopped and squatted down to study it in silence as it lay in the sunlight filtering down through the branches overhead. The dead animal was lying on its back, and the whiteness that had caught Honda's attention was the fur of its belly. The rest of its body was a sleek, velvet black. Mud was worked into the lines of its tiny, intricately formed white paws, proof of strenuous digging. As it was lying on its back, they could see its pointed beaklike mouth. Its death rictus revealed the soft, pink interior of its mouth behind the two delicate incisors.

At the same moment the two young men thought of the

black dog whose dead body had hung over the edge of the waterfall on the Matsugae estate until sent on its way with altogether unexpected funereal solemnity.

Kiyoaki picked the young mole up by its almost hairless tail and laid it gently in his palm. It was already rather shriveled, and so there was nothing distasteful about it. What was disturbing, however, was that this wretched little animal was condemned to labor blindly and without purpose. The very care and delicacy that had gone into the shaping of its tiny paws were odious.

Kiyoaki took the animal by the tail again as he stood up. At this point the path passed close to the pond, and he casually turned and threw the animal into the water.

"Why did you do that?" demanded Honda, frowning at his friend's offhandedness. This rough behavior, typical of a student, allowed him to read at a glance the depth of his friend's desolation.

 39

SEVEN DAYS PASSED, then eight, but there was still no word from Tadeshina. After ten days Kiyoaki telephoned the innkeeper in Roppongi and was told that Tadeshina was apparently ill and confined to her bed. More days went by. Then when the innkeeper told him that she was still ill, his suspicions were aroused.

Hounded by wild desperation, he went to Azabu alone one night and walked aimlessly around the streets near the Ayakura mansion. When he passed underneath the light of the gas lamps in Toriizaka, he stretched out his hands. He was shaken to see how pale their backs looked, for he remembered once hearing that invalids near to death look at their hands constantly.

The gate in front of the Ayakura mansion was shut fast. The faint light above it was scarcely enough to read even the lettering of the weather-beaten nameplate that loomed up out of the darkness. This house was always poorly lit. He knew that there would be no chance of seeing a light in Satoko's room from the street.

He looked at the latticed windows of the empty lodges that flanked the gate. He remembered how he and Satoko had stolen in there as children, and become frightened by the gloom and smell of mold in the deserted rooms. Yearning for the sunlight outside, they had rushed to the windows and grasped the wooden latticework covered with dust. The same layer of dust was still there. The leaves of the trees around the house opposite had been so lush and green that it must have happened in May. Close-worked as the lattice was, it had not shut out this greenery, perhaps because the two young faces peering through it were so small. Just then, a man selling seedlings had gone by, and the two of them, giggling to themselves, had mimicked him as he cried "Morning glories, eggplants," comically dragging out the syllables.

He had learned much in this house. The smell of ink used in calligraphy invariably had melancholy associations for him. Melancholy, in fact, was inseparably bound up with the elegance that had become part of him. All of the beautiful things that the Count had shown him—sutras copied in gold on purple scrolls, screens with the autumn flower design favored in the imperial palaces in Kyoto—must have emitted a bright ray of carnal desire, he now realized, but in the Ayakura mansion the smell of ink and mold had lain heavy on everything. But now, within these walls that shut him out tonight, that elegance and seductive brilliance had come to life again after the lapse of many years. And he was completely cut off from it.

A faint light went out on the second floor of the house, which was fairly visible from the street. Perhaps Count and Countess Ayakura had gone to sleep. The Count had always gone to bed early. Maybe Satoko was still lying awake. But her light could not be seen. He walked along the wall until he came to the rear gate. There, without thinking, he stretched out his hand to push the cracked and yellowed doorbell, but then drew back.

Stricken with shame at his cowardice, he turned and went home.

More days passed, a terrible period of dead calm. Then still more days. He went to school, but only as a means of somehow getting through each day. When he came home, he gave no thought to his studies.

All around him at school were constant reminders that many of his classmates, Honda among them, were totally absorbed in preparations for the next spring's university entrance examination. It was no more difficult to recognize the behavior of those who were planning to take the easier route of entering schools that did not have entrance requirements. These students were zealously pursuing their favorite sports. Since he had nothing in common with either camp, Kiyoaki became more and more lonely. If someone spoke to him, he often did not answer, and so his classmates began to be rather unfriendly.

One day when he returned from school, he found Yamada the steward waiting for him at the entranceway.

"His Excellency came home early today, and he expressed a desire to play billiards with the young master. He now awaits him in the billiard room," Yamada announced.

Kiyoaki felt his heart beat faster as he heard this altogether extraordinary summons. True, the Marquis did sometimes feel the whim to have Kiyoaki's partnership in a game of billiards, but this was customarily restricted to the mellow period after dinner when the Marquis still savored the effects of the wine he had been drinking.

If his father were seized by such a mood while it was still no more than mid-afternoon, he must, Kiyoaki thought, be either in exceptionally good or exceptionally bad spirits.

He hardly ever entered the billiard room during the day. He

pushed open the heavy door and walked in. The sun was shining in through the west windows, its rays slightly distorted by the glass. When he saw how the oak paneling gleamed in the sunlight, he had the feeling that he had entered this room for the first time.

The Marquis, cue in hand and face pressed close to the baize, was in the act of taking aim at a white ball. The fingers of his left hand, cradling the tip of his cue, made Kiyoaki think of the bridge under a koto string.

"Shut the door," said the Marquis to Kiyoaki, who had stopped just inside the half-opened door, still in his school uniform. His father's features were tinged by reflections from the green surface of the billiard table so close to his face, so Kiyoaki found it difficult to gauge his expression.

"Read that. It's Tadeshina's farewell," said the Marquis, straightening up at last and using the tip of his cue to indicate an envelope that was lying on a small table by the window.

"Is she dead?" asked Kiyoaki, feeling his hand shake as he picked up the envelope.

"No, she's not dead. She's recovering. She's not dead—which makes the whole thing that much more disgraceful." As he answered, the Marquis appeared to be making an effort not to march over to where his son was standing.

Kiyoaki hesitated.

"Hurry up and read it!" For the first time, there was a cutting edge to the Marquis's voice.

He unrolled the long sheet of paper on which Tadeshina had written what was intended as her deathbed testimony, and began to read, still standing in front of the window.

> When the time comes for Your Excellency to deign to take forbearing note of this letter, I would beg you to think of Tadeshina who writes it as one who has already departed this world. But before I cut the slender thread that binds this wretched creature to life—the just reward for what I contritely acknowledge to be my heinous and sinful deeds—I am writing this in anxious haste both to confess the gravity of my sins and to offer a dying plea to Your Excellency.

The truth of the matter is that it has recently become evident that, due to Tadeshina's negligence in her entrusted
duties, Miss Satoko Ayakura is pregnant. Being overcome
with dread when I learned of this, I endeavored to persuade
her that something must be done about her condition at once,
but try as I might, my words were of no avail. Realizing that
the matter would become more crucial as time went by, I went
to Count Ayakura on my own initiative and told him everything in full detail. But my master did no more than say
'What am I to do? What am I to do?' and he did not deign to
give the least indication of his intention to take definite action.
Finally, knowing full well that it would become more difficult
to settle this matter as each month passed, and that it might
become a grave affair of state, it became clear that Tadeshina,
whose disloyalty was the source of all this tribulation, now
had no other course open to her but to sacrifice herself and to
cast herself in supplication at the feet of Your Excellency.

I fear that this will anger Your Excellency, but since this
matter of Miss Ayakura's pregnancy may be something that
could be termed 'within the family' please, please, I beg of
Your Excellency that you bring to it your gracious wisdom
and discretion. Please have pity on an old woman hurrying
toward death, and deign to intercede in this matter of my
mistress. This I beg of you from the shadow of the grave.

Humbly yours.

When he had finished reading the letter, Kiyoaki sup-
pressed the momentary rush of cowardly relief that he had not
been named in it, and hoped that his look would not express a
dishonest denial to his father. Nevertheless, he noticed that
his lips were dry and his temples were throbbing feverishly.

"Did you read it?" asked the Marquis. "Did you read the
part that says she requests my gracious wisdom and discretion
because this is a matter 'within the family'? No matter how
close we've been to the Ayakuras, one would hardly describe
anything between us as a 'family matter.' But Tadeshina
dared to put that on paper. If you can possibly make a case for
yourself, go ahead and make it. Say it right here before the
portrait of your grandfather! If I happen to be wrong, I'll
apologize. As your father, I have every reason in the world

not to want to make such conjectures. Beyond any doubt it's a detestable thing, a detestable conjecture."

His frivolous hedonist of a father had never been capable of inspiring such awe in Kiyoaki before. Nor had he ever seemed possessed of such dignity. Irritably striking the palm of one hand with his billiard cue, the Marquis stood flanked by the portrait of his father and the painting of the Battle of Tsushima. This huge oil painting, which showed the vanguard of the Japanese fleet deploying before the Russians in the Sea of Japan, was more than half taken up with the massive, dark green billows of the ocean. Kiyoaki was accustomed to seeing it only at night, and the meager lamplight had prevented him from appreciating the fine detail of the waves, which merged at night into the dark irregular shadows that covered the wall. But now in daytime, he saw how the somber blue of the waves towered up in the foreground with ponderous force, while in the distance a lighter green blended in to brighten the dark water, and here and there foaming white crests topped the waves. And then the trailing wakes of the maneuvering squadron spread out with smooth uniformity over the surface of this turbulent northern sea with terrible impact. The line of the Japanese main fleet heading farther out to sea was painted horizontally on the canvas, with its plumes of smoke drifting to the right against a sky whose chilly blue contained a touch of pale green as befitted a northern May.

In contrast, the portrait of Kiyoaki's grandfather in ceremonial robes was imbued with a human warmth, despite his evident sternness. Even now he did not seem to be chiding Kiyoaki, but rather admonishing him with both dignity and affection. He felt that he could confess anything at all to this portrait of his ancestor. Here in front of his grandfather— the face with the heavy eyelids, the cheeks with their warts, the thick lower lip—he had the exultant feeling that his indecisiveness was being cured, if only temporarily.

"There's nothing for me to say. It is as you suppose," he

said, speaking the words without even dropping his eyes. "It's
my child."

Despite the Marquis's threatening pose, his actual mood
on finding himself caught up in such a situation was one of
desperate confusion. Handling such things had never been his
strong point. So now, although the stage was set for him to
proceed to a stinging rebuke, he instead began to mutter to
himself.

"Once wasn't enough for old Tadeshina," he muttered.
"She had to have a second little secret for me. Well and good
the first time—nothing but a naughty houseboy. But this time
it had to do with no less than the son of a marquis. And yet
she could not even kill herself off successfully. Intriguing old
bitch!"

The Marquis had always eluded life's more subtle problems with a hearty burst of laughter, and now that one had
cropped up calling for indignation, he was nonplussed. This
beefy, red-faced man differed strikingly from his own father
in that he was vain enough to try not to appear harsh and unfeeling to others, including his own son. He was thus anxious
to prevent his anger from appearing as old-fashioned wrath,
but his consequent bewilderment made him feel that the sus-
taining forces of unreason were draining away. At the same
time, there was an advantage in anger: it made him quite
incapable of reflection.

His father's momentary hesitation gave him courage. Like
pure water spurting from a cleft in a rock, words came out of
this young man's mouth as the most natural and spontaneous
he would ever utter: "However that may be, Satoko is mine."

"Yours, did you say? Say that again, would you? Yours, did
you say?" demanded the Marquis, happy to have his son relieve him of the task of giving vent to his outrage. Now, his
heart at peace, he could air his rage blindly. "How dare you
speak like this now! When it first became a probability that
Satoko might become engaged to Prince Toin, didn't I try to
ensure that you had no objection? Didn't I say to you, 'At this

stage things can still be reversed. If your feelings are at all involved, tell me?' "

The Marquis tried to alternate between scorn and conciliation, but in his fury he botched the attempt. Moving along the edge of the billiard table, he came so close that Kiyoaki could see his hand trembling around the cue it held. For the first time, he felt a touch of fear.

"And what did you say then? Eh? What did you say? 'I'm not at all involved'—that's how you answered me. That certainly amounted to a man's word, didn't it? But are you a man, I wonder? I regretted raising you in such a soft and easy way, but I never realized you'd turn out like this. To lay hands on someone betrothed to an imperial prince after the Emperor himself has sanctioned the marriage! To go so far as to make her pregnant! To stain your family honor! To throw mud in your father's face! Could there be any disloyalty, any breach of filial piety worse than this? If it were in times gone by, I as your father would have had to cut my belly open and die in atonement to the Emperor. You've behaved like an animal. You've done something that's rotten through and through. Do you hear me? Just what do you have to say for yourself, Kiyoaki? You won't answer me? You'll still defy me, will you?"

The instant that he perceived the panting urgency in his father's words, Kiyoaki dodged to one side to avoid the brandished billiard cue, but he nevertheless caught a solid blow across the back. His father followed that up at once with another that numbed the arm that had tried to protect his back. And as he frantically sought his only escape, the library door, a third blow, meant for his head, missed its target and struck across the bridge of the nose. At this point Kiyoaki collided with a chair in his path and stumbled to the floor, grasping the arm of the chair as he did so to break his fall. As the blood began to spurt from his nose, his father finally held off with his cue.

Each blow must have provoked a sharp cry from Kiyoaki, and now the library door opened to reveal his grandmother and mother in the doorway. The Marquise stood trembling behind her mother-in-law as her husband, still grasping his cue and panting heavily, went rigid.

"What's this?" asked his grandmother.

With that, Marquis Matsugae seemed to notice his mother's presence for the first time, though it was clear from his expression that he found it hard to believe she was actually standing in the doorway. Far less was he capable of guessing how she had got there: that his wife, grasping the drift of events, had probably gone to fetch her. His mother's setting foot outside her retreat was by no means an everyday occurrence.

"Kiyoaki has been a disgrace. You'll understand if you read Tadeshina's farewell on the table there."

"Did Tadeshina kill herself?"

"The letter came in the mail. Then I phoned the Ayakuras to find out . . ."

"And what did you find out?" asked his mother, now seated in a chair beside the small table as she slowly pulled out of her obi the black velvet case that contained the glasses she wore to boost her failing sight. She carefully opened the purselike case.

As the Marquise stood watching her mother-in-law she suddenly realized why she had not yet spared so much as a glance for her grandson. It was a sign of her determination to cope with the Marquis single-handed. Sensing this, she rushed in relief to Kiyoaki's side. He had already taken out his handkerchief and was holding it to his bloody nose. The wound hardly seemed to be grave.

"And what did you find out?" repeated the Marquis's mother, unrolling the scroll.

Her son felt that something inside him was already crumbling.

"I phoned and inquired about Tadeshina. They caught her in time and she's recovering. And then the Count asked me suspiciously how I happened to know about it. Apparently he didn't know about her letter. She took an overdose of sleeping pills and I warned the Count that he had to prevent any word of it leaking out. But since, all things considered, my son was at fault, I could not possibly put all the blame on the Count. So the whole conversation became thoroughly pointless. We have to meet as soon as possible to talk it over, I told him, but . . . At any rate, one thing at least is clear; unless I come to a decision myself, nothing at all will be done."

"Very true. Very true indeed," said the old lady absent-mindedly as she ran her eyes over the letter.

Oddly enough, her unsophisticated country vigor—the heavy forehead glowing with health, the blunt, powerful lines of the face, the skin still ruddy with the hot sun of a generation gone by, the bobbed hair dyed a simple, glossy black—her every trait harmonized perfectly with the Victorian setting of the billiard room.

"Well, it doesn't seem that Kiyoaki is mentioned anywhere here by name, does it?"

"Please, that part about 'within the family.' One glance should be enough to tell you it's an insinuation. But, whatever else, I heard it from his own lips. He confessed that it was his child. In other words, you're on your way to becoming a great-grandmother, Mother, and of an illegitimate child at that."

"Perhaps Kiyoaki is protecting someone and his confession is false."

"You'll say anything at all, won't you, Mother? Please go ahead and ask Kiyoaki yourself."

She turned to Kiyoaki at last and spoke to him affectionately, as if he were a child of five or six.

"Listen, Kiyoaki. Look at me straight, now. Look Granny straight in the eye and answer my question. Then you can't tell fibs. Now, what your father said—is it the truth?"

Kiyoaki turned toward her, mastering the pain he still felt in his back and clutching the now blood-soaked handkerchief to his nose, which was still bleeding. With tears in his eyes and careless streaks of blood clinging to the tip of his prominent nose, he seemed pathetically young, like a wet-nosed puppy.

"It's true," he said quickly in nasal tones, immediately

seizing the fresh handkerchief proferred by his mother and clapping it to his face.

His grandmother then made a speech that seemed to echo the hoofbeats of horses galloping free, a speech that eloquently tore to shreds the conventional niceties.

"Getting the betrothed of the Imperial Prince pregnant! Now there's an achievement! How many of these simpering lads nowadays are capable of anything like that? No doubt about it—Kiyoaki's a true grandson of my husband's. You won't regret it even if you are jailed for it. At least they surely won't execute you," she said, obviously enjoying herself. The stern lines around her mouth were gone now, and she seemed aglow with a lively satisfaction, as if she had banished decades of stifling gloom, dispersing at a single stroke the enervating pall that had hung over the house ever since the present Marquis had become its master. Nor was she laying the blame on her son alone. She was speaking now in retaliation against all those others, too, who surrounded her in her old age, and whose treacherous power she could sense closing in to crush her. Her voice came echoing gaily out of another era, one of upheavals, a violent era forgotten by this generation, in which fear of imprisonment and death held no one in check, an era in which the threat of both was part of the texture of everyday life. She belonged to a generation of women who had thought nothing of washing their dinner plates in a river while corpses went floating past. That was life! And now, how remarkable that this grandson, who seemed so effete at first glance, should have revived the spirit of that age before her very eyes.

The old lady stared off into space, a look of almost drunken satisfaction on her face. The Marquis and Marquise stared at it in shocked silence—the face of an old woman too stern, too full of rough country beauty to be presented to the public as the matriarch of the Marquis's household.

"Mother, what are you saying?" said the Marquis weakly, finally shaking himself out of his stupor. "This could mean the ruin of the House of Matsugae—and it's also a terrible affront to Father."

"That's very true," she replied at once. "And so what you've got to think about now is not punishing Kiyoaki but how best to protect the House of Matsugae. The nation is important, of course, but we must think of the family too. After all, we're not like the Ayakuras, who have enjoyed the imperial favor for more than twenty-seven generations, are we now? So what do you think must be done?"

"Well, we have no choice but to go through with it as if nothing had happened, right up to the betrothal ceremony and the marriage."

"That's all very fine and clear, but something has to be done about Satoko's baby as quickly as possible. And if it's done anywhere near Tokyo and the newspapers somehow find out, then you'll have a fine mess. Don't you have anything practical to suggest?"

"Osaka would be the place," replied the Marquis, after a moment's thought. "Dr. Mori would do it for us in the strictest secrecy. And I'll make it worth his while. But Satoko will have to have some plausible reason for going to Osaka."

"The Ayakuras have all sorts of relatives down there. So wouldn't it be a perfect chance to send Satoko down to visit them and tell them in person about her engagement?"

"But if she has to visit a number of relatives and they notice her condition . . . that wouldn't do at all. But wait. I have it. How about having her go to Gesshu Temple in Nara to pay her final respects to the Abbess before her marriage? Wouldn't that be best? It's a temple that's always been closely associated with the Imperial Family, and so it would only be proper to show the Abbess this honor. All things considered, it would be perfectly natural. The Abbess has been fond of her ever since she was a little girl. So first she goes to Osaka to receive the attentions of Dr. Mori. Then she rests for a day or two, then she goes to Nara. That would be best. And her mother should go with her, I suppose. . . ."

"Not just her mother. That wouldn't do," said the old lady sternly. "Count Ayakura's wife can't be expected to have our interests at heart. Someone from here has to go along with them and look after the girl both before and after Dr. Mori's treatment. And it has to be a woman. So . . . ," she pondered and then turned to Kiyoaki's mother: "Tsujiko, you go."

"Very well."

"And you've got to keep your eyes open all the time. You don't have to go to Nara with her. But once you've seen that the crucial thing is done, come back to Tokyo as quick as you can to give us a full report."

"I understand."

"Mother's right," said the Marquis. "Do just as she says. I'll talk to the Count and we'll decide what day she's to leave. Everything will have to be done so that no one gets the least hint of what's going on."

Kiyoaki felt that he had become part of the background and that his life and love for Satoko were being treated as things already terminated. Before his very eyes, his father and mother and grandmother seemed to be carefully planning the funeral, quite unconcerned that the corpse could hear every word. Even before his funeral, something seemed already to have been buried. And so on the one hand he was like an attenuated corpse and, on the other, a severely scolded child who had no one to turn to.

Everything was thus proceeding smoothly to an altogether satisfactory conclusion, although the person most intimately concerned had no role in it and the wishes of the Ayakuras themselves were being ignored. Even his grandmother, who just a moment before had been speaking so daringly, now seemed to be basking in the pleasures of coping with a family crisis. Her character was essentially different from his, with its delicacy, and while she was endowed with the intelligence to perceive the savage nobility that lay at the root of his dishonorable behavior, once family honor was at stake, this same intelligence enabled her to put aside her admiration and adroitly conceal any such noble manifestations. This faculty, one might well suppose, she owed not to the summer sun that beat down on Kagoshima Bay but to the tutoring of her husband, Kiyoaki's grandfather.

The Marquis looked directly at Kiyoaki for the first time since he had aimed his billiard cue at him.

"From now on, you are confined to this house, and you are to fulfill your duties as a student. All your energy is to go into studying for the examinations. Do you quite understand? I shall say nothing further about this matter. This is the turning point: either you will become a man or you will not. As for Satoko, I need hardly say that you are not to see her again."

"In the old days, they called it house arrest, you know," said his grandmother. "If you get tired of studying sometimes, come over and see Granny."

And then it dawned on Kiyoaki that his father could never disown him now—he was much too afraid of what the world would say.

 40

COUNT AYAKURA WAS a hopeless coward in the face of such things as injury, sickness, and death. There was quite a disturbance on the morning that Tadeshina did not get up. The suicide note left on her pillow was brought to the Countess at once, and when she in turn handed it over to her husband, he opened it at fingertips' length, as if it were germ-ridden. It turned out to be nothing more than a simple farewell note apologizing for the many defects that had marred her service to the Count and Countess, and to Satoko, and thanking them for their never-failing benevolence, the sort of note that could fall into any hands at all and still not excite suspicion.

The Countess sent for the doctor at once. The Count, of

course, did not go to see for himself, but was content to receive a full report from his wife afterwards.

"She took more than a hundred and twenty sleeping pills. She hasn't recovered consciousness yet, but the doctor told me what she'd done. My goodness, she was flailing her arms and legs and her body was convulsed like a bow—what a commotion! No one knew where the old woman could find such strength. But then, all of us held her down together and there was the injection and then the doctor pumped out her stomach—that was frightful and I tried not to look. And the doctor finally assured me that she was going to live. How wonderful to have such expertise! Before we said anything at all, he sniffed her breath and said: 'Ah, a smell of garlic. It must be Calmotin tablets.' He knew right away."

"Did he say how long it would take her to recover?"

"Yes, he was kind enough to tell me that she would have to rest for at least ten days."

"Be sure that nothing of this becomes known outside the house. You'll have to warn the women to keep their mouths shut and we'll have to speak to the doctor too. How is Satoko taking this?"

"She's shut herself in her room. She won't even go and see Tadeshina. In her present condition I think it might not be good for her to visit Tadeshina right now. And then, she hasn't said a word to her since Tadeshina raised that matter with us, so she probably feels disinclined to rush in to see her. The best thing would be to leave Satoko alone."

Five days before, Tadeshina, at her wit's end, had broken the news of Satoko's pregnancy to the Count and Countess, but instead of flying into a rage and subjecting her to the expected torrent of rebukes, the Count had in fact reacted so listlessly that she had been driven in desperation to write the letter to Marquis Matsugae and then to take an overdose of sleeping pills.

Satoko had persisted in rejecting Tadeshina's advice. Although the danger was growing more acute with each day that

passed, she not only ordered Tadeshina to say nothing to anyone, but she gave no slightest indication that she herself was
ever going to come to a decision. And so, unable to bear this
any longer, Tadeshina had betrayed her mistress by telling
her secret to her mother and father. But the Count and
Countess—perhaps because the news was such a stunning
blow—had shown no more perturbation than if the news had
been of a cat running off with one of the chickens in the back-
yard.

The day after she told him, and the day after that too,
Tadeshina happened to cross paths with the Count, but he
gave no sign of being concerned about the problem. He was,
in fact, profoundly shaken. But since the problem was at once
too vast to deal with on his own and too embarrassing to discuss with others, he made every effort to put it out of his mind.

He and his wife had agreed to say nothing to Satoko until
they were ready to take some kind of action. Satoko, however,
whose perceptions were now at their keenest, subjected Tadeshina to a cross-examination and so found out what had
happened. And with that, she shut herself in her room and
would have no more to do with her, and an uncanny silence
fell over the house. Tadeshina stopped receiving any com-
munications from the outside world, telling the servants to
say that she was sick.

The Count avoided the problem even with his wife. He was
fully aware of the fearful nature of the circumstances and of
the necessity for immediate action, but he continued to pro-
crastinate nonetheless. This did not mean that he believed in
miracles either.

Count Ayakura's paralysis did have a sort of refinement.
Although one could hardly deny that his chronic indecisiveness involved a certain skepticism about the value of any
decision at all, he was by no means a skeptic in the ordinary
sense of the word. Even though he was plunged in meditation
from morning to night, he was loath to direct his immense
emotional reserves toward a single conclusion. Meditation had
a great deal in common with *kemari*, the traditional sport of

the Ayakuras. No matter how high one kicked the ball, it would obviously come down to earth again at once. Even if his illustrious ancestor Namba Munetate could excite cries of admiration when he picked up the white deerskin ball by its thongs of purple leather and kicked it to such incredible heights that it topped the ninety-foot roof of the imperial residence itself, it must inevitably fall back again into the garden.

Since all the solutions left something to be desired in terms of good taste, it was better to wait for someone else to make the unpleasant decision. Someone else's foot would have to stretch out to intercept the falling ball. Even if one kicked the ball oneself, it was quite possible that it might be seized by some unexpected whim of its own as it reached the high point of its arc, and come sailing down in a new and unpredictable trajectory.

The specter of ruin never rose before the Count. If it was not a grave crisis to have the fiancée of an imperial prince, whose engagement had been sanctioned by the Emperor himself, carrying another man's offspring in her womb, then the world would never know a grave crisis. Still, the descending ball would not inevitably be his to kick; surely someone else's turn to cope with it would come. The Count was never one to be long vexed by worries, and as an inevitable consequence, his worries always ended up by vexing others.

And then it happened that on the day after the tumult of Tadeshina's attempt on her life, the telephone call came from Marquis Matsugae.

*

That the Marquis should have known what had happened despite all efforts to hush it up was simply incredible to the Count. He would not have been surprised to learn that there was an informer in his household. But since his prime suspect, Tadeshina herself, had been unconscious throughout the previous day, all his most likely speculations were left with the ground cut out from under them.

Having heard from his wife that Tadeshina was recovering at a good rate, that she could talk and that her appetite had even returned, the Count therefore summoned up his extreme reserves of courage and decided to visit the sickroom all by himself.

"You needn't come with me. I'll go and see her on my own. Perhaps the woman will be more inclined to tell the truth that way," he told his wife.

"But the room is in a terrible state, and if you visit her without warning, she'll be upset. I'll go and tell her first, and help her to get herself ready."

"As you wish."

The Count had to endure a two-hour wait. When the patient heard the news from the Countess, she immediately began to apply her makeup.

She had been granted the exceptional privilege of a room in the main house, but it was no more than four and a half mats large, and never caught the sun. When her bedding was laid out, it occupied almost the whole floor. The Count had never been in there before.

Finally, a servant came to escort him to the room. A chair for him had been placed on the tatami floor and Tadeshina's bedding had been put away. Dressed in a sleeved coverlet and with her elbows supported on a pile of pillows on her lap, Tadeshina bowed in reverence as the master entered. As she did so, her forehead seemed to press down on the pillows in front of her, but he noticed that, perfect as her bow was, she overcame her weakness sufficiently to preserve a slight gap between her forehead and the pillows. She was concerned about her makeup, that smooth expanse of thick, congealed white that extended right up to her scrupulously groomed hairline.

"Well, you've had quite an ordeal," the Count began, after sitting down. "But you pulled through, and that's the main thing. You shouldn't worry us so."

Although he found nothing awkward in looking down at her from his position in the chair, he felt that for some reason neither his voice nor his meaning was reaching her.

"How unworthy I am to receive Your Excellency's visit! I am altogether in a state of dread. Never can I express adequately the deep shame that I feel . . ."

Her head still bowed, she seemed to be dabbing her eyes with the tissue paper she had pulled from her sleeve, but he realized that in so doing she was again being careful to preserve her makeup.

"According to the doctor, ten days rest and you'll be your old self again. So just relax and take a good long rest."

"Oh thank you so much, Your Excellency. I am covered with shame, having failed so miserably in trying to die."

As the Count looked down at the old woman cowering in her russet chrysanthemum-patterned bedjacket, he sensed the offensive aura that surrounds someone who has gone down the road of death only to turn back. He smelled the breath of defilement that clung to everything in the small room, even to its cabinet and drawers, and he grew more and more uneasy. The very care and skill that had gone into the application of the liquid white makeup on the nape of her neck, still visible as she bowed her head, and that had arranged her coiffure so that not a single hair straggled out of place, only served to intensify his indefinable sense of fear.

"Actually," he said, putting the question as casually as he could, "I was rather taken aback to receive a telephone call from Marquis Matsugae today. He already knew what had happened. And so I thought I might ask you if you did not have some explanation for it."

But there are questions that answer themselves as soon as they are formulated. The words had hardly passed his lips before the answer came to him with startling suddenness, just as she raised her head.

The old court-style makeup covering her face was thicker than ever. She had painted her lips a bright red that covered even their innermost edge. Not content merely to subdue her wrinkles with makeup, she had applied layer upon layer of white to create a smooth surface which did not, however,

blend into her skin, roughened by her recent ordeal. The
effect was as if the makeup were clinging to her skin as though
the pores had sprouted a white mold. The Count furtively
looked away before he started to speak again.

"You wrote to the Marquis beforehand, didn't you?"

"Yes, Your Excellency," she answered, her head still raised,
her voice quite steady. "I really intended to die, and so I wrote
to him begging him to do what was necessary after I was
gone."

"You told him everything in that letter?"

"No, sir."

"There are things you left out?"

"Yes, Your Excellency, there are many things I left out,"
she replied, now cheerful.

 41

ALTHOUGH THE COUNT HAD no very clear-cut idea
of anything he might wish to keep from Marquis Matsugae,
he had only to hear Tadeshina mention her omissions to feel
suddenly uneasy.

"And the things you left out—what were they?"

"What does the master mean? I answered Your Excellency as I did, simply because you were pleased to ask me if
I had told the Marquis *everything* in the letter. There must
be something on the master's mind to make him ask such a
question."

"This is no time to talk in riddles. I've come here alone like
this because I thought we could talk freely without regard
for others. So it would be as well if you said clearly what you
meant."

"There are many, many things I did not discuss in that
letter. Among them is the matter that the master was pleased
to confide to me some eight years ago at Kitazaki's. I intended
to die with that sealed in my heart."

"Kitazaki's?"

The Count shuddered as he heard that name, which rang
like doom in his ears. He now understood what Tadeshina
had been hinting at, and as he did so his anxiety deepened.
He felt driven to tear away any vestige of doubt.

"What did I say at Kitazaki's?"

"It was an evening during the rainy season. The master can
hardly have forgotten. Miss Satoko, though she was slowly
growing up to be a young lady, was still only thirteen. Marquis
Matsugae came here that day to pay one of his rare visits.
And when he was leaving, the master's mood seemed to be
not what it should be. And so he went to Kitazaki's house for
a little recreation. And that night he was pleased to tell me
something."

The Count was fully aware of the drift of Tadeshina's
remarks. She intended to forge a weapon from his words that
night and to make her own dereliction entirely his responsibility. He suddenly doubted that she had ever really intended to
kill herself.

Her eyes now regarded him from the heavily powdered face
above the pile of pillows like two loopholes cut into the white
walls of a fortress. The darkness behind that wall was teem-
ing with things from the past and out of it could come flying
an arrow, aimed at him as he stood exposed in the bright light
outside.

"Why do you bring that up now? It was something I said
as a joke."

"Was it really?"

Suddenly those loophole eyes seemed to narrow still further.
He had the feeling that darkness itself in all its intensity was
pointed at him. Then she went on, her voice heavy, "But still
. . . that night, at Kitazaki's house. . . ."

Kitazaki, Kitazaki—that name, bound up with memories

the Count had been trying to ignore, came to the lips of this sly old woman again and again. Though eight years had passed since he last set foot there, every detail of the house now sprang vividly to mind once again. The inn stood at the foot of a slope, and although it had no gate nor entranceway to speak of, it was surrounded by quite a large garden with a wooden fence. The gloomy, damp front hall, a spot favored by slugs and snails, had been preempted by four or five pairs of black boots. Even their blotched, yellowish brown leather linings, greasy and moldy with sweat, now flashed before his eyes, as did the broad-striped name-tabs that hung out of them. That night the sound of rude and boisterous singing had greeted him at the front door. The Russo-Japanese War was at its height, and the quartering of soldiers was a respectable and sure source of income. It had given the inn a reputable appearance along with the smell of a stable. As he was led to a room at the rear, he walked along the corridor as if passing through a quarantine ward, fearful even that his sleeve might brush against a pillar along the way. He had a profound aversion to human sweat and all that related to it.

On that night in the rainy season eight years ago, the Count had been unable to regain his usual composure after ushering out his guest the Marquis. And that was the moment that Tadeshina, shrewdly gauging her master's mood from his expression, had chosen to speak.

"Kitazaki tells me that something very amusing has come his way and that he would like nothing better than to offer it to the master for his enjoyment. Would the master not consider going there tonight, just for a little recreation?"

Since she was free to do such things as "visiting her relatives" once Satoko had gone to bed, there was no obstacle to her going out and then meeting the Count at a prearranged spot.

Kitazaki received the Count with extreme obsequiousness and served him saké, then left the room to return carrying an old scroll which he laid deferentially on the table.

"It is indeed noisy here tonight," he said apologetically.

"Somebody is about to leave for the front, and is having a farewell party. It's terribly hot, but perhaps it would be well to close the rain shutters, Your Excellency."

Kitazaki meant that by so doing, the din that echoed from the second floor of the main wing would be somewhat lessened. The Count agreed and he closed the shutters. However, the falling rain immediately seemed to sound more insistently on every side, caging him into the room. The brilliant color of the Genji sliding door gave it a kind of suffocating, panting sensuality, as though the room itself were a picture rolled up within a forbidden scroll.

Sitting opposite the Count, Kitazaki reached respectfully across the table with his wrinkled but honest-looking old hands and unfastened the purple cord that bound the scroll. Then he began to unroll it for the Count, revealing first the pretentious inscription at the top. It was a koan:

> Chao Chu went to a nun one day to say, "Do you have it? Do you have it?" And when the nun in turn raised her fists at him, Chao Chu went on his Way at once, declaring: "Shallow water affords poor anchorage."

The oppressive heat of that night! Its sultry torpor, only aggravated by the breeze stirred at his back by Tadeshina's fan, seemed to the Count to equal that of a rice-steaming basket. The saké had begun to take effect; the Count heard the drumming of the rain outside as if it were striking the back of his skull; the world outside was lost in innocent thoughts of victory in war. And thus the Count sat looking down at the erotic scroll. Suddenly Kitazaki's hands flashed through the air to clap together on a mosquito. He apologized at once for the disturbance of the noise, and the Count caught a glimpse of the tiny black smudge of crushed mosquito in his dry white palm, together with a red smear of blood, an unclean image that unsettled him. Why had the mosquito not bitten him? Was he really so well protected from everything?

The first picture on the scroll was that of an abbot in a brown robe and a young widow seated facing each other in front of a screen. The style was that of haiku illustrations, done with a light, humorous touch. The face of the abbot was drawn in caricature to look like a large penis.

In the next picture the abbot sprang upon the young widow without warning, intent on raping her, and although she was putting up a fight, her kimono was already in disarray. In the next they were locked in a naked embrace and the woman's expression was now blissfully relaxed. The abbot's penis was like the twisted root of a giant pine, and his brown tongue stuck out in great delight. In accordance with this artistic tradition, the young widow's feet and toes were painted with Chinese white, and curved sharply inward. Tremors ran the length of her white, clinging thighs and ended finally at her toes, as though the tension there embodied her straining effort to hold back the flood of ecstasy that was about to gush out into eternity. The woman's exertions were altogether admirable, thought the Count.

On the other side of the screen, meantime, a number of novice monks were standing on a wooden drum and a writing table, and boosting one another onto their shoulders, desperately keen to see what was going on behind the screen while simultaneously engaged in a comic struggle to keep down those parts of their anatomy that had already swollen to massive proportions. Finally the screen fell over. And as the stark-naked woman attempted to cover herself and escape, and the abbot lay exhausted with no strength left to reprimand the novices, a scene of total disorder began to unfold.

The monks' penises were drawn to appear nearly as long as their owners were tall, the usual proportions being inadequate for the artist to convey the magnitude of their burden of lust. As they set upon the woman, the face of each of them was a comic study in indescribable anguish, and they staggered about under the weight of their own erections.

After such punishing toil, the woman's entire body turned deathly pale and she died. Her soul flew out of her and took refuge in the branches of a willow tree blown by the wind.

And there she became a vengeful ghost, her face drawn in the image of a vulva.

At this point, the scroll lost whatever humor it had once had, and became permeated with fearful gloom. Not one but many ghosts, all similar, assaulted the men, hair streaming wildly, crimson lips gaping. Fleeing in panic, the men were no match for the phantoms, who swarmed over them in a whirlwind, tearing out their penises as well as the abbot's with their powerful jaws.

The final scene was by the seashore. The emasculated men lay naked on the beach, howling desperately, while a boat weighed down with their mutilated penises was just setting sail on a dark sea. The ghosts crowded the deck, hair streaming in the wind, pale hands waving derisively, their vaginal faces mocking the wretched cries of their victims on the shore. The prow of the boat, too, was carved in the form of a vulva, and as it pointed toward deep water, a tuft of hair clinging to it waved in the sea breeze.

*

When he finally looked up from the scroll, the Count felt inexplicably depressed. The saké, far from soothing him, had only increased his feelings of apprehension. But he had Kitazaki bring more of it, and drank it in silence. His mind was still filled with the vivid image of the woman in the scroll, her toes bent inward. The lewd whiteness of her painted legs still flashed before his eyes.

What he did next could only have been due to the languid heat of that night in the rainy season and to his own disgust. Fourteen years before that wet evening, when his wife had been pregnant with Satoko, he had favored Tadeshina with his attentions. Since even then she had been past forty, this had been an extraordinary whim, and did not last long. Fourteen years later, with Tadeshina well into her fifties, he never dreamed that anything of the sort would happen again. At any rate, because of what took place this time, he was never to set foot across the threshold of Kitazaki's inn again.

Events and circumstances—the Marquis's visit, the crushing blow to his pride, the rainy night, the isolated rear parlor of Kitazaki's house, the saké, the sinister pornography—all crowded in on the Count, intensifying his mood of resentment and (it could hardly have been otherwise) inflaming him with a desire to debase himself, which drove him to do what he did. Tadeshina's response, devoid of any reproach, set the seal on his feelings of self-loathing.

"This woman," he thought, "she'll wait fourteen, twenty, a hundred years—it makes no difference to her. And no matter when she hears the voice of her master, she'll never be caught unawares."

Through circumstances which had been none of his doing, he was driven by his seething resentment to plunge into a dark wood where the ghost from the pornographic scroll was lying in wait for him. Moreover, Tadeshina's unruffled composure, her deferential flirting, the evident pride she took in her exhaustive knowledge of sexual technique, all worked on him just as coercively as they had fourteen years earlier.

Perhaps there had been some collusion between her and Kitazaki who left the room and did not return. Afterwards, in the darkness, shut in by the pervasive sound of falling rain, neither of them spoke. Then the soldiers' voices broke through once more, and this time the Count clearly heard the words of their song:

> To the battlefield
> Torn with steel and fire,
> The fate of the nation's defense
> Falls on you.
> Forward, brave comrades!
> Forward, Imperial Army!

The Count suddenly became a child again. He felt the need to unburden himself of the anger that was devouring him, and he gave Tadeshina a detailed account of something that belonged to a sphere from which servants were excluded.

For he felt that his anger was not merely his alone, but rather an emotion that incorporated the wrath of his ancestors.

Marquis Matsugae had paid a visit that day. And when Satoko had come into the room to pay her respects, he had stroked her bobbed hair. And then perhaps under the influence of the sake he had drunk, he spoke abruptly in front of the child: "What a beautiful little princess you have become! When you grow up, you will be so beautiful that nobody will find words to describe you. And as for finding a handsome husband, you just leave that to Uncle, and don't worry about a thing. If you trust Uncle completely, I'll get you a bride-groom without equal anywhere in the world. Your father won't have a thing to worry about. I'll line up a trousseau on golden satin for you when you become a bride. What a long, long, proud procession that will be!—such as has never been seen in all the generations of Ayakuras."

The Countess had given the slightest of frowns at that moment, but the Count had merely smiled. Instead of smiling in the face of humiliation, his ancestors would have revealed just enough of their elegance, and struck back. But these days —when, for example, the ancestral game of *kemari* was no more than a memory—there were no means left to dazzle the vulgar. And when such men as this imposter, overflowing with goodwill and innocent of any intention to wound a genu-ine aristocrat, offered their unwitting insults, there was noth-ing to do but laugh vaguely. However, there was a faintly mysterious element lingering in the smile that came to the lips of the cultured when confronted with the new ascendancy of money and power.

The Count had remained silent for a while after telling Tadeshina all this. If elegance was to have its revenge, he was thinking, how was it to be accomplished? Wasn't there a revenge proper to court nobles, like the revenge in which incense was inserted into the flowing sleeve of a court robe and allowed to burn slowly to a fine ash while showing hardly a trace of flame? A revenge such as this, that would leave a subtle, fragrant poison permeating the material, so that its potency would remain undiminished down the years?

At last the Count turned to Tadeshina and said: "I am going to ask you, long in advance, to do something. When Satoko grows up, I am afraid that everything will go exactly according to Matsugae's wishes, and so he will be the one to arrange a marriage for her. But when he's done that, before the marriage takes place, I want you to guide her into bed with some man she likes, a man who knows how to keep his mouth shut. I don't care about his social position—just so long as she is fond of him. I have no intention of handing Satoko over as a chaste virgin to any bridegroom for whom I have Matsugae's benevolence to thank. And so I'll give Matsugae's nose a twist without his knowing a thing about it. But nobody is to know about this, and you're not to consult me about it. It's something you must do just as if it were a sin committed on your initiative alone. And there's one more aspect to it: since you are the equivalent of a master of arts in all sexual matters, it's not asking too much, is it, for you to instruct Satoko thoroughly in two rather different accomplishments? The first is to make a man think he's taking a girl as a virgin when he's not. And the second, on the contrary, is to make him think that she's already lost her virginity when in fact she has not."

"You need say no more, master," Tadeshina replied, her voice betraying no sign of hesitation or dismay. "There are such effective techniques with regard to both that there is no danger of arousing the suspicions of even the most experienced and libertine gentlemen. And so I will take great pains to educate Miss Satoko in them. However, might I be permitted to wonder what the Marquis has in mind as concerns the second of these?"

"So that the person who makes a conquest of someone else's bride before the wedding doesn't become too exultant about it. If he knows that she's a virgin, he may become presumptuous about his conquest, and that just won't do. And so I'm entrusting you with this as well."

"Everything is quite understood," answered Tadeshina.

Instead of a simple "As the master wishes," she undertook
her appointed task with a grave and formal agreement.

*

And Tadeshina was now alluding to what had happened
that night eight years before. The Count was only too aware
of what she wanted to say. But at the same time, he was quite
sure that the significance of the unforeseen course of events
after she had accepted her commission could not have been
lost on a woman of Tadeshina's shrewdness. The prospective
bridegroom had turned out to be a prince of the Imperial
Family, and although credit was due to the Marquis, a marriage as fortunate as this would mean the resurgence of the
House of Ayakura. In short, the circumstances were very
different from those he had envisaged eight years before when
he had given Tadeshina his instructions in a burning rage. If,
despite all this, she had carried out her task in scrupulous
accordance with that ancient promise, the reason must lie in
her own desire to do so. Furthermore, the secret had already
been spilled to Marquis Matsugae.

Was it possible that she had taken aim against the House
of Matsugae out of some grand design, intending to bring
down a disaster that would achieve the revenge the Count's
own timidity and listlessness had put beyond his reach? Or
was it that her revenge was directed not at the Matsugaes
but at none other than the Count himself? Whatever he did,
he was at a disadvantage—he could not afford to let her tell
the Marquis that bedtime story of eight years before.

He felt it best to say nothing. What was done was done.
And as for the Marquis knowing about it, he had to be prepared for a more or less severe rebuke on that score. Still, he
reflected, the Marquis would use his immense influence to
devise some ploy that would save the situation. Now was the
time to entrust the whole matter to somebody else.

About one thing, however, he was quite certain: Tadeshina's state of mind. However much she professed her guilt,
she was in fact quite disinclined to beg forgiveness for what

she had done. There she sat, the old woman who had tried to kill herself, still indifferent to his pardon, the russet coverlet about her shoulders, the white makeup clinging to her face as thickly as if she were a cricket that had tumbled into a box of powder. And tiny as her figure was, it somehow seemed to fill the whole wide world with melancholy.

He suddenly noticed that this room was the same size as the rear parlor of Kitazaki's inn. All at once he could hear the rustling murmur of the rain and, quite out of season, the stifling heat that brings decay struck his cheek as it had done before.

She raised her whitened face once more to say something. Her dry, wrinkled lips were slightly parted and the wet, red cavern of her mouth gleamed in the light of the electric bulb as brightly as the deep scarlet of her court lip rouge.

He could guess what she was about to say. Wasn't what she had done the result, just as she herself had said, of the events of that night eight years before? And hadn't she done it for no other reason than to give the Count a forcible reminder of what had occurred that night, since he had never again shown the slightest interest in her?

Suddenly he felt the urge to ask the sort of ruthless question of which only a child is capable.

"Well, happily your life was saved . . . but did you honestly mean to kill yourself?"

He thought that she might either become angry or burst into tears, but instead she merely laughed politely.

"Well now, if the master had deigned to say to me, 'Kill yourself,' perhaps I would really have been in the mood to die. And if he should so order me even now, I would try once more. Eight years from now, however, the master might naturally enough have forgotten what he had said, once again."

42

WHEN MARQUIS MATSUGAE met with Count
Ayakura, he was taken aback to see how little concern the
Count evinced at the course of events. But when the Count
readily agreed to the proposal he had so strongly urged, high
spirits returned. The Count assured him that everything
would be done just as he wished. He was immensely heartened,
he said, to hear that the Marquise herself would accompany
Satoko to Osaka. And as for being able to entrust everything
to Dr. Mori in the strictest confidence, this was an undreamed-
of blessing. Everything would be carried out in accordance
with the Matsugaes' instructions, and he therefore begged
that the Marquis be so gracious as to continue his kind efforts
on behalf of the Ayakuras. Such was the tenor of his reply.

The Ayakuras had but one, extremely modest request,
which the Marquis could hardly help but grant. This was
that Satoko and Kiyoaki be allowed to see each other just
before she left for Osaka. There was of course no question
of permitting them to be alone together. But if they could
meet face to face for a brief moment with their parents at
hand, that would satisfy the Ayakuras. And if this request
could be granted, the Ayakuras would give every assurance
that Satoko would never be allowed to see Kiyoaki again.
The request originated with Satoko herself, but, as the Count
explained with some embarrassment, he and his wife felt that
it would be best to grant her this much.

The circumstance of the Marquise accompanying Satoko
to Osaka could now be utilized to give the meeting with
Kiyoaki an uncontrived appearance. Nothing would be more

natural than a son coming to the station to see his mother off, and at such a time no one would have any cause to look askance if Kiyoaki exchanged a word or two with Satoko.

With matters thus concluded, the Marquis, at the suggestion of his wife, secretly summoned Dr. Mori to Tokyo, even though he was fully occupied with his Osaka practice. The doctor stayed with the Matsugaes for a week prior to Satoko's departure on November 14, always in reserve in case she should need him. For if a message came from the Ayakuras, he was ready to rush over there at once. It was the danger of a miscarriage, looming from moment to moment, that made these precautions necessary. If such a thing did occur, Dr. Mori himself would have to attend to it and in such a way that no word would escape. Furthermore, he was to be on hand during the long and extremely perilous train trip to Osaka, traveling inconspicuously in another car.

A renowned obstetrician thus surrendered his freedom and put himself at the beck and call of the Matsugaes and Ayakuras, something that only the Marquis's money could have achieved. And if things progressed as he hoped, the trip to Osaka would itself greatly contribute to keeping the truth hidden from the world. For who would imagine a pregnant woman undertaking any venture such as a train journey?

Although Dr. Mori wore suits tailored in England and was the very model of a Western gentleman, he was a stumpy little man, and there was something about his face that put one in mind of a clerk. Before he examined each of his patients, he spread a fresh layer of high-quality paper over the pillow for her, and would carelessly crumple it up and throw it away afterwards, a practice that enhanced his reputation. He was flawlessly polite and his smile never waned. He had numerous patients among women of the upper class. His skill was unsurpassed and his mouth as tight as an oyster.

He enjoyed talking about the weather, and apart from this, there seemed to be no topic capable of capturing his interest. However, he was able to muster enough charm for his patients merely by remarking how terribly hot it was today or that it was getting warmer after each shower. He was skilled in Chinese poetry and had expressed his impressions of London in twenty Chinese poems in the seven-line form, which he had published privately under the title *London Poems*. He wore a huge, three-carat diamond ring, and before examining a patient he would screw up his face ostentatiously and pull off the ring with apparent difficulty, throwing it brusquely on whatever table was close at hand. However, no one ever noticed him forgetting to pick it up again. His stiff moustache had the subdued luster of a fern after rain.

It was incumbent on the Ayakuras to accompany Satoko to the Toinnomiya residence so that she could pay her respects before her trip to Osaka. Since a trip by carriage would increase the risks involved, Marquis Matsugae furnished them with an automobile. Moreover, Dr. Mori accompanied them disguised as a butler, sitting up beside the driver and wearing an old suit of Yamada's. By a stroke of good fortune, the young prince himself was away on maneuvers. Satoko was able to greet Princess Toin just inside the entranceway and then withdraw. The perilous expedition was thus completed without mishap.

Though the Toinnomiyas planned to dispatch a household official to the station to see Satoko off on November 14, the Ayakuras politely declined this favor. Everything was going exactly according to Marquis Matsugae's plan. The Ayakuras would meet Marquise Matsugae and her son at the Shimbashi station. Dr. Mori was to board a third-class carriage without so much as a glance in their direction. Since the purpose of the trip was supposedly the perfectly laudable one of paying a farewell visit to the Abbess of Gesshu, the Marquis did not hesitate to reserve the entire observation car for the Ayakuras and his wife. This belonged to a special express bound for Shimonoseki which left Shimbashi station at nine thirty in the morning and arrived at Osaka eleven hours and fifteen minutes later.

Shimbashi station, designed by an American architect, had been built in 1872 at the beginning of the Meiji era. It had a timber frame, but its walls were of dark, speckled stone cut from quarries on the Izu Peninsula. Now, on this clear, bright November morning, the sunshine sharply etched the shadows cast by the projecting cornice onto their austere surface. Marquise Matsugae, rather tense at the prospect of setting out on a trip from which she would have to return on her own, arrived at the station having said hardly a word on the way either to Yamada, who was carrying her baggage with his usual deference, or to Kiyoaki. The three of them climbed the long flight of stone steps that led to the platform.

The train had not yet pulled in. The slanting rays of the morning sun poured down on the broad platform and the tracks to either side of it, and motes of dust stirred in the brilliant air. The Marquise was in such a state of anxiety about the trip that confronted her that she heaved deep sighs at frequent intervals.

"I don't see them yet, I wonder if something has happened?" she said from time to time, but she could get no response from Yamada but a reverent and meaningless "Ah!" Although she had known what to expect, she could not refrain from her question.

Kiyoaki realized how disturbed his mother was, but being in no mood to alleviate her distress, he stood some distance away. He felt faint, and his stiff posture was expressive of the effort he was making to keep a grip on himself. It seemed as if he might topple over still rigid like a statue, cast in one piece but lacking any vital strength to sustain it. The air on the platform was chilly but he threw out his chest under his braided uniform jacket. The bleak distress of waiting seemed to have frozen him to the marrow.

The train backed into the station with ponderous dignity while the sun streaked the tops of the cars with brilliant ribbons and flashed from the rail at the rear of the observation car. Just at this moment, the Marquise picked out Dr. Mori by his neat moustache, in the midst of a group waiting some way down the platform. She felt a measure of relief. It had been agreed that, barring some emergency, the doctor would keep to himself throughout the trip to Osaka.

The three of them climbed into the observation car, Yamada carrying the Marquise's luggage. While she was giving Yamada further instructions, Kiyoaki stared out of the window at the platform. He was watching Countess Ayakura and Satoko approaching through the crowd. Satoko was wearing a rainbow shawl wrapped around her shoulders. When she reached the bright flood of sunlight that poured past the edge of the platform roof, her expressionless face looked as white as curds.

His heart beat wildly both with distress and joy. And as he watched her, with her mother at her side, drawing steadily closer but moving at a slow and measured pace, he was taken for a moment with the fancy that he was the bridegroom waiting there to receive his bride. And the solemn ceremonial march, like a cumulative weariness that settled over him particle by particle, stirred a joy that was painfully intense and left him quite enervated.

Countess Ayakura stepped up into the car, and, leaving the servant to carry Satoko's luggage, offered her apologies for being late. Kiyoaki's mother naturally greeted her with the utmost courtesy, but a certain contraction still visible in her forehead gave adequate expression to the haughty displeasure she felt.

Satoko covered her mouth with her rainbow shawl and kept herself hidden behind her mother. She exchanged the normal greetings with Kiyoaki and then, urged by the Marquise, sat down promptly in one of the deep scarlet upholstered chairs which furnished the car.

Kiyoaki then realized why she had arrived so late. She must have delayed her arrival at the station for no other reason than to shorten, even by a fraction, the length of their parting. In the light of this November morning, clear as bitter medicine, they would have no time to say anything to each other. While their mothers were talking, he stared down at her as she sat with bowed head, and in so doing, he began to be concerned about the rising intensity of passion that must be evident in his gaze. His whole heart was in it, but he feared that, like too powerful sunlight, it might scorch Satoko's fragile pallor. The forces at work within him, the emotion he wanted to communicate, had to have subtlety and grace, and he realized how crude a shape his passion had given it. He now felt something that had never touched him before, and he wanted to beg her forgiveness.

As for her body, now covered by her kimono, he knew all there was to know about it, even its tiniest recesses. He knew where her white flesh would first flush crimson with embarrassment, where it would yield, where it would throb with the wingbeat of a snared swan. He knew where it would express joy and where it would express sorrow. Because he knew it in its totality, it seemed to give off a faint glow which could be sensed even through her kimono. But now something he didn't recognize within that body, deep within her very heart, which she seemed to be protecting with the flowing sleeves of her kimono, was pushing its way into life. His nineteen-year-old imagination could not deal with a phenomenon such as that of a child, something that, however intimately bound up with dark, hot blood and flesh, seemed altogether metaphysical.

But even so, the only thing of his that had entered Satoko and become part of her had to be a child. Soon, however, this part would be torn from her and their flesh would become separate once again. And since he had no means whatever of preventing this, there was nothing to do but stand by and let it happen. In a way the child involved here was Kiyoaki himself, for he was still lacking in the power to act independently. He trembled with the bereft loneliness and bitter frustration of a child forced to stay at home as a punishment for a misdeed while the rest of the family went happily off on a picnic.

She raised her eyes and stared vacantly out of the window on the platform side of the train. She seemed entirely absorbed in the vision of what would be cast out from her and he was sure that there was no hope he would ever be reflected in them again.

A piercing whistle sounded a warning. She stood up. It seemed to him that her action was a decisive effort that had demanded all her strength. Her anxious mother reached out and seized her arm.

"The train's about to leave. You'll have to get off," Satoko said to him. Her voice sounded almost cheerful, but it was a trifle shrill.

Inevitably there ensued a hurried conversation between him and his mother, consisting of the usual admonitions and good wishes exchanged between mother and son before she goes off, leaving him behind. He wondered at the skill he was able to bring to supporting his role in this little skit.

When he had finally freed himself from his mother, he turned to the Countess and quickly ran through the correct formulas of farewell with her. Then, as though nothing could be more casual, he said to Satoko, "Well, take care of yourself now." At that moment he felt able to lend lightness to his words, and this was reflected in an impulse to put out his hand and lay it on her shoulder. But at the next moment, his arm seemed stricken with paralysis and hung useless at his side, for he had met her gaze in its full intensity.

Her large, beautiful eyes were certainly wet with tears, but tears quite different from those he had been dreading up to now. They were something living that was being cut to pieces. Her eyes held the terrible glance of a drowning man, and he could not bear this gaze. Her lovely long eyelashes spread wide, like a plant bursting into flower.

"You too, Kiyo. Good-bye," she said in one breath, her tone quite proper.

He fled from the train as if pursued, just as the station-master, wearing a short sword at the belt of his black five-button jacket, raised his hand in signal. Once more the conductor's whistle sounded. Although restrained by Yamada's presence beside him, he called her name in his heart again and again. The line of cars gave a brief shudder and then, like a length of yarn being unwound from a spool, the train began to move. In a few brief moments the observation car and its rear railing were far away, and neither Satoko nor the two mothers had shown themselves. The trailing smoke that poured over the platform testified to the power unleashed in the train's departure. Its acrid smell filled the untimely darkness that it had left behind.

43

ON THE MORNING after two days in Osaka, Marquise Matsugae left the inn where she was staying and went to the nearest post office to send a personal telegram. Her husband had given her strict instructions that she was not to delegate this task to anyone. This being the first time in her life that she had entered a post office, she was thoroughly flustered, although in the midst of her confusion she somehow happened to recall a princess, recently deceased, who was convinced that money was filthy and passed her life without ever laying hand on it. But willy-nilly, she sent a telegram couched in the wording agreed on with her husband: "Visit safely accomplished."

She felt a surge of relief sweep through her as if a heavy burden had slipped from her shoulders. She returned to the inn to pay her bill and then went to Osaka station, where Countess Ayakura was waiting to see her off on her solitary return trip to Tokyo. In order to pay her these respects, the Countess had momentarily slipped away from Satoko's bedside in the hospital.

Satoko had entered Dr. Mori's private clinic under an assumed name, in conformity with the doctor's insistence on two or three days of complete rest. The Countess had been with her constantly, but although her physical condition was excellent, she had not said a word to her mother since the operation, an attitude that pained the Countess deeply.

Since the comfortable stay in the hospital was prescribed merely as a precautionary measure, when Dr. Mori gave his permission for her to leave, she was quite fit to move about, almost as if in perfect health. Now, with her morning sickness a thing of the past, she should have become more buoyant both physically and mentally, but she obstinately held to her silence.

According to the plan arranged for them, they were to go to Gesshu Temple next for Satoko's farewell visit to the Abbess. They would stay there one night and return to Tokyo the next morning.

In the middle of November 18, then, the two of them got off a Sakurai Line train at Obitoké station. It was a warm and beautiful autumn afternoon, and despite her uneasiness over her taciturn daughter, the Countess felt more at rest.

Since she had wanted to avoid putting the old nuns to any inconvenience, she had not informed the convent of their time of arrival. Now, however, though she had asked a station attendant to call two rickshaws for them, there was still no sign of them. While they were waiting, the Countess, who had a fondness for exploring unfamiliar places, went for a stroll in the quiet vicinity of the station, leaving her daughter to her own reflections in the first class waiting-room. Just outside, she came across a signboard directing visitors to the Obitoké Temple nearby.

OBITOKÉ TEMPLE OF MT. KOYASU.
The Bodhisattva Obitoké Koyasu Jizo is revered here. Japan's most ancient and hallowed place of prayer for obtaining the favor of children and their safe birth. Sanctified by the imperial prayers of the Emperors Montoku and Seiwa and the Empress Somedono.

She felt it just as well that these words had escaped Satoko's eye. To lessen the chance of her daughter seeing the signboard, she would have to let the rickshaw pull in deep under the station roof and help her in. It seemed to her that the words were unexpected drops of blood tainting this lovely scenery underneath so brilliant a November sky.

Obitoké station had a well beside it, and white walls under a tiled roof. Opposite it stood an old-fashioned house surrounded by a roofed-in mud wall and boasting an imposing storehouse at the back. Although the white storehouse and mud wall made the bright sunlight dance, an eerie silence hung over the scene. The road surface was gray with thawing mud and glinted with traces of frost, which made for difficult walking. However, her eye was caught by an attractive splash of yellow in the distance. This lay at the approach to a small bridge; it crossed the railway line at a spot where the tall bare trees that bordered the track in ascending ranks came to an end, although they seemed to file on into infinity. So she gathered up her skirts and began to make her way up a slight gradient in the direction of this diversion.

As it turned out, the bridge approach had been decorated with flowerpots of trailing chrysanthemums. Any number of them were dotted about haphazardly in the shelter of a pale green willow that stood beside the path leading onto the bridge. Though it served its purpose as an overpass, it was unpretentious, made of wood, and seemed barely larger than a saddle. Some checkered quilts, hung out to air, were draped over its railing, soaking up the sun and fluffed out as they swung gracefully in the breeze. In the yard of a house close by, diapers were drying in the sun and a length of red material was stretched out and secured by clothespins. The dried persimmons that lined the eaves still had a luster like the glow of sunset. And there was no one to be seen anywhere.

Far down the road, she caught sight of the swaying black hoods of two rickshaws coming in her direction. She hurried back to the station to tell Satoko.

*

Because the weather was so pleasant, she had the men lower the rickshaw hoods. They left the town and its two or three inns behind them and traveled for a time along a road

bordered with rice paddies. If one looked up carefully at the
mountains, one could pick out Gesshu Temple at the very
heart of them.

Some distance farther on, the road was lined with persim-
mon trees, whose branches, although bare of almost all their
leaves, were heavy with fruit. All the rice fields looked festive,
decked all over with a maze of drying racks.

The Countess, in the first rickshaw, turned around from
time to time to look back at her daughter. Satoko had folded
her shawl and laid it in her lap. When her mother saw that
she was looking around her as though she were enjoying the
scenery, she felt somewhat relieved.

As the road entered the mountains, the pace of the rickshaw
men slowed down. Both of them were old men, and their legs
were evidently not what they had been. However, there was
no reason to hurry. On the contrary, thought the Countess, she
and Satoko were fortunate to be able to have such a leisurely
view of the countryside.

They were approaching the outer stone gate of Gesshu, and
once they had passed through it, the scenery became limited
to the gently sloping path itself, a broad expanse of pale blue
sky partially obscured by the tall, white-bearded grass along
the path, and a low range of mountains far in the distance.

The rickshaw men finally stopped for a rest, and as they
talked and wiped away their sweat, the Countess raised her
voice to carry over theirs and called back to Satoko: "You'd
better take your fill of the scenery from here to the convent.
People like me can come here at any time, but you will soon
be in a position where you won't be able to go on outings so
easily."

Her daughter did not reply, but she gave a slow smile and
nodded her head slightly.

The rickshaws moved on again, and the path continued
to slope upwards, which slowed the pace still further. After
they had entered the convent grounds, however, the trees on
either side of them grew denser, lessening the heat of the sun.

The Countess's ears still echoed faintly with the autumn

midday humming of the insects she had been listening to while
the rickshaw men were having their rest. But then the per-
simmon trees that had begun to appear on the left-hand side
of the road caught her eye and enchanted her with their clear,
glowing fruit. Flashing in the sunlight, some of the persimmons that weighed down each branch were casting lacquered
shadows on the others. One tree was rich with orange-red fruit
which, unlike flowers, resisted the wind and left only the dry
leaves to stir. Its mass of ripe fruit was thus spread out against
the sky as if fixed firmly to the spot against a field of blue.

"I don't see any maple leaves at all. I wonder why," she
called back to Satoko, nearly shrieking with the effort but
not drawing any response.

Even scrub maples were scarce along the road. There was
little to catch the eye now but the green of radish fields to the
west and bamboo thickets to the east. The radish fields were
covered with a thick growth of leaves that filtered the sunshine
into subtly complex patterns. Then they gave way to a line of
tea bushes separated from the road by a marsh. Red-berried
vines of magnolia covered this tea hedge, and beyond appeared the still waters of a larger marsh. A little farther on,
the road darkened abruptly as the rickshaws passed into the
shade of some ancient cedars. The sun spilled down in flecks
of light on the bamboo grass beneath the trees, and one tall,
isolated stalk flashed with a singular intensity.

She felt a sudden chill in the air. Turning again toward
the rickshaw behind her, she mimed the clutching of her shawl
about her shoulders. Although she hardly dared hope for a
response, when she glanced backward a few minutes later,
she caught the iridescent colors of Satoko's shawl in the corner
of her eye, fluttering in the breeze. Although her daughter still
had no inclination to talk, the Countess could at least take
consolation in her obedience.

Once the rickshaws had passed through a black-painted
gate, the scenery around them took on the more formal aspect
of a garden, as might be expected of the immediate surroundings of the convent. Its red maple leaves—the first she had

seen along the way—caught the Countess by surprise, and she gasped with admiration.

There was nothing gaudily charming about the colors of these maples here within the black gate. Their deep scarlet was a shade that was blended only in the depths of the mountains, a color that seemed to speak to the Countess of sins as yet unpurged. She suddenly felt a chill edge of anxiety cut into her, and thought of Satoko in the rickshaw behind.

The screen of slender pines and cedars that formed a backdrop to the maples was not thick enough to shut out the broad, bright expanse of sky. Its brilliance flooded through them, striking the maples from behind and turning their extended red-leaved branches to scattered clouds caught in the radiance of the morning sun. As she looked up at the sky from beneath the branches, she admired the subtly delicate way the leaves were interwoven, and imagined that she was seeing the heavens through a tracery of deep scarlet.

Finally the rickshaws stopped and the Countess and Satoko stepped down in front of a Tang Dynasty gate, behind which was a stone-paved lane and the main entrance to the convent of Gesshu.

  # 44

A FULL YEAR HAD GONE BY since Satoko and her mother had last paid their respects to the Abbess on the occasion of her trip to Tokyo. And now, as they waited in a large parlor, the senior nun assured them that Her Reverence had been delighted at the prospect of this visit. She was still speaking as the Abbess herself entered, the junior nun leading her by the hand.

After the Countess had imparted the news of Satoko's engagement, Her Reverence congratulated her, saying, "The next time you are kind enough to honor us with a visit, it will not do for you to be lodged anywhere but in the pavilion." The pavilion was a villa in the convent grounds reserved for members of the Imperial Family.

Now that she was here at Gesshu, Satoko could not very well keep silent any longer, and she answered, however briefly, whenever she was spoken to. Her withdrawal might have been taken for mere shyness. The Abbess, of course, being a woman of immense discretion, gave no sign that she noticed anything amiss.

"A man in the village who cultivates them brings some every year," said the Abbess in response to the Countess's lavish praise of the potted chrysanthemums that were standing in rows in the courtyard. "He gives us such a lecture about them." Then she made the senior nun repeat the chrysanthemum enthusiast's explanations—this was a crimson single-fold chrysanthemum, bred to blossom in a pattern of parallel stripes; this a yellow tubular chrysanthemum bred in the same way, and so on. Finally Her Reverence herself led Satoko and her mother into the drawing room.

"Our maples seem to be late in turning this year," she said after the senior nun had pulled open the sliding door to reveal the beauty of the inner garden, with its simulated mountains and its now fading grass. It contained several huge maple trees that were crowned with red, but as one looked down at the lower branches, this paled to an orange that gave way to a yellow that finally merged into a light green. The red at the very top was dark, with a quality suggestive of congealed blood. The sasanquas had already begun to bloom. And in one corner of the garden, the smooth curve of a dry branch of crape myrtle added a beautiful touch of luster.

They returned to the parlor, and while Her Reverence and the Countess engaged in polite conversation, the short autumn day drew to a close.

Dinner was a festive affair, complete with the rice and red

beans reserved for holidays, and the two nuns did their best
to enliven the company, but nothing seemed able to lighten
the mood of the evening.

"This is the day of the fire kindling at the Imperial Palace,"
said the Abbess. The fire kindling was a court observance
built around the kindling of a huge flame in a hibachi while
a court lady stood in front of it chanting an incantation. The
senior nun, who had seen it during her years of service at the
palace, chanted it from memory.

It was an ancient ritual that took place in the presence of
the Emperor on the eighteenth of November. After a flame
was struck in the hibachi and soared almost to the ceiling, a
court lady, swathed in white ceremonial robes, would begin
the chant with the words: "Upwards! Upwards! Let the holy
flame be kindled! If these tangerines and these *manju* should
please you . . ." The tangerines and bean-jam dumplings
were then thrown onto the fire, heated through, and then
offered to the Emperor.

One might well feel that the nun's reenactment of so solemn
an observance was bordering on the sacrilegious, but the
Abbess realized that the old woman's sole intention was to
provide some badly needed cheer, and she did not utter a
word of reproof.

Night came early at Gesshu. By five in the evening, the
front gate was already bolted. Shortly after dinner, the nuns
retired to their sleeping quarters, and the Countess and her
daughter were led to their room. They would stay until the
following mid-afternoon, allowing for a leisurely farewell.
Then they were to board a night train that evening for Tokyo.

The Countess had intended to reprimand Satoko once they
were alone together for having let her sadness affect her good
manners during the day. But after some reflection on her state
of mind after the Osaka experience, she decided against it
and went to bed without a word to her daughter.

Even in the unrelieved darkness of the night, the sliding
door's paper paneling loomed white and insistently mournful
in the guest parlor of Gesshu. It was as if the frost air of the

cold November night had penetrated the thin skin of the paper. The Countess could easily distinguish the paper patterns of sixteen-petal chrysanthemums and white clouds that decorated the door catches. Up in the direction of the darkened ceiling, metal rosettes of six chrysanthemums grouped around kikkyo blossoms masked each of the pegs, accentuating the blackness around them. Outside there was no wind at all, with not even the sound of a breeze stirring in the pines to be heard. Nevertheless, one was distinctly aware of the expanse of forest and mountain.

The Countess was overcome with a sense of relief. Whatever the cost, she and her daughter had faithfully carried out the painful duty that was their lot, and now she felt that everything would be calm and serene. And so, despite her consciousness that her daughter was tossing and turning beside her, she soon fell asleep.

When she opened her eyes, Satoko was no longer at her side. Stretching out her hand in the pre-dawn darkness, she came upon her daughter's nightgown neatly folded on top of the quilt. Anxiety surged through her, but she told herself that Satoko had merely gone to the lavatory, and she determined to do nothing for a few moments. But although she tried to wait, her chest was tight with a dull coldness and she got up to make sure. The lavatory was empty. There was no sign of anyone else about. The sky was now tinged with an uncertain blue.

Just then she heard the sound of movement coming from the kitchen. A few moments later, an early-rising serving maid, startled at the Countess's sudden appearance, went down on her knees.

"Have you seen Satoko?" she asked her, but the maid was terrified and could do nothing but shake her head frantically, nor would she budge an inch to help in the search.

After this, however, while the Countess was pacing the convent passages in aimless desperation, she happened to meet the junior nun. The nun was startled at her news and began at once to guide her in her search.

At the far end of a connecting corridor, the flickering glow
of candles came from the main hall of worship. It was hardly
likely that a nun would already be at her devotions at this
hour of the morning.

Two burning candles traced with the flower-wheel pattern
were illuminating the image of Buddha before which Satoko
was sitting. Seeing her daughter from the rear, the Countess
did not recognize her for some moments. For Satoko had
cropped short her hair. She had placed the shorn strands on
the sutra stand, as though in offering, and, beads in hand, was
lost in prayer.

Her mother's first reaction was relief at finding her daughter alive. She then realized that until that moment she had
been certain that Satoko was dead.

"You've cut off your hair," she cried as she embraced her.

"Yes, Mother. There was nothing else to do," Satoko answered, finally looking her mother directly in the eye. The
small, wavering candle flames flickered in her pupils, but the
whites of her eyes already held the brilliance of the dawn.
Never had the Countess seen so fearful a daybreak as she now
saw mirrored in her daughter's gaze. And the same white
glow, growing stronger by the minute, shone in each of the
crystal beads of the string wrapped around her fingers. Like
a force of will so intense that it transcends mere willing, the
dawn light seemed to flow with equal force from every one of
the cold crystals.

The junior nun hurried off to break the news to her senior.
And then, having completed her report, she withdrew, leaving
it to the senior nun to conduct Countess Ayakura and her
daughter to the Abbess.

"Your Reverence, have you arisen yet?" she called from
outside the door of the Abbess's quarters.

"Yes."

"Please forgive us."

The old nun then slid open the door to reveal the Abbess
sitting upright on her quilted mattress. The Countess began
haltingly.

"What has happened, Your Reverence, is that Satoko, just now, in the chapel, cut off her hair."

The Abbess gazed out into the corridor as her eyes absorbed the change that Satoko had worked on herself. But her features betrayed no sign of surprise.

"Well, well. I was wondering if things might not turn out something like this," she said. After a pause, as if a new thought had just struck her, she went on to say that as the circumstances appeared to be rather involved, she thought it best for the Countess to be kind enough to leave her daughter alone with her so that she and Satoko could have a heart-to-heart talk. The Countess and the senior nun acquiesced, and withdrew.

The nun, left alone with Countess Ayakura, did her best to entertain her, but the Countess was so distraught that she could not eat a bite of breakfast. The nun could well imagine her distress and was unable to think of any topic of conversation that might divert her. A long time passed before a summons finally came from the Abbess's quarters. And there, in Satoko's presence, the Abbess informed the Countess of a piece of news of shattering significance: since there was no mistaking the genuineness of Satoko's desire to renounce the world, Gesshu Temple would receive her as a novice.

For most of the morning so far, the Countess's mind had been wholly involved in concocting a variety of stopgap measures. She could not doubt that Satoko's decision was firm. And then some months or even half a year would be required to restore her daughter's hair to normal, but if only she could be dissuaded from taking the tonsure, these months could be accounted for a period of convalescence from some illness incurred during the trip, and the Ayakuras could thus obtain a postponement of the betrothal ceremony. Then the persuasive powers of her father and Marquis Matsugae could be brought to bear on her in the interval, and perhaps she could be induced to change her mind.

And now, hearing the Abbess's words, her determination, far from weakening, became all the more set. The usual procedure, when one was to be accepted as a novice, was to undergo a year of ascetic discipline before receiving the tonsure at the formal induction ceremony. Whatever else, the restoration of Satoko's ravaged hair was of prime importance. Then, in the event that she could be persuaded fairly soon to reject her vocation . . . the Countess's mind was filled with marvelous ploys: if events quickly took a favorable turn, perhaps Satoko could get through the betrothal ceremony safely with the help of a carefully made wig.

Countess Ayakura came to her decision: for the present, her only course was to leave Satoko here and return to Tokyo as quickly as possible to work out a plan of action.

"I appreciate the sentiments expressed by Your Reverence," she said in reply. "However, not only has this come up suddenly in the midst of a journey, but it is also a matter that involves disturbing the Imperial Family. I therefore think it best to beg your indulgence to return temporarily to Tokyo to consult my husband before coming back here. And in the meantime I will entrust Satoko to your care."

Satoko heard her mother out without so much as a raised eyebrow. The Countess was now afraid even to speak to her own daughter.

45

UPON HIS WIFE'S RETURN, when Count Ayakura learned of this astonishing development, he let an entire week pass without doing anything at all, a procrastination that was to provoke the wrath of Marquis Matsugae.

The Matsugae household was resting secure in the assumption that Satoko had already returned to Tokyo and that due notice of this had been conveyed to Prince Toin's family. A miscalculation of this sort was out of character for the Marquis, but once his wife had come back from Osaka and told him that his meticulous planning had been carried out without a hitch, complacency got the upper hand, and he felt assured of a successful conclusion.

Count Ayakura's abstraction persisted. He believed that only a vulgar mentality was willing to acknowledge the possibility of catastrophe. He felt that taking naps was much more beneficial than confronting catastrophes. However precipitous the future might seem, he learned from the game of *kemari* that the ball must always come down. There was no call for consternation. Grief and rage, along with other outbursts of passion, were mistakes easily committed by a mind lacking in refinement. And the Count was certainly not a man who lacked refinement.

Just let matters slide. How much better to accept each sweet drop of the honey that was Time, than to stoop to the vulgarity latent in every decision. However grave the matter at hand might be, if one neglected it for long enough, the act of neglect itself would begin to affect the situation, and someone else would emerge as an ally. Such was Count Ayakura's version of political theory.

Once back at the side of such a husband, the Countess became daily less concerned with the anxiety that had oppressed her at Gesshu. In the present circumstances, it was lucky that Tadeshina was away and unable to act blindly on one of her rash impulses. The Count had been kind enough to send her off for a leisurely convalescence at the hot springs of Yugawara.

After a week, however, there was a phone call from Marquis Matsugae, and even Count Ayakura could no longer keep the matter secret. The Marquis was temporarily struck dumb when he heard the Count tell him that as a matter of fact Satoko had not yet returned and he felt the stirrings of all sorts of nasty premonitions.

The Marquis and his wife lost no time in paying a visit to

the Ayakuras. At first the Count offered one vague response
after another as he was questioned. And then when the truth
finally came out, the Marquis was so furious that he struck
the table in front of him with his fist.

*

So it came about that this ten-mat parlor awkwardly re-
done to become the sole Western-style room in the mansion
became the scene for the first occasion in their long acquaintance that these two couples confronted each other stripped of
all niceties. The women averted their eyes and each from
time to time stole a look at her husband. Though the two men
faced each other, Count Ayakura tended to hang his head. His
hands, resting on the table, were small and white, the hands
of a doll in a puppet play. In contrast, despite his essential
weakness, the Marquis's coarse, florid features could have
served as a Noh mask of the angry devil with the fiercely
contorted eyebrows. Even in the eyes of the wives, the Count
appeared to have no chance.

As it turned out, the Marquis's anger swept all before it for
a time. But even while he was letting himself rage, he began
to feel a little embarrassed over his display of self-righteous-
ness. For after all, his own position in this affair was safe from
first to last. Moreover, he could hardly have been matched
with a weaker, more pitiful antagonist than the one who now
confronted him. The Count's color was unhealthy. As he sat
there in silence, an expression, part sorrow, part dismay, came
over his face, which seemed to be carved out of yellow ivory,
the features delicately chiseled and quite composed. The crin-
kled eyelids emphasized the deep-set cast of the habitually
downcast eyes as well as their melancholy. The Marquis had
the feeling, not for the first time, that they were women's
eyes.

Count Ayakura's languid reticence, his manner of slump-
ing casually in his chair, clearly bespoke the graceful elegance of ancient tradition—something that was nowhere to
be found in the Marquis's pedigree—now displayed at its most

deeply injured. It had something of the soiled plumage of a dead bird, a creature that had once sung beautifully but whose flesh was tasteless and so inedible after all.

"It's quite unbelievable! A positively wretched thing to happen. What apologies could we offer to the Emperor, to the entire nation?" the Marquis declaimed heedlessly, intent on letting his anger sweep along on a stream of orotund syllables but aware that its supporting lifeline might snap at any minute. Anger was useless against the Count, who was neither acquainted with logic nor remotely inclined to initiate any course of action. Worse still, the Marquis gradually came to realize that the more enraged he became, the more the force of his passion was turned relentlessly back against itself.

He could not believe that the Count had plotted just such a result from the very beginning. But nonetheless he now saw with painful clarity that the Count had been able to use his endemic listlessness to forge so impregnable a position that, however monumental the catastrophe, the blame for it would come to rest not on himself but on his ally.

After all, it was the Marquis who had asked the Count to give his son an upbringing that would imbue him with a sense of elegance. It was undoubtedly the desires of the flesh in Kiyoaki that had brought on this misfortune, and one might well argue that this was the consequence of the subtle poison that had begun to infect his spirit after his arrival in the Ayakura household as an infant. But the ultimate instigator of this was none other than the Marquis himself. Furthermore, in this latest twist of the crisis, it was the Marquis who had insisted on sending Satoko down to Osaka without any forethought that something like this might occur. Everything thus conspired to turn the force of the Marquis's wrath against himself.

Finally worn out by his exertions and unnerved by his growing anxiety, the Marquis held his tongue. The ensuing silence lengthened and grew more profound until it seemed as if the four of them had gathered in this room to practice group meditation. The noonday clucking of the chickens came

from the yard behind the house. Each time the early winter
wind blew through the trees outside, the pine needles that
stirred at the slightest touch flashed brightly. There was no
sound of human activity from anywhere else in the house, and
the silence seemed to be in deference to the eerie atmosphere
in the parlor.

The Countess finally broke the spell.

"It was my negligence that caused this. There is no way
that I can apologize sufficiently to you, Marquis Matsugae.
However, things being as they are, wouldn't it be best to try
and make Satoko change her mind as soon as possible and
have the betrothal ceremony take place as planned?"

"But what about her hair?" was the Marquis's immediate
retort.

"Well, as to that, if we are quick and arrange to have a
wig made, it would mislead the public eye for a while . . ."

"A wig!" the Marquis exclaimed, breaking in before the
Countess had finished with a slightly shrill note of joy in his
voice. "I never thought of that."

"Yes, of course," said his wife, chiming in at once. "We
never thought of that."

And from then on, as the others were infected with the
Marquis's enthusiasm, the wig was all they could talk about.
For the first time, laughter was heard in the parlor as the four
of them competed to pounce first on this bright idea as if it
were a scrap of meat.

Not all of them, however, placed the same degree of faith
in the Countess's novel idea. The Count, for one, did not trust
its efficacy. The Marquis may well have shared his skepticism, but he was capable of feigning belief with dignity. And
the Count himself hastened to profit by his example.

"Even if the young prince gets a bit suspicious about Satoko's hair," said the Marquis, lowering his voice to a forced
whisper while he laughed, "he's certainly not going to touch
it to see for himself."

An atmosphere of cordiality pervaded the room, however
fragile the fiction that sustained it. For the fiction supplied

them with that tangible element so vital at this moment. No one considered Satoko's soul; it was her hair alone that pertained to the national interest.

The Marquis's father had dedicated all of his fierce strength and passion to the cause of the imperial restoration. His mortification would have been bitter had he known that the glory he had earned for the family name would one day depend on a woman's wig. This sort of intricate and shady maneuvering was hardly the forte of the House of Matsugae. It was, in fact, far more characteristic of the Ayakuras. But the present Marquis, instead of leaving elegantly refined deceptions to the Ayakuras, who were bred to that kind of thing, had become fascinated by it, and so the House of Matsugae was now compelled to share an unaccustomed burden.

The truth of the matter was that this wig as yet only existed in their imaginations and was totally irrelevant to Satoko's intentions. However, once they succeeded in dressing her in a wig, they would be able to construct a flawless picture from the pieces of a shattered jigsaw puzzle. Everything thus seemed to depend on the wig, and the Marquis gave himself over to the project with enthusiasm.

Each of the foursome in the parlor contributed wholeheartedly to the discussion of the nonexistent hairpiece. Satoko would have to wear one dressed in a long, straight hairstyle for the betrothal ceremony, but for everyday use, a wig done in the Western fashion would be necessary. And since there was no telling when someone might catch sight of her, she must not take it off even when she took a bath. And each of them began to use his or her imagination to picture this wig with which they had already decided to crown her: abundant, jet-black hair, even more glossy than her own. Such sovereign power would be hers despite herself, the grandeur of a towering, gracefully arranged coiffure radiating a dark fascination moreover that would imbue the flat brightness of midday with something of the essence of night. Each of the four was well enough aware that it would be no simple mat-

ter to achieve this—that beneath this peerless wig there would
be a face marked with unhappiness, but no one was willing to
dwell for long on this aspect of the problem.

"This time I would appreciate it greatly if you yourself,
Count, went down there to impress upon your daughter how
firmly your mind is made up. Countess, I'm so sorry that you
must go to the trouble of a second trip, but I'll arrange for
my wife to accompany you again. Of course, I, too, should
really go. However . . ." Here, the Marquis, who was sensitive to appearances, faltered slightly. "If I should go, you see,
it might well make people wonder. So I'll stay here. I would
like the whole trip to be accomplished in the greatest secrecy
this time. As far as my wife's absence is concerned, we can let
it be known that she's ill. And in the meantime here in Tokyo,
let me look around and I'll hire the best craftsman available
to make us a fine wig without anyone being the wiser. If a
newspaper reporter should get wind of it, we'd have a pretty
situation on our hands. But just you leave that question
to me."

 46

KIYOAKI WAS SURPRISED to see his mother once
again getting ready for a trip. However, she refused to tell
him either the destination or the purpose of her journey, saying only that he was not to mention it outside the house. He
sensed that something alarming was afoot and that it had to
do with Satoko, but with Yamada constantly at his side to
keep an eye on him, there was no way he could find out any
more.

When the Ayakuras and Marquise Matsugae arrived at Gesshu Temple, they were met with an appalling state of affairs. Satoko had already received the tonsure.

*

The circumstances that had led so rapidly to her renunciation of the world were as follows. When the Abbess had heard the entire story from Satoko that first morning, she had known at once that she must allow the girl to become a nun. Keenly aware that each of her predecessors at Gesshu had been an imperial princess, she felt bound to revere the Emperor above all else. And so she had come to the decision that she had to allow Satoko to enter even if this involved a temporary thwarting of the imperial will. She had concluded that, given the circumstances, there was no other way to discharge her loyalty to the Emperor. She had happened to uncover a plot directed at him, and she could not allow it to proceed unchecked. She was not one to countenance a breach of loyalty, no matter how elegant the cunning that disguised it.

Thus it was that the normally so discreet and gentle Abbess of Gesshu made up her mind, determined to give in neither to the force of authority nor the threat of coercion. Even if all the world should be ranged against her, even if she were forced to ignore a particular imperial decree, she would persist in what she had to do—to be a silent guard of the sacred person of His Majesty.

Her resolve had a profound effect on Satoko, who became all the more determined to turn her back on the world. She had not expected the Abbess to grant her request so readily. She had had an encounter with the Lord Buddha, and the Abbess, her eye as keen as a crane's, had immediately discerned the firmness of the girl's decision.

Although it was customary for a novice to undergo a year of ascetic discipline before her formal induction as a nun, both Satoko and the Abbess felt that in the present circumstances this period should be dispensed with. But the Abbess could not bring herself to disregard the Ayakuras so com-

pletely as to allow Satoko to take the tonsure before the
Countess returned from Tokyo. Moreover, there was the matter of Kiyoaki. Would it not be wise, she thought, to allow
him and Satoko to bid each other a long farewell before she
sacrificed what hair she had spared so far?

Satoko could hardly endure the delay. She came to the Abbess every day and, like a child teasing her mother to give her
candy, begged to be allowed to take the tonsure. Finally, the
Abbess found herself prepared to yield.

"If I were to allow you to take the tonsure," she asked Satoko, "you would never be allowed to see Kiyoaki again. That
wouldn't trouble you?"

"No."

"Well, once you make the decision not to see him ever again
in this world and so advance to initiation, any later regrets
would indeed be bitter ones."

"I will have no regrets. In this world I shall never set eyes
on him again. As for parting, we've had farewells enough. So
please . . ."

Her voice as she replied was clear and firm.

"Very well. Tomorrow morning, then, I will preside at the
tonsure ceremony," the Abbess replied, allowing one more
day of grace.

Countess Ayakura did not return in the interval.

From that first morning at Gesshu, Satoko had plunged
herself, of her own volition, into the disciplined routine of
convent life. The distinctive character of Hosso Buddhism
was in placing greater emphasis on the cultivation of the mind
than the practice of religious austerities. Gesshu Temple,
furthermore, was traditionally dedicated to praying for the
welfare of the whole nation, and there were no households
registered with it as parishioners. Sometimes the Abbess
would observe with gentle humor that the "Grace of tears"
was something never encountered in Hosso Buddhism, thus
underlining the contrast with the more recently arisen Amida
cult of Pure Land Buddhism, with its great stress on ecstatic
prayers of gratitude.

Then, too, in Mahayana Buddhism in general, there were no precepts to speak of. But for the rules of its monastic life the precepts of Hinayana Buddhism were often borrowed. In convents such as Gesshu, however, the rule was the "Precepts of a Bodhisattva" contained in the *Brahamajala Sutra*. Its forty-eight prohibitions began with ten major injunctions against such sins as the taking of life, stealing, excess of any sort, and lying, and it concluded with an admonishment against destroying Buddhist teachings.

Far more severe than any commandment, however, was the monastic training. In the brief time she had been at Gesshu, Satoko had already memorized both the "Sutra of the En-lightened Heart" and the "Thirty Verses" expounding the doctrine of *Yuishiki*. Each morning she got up early to sweep and dust the main hall of worship before the Abbess came for her morning devotions, in the course of which she then had an opportunity to practice the chanting of the sutras. She was no longer treated as a guest, and the senior nun, whom the Ab-bess had placed in charge of her, was now a changed woman in her severity of manner.

On the morning of the initiation ceremony, she carefully performed the prescribed ablutions before putting on the black robes of a nun. In the hall of worship, she sat with her string of beads wrapped around her hands, which she held clasped together in front of her. After the Abbess herself had first taken the razor and begun the tonsuring, the old nun in charge of her took over. And as she shaved steadily with a skilled hand, the Abbess began to chant the "Sutra of the En-lightened Heart," accompanied by the junior nun.

> When she had consummated the works of perfection,
> The Five Aggregates of|living being became as
> Things void before the Bohdisattva Kannon's eyes,
> And stricken from her was the yoke of human suffering.

Satoko, too, took up the chant, her eyes closed. And as she did so, her body became like a boat that is gradually lightened of all its cargo and freed of its anchor, and she felt herself

being swept along on the deep swelling wave of chanting
voices.

She kept her eyes shut. The main hall had the penetrating
chill of an ice house. and so, although she herself was floating free, she imagined a vast expanse of pure ice gripping all
the world about her. Suddenly the cry of a shrike came from
the garden outside, and a crack raced across this icy plane
with the swiftness of a jagged steak of lightning. But it sealed
itself almost at once, and the ice became whole once more.

She felt the razor working its way with scrupulous care
across her scalp. Sometimes she imagined the frenetic gnawing of a mouse's tiny white incisors, sometimes the placid
grinding of the molars of a horse or cow.

As lock after lock fell away, she felt her scalp begin to
tingle with a refreshing coolness that was quite new to her.
The razor was shearing off the black hair that had separated
her from the world for so long, sultry and heavy with its sorry
burden of desire; but her scalp was now being laid bare to a
realm of purity whose chill freshness had not been violated
by any man's hand. As the expanse of shaved head broadened,
she began to feel the skin coming more and more alive, just
as if a cool solution of menthol was spreading over it.

She imagined that the chill must be like the surface of the
moon, directly exposed to the vastness of the universe. The
world she had known was falling away with each strand. And
as it did so, she became infinitely removed from it.

In one sense, it seemed as though her hair were being har-
vested. Shorn black clumps, still saturated with the stifling
brilliance of the summer sun, piled up on the floor around her.
But it was a worthless crop, for the very instant that the luxuriant black handfuls ceased to be hers, the beauty of life went
out of them, leaving only an ugly remnant. Something that
had once been an intimate part of her, an aesthetic element of
her innermost being, was now being relentlessly thrown aside.
As irrevocable as the amputation of a limb, the ties that bound
her to the world of transience were being severed.

When her scalp at last shone with a bluish glint, the Abbess addressed her gently.

"The most crucial renunciation is the one that comes after formal renunciation. I have the utmost trust in your present resolution. From this day on, if you seek constantly to purify your heart in the austerities of our life, I have no doubt that one day you will become the glory of our sisterhood."

*

This was how Satoko's premature tonsuring came about. Neither Countess Ayakura nor Marquise Matsugae, however, was prepared to give up, no matter how shattered they were by Satoko's transformation. After all, there remained the wig, a potent weapon still held in reserve.

 47

COUNT AYAKURA ALONE among the three visitors maintained an appearance of affability from first to last. He engaged the Abbess and Satoko in casual, unhurried conversation about the world in general, and at no time gave the slightest hint that he might want Satoko to change her mind.

A telegram arrived every day from Marquis Matsugae demanding a report on the situation to date. Finally the Countess broke down and wept as she pleaded with her daughter, but this gained her nothing, and so on the third day after their arrival, the Countess and the Marquise left for Tokyo, putting all their trust in the Count, who remained at Gesshu. The strain had worked such ravages in the Countess that she took to her bed as soon as she returned home.

As for the Count, he spent a week at Gesshu doing nothing at all. He was afraid to return to Tokyo. Since he had made no attempt whatever to persuade Satoko to return to secular life, the Abbess relaxed her guard and gave him and his daughter the chance to be alone together. The senior nun, however, kept a casual eye on them from a distance.

The two of them sat facing each other in silence on a veranda that caught some share of the winter sunshine. Beyond the dry tree branches, some scattered clouds reemphasized the blue of the sky. A flycatcher called timidly from a crape myrtle. They had been sitting without a word for a long time. Finally Count Ayakura spoke, with a hint of an ingratiating smile.

"I won't be able to mix much in society from now on, because of you."

"Be kind enough to forgive me," Satoko answered calmly, without a trace of emotion.

"My, you have all sorts of birds in this garden, haven't you?" he said after a few moments.

"Yes, we have all sorts."

"I took a little stroll around this morning. By the time the persimmons here are ripe enough to fall, it looks as though the birds have already been at them. There seems to be no one to pick them up."

"Yes, that's exactly what happens."

"I should think we'll have some snow before too long," he added, but there was no answer. And so the two of them sat in silence, gazing down at the garden.

The following morning Count Ayakura finally left Gesshu. And when he confronted Marquis Matsugae in Tokyo, having failed completely in his mission, he found that the Marquis was no longer angry.

It was already December 4, which left a mere week until the betrothal ceremony. The Marquis secretly summoned the superintendent-general of the metropolitan police to the Matsugae residence. His plan was to invoke the power of the police to effect Satoko's forcible removal from the convent.

The superintendent-general sent a confidential order to the Nara police. Since this was a matter of setting foot in a convent whose Abbess was traditionally an imperial princess, however, the Nara police were afraid of incurring the wrath of the Imperial Household Ministry. As long as the temple was receiving assistance from imperial funds—be it only a thousand yen a year—the slightest violation of its autonomy was unthinkable. The superintendent-general himself therefore went down to Nara in private, accompanied by a trusted subordinate in civilian clothes. The Abbess did not show the slightest sign of alarm when the senior nun handed her his card.

After spending an hour chatting with the Abbess over tea, he finally had to withdraw, yielding to the force of her massive dignity.

The Marquis had played the last card in his hand, and had come to the realization that there was nothing else to do but to request the Toinnomiyas to accept Satoko's withdrawal from the proposed marriage. In recent weeks, Prince Toin had sent an official to the Ayakuras several times, and was concerned over their strange behavior.

The Marquis summoned the Count to his home and told him that they had no choice but to accept the situation. Then he outlined the strategy they were to follow. They would present the Toinnomiyas with a certificate signed by a reputable doctor testifying that Satoko had been stricken by a severe nervous breakdown. The shared responsibility of preserving this secret might unite the Toinnomiyas with the Ayakuras and Matsugaes in mutual trust, and this might soften the Prince's anger. As for the general public, all that need be done was to spread the rumor that the Toinnomiyas had released a curt, vaguely worded statement that the engagement was at an end and that Satoko had turned her back on the world and fled to a convent. As a result of this inversion of cause and effect, the Toinnomiyas, although obliged to some extent to play the villain, would nonetheless maintain face and prestige. And the Ayakuras, while incurring a measure of shame, would nevertheless benefit from public sympathy.

It would never do, however, to let things get out of hand. If that were to happen, altogether too much sympathy would accrue to the Ayakuras, and the Toinnomiyas, faced with the stirrings of unjustified hostility, would be compelled to clarify matters, and so have to make public Satoko's medical certificate. It was essential to present the story to the newspaper reporters without making too much cause and effect out of the Toinnomiyas' breaking of the engagement and Satoko's becoming a nun. They must be presented as separate events—but their chronological sequence would have to be reversed. The reporters themselves, however, would hardly be content with such an explanation. Should this be the case, a bare hint would be dropped to them that there was indeed a causal relationship but the families involved requested that they refrain from disclosing this.

As soon as he obtained Count Ayakura's agreement to this plan, the Marquis immediately put in a call to Dr. Ozu, the director of the Ozu Mental Clinic, and requested that he come to the Matsugae residence at once to conduct an examination in the strictest secrecy. The clinic had an excellent reputation for protecting the privacy of its eminent patients when emergencies of this sort arose. Dr. Ozu took a long time to arrive, however, and in the interval the Marquis was no longer able to hide his irritation from the Count, who was forced to wait for the doctor with him. But since it would have been improper in the circumstances to send a car from the Matsugae residence, the Marquis could do nothing but grit his teeth.

When the doctor arrived, he was brought to the small second-floor parlor of the Western-style house, where a fire was burning brightly in the fireplace. The Marquis introduced himself and the Count in turn and offered the doctor a cigar.

"And where would you like me to examine the patient?" asked Dr. Ozu. The Marquis and the Count exchanged glances.

"Well," the Marquis replied, "the truth of the matter is that the patient isn't here at the moment."

As soon as he learned that he was being asked then and

there to sign a medical certificate for a patient he had never set eyes on, the doctor went red with anger. What particularly provoked him was the look that he was sure he had caught in the Marquis's eyes: a flicker of presumption that his signature would indeed be forthcoming.

"What's the meaning of this preposterous request?" he demanded. "Do you by any chance take me for one of your society doctors who can be bought and paid for?"

"Believe me, Doctor," the Marquis replied, "we have by no means mistaken you for a gentleman of that sort." He took his cigar out of his mouth and began to pace the room. Then, gazing across at the doctor and noting how his plump, healthy ruddy cheeks were quivering in the firelight, he addressed him in a deep, solemn tone: "As for this medical certificate, it is something that is essential to the continued tranquillity of His Sacred Majesty."

*

When the Marquis had the signed certificate in his hand, he at once requested a meeting with Prince Toin at his earliest convenience, and went next night to the Prince's residence.

Fortunately enough, the young prince was away again on regimental maneuvers. Since the Marquis had specifically requested an audience with Prince Haruhisa, the Princess was not at her husband's side when he greeted the Marquis.

Prince Toin seemed to be in a jovial mood as he urged a fine French wine on his guest and spoke of this and that, not forgetting to declare once again how fine the entertainment had been at the blossom festival the previous spring. Quite some time had passed since the two had had a chance to talk together like this, and the Marquis again recalled the experiences they had shared during the Paris Olympics of 1900 and went on to entertain the Prince with a variety of anecdotes about their well-remembered cabaret at the champagne fountain. It seemed as if neither had a care in the world.

Nevertheless the Marquis was well aware that beneath the Prince's dignified and unruffled composure, he was in fact waiting with anxiety and misgiving to hear what he had to tell him. The Prince had not said a word about the betrothal ceremony, now only a few days distant. Like sunlight falling on a sparse grove of trees, the lamplight on the handsome gray moustache revealed a fleeting expression of uneasiness which from time to time contorted the mouth beneath.

"Well now, as regards my intruding on you here to-night . . . ," the Marquis said, broaching the crucial topic in a deliberately frivolous tone, as agile as a bird that darts straight to its nest after flying around for a time with careless ease. "I have the unpleasant task of imparting some unfortunate news that is not at all easy to express. Ayakura's daughter has gone out of her mind."

"What?" The Prince's eyes opened wide with shock.

"Ayakura, being the sort of fellow he is, kept it completely hidden. Without even consulting me, he put Satoko into a convent, hoping to avoid a scandal, and yet up until now he hasn't been able to summon enough courage to inform Your Highness of what has happened."

"Why, this is incredible! Waiting until now!"

The Prince pressed his lips firmly together, and the edges of his moustache dipped downward. He stared for some moments at the pointed toes of his shoes glinting in the light cast by the fireplace.

"This is a medical certificate signed by Dr. Ozu. Indeed, as you see, it's dated a month ago, but Ayakura didn't show it to me. All this is due to my failure to keep a sharp eye on everything, and there is no way for me adequately to express my sorrow . . ."

"If she's ill, she's ill. It can't be helped. But why didn't he tell me about it earlier? And so that's what the trip to the Kansai was about! Now that you mention it, when they were here to pay their respects before leaving, her color wasn't good at all, and Princess Toin was concerned about it."

"Her mind hasn't been right since last September, and she's been doing all sorts of odd things, they say, until finally her behavior was brought to my attention."

"Well, that's how the situation stands; nothing can be done about it," said the Prince. "I'll go to the palace early tomorrow to express my apologies to the Emperor. I wonder how His Majesty will take it? You'll let me take this certificate, then, won't you? I'll have to show it to him."

Prince Toin's exquisite breeding was evident in that he said not one word about young Prince Harunori. As for the Marquis, he kept his shrewd eyes fixed throughout the interview on each shift of expression in the Prince's face. In it, he had seen dark threatening waves rise and fall and rise again. And after he had watched the process for some time, he felt his own anxiety receding. The moment of greatest danger had passed.

The Prince summoned his wife, and after the three of them had gone well into the night discussing the best plan to follow, Marquis Matsugae finally took his leave.

*

The following morning, Prince Harunori happened to return from maneuvers just at the awkward moment when his father was about to leave for the Imperial Palace. Prince Toin took his son aside and broke the news to him. There was no trace of emotion on his young, sturdy face as he replied that he would behave entirely according to his father's wishes in the matter. And so, far from being resentful, the young man showed no signs even of being perturbed at the course of events.

Since he was tired after the all-night maneuvers, he went to bed as soon as he had seen his father off. His mother, however, feeling sure that he would be unable to sleep after such news, came to his room.

As he raised his eyes to her, she noticed that they were slightly bloodshot from lack of sleep, but his look was as direct and unflinching as ever.

"So it was just last night," he said to her, "that Marquis Matsugae came to tell us about it."

"Yes, just last night."

"You know, Mother, I just happened to think of something that took place a long time ago, when I was a lieutenant at the palace. I told you about it then, didn't I? Anyway, I was going for an audience with the Emperor and I happened to run into Marshal Yamagata in the corridor. I'll never forget it, Mother. It was the corridor that ran along the side of the front reception room. The Marshal was just coming from an audience, I think. As usual, he was wearing that uniform overcoat with the wide lapels, the peak of his cap was down over his eyes, and his hands were sticking in his pockets as if he didn't give a damn about anybody. He was coming toward me down that dark corridor with his sword almost dragging at his side. I instantly stepped aside, stood to attention and saluted him. He glanced at me quickly from under the peak of his cap with those eyes that never smiled. Surely, Mother, Marshal Yamagata must have known who I was. But he turned his head away abruptly, looking annoyed, threw back his shoulders inside that overcoat at the same time, and swaggered away down the corridor without so much as returning my salute. Now why, Mother, do you suppose I happened to remember that just now?"

*

An article in next day's paper informed the general public that they were going to be deprived of the festivities they had been anticipating with such pleasure. There would be no betrothal ceremony. The engagement had been dissolved "because of circumstances in the family of His Imperial Majesty Prince Harunori." And so it came about that Kiyoaki, who had been told nothing at all about recent events, finally learned what had happened from a newspaper.

48

AFTER THE BROKEN ENGAGEMENT became known, the family watched over Kiyoaki even more closely, and the steward Yamada accompanied him even to school. His classmates, having no inkling of the circumstances, did not know what to make of such solicitude, ordinarily shown only to the youngest of the grade-school boys. Furthermore, his father and mother no longer uttered a word about the affair in his presence, and everyone else in the household behaved in front of him as though nothing had happened.

Society, however, was agog. Kiyoaki was surprised to find that even the sons of the most prestigious families at Peers were so much in the dark over this event that some of them asked him, of all people, what he thought of the affair.

"Everybody's so sympathetic toward the Ayakuras, but do you know what I think?" one student demanded. "I think that this is going to undermine people's reverence for the Imperial Family. Isn't everybody saying that they found out later that this Miss Ayakura wasn't quite right in her mind? But I want to know why this only came out right now."

While Kiyoaki was wondering how best to answer, Honda, who was standing beside him, stepped into the breach.

"Even if someone is sick, there's no way of knowing until the symptoms appear, is there? Why don't you stop gossiping like a schoolgirl?"

But this kind of appeal to masculinity was ineffective at Peers. To begin with, Honda's family did not have the status to qualify him as a person in the know, who could provide a plausible ending to this sort of exchange. In order to qualify

as a person in the know, one had to be able to say something
like: "She happens to be my cousin," or perhaps, "He is the
son of my uncle's mistress." A boy such as this had to show
that he was proud to have faint blood ties to crime and scandal, and yet at the same time parade his own noble aloofness
intact. And so with a slight curl to his lip, he would drop
enough of a hint to indicate that, unlike the rumormongering
rabble, he had access to behind-the-scenes information. At this
school, mere boys of fifteen or sixteen were apt to put on airs
and say: "It's given the Home Minister quite a headache, you
know. He called up late last night to talk to Father about it";
or again: "Everyone thinks that the Home Minister is laid up
with a cold, but the truth is that he was in such a hurry to get
to an imperial audience that he missed the step getting out of
his carriage and sprained his ankle."

Strangely enough, Kiyoaki's habitual secretiveness seemed
to have worked to his advantage in this business. For other
than Honda, none of his classmates had any idea of his relations with Satoko, nor was anyone aware of Marquis Matsugae's role in the matter. There was, however, a son of the
ancient court nobility who was related to the Ayakuras and
vehemently insisted that someone as beautiful and gifted as
Satoko could not possibly have gone mad; but all he provoked
were scornful smiles from his classmates, who thought him
simply anxious to defend his own kind.

All of this caused Kiyoaki constant pain. In comparison
with Satoko's public humiliation, however, he did not even
have a slighting remark to contend with. And however acute
his private agony, it was, after all, the torment of a coward.

Whenever this business came up with his classmates or he
heard Satoko's name on their lips, he would look out of the
window of the second-floor classroom as though absorbed in
the view of the distant mountains, now wholly in the grip of
winter, their snow-covered slopes sparkling in the clear morning air. He would imagine Satoko herself, now remote and
unapproachable, presenting a similar purity to the world at
large, without a word in her own defense. The brightness,

distant yet almost painful, was visible to Kiyoaki alone. Its flawlessness struck him to the heart. By accepting everything —sin, shame, the imputation of madness—she had absolved herself. But what of him?

There were times when he wanted to shout out his guilt at the top of his voice. But then her terrible self-sacrifice would be in vain. Would it really be an act of courage to nullify that for the sake of quieting his conscience? Or did true courage demand rather that he silently endure his present existence as a virtual prisoner? It was too complex an evaluation for him. But at any rate, to continue as he was, despite the worsening pain, in other words to submit to the will of his parents and the whole household, was to persist in a course of action that was becoming more and more difficult.

There had been a time when idleness and melancholy seemed to be the intrinsic elements of life as he wanted it to be. How had he happened to lose his capacity for such enjoyment, his ability to luxuriate in it without ever getting bored? It was gone, as unnoticed as an umbrella forgotten at someone's house.

Now he needed something to hope for if he was to endure idleness and melancholy. And since there was nothing even remotely encouraging about his situation, he began to construct a hope of his own.

"The rumor about her insanity is too incredible even to bother discussing," he thought. "I just don't believe it. So why couldn't it be true that her running away from the world and becoming a nun is only a trick? Maybe she staged this daring comedy just to gain time and get out of that marriage —for my sake, in other words. If it's true, then we must unite to keep perfect silence, even though such a distance separates us. That accounts for her not even writing me so much as a note. It's obvious! What else could her silence mean?"

If Kiyoaki had truly understood her character, he would have known immediately that his fiction was an impossibility. After all, wasn't the image of a domineering Satoko no more

SPRING SNOW   [349]

than an illusion he had created out of his own timidity? If so, then she was perhaps no more substantial than a flake of snow that had melted in his arms. His eyes had been fixed on one single aspect of the truth. So much so, that now he almost believed in the eternal validity of the pretense in whose shadow this truth had found a precarious existence. Thus his hope made him a prey to self-deception.

It was a hope tinged with baseness. For if he had really surrendered to the vision of her beauty, he could not have left any room for hope. Without his noticing it, his coldly glittering heart had begun to melt with pity and tenderness, like ice under the rays of the setting sun. He felt the urge to be gentle with people. And he began to take a closer look at the world about him.

There was a student at Peers, the son of a marquis whose family lineage was extremely ancient, who had been nicknamed "the Monster." Rumor had it that he was a leper, but since it was unthinkable that a leper would be allowed to attend classes, it could only be that he had some other disease, which was not contagious. Half his hair had fallen out. His complexion was ashen and his skin lackluster. His back was hunched. No one knew what his eyes were like because he kept them well covered with the peak of his school cap which he had special permission to wear even in the classroom. He sniveled constantly, and made a noise like water at a low boil. As he never talked to anyone, he would take a book during recess and walk to the far edge of the lawn in front of the school before he sat down to read it.

Kiyoaki too, of course, had never had anything at all to do with this student, who, besides everything else, was in a different course. Even though their fathers were nobles of the same rank, Kiyoaki seemed to embody beauty more than any other boy in the school, whereas the other was like the chosen emissary of ugliness and sinister shadow.

Although the dry grass in the corner of the lawn that was the Monster's chosen spot caught more than its fair share of sun on this particular early winter day, everyone else avoided

it. When Kiyoaki came up and sat down beside him, he shut
his book and went tense as he prepared to flee, as he always
did. Only the muffled sound of his sniveling, like the steady
dragging of a light chain, broke the silence.

"What's that you're always reading?" asked the Marquis's
son who was beautiful.

"Nothing . . . ," replied the Marquis's son who was ugly.
He thrust the book behind him, but not before Kiyoaki's eye
caught the name Leopardi printed on the spine. The gilt lettering cast a faint reflection that flashed over the dry grass
and was gone.

Since the Monster was not disposed to talk, Kiyoaki edged
away from him without getting up, then stretched out his legs
and lay on his side, supporting himself on one elbow and ignoring the numerous blades of dry grass now clinging to his
woolen uniform. Still directly opposite him, the Monster sat
huddled in obvious distress, shutting the book that he had
once more spread out in front of him. Kiyoaki felt that he was
looking at a caricature of his own misery, and his gentleness
began to give way to indignation. As the unseasonably warm
sun continued its prodigality regardless, Kiyoaki saw the ugly
figure of the Marquis's son begin to undergo a gradual transformation. His crumpled legs cautiously stretched out as he
lay down on the grass and propped himself on his elbow opposite Kiyoaki. His form became Kiyoaki's own, down to the
very angle of the head and the set of the shoulders. They had
become as like as a pair of lion-dogs guarding a temple gate.
Beneath the lowered brim of his cap, the other's lips, though
not exactly smiling, at least gave a hint that their owner was
in a cheerful mood.

And so the two Marquis's sons, one ugly, one beautiful,
made a pair. The Monster had handled Kiyoaki's whim of pity
and solicitude by showing neither gratitude nor resentment
but by calling on his profound self-awareness, the mirror-
image of Kiyoaki's own, and by so doing, he had acquired a
form that was somehow a match for Kiyoaki's. If one disre-
garded their faces, the two of them presented a remarkable

symmetry there on the warm, dry grass, from the braid that
trimmed their jackets to the cuffs of their trousers.

Kiyoaki's attempt to penetrate the other's reserve could
hardly have been rebuffed more completely, yet with greater
gentleness. He felt enveloped in the warmth and kindness
that had accompanied it.

From the nearby archery range came the twang of a bowstring—a sound that made him think of the cold bite of the
winter wind—followed by the dull thud of the arrow striking
home as if the target were a slack-tuned drum.

His own heart seemed to him to be much like an arrow
stripped of the flashing white feathers that gave it direction.

 49

WHEN SCHOOL ENDED for the winter vacation, the
studious among Kiyoaki's classmates devoted themselves to
studying for the pre-graduation exams, but the mere prospect
of opening a book filled him with horror. No more than a third
of his class, including Honda, intended to go on after the
spring graduation to sit for the university entrance exams
that were held in the summer. Most of them intended to use
their privilege as graduates of Peers to receive dispensation
from the entrance examinations and either apply to those de-
partments of Tokyo Imperial University that were always
under-subscribed, or perhaps enter one of the other imperial
universities, such as Kyoto or Tohoku. Kiyoaki too, regardless of what his father might think, would probably follow
the line of least resistance. If he entered Kyoto University, he
would be that much closer to Satoko's convent.

For the present, therefore, he was free to drift in privileged idleness. There were two heavy snowfalls in December, but he was in no mood to feel boyish glee at the sight of the snow-covered grounds that greeted him one morning. He pushed aside the curtain of the window beside his bed and looked out with indifference at the winter scene, the island now a patch of brilliant white in the middle of the pond. He did not stir from his bed for hours. At other times an idea would strike him and his eyes would flash at the prospect of getting back at Yamada, who supervised him even while he was walking around the estate. He chose a night when a particularly gusty north wind was raging, and went for a brisk climb up the maple hill. Yamada, flashlight in hand and neck buried in the collar of his overcoat, had to come striding after him despite his feebleness. The creaking of the branches, the crying of the owl, the treacherous footing underneath—everything filled him with delight as he felt himself moving onward and upward as irresistibly as a devouring flame. With each step he imagined himself crushing the darkness beneath his heel as if it were something soft and alive. At the crest of the hill, the brilliant, star-filled winter sky was spread wide.

*

Just before the year's end, a gentleman came to the Matsugae residence to call the Marquis's attention to a newspaper article written by Iinuma. The Marquis was enraged at this evidence of his disloyalty to the family.

The paper had a small circulation and was the organ of a right-wing group. The Marquis protested that it was the kind of muckraking sheet whose practice was to extort money from those in high society under the threat of exposing some scandal or another. It would have been quite something else if Iinuma had degraded himself to the extent of coming to ask for money before publishing the article. But to go ahead and write such a thing without even attempting this was nothing less than an open and provocative breach of his obligations.

Under a heading with a decidedly patriotic flavor, "A Disloyal and Unfilial Marquis," the burden of the indictment was as follows: the man intimately involved behind the scenes in the present affair of the broken engagement was, in fact, Marquis Matsugae. Any marriage involving a member of the Imperial Family had to be subjected to close scrutiny in accordance with the provisions of the Imperial Household Code because such a marriage, no matter how remote the possibility, might affect the imperial succession. These then were the grave circumstances under which Marquis Matsugae had taken it upon himself to sponsor the daughter of an ancient family, a girl whose mental instability he claimed to have been unaware of at the time, going so far as to obtain an imperial sanction for her marriage, only to have his plans fall through, almost on the eve of the betrothal ceremony. Despite all this, however, simply by being lucky enough to have succeeded in keeping his name out of the affair, Marquis Matsugae today was going tranquilly about his business, thus displaying not only a brazen disloyalty to His Majesty the Emperor, but also a lack of reverence toward his own father, one of the pillars of the Meiji Restoration.

If the article provoked the Marquis to fury, it aroused misgivings in his son. He noticed at once that Iinuma had made a point of appending his name and address to it and also that, although he was fully aware of what had happened between Kiyoaki and Satoko, he had written as though he really believed Satoko had had a nervous breakdown. Up to then, Kiyoaki had had no idea where he was living. And now the thought struck him that Iinuma had written this in the knowledge that he would incur the stigma of someone dead to all sense of obligation, because he had wanted Kiyoaki to read it at all costs and know where he was, without seeming to inform him directly. At any rate, he was sure that the article contained a hidden message that was aimed at him alone: Don't be like your father.

All at once, he felt a rush of nostalgia at the thought of Iinuma. To have his awkward devotion once more, to mock it playfully—he could think of nothing that would cheer him more in his present mood. However, to try to see him now while his father's anger was at its peak, would be to court further reprisals, and his sense of nostalgia was not strong enough to make him want to run that risk.

On the other hand, he knew that arranging a meeting with Tadeshina would be far less dangerous. Ever since the old woman's thwarted suicide, however, he could only think of her with indescribable disgust. To judge by her having betrayed him to his father in her farewell letter, he was convinced that some twist of character made her derive a peculiar pleasure from betraying all those without exception whom she had brought together. He had come to realize that she was like those people who would tend their gardens scrupulously just for the pleasure of tearing up their flowers once they had bloomed.

His father almost never spoke to him. And his mother, not wishing to cross her husband, tried her best to leave her son alone.

The reality at the heart of his father's anger was worry and fear. He hired a private policeman to stand guard at the front gate, and had two more posted at the rear. The old year ended, however, with neither private threat nor the rise of public antagonism to confront the Matsugaes. Iinuma's disclosure had apparently failed to set off any repercussions in official circles.

It was customary for the two foreign families who rented from the Matsugaes to send over invitations for Christmas Eve. But since to gratify one family would be to disappoint the other, the Marquis made it a practice to accept neither invitation, but rather to send over presents for each family's children. This year, however, feeling that he might find something to divert him in the holiday mood of a foreign household, Kiyoaki asked his mother if she would intercede with his father to let him go. But the Marquis would not hear of it.

The reason he gave was not the usual one of being unwilling to disappoint one family or the other. Instead he said that it was beneath the dignity of the son of the nobility to accept

an invitation from a tenant family. One of the implications
in this was clear enough to Kiyoaki: his father still had little
faith in his son's ability to maintain his dignity.

The Matsugae household was in a flurry of activity during
the last days of the year, as the traditional massive house-
cleaning that preceded the New Year's holidays could not be
completed in a single day. Kiyoaki had nothing to do. The
feeling that the year was ending was a knife in his heart—
this year above all years—for it would never come again. In
these last, waning days, he had come to realize that this year
had seen the peak of his life.

He left the house and all its bustle behind him and walked
alone toward the pond, in the mood to go rowing. Yamada
came hurrying after him with an offer of company that was
harshly rebuffed.

As the prow of the boat pushed through dry reeds and broken remains of lotus leaves, a small flock of wild ducks took
to the air. In the midst of their frantic flapping, he saw their
small, flat bellies flash for a second in the clear winter air
with not a drop of water to mar the silken sheen of their
feathers. A reflected gleam raced crookedly across the tangled reeds.

He looked down at the cold image of clouds and blue sky
reflected in the surface of the water, and wondered at the
sluggish ripples stirred by his oars. As the reflection broke
up, the dark, muddy water seemed to be telling him something quite alien to the crystalline clouds and winter sky.

He rested his oars and looked toward the main reception
room of the house, watching the servants busy at work as if
they were actors scurrying about on a distant stage. The waterfall had not frozen, but its sound was muffled and discordant. His view of its lower reaches was blocked by the island, but farther up, on the north side of the maple hill, the
bare tree branches revealed the dirty remnants of snow on the
banks of the stream.

He finally steered his boat into the tiny island inlet, fastened it to a stake, and made his way up to the faded green pines that crowned the knoll. As he looked at the three metal cranes, the beaks of the two that had outstretched necks seemed like a pair of blunt arrowheads aimed at the December sky.

He threw himself down at once on the dry brown grass warmed by the heat of the sun, and lay there, face up, knowing that he was completely alone, secure from every eye. Then as he sensed the numb chill that came from rowing in the fingers that cradled his head, he was suddenly overwhelmed by a wild rush of misery that he had been able to fend off while he was in the presence of other people.

"This year was mine—and now it's gone," he cried out to himself. "It's gone! Just like a cloud dissolving." The words poured out of him, cruel and unrestrained, lashing him, intensifying his agony. Never before had he given way to such wildness. "Everything has turned sour, I'll never be carried away with joy again. There's a terrible clarity dominating everything. As though the world were made of crystal so that you only have to flick part of it with your fingernail for a tiny shudder to run through it all. . . . And then the loneliness— it's something that burns. Like hot thick soup you can't bear inside your mouth unless you blow on it again and again. And there it is, always in front of me. In its heavy white bowl of thick china, dirty and dull as an old pillow. Who is it that keeps forcing it on me?

"I've been left all alone. I'm burning with desire. I hate what's happened to me. I'm lost and I don't know where I'm going. What my heart wants it can't have . . . my little private joys, rationalizations, self-deceptions—all gone! All I have left is a flame of longing for times gone by, for what I've lost. Growing old for nothing. I'm left with a terrible emptiness. What can life offer me but bitterness? Alone in my room . . . alone all through the nights . . . cut off from the world and from everyone in it by my own despair. And if I cry out, who is there to hear me? And all the while my public self is as graceful as ever. A hollow nobility—that's what's left of me."

A huge flock of crows was perched in the bare branches of the maples on the hill. He listened to their discordant shrieks and to the beating of wings as they flew overhead toward the low hill where Omiyasama was enshrined.

50

EARLY IN THE NEW YEAR it was customary for the Imperial Poetry Recitation to be held at the palace. Ever since Kiyoaki was fifteen, Count Ayakura had sent him an invitation each year without fail, a kind of abiding token of the training in elegance he had once received from the Count. And this year too, though one would hardly have been surprised if it had been otherwise, an invitation came as usual through the Imperial Household Ministry. The Count was going to assume his role as an imperial lector once again, unhindered by any shameful scruples, and it was clearly he who had arranged Kiyoaki's invitation.

When he showed his father the invitation, the Marquis frowned at the sight of the Count's signature among those of the four lectors. He was seeing elegance in a new light: it confronted him with tenacity and impudence.

"Since it's a regular event, you'd better go," he said at last. "If you didn't this year, it might start people talking about some rift between the Ayakuras and us. In essence, we are not supposed to have any connection with them where that affair is concerned."

Year by year the poetry ceremony had grown on Kiyoaki, and he had come to appreciate it greatly. At no other time did the dignity of Count Ayakura's bearing show to such advantage as it did on these occasions, nor could Kiyoaki imagine any role more suited to him. Now of course, the sight of the Count would be a painful one, but even so he felt that he wanted to see him. He felt the desire to take a steady look at the shattered fragments of a poem that had once been alive inside him too, until he had grown weary of looking. He thought that if he attended, the image of Satoko would fill his mind.

He no longer believed himself to be a thorn of elegance jabbed into the sturdy fingers of the Matsugaes. But he had not changed to the point of thinking that he actually was one of those fingers either. Only the elegance that had been so conscious a part of him had withered. His heart had become desolate. Nowhere in himself could he find the kind of graceful sorrow that inspires poems. He was empty now, his soul a desert swept by parching winds. He had never felt more estranged from elegance and from beauty as well.

Yet perhaps all this was essential to his attaining true beauty—this inner emptiness, this loss of all joy, even this utter inability to believe that the oppressive weight of each moment was something real, that his pain, at least, was something that was his. The symptoms of a man afflicted by true beauty are much like those of leprosy.

Since he no longer looked in the mirror, he had no way of knowing that the sad and haggard cast of his features had evolved into the classical expression of youth pining away for love.

One evening when he was eating dinner at a table laid for him alone, the maid set down a small wineglass beside his plate, with cut-glass sides that were darkened by the crimson liquid they contained. Without bothering to ask the girl, he presumed it to be wine and drained the glass without hesitation. But then a strange sensation, a thick, slippery aftertaste lingered on his tongue.

"What was this?"

"The blood of a snapping turtle, sir," the maid answered. "I was ordered not to tell you unless you asked what it was. It was the cook, sir. He said that he wanted to make the young master fit and healthy again. So he caught a turtle from the pond and prepared it for you."

As he felt the unpleasantly smooth liquid sliding down his throat, he remembered the story the servants had so often used to frighten him when he was a child. Once again he saw the disturbing picture he had formed at that time of a snapping turtle raising its head like a sinister ghost from the dark waters of the pond, its eyes fixed on him, a creature that usually lay buried in the warm mud on the bottom, but never failed to force its way up to the surface time and again, pushing through the hostile weeds of dreams that conquered time, to fix its eyes on him at every stage of his life. But now, suddenly, the spell was broken. Death had overtaken the turtle, and he had just drunk its blood without knowing it. And with that, a whole era seemed suddenly at an end. Inside him, the terror was being docilely transformed into this unfamiliar energy that was coursing through him with a force whose intensity he could only guess.

*

The order of procedure each year at the Imperial Poetry Recitation was to read the selections according to the status of the writer, beginning with poems written by those of lower rank. With these first poems, the lector began by reading the poet's brief words of introduction, and then gave his office and rank. With the later poems, however, the lector first gave office and rank and then immediately began to recite the poem itself.

Among those who functioned as imperial lectors, Count Ayakura held the honored position of chief. Once more today both their Imperial Majesties and His Imperial Highness the Crown Prince graced him with their attention as the clear tones and beautifully modulated voice sounded through the chamber.

No tremor of guilt blurred its clarity. On the contrary, it was so brilliant as to stir sadness in the hearts of his audience. As he read each poem, the languid cadence of his words kept the pace of a Shinto priest's gleaming black-shod feet climbing, one by one, the stone steps of a shrine bathed in the strange warmth of the winter sun. It was a voice whose tone was neither masculine nor feminine.

Not a single cough marred the silence of the audience. But although his voice was supreme in the palace chamber, it was never sensual, nor called attention to itself at the expense of the poem itself. What poured smoothly from his throat was the very essence of elegance, impervious to shame, and its paradoxical blend of joy and pathos flowed through the room like the rolling mist in a picture scroll.

Up to now, each of the poems had been repeated only once, but when the Count concluded the Crown Prince's poem with the formula, "Such being the most eminent composition of His Majesty the Heir to the Imperial Throne," he went on to recite it twice more.

The Empress's poem was recited three times. The Count read the first verse, and then from the second verse on, all four lectors recited it in unison. With the exception of the Emperor himself, the rest of the Imperial Family, including the Crown Prince, and of course everyone else in the audience, stood up to listen.

This year, Her Imperial Majesty had composed a poem of exceptional grace and nobility. As he stood listening to it, Kiyoaki stole a glance at Count Ayakura, who was standing some distance from him. He noticed how the paper bearing the poem rested folded in the Count's small, white hand, so like a woman's. The fine tissue was a light plum color.

Although an affair that involved the Count and that had shaken the whole country was barely concluded, Kiyoaki was not surprised to hear no trace of a nervous quiver in his voice, much less the deep sorrow of a father whose only daughter has been lost to the world. The voice went on, clear, beautiful, never strident, performing exactly what had been entrusted to it. Let a thousand years go by, the Count would still be serving his Emperor as he served him now, like the rarest of songbirds.

The Imperial Poetry Recitation came to its climax at last. It was the moment for the reading of the poem of His Imperial Majesty himself.

Count Ayakura made his way reverently into the immediate vicinity of the Emperor and gravely took the imperial composition, which had been placed on the cover of an inkstone case in the traditional manner, and raised it to the level of his forehead. He then recited it five times.

As he read, the purity of his voice became, if anything, more pronounced, until he came at last to the end of the fifth recitation and concluded with the words "Such being the most august composition of His Sacred Majesty."

Kiyoaki, meantime, glanced up fearfully at the Emperor's face, his imagination quickened by the memory of the late Emperor's having patted him on the head when he was a boy. His Majesty seemed to be rather more frail than his imperial father had been, and although he was listening to the reading of his own composition, his face showed no sign of complacency, but retained an icy composure. Kiyoaki suddenly shook in fear at the totally improbable notion that His Imperial Majesty was in fact suppressing an anger that was directed at him.

"I've dared to betray His Majesty. There's nothing to do but to die."

He held fast to that one thought as he stood there, the atmosphere around him heavy with the rich fragrance of incense, feeling as though he might collapse at any moment. A thrill ran through him, but whether of joy or dread he could not tell.

51

I⟨т⟩ ⟨was⟩ F⟨ebruary⟩. With the pre-graduation exams
looming over them, all Kiyoaki's classmates were now wholly
caught up in their work. And he, who was indifferent to anything of the sort, stood more aloof than ever. Honda was certainly willing to help him with the preparation for his tests,
but he held back, feeling that Kiyoaki would have none of it.
He knew only too well how Kiyoaki reserved his keenest displeasure for any excessive show of friendship.

One day, just at this time, the Marquis suddenly presented
his son with the suggestion of entering Merton College, Ox-
ford. His admission could be arranged with no great difficulty,
especially since the Marquis was on good terms with the dean
of this famous institution founded in the thirteenth century,
but in order to qualify, Kiyoaki would at least have to get
through the final exams at Peers. The Marquis had, in fact,
been painfully aware that Kiyoaki was becoming more pale
and haggard by the day, and he had finally devised this means
of saving his son, who was to attain a court rank of at least
fifth degree, junior grade, before long. Since the plan of salva-
tion was so unexpected, Kiyoaki's interest was certainly
aroused. He therefore decided that he would give every appearance of being delighted with his father's proposal for the
present.

Prior to this, he had cherished a moderate sort of desire to
see something of the West. But now that his whole existence
was focused on a single object, a tiny, exquisitely beautiful
part of Japan, he could look at the map of the world spread
out before him, and be filled with a sense of crudity, not only

by the vast array of foreign countries, but even by the red-painted image of his own, curving like a shrimp against the flank of Asia. His Japan was light green, a country without shape, full of a pathos, as pervasive as rising mist.

His father bought a huge new map and had it hung on the wall in the billiard room. His intention was obviously to arouse great thoughts in Kiyoaki. However, its flat, lifeless seas failed to excite him. What came to his mind instead was the memory of a night sea like a huge, black beast with a living warmth, a pulse of its own, and blood that cried out—the sea at Kamakura, whose awesome rumbling had tormented him to the limit of endurance on a summer night.

Though he had mentioned it to no one, he had recently been troubled with frequent headaches and dizzy spells. He slept less each night. As he lay in bed, he told himself that the next day would surely bring a letter from Satoko. She would set a time and place for them to meet so that they could run away together. He would find her in some small, unfamiliar town, perhaps on a corner in front of an old-fashioned storehouse converted into a bank. She would run up to him and he would take her in his arms and hold her as he had been longing to do. Over and over again, he visualized the scene down to its last detail. But the image he cherished in this way was formed in a mirror backed with thin, brittle foil that was easily torn away to reveal nothing but a dismal blankness. His tears soaked his pillow and he called her name again and again through the night in helpless frustration.

As he did so, there were moments when her image was suddenly there beside him, somewhere between dream and reality. His dreams ceased to tell stories objective enough to be recorded in his journal. Hope and despair, dream and reality, now came together to cancel each other out, the border between them as vague as the shoreline against which the rolling waves break without cease. There for an instant, on the surface of the water that lapped back over the smooth sand, he saw the reflection of her face. Never had she seemed more lovely nor more grief-stricken. And when he put his lips close to this face that glimmered like the evening star, it vanished.

A frantic desire to break out of his plight grew more intense every day. Although everything had one single message for him—be it every hour, every morning, every noon and night, or the sky, the trees, the clouds and wind all telling him to give her up—he was still tormented by uncertainty. He felt a desperate need to lay hands on one thing at least that was sure and certain, to hear no more than a single word from her own lips, if he could only know that it was true. And if a word was too much to ask, he would be satisfied with just a glimpse of her face. He could no longer endure his racking anxiety.

In the meantime, the storm of rumors had quickly subsided. People did not take long to forget even so unprecedented and inexplicable an affair as an engagement sanctioned by imperial decree being broken on the very eve of the betrothal ceremony, especially since a naval bribery scandal had recently come to light to attract their indignation.

He made up his mind to leave home. Since his parents were on their guard, however, they had stopped giving him any allowance, and so he didn't have so much as a sen of his own.

Honda was taken aback when Kiyoaki approached him for money. In accordance with his father's ideas, he had been given a bank account of his own, which he was free to manage as he saw fit. He now withdrew the entire amount and gave it to Kiyoaki without asking a single question about what he intended to do with it.

It was the morning of the twenty-first of February when Honda brought the money to school and handed it over to his friend. The sky was bright and clear, but the morning air was bitterly cold.

"You've about twenty minutes left before class," said Kiyoaki after taking the money. His voice sounded a little timid. "Won't you come along and see me off?"

"Where are you going?" asked the startled Honda. He knew that Yamada must be standing guard at the front gate.

"That way," Kiyoaki answered, smiling and pointing toward the woods.

Honda was pleased to see his friend showing signs of energy for the first time in months, but no healthy glow had returned to his face. On the contrary, his gaunt features were pale and strained, making Honda think of a thin sheet of ice in early spring.

"Do you feel all right?"

"I think I have a cold. Otherwise I'm fine," Kiyoaki replied, leading the way cheerfully along the path that ran through the woods.

It had been a long time since Honda had seen him walking so briskly. Moreover, he had a good idea where his steps were leading, but said nothing. They passed a marsh whose icy surface, laced with intricate designs of frozen driftwood, dully reflected the slanting rays of the morning sun. And then, leaving the wood and its chattering birds behind, they came to the eastern edge of the school property.

They were now at the top of a slope, across the bottom of which stretched a line of factories. Strands of barbed wire had been carelessly strung along here in place of a fence, and the neighborhood children often slipped through the breaks into the campus. Beyond the wire, the grassy hill extended as far as the road, where a rough wooden fence had been put up over a low stone wall.

At this point the two of them came to a halt. Off to the right was a streetcar line. Directly below, the sun glinted from the jagged slate factory roofs as they caught the force of its morning rays. The motley collection of machines gathered under these roofs, already running at full throttle, set up a dull roar like the sea. The smokestacks stretched bleakly toward the sky. The smoke that poured from them left a shadow that crawled over the tops of the factories and shut out the sun from the washing that was hung out beside a row of hovels. But there were also some houses with makeshift shelves hung from the roof to display a number of bonsai. Here and there, one saw constant flashes of light. Once it was the reflection from a pair of pliers on the hip of an electrician climbing a pole. Another time it was the eerie glow of a flame seen through the windows of a chemical plant. In one factory, when the roar of machines ceased, there arose the sustained din of hammers beating on steel plating.

Far away, there was the clear sun. Below, skirting the school property, ran the road over which Kiyoaki was about to escape. The shadows of the small houses that lined it were etched upon its dusty white surface. A man was riding a dull, rusted bicycle past a group of children who were kicking a stone about.

"Well, I'll be seeing you," said Kiyoaki.

These were clearly words of farewell. They were graven on Honda's mind: for once, Kiyoaki had come up with a cheerful expression typical of a young man.

Kiyoaki had even left his book bag in the classroom. All he had on was his uniform and his overcoat trimmed with two rows of brass buttons and the cherry-blossom insignia running down the front of it. He had stylishly spread the collar open, exposing the tight, navy-style collar of his jacket, together with the strip of white celluloid inside it, pressed against his young throat as he now smiled at Honda, his face shadowed by the peak of his cap. Then still smiling, he turned and, bending apart some broken strands of wire with his gloved hands, climbed through the barrier.

*

His disappearance was immediately reported to his parents, who were thoroughly upset. Once again, however, it was his grandmother's decisiveness that restored order.

"Don't you see the way it is? He's happy about going to school in England. And since he intends to go, he wants to see Satoko first and say good-bye to her. But since you wouldn't have let him do it if he'd told you about it first, he's gone down there without telling you. Is there any other likely explanation?"

"But surely Satoko won't see him."

"If that's what happens, he'll give up and come home. Kiyoaki's a young man. You've got to let him have his head until he gets this out of his system. It's because you tried to keep too close a rein on him that this sort of thing had to happen."

"But Mother! After what's happened the precautions we took were only to be expected."

"All right, and this was only to be expected too."

"That's as may be, but it will be just terrible if this gets out. What I'll do is get in touch with the superintendent-general at once and have him start a search in absolute secrecy."

"A search! Why a search? You already know where he's going."

"But unless he's caught and brought back . . ."

"You'll regret it!" the old woman shouted, her eyes burning with anger. "He might do something really terrible this time. It's quite all right for safety's sake to have the police look into things quietly. If they let us know just where he is as soon as they find out, that will be useful. But since we know perfectly well where he's going and why, they're to keep their distance, and they must absolutely not let him suspect anything. Right now the boy is to be left completely free, and not to be interfered with. Everything must be done quietly. We must get through this without turning it into a big drama. That's what's essential. If there's any blunder now, the results could be disastrous. That's what I want you to understand."

*

The night of February 21, Kiyoaki stayed at a hotel in Osaka. The next morning he paid his bill and took a Sakurai Line train to Obitoké, where he rented a room at a merchant's inn called the Kuzonoya. No sooner had he done this than he hired a rickshaw to go to Gesshu. He hurried the rickshaw man through the temple gate and up the slope that led to the Tang front entrance, where he got out. Confronted by a blank expanse of tightly shut sliding door, he called out. The convent janitor appeared, asked him his name and business, and then left him standing there. After a short wait, the next to appear was the senior nun. And she, without even allowing him to step up into the front hallway, rebuffed him by saying with thinly veiled displeasure that Her Reverence the Abbess would not see him and that furthermore it would be unthinkable for a novice to be permitted to do so. Since he had more or less expected this reception, he did not press the issue, but left then and there and returned to the inn.

He deferred his hopes to the next day, and when he thought over his initial failure in solitude, he concluded that it was due to his presumption in taking the rickshaw right up to the very entrance of the convent. He had been driven to it by his anxiety and haste, of course, but since seeing Satoko again was a kind of supplication, he decided that he should have got out at the gate and walked from there, whether the nuns took note of this show of devotion or not. He had better do some kind of penance.

His room at the inn was dirty, the food was tasteless, and the night cold. But the thought of Satoko now nearby gave him a feeling of deep contentment. That night, for the first time in months, he slept soundly.

The next day was the twenty-third; he felt more energetic and went to the convent twice—once in the morning and again in the afternoon—leaving the rickshaw at the gate and climbing the long sloping path as a pilgrim would. However, his reception was no warmer than the day before. On the ride back, he began to cough, and felt a slight pain deep inside his chest. He decided against using the hot bath at the inn.

His dinner that night proved to be of a quality wholly unexpected at a country inn of this sort. Furthermore, not only had everyone's behavior toward him markedly improved but despite his protests, he had been moved into the best room the inn had to offer. When he demanded an explanation from the maid, she tried to put him off. Finally, however, when he became angry with her, the mystery was solved. She told him that while he had been out that day, a local policeman had come and questioned the innkeeper closely about him. The policeman then said that Kiyoaki was from an extremely exalted family. He was therefore to be treated with the utmost deference, but on no account was he to learn of the policeman's

visit. Furthermore, should he move out of the inn, the police
were to be informed immediately. Kiyoaki felt a rush of fear.
He realized that he had no time to lose.

When he got up next morning, the twenty-fourth of February, he felt very much out of sorts. His head was stuffy and
he was listless. Nevertheless, his mind was made up. If he was
ever to see Satoko again, he had to commit all his strength to
the penance he must undergo, whatever hardship it entailed.
In this mood he set out from the inn, and, without hiring a
rickshaw, started on the more than two miles to Gesshu. Fortunately it was a beautiful morning. The road itself, however,
was none too easy. Moreover his cough grew worse as he
walked, and he had a sensation in his chest like the settling of
metallic dust. A severe fit of coughing overtook him at the
very entrance to Gesshu. The expression on the face of the
senior nun who met him remained unaltered as she refused
his request in precisely the same terms.

The next day, the twenty-fifth, he began to have chills and
fever. Although he realized that it was unwise to go out, he
hired a rickshaw once more and went to the convent, only to be
rebuffed just as before. His hope at last began to fail. Hin-
dered by the fever that clouded his mind, he tried to evaluate
the situation, but no feasible course of action occurred to him.
Finally, he told the clerk at the inn to send a telegram: "Please
come at once. Am at the Kuzonoya in Obitoké on Sakurai Line.
Not a word to my parents. Kiyoaki Matsugae."

This done, he passed an uncomfortable night before waking
groggily on the morning of the twenty-sixth.

52

I‌T WAS A MORNING when light flakes of snow
danced in the brisk wind that swept over the plain of Yamato.
They seemed too fragile even for spring snow, but were rather
more reminiscent of a swarm of summer insects. When the
sky remained overcast, they disappeared against the clouds.
Only when the sun shone through did one become aware of
the powdery, swirling snow. The cold in the air was worse
than it would have been on a day of heavy snow.

As he lay with his head on his pillow, he considered how he
could prove his ultimate devotion to Satoko. The night before
he had at last decided to appeal to Honda for help, and he was
sure that his friend would come today without fail. With
Honda to sustain him, perhaps he might be able to soften the
Abbess's unyielding attitude. But before that there was one
thing he had to do. He had to try it. All by himself, with no
one's help, he had to demonstrate the purity of his devotion.
On looking back, he realized that up to now he had not even
once had the opportunity of proving this devotion to Satoko.
Or perhaps, he thought, his cowardice had made him flee any
such opportunity until now.

Today, there was only one thing for him to do. To go out,
ill as he was, to risk worse illness, was a significantly great
penance. Devotion so overwhelming might stir a response
from Satoko, or then again it might not. Whatever the result,
even if there were not the faintest hope of her being moved,
he had now reached a state of mind where he would have no
peace until he had done this thing, done it as a penance that he
demanded of himself. He had begun his journey completely

obsessed by a single thought: to have even a single glimpse of
her face. In the meantime, however, his heart had formed another resolution of its own, that overrode his intentions and
desires.

The only force to counter this wayward urge in his heart
was his body itself. He was in the grip of an aching fever. A
heavy gold thread had been strung through every part of it,
embroidering his flesh with pain and heat. The strength had
gone out of him. If he lifted his arm, the pale skin immediately
turned blue and cold, and the arm itself became as heavy as a
full bucket in a well. His cough seemed to come from deeper
and deeper in his chest, like the constant rumble of distant
thunder on a darkened horizon. His body balked at his demands, weak and enervated to the very fingertips under the
assault of the burning fever that shot through him.

He called Satoko's name more and more desperately. The
empty hours dragged by. This morning, for the first time, the
servants at the inn realized that he was ill. They warmed his
room and anxiously set about doing all they could to make him
comfortable, but he stubbornly refused to allow them either
to treat him themselves or call a doctor.

Finally in the afternoon, he told the maid to hire a rickshaw
for him. She hesitated, and went to tell the innkeeper. When
the man came up to his room and tried to persuade him to
stay indoors, he struggled to his feet, got into his uniform and
put on his overcoat without help, to put on a show of health. A
rickshaw came. He set out in it, his legs wrapped in a blanket
that the inn maids had thrust in after him. Despite its protection, however, he was attacked by the terrible force of the cold.

His eye was caught by the stray snowflakes swirling in
through the openings left by the black canvas rickshaw
cover. Suddenly the vivid memory of the ride through the
snow with Satoko just a year before came to him, and his chest
tightened with emotion and a grating pain.

He could no longer cower in the gloom inside the swaying
rickshaw, doing nothing but trying to endure the pain in his
head. He loosened the front flap of the bonnet and then pulled

his muffler up over his mouth and nose and looked out at the passing scenery, his eyes watering with fever. He wanted to rid his mind of any image that would drive his thoughts back upon the pain that racked him.

The rickshaw had already passed out of the narrow lanes of Obitoké. Powdered snow fell on the fields and paddies to either side of the flat road that led directly to where Gesshu stood among the mountains shrouded in cloud. It fell on the rice shocks left in the paddies, on the withered mulberry leaves, on the blurred green of the pak-choi leaves that separated the rice and mulberry fields, on the rust-colored reeds and bulrushes on the marshes. It kept falling noiselessly, but was not enough to cover the ground. Even the flakes that fell on his blanket vanished without leaving obvious drops of moisture.

He saw the flat white of the sky grow gradually brighter until a pale sun at last shone through the clouds. The falling snow blended into this new brightness more and more, until it was like a fine white ash floating in the air.

All along the road, the tall, dry grass swayed in the light wind, its feathery plumes having a faint glint of silver in the cold sunlight. Just beyond the fields, the foothills were shrouded in gray, but in the distance was a corner of clear blue sky and the snow-capped mountains were dazzling white.

As he gazed out at the scenery around him, his ears ringing with fever, he felt that he was really in touch with external reality for the first time in long months. The world around him was absolutely still. The swaying of the rickshaw and the heaviness of his eyelids may well have confused what he saw out there, but whatever the incidental distortion, this was a clear enough confrontation. And since he had been floundering about for so long in a chaotic darkness of sorrow and worry, the experience struck him with all the force of novelty. Wherever he looked, moreover, there was no sign of human life.

The rickshaw was already getting close to the thick growth of bamboo that covered the mountainside and surrounded

Gesshu itself. Up ahead, towering over the bamboos, stood
the pines that lined the road as it began its upward climb inside the gate. When he saw the austere stone gate posts at the
end of the winding length of road that led out of the fields, he
was convulsed by a spasm of poignant fear.

"If I go in through the gate in the rickshaw," he told himself, "and then the four hundred or so yards up to the front
door—if I ride all the way, I have the feeling that they won't
let me see Satoko today either. Maybe things have changed a
little since last time. Maybe the old nun took my part with the
Abbess, and now she's relented a bit. And then if they see that
I've walked up through the snow, she might let me see Satoko,
if only for a moment. But if I ride all the way, that could make
a bad impression on them and provoke an instinctive reaction
against me. Then the Abbess might decide never to let me see
Satoko. All my efforts should bring about some change of
heart in them. It's like a fan made with hundreds of thin, delicate slats held together by a single rivet. If I'm at all careless,
the rivet will come loose, and the whole thing will fall apart.
And then, if I rode all the way to the front door and wasn't
able to see Satoko, I'd feel it was my fault. I'd tell myself it
was because I was insincere. I'd know in my heart that if only
I had got out of the rickshaw and walked, no matter how weak
I felt, then such sincerity—even if she was unaware of it—
would have affected her, and she would have seen me. That's
it then. There's no reason to have such regrets. I have no
other choice but to risk my life if I want to see her. To me,
she's the essence of beauty. And it's only that which has
brought me this far."

He himself no longer knew whether his reasoning was ordered or wildly disturbed by fever. He told the rickshaw man
to stop at the gate. Then after getting out and telling him to
wait there, he began to walk up the slope. The sun was coming through again, and the snowflakes danced in its pale rays.
From the bamboo groves on either side of him he heard a
chirping that sounded like a lark. Green moss grew on the
trunks of the bare cherry trees that were scattered among the

pines along the roadside. A single plum tree bloomed white in the midst of the bamboos.

Having come this way six times in the last five days, it would seem that there was nothing left to catch him unawares. But as he began to make his way upward from where he had left the rickshaw, with unsteady legs and stumbling feet, he looked around him and the world took on a mournful clarity in his fevered eyes. The scenery that had become familiar in recent days now had a strange novelty about it that was almost unnerving. And at every moment, sharp-pointed silver arrows of cold shot through his spine. The ferns along the road, the red-berried spearflowers, the pine needles rustling in the wind, the bamboos with their green trunks and yellowed leaves, the abundance of tall dry grass, the road itself, rutted and white with frost as it passed through the midst of it all— Kiyoaki's eyes followed everything until it finally merged into the black shadow that lay across the road ahead as it rose through a grove of cedars. Surrounded by unbroken silence and utter clarity was a world untouched by blemish of any kind. And at its center, so inexpressibly poignant, at its innermost heart, he knew, was Satoko herself, her figure as quiet and still as an exquisite gold statue. But could such a still and perfect world, which eschewed all intimacy, really bear any relation to the familiar world he knew?

His breath grew harsh as he walked. Stopping to rest, he sat down on a large rock beside the road, only to be struck to the bone immediately by its intense chill, as though his layers of clothing could do nothing to hinder it. He coughed deeply, and as he did so, he saw that the handkerchief he held over his mouth was covered with rusty phlegm.

After his fit had gradually subsided, he looked up dizzily at the distant snow-covered mountain peaks that rose up beyond the sparse growth of trees. As his eyes were filled with tears from his coughing spell, his blurred vision seemed to heighten the sparkle of the snow. At that instant a memory of his thirteenth birthday came back to him. He was an imperial page once more, looking up at Princess Kasuga ahead of him as he

held her train. The snowy peaks before his eyes today were
the very image of the white that had dazzled him that day—
the pure color of the nape of her neck under the lustrous black
of her hair. That had been the moment in his life when a di-
vine female beauty had first moved him to adoration.

The sun disappeared once more. Gradually the snow came
down more heavily. He took off his glove and caught some
flakes in one hand. His palm was hot with fever, and they
melted before his eyes as soon as they touched it. How well he
had looked after his beautifully shaped hand, he reflected—
it had never been dirtied, never known a blister. He had used
it, but only in emotion.

Finally he got to his feet and started walking again, wondering whether he would be able to plod through the snow and
reach the temple. By the time he had climbed as far as the
cedar grove, the wind had grown much worse and its harsh
whine throbbed in his ears. The cedars thinned to reveal a
small pond, its chill surface a froth of ripples under the leaden
winter sky. Once past the pond, the gloomy darkness of the
thick old cedars closed in on him again, their branches deflect-
ing the force of the pelting snow.

By now he had but one objective: to keep putting one foot
in front of the other. All his recollections of the past had
crumbled away. He now knew that the future would only reveal itself at this pace, foot by foot, yard by yard, as he painfully struggled forward.

He went through the black gate without realizing it, and
when he looked up, he saw the Tang entrance itself in front
of him. Snow clung to the row of chrysanthemum tiles that
formed its eaves.

Collapsing in front of the sliding door, he broke into such a
violent fit of coughing that there was no need to call out.

The senior nun opened the door and immediately began to
rub his back to relieve his spasm. In a kind of trance, he had
the indescribably blissful feeling that Satoko had come, that
her hands were now caressing him.

The old nun did not refuse him at once today as she had before. Instead she left him there after a few moments and went back inside. He waited for a long time, feeling the minutes stretch out interminably. And as he waited, a mist seemed to cloud his sight. His pain, his joyful hope, both dissolved gradually into a single vague state of consciousness.

He heard women's voices in a flurry of conversation. Then silence again. More time passed. When the door slid open once more, the senior nun was alone.

"I'm sorry. Your request for a meeting cannot be granted. No matter how many times you come here, sir, I shall be forced to give you the same answer. I will arrange for a servant of the convent to accompany you, so please be kind enough to leave."

Helped by the janitor, who was fortunately a strong man, he went back down the road to where his rickshaw was waiting.

 53

HONDA ARRIVED AT THE INN in Obitoké late on the night of February 26. As soon as he saw how critical Kiyoaki's condition was, he was all for taking him back to Tokyo at once, but his friend would not hear of it. He discovered that the local doctor who had been summoned earlier in the evening had said that the symptoms indicated pneumonia.

Kiyoaki pleaded with him desperately. He wanted his friend to go to Gesshu next day, to talk to the Abbess, make every effort to soften her attitude. Since Honda was not involved, his words might perhaps have some effect on Her Reverence. And if she should relent, he wanted Honda to take him up to the temple.

Honda resisted for a time, but finally gave in, agreeing to delay their departure by one day. At all costs he would try to obtain an interview with the Abbess next day and do all he could on Kiyoaki's behalf. But he made his friend promise faithfully that if she should still refuse, he would go back to Tokyo with him immediately. Honda stayed up all that night, changing the wet dressings on Kiyoaki's chest. By the light of the dim lamp in the room, he saw that his skin, white as it was, now had a slight tinge of red from the dressings that covered it.

The final exams were only three days away. He had had every reason to expect his parents to be opposed to his making any trip at all right now. But when he had shown Kiyoaki's telegram to his father, surprisingly he had told him to go ahead, without asking any further details. And his mother had quite agreed. Justice Honda had once been ready to sacrifice his career for the sake of his old colleagues who were being forced to retire because the system of life tenure was being abolished. Now he intended to teach his son the value of friendship. During the train ride to Osaka, Honda had worked intently, and even now, as he held watch at Kiyoaki's bedside, he had his logic notebook open beside him.

In one circle of pale yellow light the lamp above them caught the ultimate symbols of two diametrically opposed worlds to which these young men had given themselves. One of them lay critically ill for the sake of love. The other was preparing himself for the grave demands of reality.

Kiyoaki, half asleep, was swimming in a chaotic sea of passion, seaweed clutching at his legs. Honda was dreaming of the world as a creation securely based on a foundation of order and reason. And so throughout a bitter night in early spring, in the room of an old country inn, these two young men's heads were close together under the light, one coolly rational, one burning with fever, each in turn finally bound by the rhythm of his own particular world.

In all their friendship, Honda had never been more aware than he was now of the utter impossibility of seeing into Kiyoaki's thoughts. He lay in front of him, but his spirit was off racing somewhere else. Sometimes he would deliriously call Satoko's name, and his cheeks would flood with color. His face lost its haggard look and instead seemed more than normally healthy. His skin glowed as if it were fine ivory with a fire inside it. But Honda knew that there was no way for him to reach that essence. Here before him, he thought, was passion in its truest sense. The kind of thing that would never take possession of him. But more than that, he thought, wasn't it true that no passion whatever would succeed in sweeping him away? For he realized that his nature seemed to be lacking in the quality that made this possible. It would never assent to such an invasion. His affection for his friend was deep, he was willing enough to weep when required—but as for feelings, he was lacking in something there. Why did he instinctively channel all his energies into the maintaining of a suitable inner and outer decorum? Why, unlike Kiyoaki, had he been somehow unable to open his soul to the four great inchoate elements of fire, wind, water, and earth?

His eyes returned to the notebook in front of him and his own neat, precise handwriting.

> Aristotle's formal logic dominated European thought until almost the end of the Middle Ages. This is divided into two periods, the first of which is called "Old Logic." The works expounded were the "Theses" and the "Categories" from the *Organon*. The second is called "New Logic." It may be said that this period received its initial impetus from the complete Latin translation of the *Organon* which was finished by the middle of the twelfth century . . .

He could not help thinking that these words, like inscriptions cut into stone exposed to the weather, would fall from his mind, flake by flake.

54

HONDA HAD HEARD that the convent day began early, so he shook himself out of a brief doze just as dawn was breaking. After a hasty breakfast, he told the maid to hire a rickshaw and got ready to leave.

Kiyoaki looked up at him from his bed, tears in his eyes. All he could manage was a look of entreaty as he lay with his head on the pillow, but it pierced Honda like a knife. Up until that moment, his intention had been to make a perfunctory visit to Gesshu and then get his gravely ill friend back to Tokyo as quickly as he could. But once he had seen the look in Kiyoaki's eyes, he knew that whatever the cost, he had to make every effort to effect a meeting between his friend and Satoko.

Fortunately it was a warm springlike morning, perhaps a good omen. As his rickshaw approached the convent entrance, he noticed that a man who was sweeping there took one look at him from a distance, abruptly put down his broom and rushed inside. His school uniform, which was the same as Kiyoaki's, must have put the man on guard, he thought, making him hurry in to sound the warning. The nun who appeared at the door had an expression of forbidding determination even before he could say who he was.

"Excuse me, Sister. My name is Honda. I am sorry to intrude, but I have come all the way from Tokyo because of this matter of Kiyoaki Matsugae. I would be extremely grateful if the Reverend Abbess would consent to see me."

"Please wait for a few moments," the nun replied.

He stood there for a long time on the front step, and then while he was involved in turning over in his mind the various counter-arguments to be used in the event of a refusal, the same nun surprised him by coming back and conducting him to a parlor inside. Hope, however faint, began to stir in him.

In the parlor he was again left to himself for a long time. The song of warblers came from the inner garden, though the sliding door was fully shut and he had no view. In the shadows he could just make out the intricate paper crest design of cloud-and-chrysanthemum on each door catch. The flower arrangement in the *tokonoma* alcove combined rape blossoms and peach buds. The bright yellow flowers seemed to pulse with the vigor of the spring countryside, and the dull bark and pale green leaves of the peach branch brought out the beauty of its swelling buds. The sliding doors were plain white, but he noticed a folding screen by the wall that seemed to be something precious, and he walked over to it.

He inspected it in detail. It was a screen depicting scenes of each of the twelve months of the year, done predominantly in the style of the Kano school, but enriched with the vivid colors that were traditionally Yamato.

The flow of the seasons began with spring at the right-hand edge of the screen. Courtiers enjoyed themselves in a garden beneath pines and white plum trees. A mass of golden cloud hid all but a fraction of a pavilion surrounded by a cypress hedge. A little to the left, young colts of various colors frolicked about. The pond in the garden at some point became a paddy and here young girls were at work planting rice shoots. A small waterfall burst from the golden cloud and tumbled down in two stages into another pond. The green shade of the grass at the water's edge bespoke the arrival of summer. Courtiers were hanging white paper pendants for the Mid-summer Purification on the trees and bushes round the pond, with minor officials and crimson-robed servants in attendance. Deer were grazing contentedly in the garden of a shrine, and a white horse was being led out through its red torii gate. Imperial guards, bows slung over their shoulders, were busy making preparations for a festival procession. And the red maple leaves already reflected in the pond foretold the chill of

winter that would soon take its toll. Then a bit farther on, still
more courtiers were setting out on a day's falconry in gold-
tinted snow. The sky too was golden, shining through the
snowy branches of a bamboo grove. A white dog was in bay-
ing pursuit of a partridge with a touch of red at its neck; it
streaked through the dry reeds like an arrow and escaped up
into the winter sky. The hawks at the courtiers' wrists kept
their arrogant eyes riveted on the fleeing partridge.

He returned to his place after a leisurely examination of the
Tsukinami screen, but there was still no sign of the Abbess.

The nun returned, knelt down, and served him with tea and
cake. She told him that the Abbess would be with him in just
a few minutes, and asked him to make himself comfortable
while he waited.

A small box decorated with a picture relief lay on the table.
It must have been a product of the convent, and furthermore,
there was something unskilled about its workmanship that
made him wonder if Satoko's inexperienced hand had been at
work on it. The paper glued to the sides and the padded picture
mounted on the lid were both highly colored after the taste of
the old Imperial Court, lavish and oppressively gaudy. In the
picture, a boy was chasing a butterfly. As he raced after the
red-and-purple-winged insect, his face, his satiny white skin
and his plump nakedness all suggested the sensuous grace of a
court doll. After his ride through the dark, early spring fields
and up the mountain through the still desolate woods, he felt
that here in this shadowy parlor at Gesshu he had finally experienced the heavy, syrupy sweetness that was the essence of
womanhood.

He heard the rustle of clothing, and then Her Reverence
herself came in through the doorway, leaning on the arm of
the senior nun. He stood up straight, but was unable to control the beating of his heart.

The Abbess must certainly have been advanced in years,
but the small features in the clear-skinned face above the
austere purple robe seemed to be carved out of fine yellow
boxwood and showed no trace of age. They had a warm ex-

pression as she now sat down opposite him. The old nun took a seat to one side.

"So, they tell me that you have come all the way from Tokyo?"

"Yes, Your Reverence." He had difficulty in getting his words out in front of her.

"This gentleman says that he is a school friend of Mr. Matsugae," said the old nun by way of contribution.

"Ah yes!" said the Abbess. "To tell the truth, we have been feeling so sorry for the Marquis's son. However . . ."

"Matsugae has a terrible fever. He's in bed back at the inn. I received a telegram from him and I came down here as quickly as I could. Today I've come here in his place to make the request he asked me to make." At last Honda found himself able to talk freely.

This, he thought, was most probably the way a young lawyer felt when he stood before the court. Regardless of the mood of the judges, he must plunge ahead, wholly intent on his plea and concerned only with the vindication of his client.

He told the Abbess of his friendship with Kiyoaki, he described his illness, and made it clear to her that Kiyoaki was risking his life for the sake of even the briefest of meetings with Satoko. He did not hesitate to say that if all this came to a tragic end, Gesshu itself would not be free of cause for remorse. He grew hotter and hotter as his fervent words poured out, and although the room was rather cold, he felt his ears and forehead burning.

As might be expected, his speech seemed to move the Abbess and the senior nun but they both remained silent.

"And then I do wish you would be kind enough to try to understand my own position. I lent my friend money because he told me he needed it. And that's what he used to come down here. Now he's fallen ill. I feel responsible to his parents for all this. And furthermore, as you must be thinking yourselves, the proper thing for me to do is obviously to get him back to Tokyo as soon as possible. I also realize that it's the only sensible solution. But I haven't done it. Instead, without even dar-

ing to contemplate how upset his parents are going to be with
me, I've come to you now like this to beg you to grant Matsugae's request. I'm doing it because after seeing the look of
desperate hope in his eyes, I do not feel that I have any other
choice. If Your Reverence could only see that look, I'm sure
that you too would be moved. As for me, I can't help but believe that it's far more important now to grant him what he
wants than to worry about his illness. It's a frightening thing
to say, but I somehow feel that he's not going to recover. So I
am really giving you his dying request. Would letting him see
Satoko for just a moment or two be quite outside the scope of
the Lord Buddha's compassion? Won't you please permit it?"

Her Reverence still did not answer. Although he was completely wrought up, he stopped there, afraid that if he said
anything further his words would only make it less likely that
the Abbess would change her mind. The chilly room was
hushed. The light that filtered through the pure white paper
of the latticework doors made Honda think of a thin mist.

At that moment he thought he heard something. It was not
by any means so close as to be in the next room, but close
enough, coming perhaps from a corner of the hallway or from
the next room but one. It sounded like a muffled laugh, as faint
as the opening of a plum blossom. But then after a moment's
reflection, he was sure that unless his ears had deceived him,
the sound that had carried to him through the chill convent
atmosphere on this spring morning was not a muffled laugh,
as he had thought, but a young woman's stifled sob. It did not
have the weight of a woman fighting down her tears. What he
had heard, as dark and faint as the sound of a cut bowstring,
was the trailing echo of a hidden sob. But then he began to
wonder if it was no more than a momentary quirk of his imagination.

"Ah," said the Abbess, breaking her silence at last, "no
doubt you think me unduly severe. You may feel that I am
the one who is using every means to keep these two apart.
However, surely it may well be that some superhuman agency
is at work here. It began when Satoko herself made a vow be-

fore the Lord Buddha. She swore never to meet this man again
in this world. I therefore think that the Lord Buddha in his
wisdom is making sure that she does not. But for the young
master, what a tragedy it is."

"Despite everything then, Your Reverence will not give
permission?"

"No."

Her voice had an inexpressible dignity, and he felt quite
powerless to answer her. The simple *no* seemed powerful
enough to tear apart the very sky like fragile silk.

After that, seeing his deep distress, the Abbess's beautiful
voice began to direct an exalted monologue at him. Although
he was by no means eager to leave and have to face Kiyoaki's
dejection, his distress prevented him from paying more than
half-hearted attention to what she was saying.

The Abbess referred to the net of Indra. Indra was an Indian God, and once he cast his net, every man, every living
thing without exception was inextricably caught in its meshes.
And so it was that all creatures in existence were inescapably
bound by it.

Indra's net symbolized the Chain of Causation or, in Sanskrit, *pratitya-samutpada. Yuishiki* (Vijñaptimātrata or Consciousness), the fundamental doctrine of the Hosso Sect, to
which Gesshu belonged, was celebrated in *The Thirty Verses
of Yuishiki*, the canonical text attributed to Vasubandhu,
whom the sect regarded as its founder. According to the
Verses, *Alaya* is the origin of the Chain of Causation. This
was a Sanskrit word that denoted a storehouse. For within the
Alaya were contained the karmic "seeds" that held the con-
sequential effects of all deeds, both good and evil.

Deeper within man than the first six forms of consciousness
—sight, hearing, smell, taste, touch, and mind, with which
sentient beings are endowed—there was a seventh called
Mana or self-awareness. But *Alaya*, the ultimate form of consciousness lay deeper yet.

Just as *The Thirty Verses* expressed it, "Like unto a violent torrent, ever flowing, ever changing," this eighth form

of awareness, like a raging river, changed incessantly, never ceasing to flow onward. In constant flux, *Alaya* is the source of all sentient beings and the sum of all effects on them.

Asanga, the co-founder along with Vasubandhu of the Yuishiki school, in a doctrinal work called *The Providence of the Greater Vehicle*, evolved, on the basis of the eternally mutative nature of *Alaya*, a unique theory of the Chain of Causation in terms of time. It dealt with the interaction of the *Alaya* consciousness and the Law of Defilement that gave rise to what was termed "the ever-recurring cycle of annihilation and renewal of causality." According to the doctrine of *Yuishiki*, "awareness only," each of the various dharmas, which were actually nothing other than consciousness, far from enjoying permanence, existed purely for the moment. And once the instant was past, they were annihilated. At the present moment, the *Alaya* consciousness and the Law of Defilement exist simultaneously, and their interaction gives rise to the causality of the present moment. Once this moment is past, both *Alaya* and the Law of Defilement are annihilated, but with the next moment, both are reborn, and both once again interact to give rise to a new causality. Beings in existence thus are annihilated from moment to moment, and this gives rise to time. The process whereby time is engendered by this moment-to-moment annihilation may be likened to a row of dots and a line.

*

As the minutes passed, Honda gradually found himself being drawn into the Abbess's profound doctrinal exposition. But his present circumstances prevented any stirring of his instinctive spirit of rational inquiry. The sudden burst of complex Buddhist terminology put him off, and then there were many difficult points over which he had doubts. Karma, he thought, should operate eternally, a process without beginning, that by its nature contained within itself elements of time. It seemed contradictory to him that, on the contrary, time was to be understood as arising from the dissolution and regeneration of each present moment's causality.

His various misgivings thus prevented him from giving wholeheartedly respectful attention to Her Reverence's learned discourse. The old nun also irritated him with her interjections. At appropriate intervals, she would chime in with "How very true!" . . . "Indeed, just so!" . . . "How could it be otherwise?" and the like. So he contented himself by memorizing the titles of *The Thirty Verses* and *The Providence of the Greater Vehicle* and thought that he could look into them when he had the leisure and then come back here to ask questions. Given his present mood, then, he did not realize from what perspective and with what clarity the Abbess's words were illuminating Kiyoaki's fate as well as his own, though on the face of it they might seem remote and irrelevant. It was just the same way that the moon, at its zenith, subtly lights up the dark waters of a lake.

He murmured a polite farewell and took his leave of Gesshu as quickly as he could.

 55

DURING THE TRAIN RIDE back to Tokyo, Kiyoaki's all too evident pain was a constant source of distress to Honda. He put aside his books entirely, his sole concern now to get his friend home as soon as possible. As he looked down at Kiyoaki lying gravely ill on his berth, being carried back to Tokyo without having achieved the meeting he had so desired, he felt a gnawing regret. He was now wondering if it had really been the act of a friend to give him that money.

Kiyoaki had fallen into a doze. Honda, on the other hand, was more alert than ever, despite having gone without sleep for so long. He allowed a multitude of thoughts to come and go unchecked. Among these, the memory of the Abbess's sermons on two occasions came to him, each with an entirely different effect. In the autumn of the previous year, he had heard his first sermon from her, the parable of drinking the water from the skull. He had taken that principle and made a parable of his own from it, one dealing with human love. And he had concluded by thinking that it would unquestionably be wonderful if a man could really make the substance of the world truly conform to that of his innermost heart. Later, in the course of his legal studies, he had given considerable thought to the doctrine of reincarnation as expressed in the Laws of Manu. And this morning, he had heard the Abbess speak again. He now felt as though the only key to the riddle that had been vexing him had dangled momentarily on a cord before his eyes, swinging back and forth with so many confusing jumps and twists that the riddle itself seemed to have become all the more complex.

The train was due at Shimbashi Station at six in the morning. The night was already well advanced. The heavy breathing of the passengers mingled with the rumble of the wheels. He would stay awake until dawn, watching Kiyoaki in the lower berth directly opposite him. He had left the curtains open so that he would know at once if there was any change at all in Kiyoaki's condition, and now he stared out of the window at the fields clothed in darkness.

Though the train was racing through the night, the darkness was so thick and the sky so overcast that the fields and mountains beyond were almost blotted out, leaving nearly nothing to mark the forward progress of the train. From time to time, a tiny flash of light or the brief glow of a lantern tore a brilliant rent in the curtain of blackness, but these could not provide any orientation. It was not the train that made this rumbling noise, Honda mused. It was something else. Something that enveloped this little thing as it made its insignificant way through the night. The roaring issued from the massive darkness itself.

While Honda had been hurriedly packing to leave the inn at Obitoké, Kiyoaki had obtained a few sheets of cheap stationery from the innkeeper and had written a note which he had then given to Honda, asking him to deliver it to his mother the Marquise. Honda had placed it carefully in the inside pocket of his jacket. Now, for want of anything better to do, he took it out and read it by the poor light of the bulb hanging from the roof of the car.

It was written in pencil, and the hand was unsteady, quite unlike Kiyoaki. He had never drawn his figures with much grace, but there had always been an abundantly vigorous touch to them:

> Dear Mother,
>
> There is something that I would like you to give Honda for me. The dream journal in my desk. He'd like it. And since nobody else would want to read it, please see that he gets it.
>
> Kiyoaki

Honda could see that he had used his last reserves of strength to write this as a kind of will. But if it really had been that, he should surely have included a word or two for his mother herself, instead of addressing her in this curt and businesslike fashion.

A groan came from the opposite berth. He quickly put away the note and was beside Kiyoaki in a flash, looking down at his face.

"What is it?"

"My chest hurts. It feels as if I'm being stabbed here."

Kiyoaki's breathing was harsh. His words came in spurts. Honda, not knowing what else to do, gently began to massage the lower left side of his chest, the spot where he said the pain was most intense. But in the faint light, he saw that his friend's face was still contorted.

Despite the contortions, however, it was beautiful. Intense suffering had imbued it with an extraordinary character, carving lines into it that gave it the austere dignity of a bronze mask. The beautiful eyes were filled with tears. Above them, however, the eyebrows were tightly puckered, and the masculine force they conveyed made a striking contrast with the pathos of the flashing dark, wet pupils. As he fought the pain, his finely chiseled nose jutted upward as if he were trying to probe the darkness around him, and his lips, parched with fever, were drawn back to reveal the palely gleaming mother-of-pearl of his teeth.

Finally, the racking pain seemed to subside.

"You're asleep? Good. It's what you need," said Honda. He wondered about the tortured look he had seen on his friend's face just a moment before. Hadn't it in fact been an expression of intense joy, the kind to be found nowhere but at the extremity of human existence? Perhaps Kiyoaki had seen something, and Honda envied him that, an emotion that in turn stirred an odd shame and self-reproach in him.

He shook his head slightly. He had begun to feel the numbing weight of grief. Deep within him, as subtly and persistently as the spinning of a silkworm's thread, an emotion had gradually taken shape. Its significance eluded him, and he was disturbed by it.

Then Kiyoaki, who seemed to have dozed off for a moment, suddenly opened his eyes wide and reached for Honda's hand. He grasped it tightly as he spoke.

"Just now I had a dream. I'll see you again. I know it. Beneath the falls."

His dream, Honda thought, had taken him to the park around his father's house. And there, the most vivid of all the images must have been the falls, tumbling down from the crest of the hill in its nine stages.

Two days after his return to Tokyo, Kiyoaki Matsugae died at the age of twenty.

ABOUT THE AUTHOR

ON NOVEMBER 25, 1970, Yukio Mishima committed *seppuku* (ritual suicide). Forty-five years old and at the peak of a brilliant literary career, he had that morning written the last word of the final novel of his tetralogy, *The Sea of Fertility*. "The tetralogy is his masterpiece, as he knew," Donald Keene has said.

Mishima had written much about suicide and early death, and often told his friends he wished to die young. After he conceived the idea of *The Sea of Fertility* in 1964, he frequently said he would die when it was completed. In fact the second of the four novels, *Runaway Horses*, is a remarkable literary rehearsal of his *seppuku*. Just before his suicide, he wrote his closest friends that he felt empty, having put into the tetralogy everything he thought and felt about life and this world. "The title, *The Sea of Fertility*," he told Keene, "is intended to suggest the arid sea of the moon that belies its name. Or I might say that it superimposes the image of cosmic nihilism on that of the fertile sea."

Mishima's works have been compared to the works of Proust, Gide, and Sartre, and his obsession with courage and the manly virtues has been likened to Hemingway's. Arthur Miller said, "I felt Mishima had an admirable style. He was surrealistic. He was very erotic. He had an economy of means to create enormous myths—his novels are compressed visions." A British magazine called him "one of the outstanding modern writers of fiction, possessing a complex, subtle and frightening imaginative power."

He was often wrongly called a rightist because of his private "army" of a hundred unarmed young men, but it was not on the blacklist of the careful Japanese police because it had never been involved in violence and differed from conventional rightist organizations. It was a theatrical fantasy conceived by a poet, as was his death, about which Selig Harrison of the Washington *Post* wrote, "He forced the Japanese to consider where they are going more dramatically than anyone else since World War II, and he has done so with a distinctively Japanese symbolism."

Mishima was born into a samurai family and imbued with the code that apotheosized complete control over mind and body, and loyalty to the Emperor—the same code that produced the austerity and self-sacrifice of Zen. Much of the tetralogy shows that he viewed the self-seeking arrogance and corruption of the militarists of the thirties (and their contemporary successors) as inimical to the samurai code.

His first novel was published in his school magazine when he was thirteen. A perceptive teacher encouraged him and persuaded a magazine to publish a story, *The Forest in Full Bloom*, in 1941, when Mishima (a pen name the teacher suggested) was sixteen. Three years later, when he entered Tokyo Imperial University, his first collection of stories was published under the same title and pen name. The first printing sold out in a week. In 1946 he brought two essays in manuscript to Kawabata, later the Nobel Prize winner, whose protégé he became. Altogether, 257 books by him, including 15 novels, have been published in Japan, and 77 translations here and in Europe.

Mishima reverenced and mastered the martial arts of Japan, creating a beautiful body he hoped age would never make ugly. He began to practice body-building in 1955, and *kendo* (dueling with bamboo staves) in 1959. In 1966 he took up *karate* as well. By 1968 he had become a *kendo* master of the fifth rank.

He traveled widely and often, and two travel books and many collections of articles are among his works. He also wrote countless short stories and thirty-three plays, in some of which he acted. Some ten films have been made from his novels; *The Sound of Waves* (1954, American edition 1956) was filmed twice, and one of the director Ichikawa's masterpieces, *Enjo*, was based on *The Temple of the Golden Pavilion* (1956, American edition 1959). Also available in English are *Five Modern Nō Plays* (1957) and the novels *After the Banquet* (1960, American edition 1963), *The Sailor Who Fell from Grace with the Sea* (1963, American edition 1965), *Forbidden Colors* (1951, American edition 1968), and *Thirst for Love* (1950, American edition 1969).

A NOTE ON THE TYPE

THIS BOOK was set in Monticello, a Linotype revival of the original Roman No. 1 cut by Archibald Binny and cast in 1796 by the Philadelphia type foundry Binny & Ronaldson. The face was named Monticello in honor of its use in the monumental fifty-volume *Papers of Thomas Jefferson*, published by Princeton University Press. Monticello is a transitional type design, embodying certain features of Bulmer and Baskerville, but it is a distinguished face in its own right.

The book was composed, printed, and bound by Kingsport Press, Inc., Kingsport, Tennessee. Typography and binding design by Kenneth A. Miyamoto.

0

Mishima   3724

Spring snow